LOVELY

Darkness

DEMONS WITHIN

USA TODAY BESTSELLING AUTHOR

LOVELY DARKNESS

DEMONS WITHIN

R SULLINS

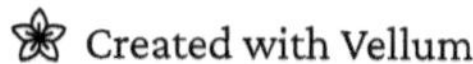 Created with Vellum

INTRODUCTION

The first time she knew real happiness was when she found out that the man who raised her wasn't her real father.

She knew that there couldn't be monsters in the world that were any worse than the monster she had called 'daddy' for most of her life.

Then she stumbled into the world of demons.

The Demon King knew the second his fated mate had been brought into the world.

After living years too numerous to count, it meant little to him other than to keep him from living as he had.

He now belonged to only one female - and he would have to wait years for her to mature enough to matter.

How stupid and vain he had been to think that his fated wouldn't matter.

The very moment she entered his club he knew he had been wrong to ignore fate.

She was **his.**

And he was going to destroy everyone that hurt her, even if he had to burn the Earth realm to the ground.

Note from author:

This book is a safe read when it comes to the relationship of the main characters. However, there is content that could possibly bother certain readers. In particular, there is violence against a child. If you prefer to not read this part, you can skip the PROLOGUE.

Happy reading! And, thank you for choosing to read my story...

DEDICATION

This is for everyone that had a shitty childhood...and wished they could have gotten some vengeance.

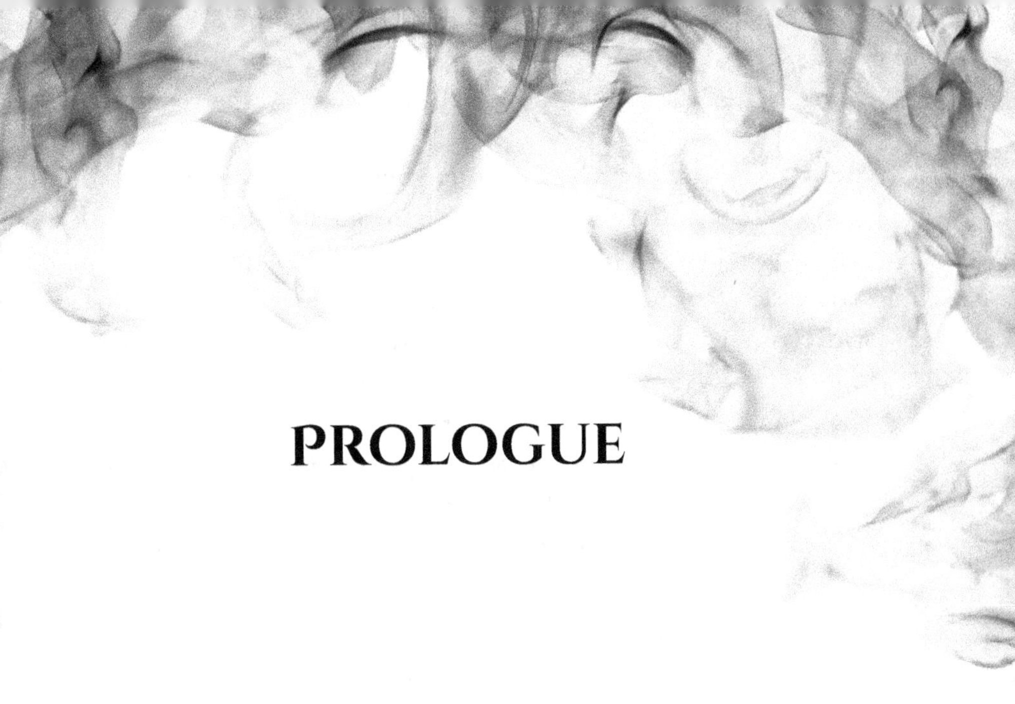

PROLOGUE

21 YEARS AGO

VAREK

I walked around the desk and leaned my hip against the sturdy wood, knowing that it could hold my weight. Crossing my arms over my chest, I slowly shook my head before tilting it to the side as I took in the demon on his knees before me. The thick sheet of plastic rustled as he adjusted his weight.

Long seconds passed as I watched his face change from the cocky smirk he'd had when first brought into my office, to the anxious, panicky look that morphed over his countenance the longer I left him stewing in silence.

I picked up a letter opener from my desktop and admired the detail in the handle. I didn't know the maker of this particular item, but was impressed by the craftsmanship. I had an undeniable soft spot for artists and made a point to support as many as I reasonably could, usually by purchasing from them, but sometimes I would sponsor them anonymously as they were building their careers.

I looked back at the demon in front of me and bit back a sound of satisfaction that he was watching the letter opener with dread laced with terror. His slitted green pupils were almost comically wide as he followed every movement of the sharp blade.

"We've been here before, haven't we, Greg?" I flipped the letter opener in my hand and checked the weight, balancing the metal on my finger. I grunted in satisfaction and set it down with a mental note to find out who the artist was. "How long ago did we have Greg here, in this very position, Talon?"

My head of security grunted from where he was standing at the door with two of his newest recruits. He had his hands folded behind his back and had his usual stoic expression on his face. "Two weeks ago, sir."

"Two weeks? Well, Greg, you've been busy since we last spoke," I paused, and looked him dead in the eyes, "haven't you?"

His gray skin took on a sickly yellow cast that I was certain wasn't a good sign in this breed of demon. The man knew he had fucked up.

"Y-yes, sir."

"Really? That's all you have to say about your recent activities? Yes, sir?" I stood and slowly walked around his kneeling body, my footsteps crinkling on the heavy tarp. I stopped when I was back to standing in front of him, the toes of my polished black oxfords just shy of grazing his disgustingly filthy jeans. I hitched up the heavy material of my slacks, so I could squat down to face the demon that had broken my rules for the last time. "You drugged and raped a demoness two weeks ago. She swore that the two of you had an ongoing agreement for some pseudo-relationship, and that the two of you would sometimes let your activities get out of hand."

I picked a small piece of lint off my slacks. "So, color me surprised when three -three, Greg- *three* more reports came in from other demonesses this morning. Ones that did not have prior relations with you, zero agreements, but yet, you took them while they were... unwilling." I stood back up and stepped back to lean against my desk again.

"Tell me something, Greg... what is my number one rule?"

He began shaking, and the smell of his terror began to fill the room with its pungent, sour odor.

"N-n-never h-harm a human." His swallow was loud in the room. "S-sir."

"Never. Harm. A. Human. Do you know why that is the number one rule, Greg?"

"So w-we don't ex-expose-"

"So, we don't expose ourselves!" My shout echoed around the room, and I sighed as the scent of urine filled the air. "You would have died for what you did to the demonesses, but what you did to that human woman..." I shook my head in disgust. "She was barely old enough to be even admitted into this club, and you stole her innocence and then her life."

His sizable gray body shook, his yellow eyes filled with tears, and his large, bulbous nose began to run.

"Pl-please, sir, I swear I will never hurt another hu-human..."

"Quiet." He immediately clamped his sharp teeth closed, his large, tusk-like fangs protruding from inside his thick upper and lower lips. "I don't know why you decided to hurt those demons, and I really don't know what made you insane enough to hurt that human girl, but you have already sealed your fate."

I lifted my hand and watched as tendrils of his soul leaked from his chest and disappeared into my waiting palm. I watched as he, with large, bulging eyes filled with pain and terror, clutched at his chest with both hands as if he could keep his essence from leaving his body. It was impossible. If I called on a soul, nothing could keep it from me.

When he was nothing more than a husk of a demon, barely breathing in front of me, I closed my fist and cut off the flow. I was told that pulling on the soul was painful, but I had the ability to make it excruciating or unnoticeable. Since most demons needed to be taught a painful lesson, I made sure to make it as agonizing as possible.

I walked around to the back of what was left of Greg and placed my hands on his head. There was another lesson that many demons needed to remember, and Greg was a perfect example and would do well as a reminder. I twisted to the left and then pulled the head toward me, carefully keeping it at an angle. It was impossible to clean blood out of fine wool suits. After eons, one learns the proper way to remove a head without getting any blood spatter on oneself.

I walked to the door, ignoring the sick-looking recruits, and opened it to reveal one of many guards standing alert in the hallway and tossed the head at him. "Make sure this gets displayed properly, where all our guests will receive the message." I took the cloth handkerchief out of my pocket and wiped my hands before dropping it on Greg. I shook my head. What self-respecting demon was named Greg? These younger demons born within the last few decades have been given, or taken, names that definitely fit in more with the humans. "Have someone clean this up, will you, Talon?"

"Of course, sir. The witch is already on her way."

"Thank you, Talon. And have someone open the window, please." Talon gestured to one of the recruits, who was swallowing rapidly and was paler than he presumably was normally. We both turned to walk out of the room together without looking back. Whatever orders were given were sure to be followed precisely.

I straightened my sleeves as we walked down the long hallway, back toward the club proper. "The stench of fear likes to cling for hours."

"Of course, sir."

I gave him a sideways glance and raised a straight black eyebrow. He chuckled and relaxed marginally. "Varek, you just had to show off with the whole head ripping thing, didn't you?"

"You want your recruits to understand what it could be like working for me?"

He sighed and then grinned. "I thought Sam was going to puke on his new boots."

"Well, they both handled the whole thing surprisingly well. I hope these last."

"If you didn't scare them off. I have high hopes for them."

We stopped at the heavy black door that opened up into the interior of the club. It was a Saturday night, and the place was already at capacity with a line down the block. It was like that each night, every week. As the central neutral zone for demons in this part of the country, it was always guaranteed to stay busy. As a trendy hotspot, humans couldn't resist either. Though the humans often found themselves waiting outside for relatively long periods of time, while the demons were able to enter immediately as VIPs.

I often fielded requests for VIP passes from the wealthier humans who thought they were important enough to be treated superior, not knowing it wasn't a pass that allowed the demons in; it was the bouncer knowing that all demons had priority. It was a demon only zone, after all. If the humans wanted priority, there were plenty of places that were available just for them.

The heavy bass that always managed to penetrate the thick door to the club entrance suddenly became just shy of overwhelming when the door swung open to admit two demons into the hallway. Talon and I stepped to the side to allow the hopeful looking male and the shyly giggling female to pass. The female looked up at me through her eyelashes, interest immediately lighting her eyes. She was a cute little thing in her human form, but she was an Annis demon under her glamor. Her skin was a lovely shade of blue, and her iron claws were carefully tended to. If I didn't already have plans for the evening with a human woman, who was probably getting impatient at the wait, I might have been tempted to take this female up on her offer.

I nodded to the couple and waited until they both walked to the door just inside the hallway entrance that led to the real reason for this building. The demon zone was the one place where all demons could go and be completely free to be themselves - within reason. This wasn't the Underworld, after all. Brimstone was what the humans knew as the dance club. It was open to all; human and demon alike. Beyond those doors, on the other hand, was an eclectic mix of entertainment that any demon would be able to find to suit them. The Tower housed a dance club, a sex club, a fighting ring, gambling den, and an all-around safe place for demons to hang out and play without fear of exposure to humans and the attention of the human police force.

Brimstone was large and popular. The entertainment in the rest of the building was much larger than the humans would ever know. The building it was housed in was warded. Human eyes just were unable to see that the building was several stories higher than the two that they actually saw. An elevator took demons to different levels within The Tower, depending on what type of entertainment they were itching for,

Inside Brimstone, I placed and maintained wards to keep demons from being able to drop their glamor. They were also obligated to follow all demon laws when involving humans. As the master of all demons on earth, I was duty-bound to punish those who chose to break those rules. The rules regarding demon exposure to humans were amongst the strictest and held some of the highest penalties.

I entered through the door and nodded to the guards standing at the entrance. This door was always heavily guarded as well as warded against humans. Human eyes should pass over the doorway as if it didn't exist. I walked to the side of the bar closest to the main entrance as well as the hallway to the office from which I had just come. The club was designed so the demons who wanted to enter The Tower didn't have to go far and so the humans wouldn't get overly curious from seeing so many walk through the club just to disappear. Most humans didn't stay at the front of the club as the dance floor and the music drew them further in and past The Tower entrance. And, of course, the wards in place helped to ensure humans did not want to linger. Still, a small bar was set up for those who chose to mingle without having to shout to be heard over the pounding music. It was still loud, but not as deafening as it would be once they passed through the wide, open archway.

I glanced around, looking for the woman that was supposed to be my entertainment for the evening. My eyes caught on a green dress at the other end of the bar from where I was standing. The brunette had her head thrown back, laughing at something the bartender had said. Her emerald gown was likely a nod to my eye color. I wondered if she had any idea how many women had done precisely the same thing in an effort to gain my attention for more than a moment.

Her gown was held by two narrow straps over her thin shoulders, and the front draped loosely, dangerously low over very generous breasts. The rest of the dress left little to the imagination as it hugged every inch of her waist, hips, and ass. Her long hair hung over one shoulder, brushing teasingly over one large breast, and her plush lips were painted a deep red that looked almost black in the low lighting above the bar.

The rest of the club was mostly lit up by red lights covered by black sconces against the black painted walls, but the bars needed a bit more light than that. Not for the bartenders since they were all demons, and therefore saw in the darkness much better than humans, but for the humans themselves.

The woman must have felt my stare because she looked around slowly before her eyes finally met mine. She smiled with one side of her mouth lifted in what was a very coy smile, and probably had men of all ages eager to drop what they were doing to rush to her side. I stood there, continuing to stare at her.

Her smile lost some of its cockiness as I made her wait for a reaction from me. This woman was nothing special to me. She would be a, hopefully, interesting distraction for the evening, nothing more. I wouldn't allow her to think she had a fleeting chance in hell of getting more than tonight with me. I had made the mistake of being too attentive or too nice in the past, and it never worked out well for the women. And having to convince a woman who felt she had been scorned, and whose name I couldn't even remember, that I would never be interested in more than a moment of distraction was bothersome at best. Nothing much had changed over the centuries.

Finally, I started to step toward her when a burning sensation halted me and had me grabbing my wrist. The pain was excruciating, and I had to grind my teeth to keep the yell back. As it was, I couldn't contain the grunt that escaped. I looked over at Talon, who was still standing at the door, saw his eyes had widened, and he was staring where I was holding my inner wrist tightly.

I looked down and slowly lifted my right hand to reveal what I knew would be there. An intricate symbol in a deep, blood-red had appeared branded onto my inner left wrist. The mark was in our demonic language and was the same symbol every bonded demon received. I watched as the pain receded as quickly as it had risen, and the writing faded into a flesh-colored, slightly raised brand. It would remain so until I came into contact with my fated mate for the first time.

Once we met, it would darken - once we bonded, it would turn blood red again and stay that way all our lives, forever marking us as a bonded pair, forever warning any others that we were unavailable until we died. It was more than a human wedding band could ever be. It was irreversible. It was also nearly impossible to resist the pull of one's mate once they finally met. And why would anyone really want to? A bond was said to complete a demon in an indescribable way.

I lifted my head and glanced around to see if anyone else had seen what had just happened to me. My date for the evening had a confused look on her face, but she began to move toward me. She swayed her hips invitingly as she walked, likely becoming impatient at being made to wait. Fortunately, it seemed that Talon was the only one to notice that something was wrong. I grit my teeth so hard, I felt my jaw ache.

I stalked back over to Talon and said, "Get rid of her," as I flung open the door without waiting for the security guard to do it for me, and strode back down the hallway and into my office. I barely noticed the open window letting in a cool breeze or that the stench from earlier and the mess were gone from the room. I took a seat at the desk and pulled out a folder from a drawer with the paperwork I needed to go over for some investments I had made in Europe.

There was no sense in taking a night off now...or in the foreseeable future. I was essentially neutered and would never be fully satisfied by any woman other than my bonded female ever again.

I looked at the clock and noted the date and time. My mate had just been born.

JULIETTE - AGE 6

I LAY ON MY SIDE, holding my tummy. It hurt so much. Usually, I could wait until Monday morning when the lunch lady would give me breakfast. Most of the time, she gave me extra that I would usually stick in the bottom of my school bag or hide in my desk for later.

This time, though, I didn't get to eat my food at lunch on Friday because Mary from room four knocked it to the ground when the lunch lady wasn't looking. I tried to pick it back up right away so I could claim the five-second rule, but Mary's friend, Sally, stepped on it and rubbed her pretty pink sneakers in it until the piece of pizza was dirty and smeared, the lights on her shoes flashing mesmerizingly. I had stared down at the lights, then at my dirty shoes with the holes in the big toes. I then looked over at Mary's shiny black dress shoes and her pretty white socks with the lace around the edges. They were so pretty and so clean.

I blinked quickly so no one would see me cry. I wasn't a cry baby. *I wasn't.*

So, because the pretty girl who was always clean and didn't smell, who liked to laugh at me, ruined my lunch on Friday, I was lying there on Sunday, trying to ignore the pain. I tried to sleep, but I just couldn't.

The house was so quiet I thought daddy must have been asleep already. So I thought maybe I could go see if there was anything in the kitchen I could eat until tomorrow morning when I could eat at school.

I got up off my mattress on the floor as quietly as possible, trying to avoid the one spring that liked to poke up and scratch my knee every time I crawled off it. For once, I was lucky and didn't get scratched, but it did snag on my nightgown and tore another hole in it.

I walked as quietly as a mouse on my tippy toes to the door, and put my ear against the wood, but I couldn't hear anything over the grumbles my tummy was making.

I carefully pulled the door open since it didn't close completely. The frame was crooked or something; I just knew that daddy would complain about the crooked house a lot. I didn't hear anything as I tippy-toe walked down the short hall and peeked around the corner. Daddy was asleep in his recliner with the tv on. People were doing weird things to each other on the screen, but I turned my head quickly so I couldn't see. A while back, I got in trouble for asking daddy what they were doing. I wasn't allowed to watch tv.

I was so scared, my heart was beating so fast, and I was afraid that my knees would collapse, but I was so hungry. I bit my lip and took the first step past the living room. I was careful to avoid the spot that liked to creak really loudly when it got stepped on.

I made it to the kitchen as quickly as I could and stood there for a second to make sure daddy hadn't woken up. I couldn't see him anymore from where I was, so I was scared that he would wake up and I wouldn't hear him.

I looked around the kitchen and knew I couldn't open the fridge. It made a really loud sound when you opened it, and the light would be too bright. I had to look in the pantry. The pantry was a tall cabinet with a lot of shelves. Daddy kept most of the food higher up, so I couldn't reach any of it. He told me all the time that he didn't want me to steal food from him. I looked over at the small table in the corner and the two chairs there. I shook my head. No way would I be able to move a chair without dragging it. Then daddy would catch me for sure.

I opened the pantry door and hoped for the best. The first thing I saw was a can with no label, but I couldn't open it anyway, so I ignored it. There was nothing else on the bottom shelf or the next one, so I put my hands on the next shelf and pulled myself as high as I could to peek at what might be on the next one. I gasped and almost fell backward when a mouse ran past my fingers and into the dark of the pantry shelves.

I took a deep breath and looked at what I could see on the shelf. There were a few more cans of food. Most were vegetables. A couple of them were dented, and one was rusted. I couldn't tell what a few of them were, but I ignored them all because I had no way to open them, just like the can without a label on the lower shelf.

Then I saw it. There, behind a can, was an open package of square crackers. I licked my lips and ignored how hard my belly twisted with hunger. I had to reach those crackers. I stretched out my arm as far as possible while balancing on my tippy-toes. I carefully pushed aside the can of green beans that was in front of the open white plastic package. My fingertips just barely brushed the plastic, so I had to push up onto one toe and pull myself higher with one hand while reaching with the other. Finally, I could touch the plastic enough to drag it closer to me.

My heart beat harder as I watched the crackers get closer. I pushed away the roach that crawled out of the plastic and carefully picked up the pack of crackers, still trying not to make any sound. In the dark, I could make out the little bits of salt on the top of the cracker in front of the pack. I licked my lips as my mouth watered, and my tummy twisted again.

I dropped back down to my feet. The crackers were right in front of me, but I knew the plastic would be so loud. I had these crackers before, once when daddy let me have two with a bowl of tomato soup. I remember how loud the plastic crinkled when he reached in to pull them out. I also remembered how the tiny pieces of salt tasted so good. I had let the cracker sit on my tongue until the flavor of the salt went away and then, finally, started to chew it. Daddy had yelled at me to hurry up or he would take it away, so I ate more quickly after that.

I listened for any sound coming from the living room and breathed out a little sigh of relief when it was still quiet and slowly, carefully slid the crackers off the shelf. I stared at them, and I just couldn't wait anymore. I reached into the plastic, pinched the first one with my fingers, and stuck it to my tongue, tasting those little pieces of salt. My stomach twisted harder than ever, and I couldn't resist taking a bite and then just pushed the whole thing into my mouth.

I started chewing quickly and almost groaned at the flavor. But when I tried to swallow, I couldn't. The cracker had made my mouth so dry I couldn't swallow and needed to cough. I tried so hard to hold it in, but I just couldn't. I held my hand tight over my mouth and nose to hold in the sound and choked a cough into my hand. Tears leaked from my eyes, and my hand holding the package of crackers accidentally squeezed the plastic.

I froze and opened my eyes wide. I listened as my daddy grunted, and then his chair squeaked as he lowered the footrest. Oh no, oh no! I looked around wildly, looking for a place to hide, but it was too late. Daddy filled the doorway of the small kitchen and glared at me with red eyes.

"Whatcha doin', girl?" His voice was deep and rough. I squeezed my legs together hard because I suddenly had to pee really badly.

All I could do was shake my head. I started trying to swallow harder and choked and coughed a little more, but I was finally able to get the cracker down and swung my arms behind my back, clenching the bag of crackers in my hands and hoping he couldn't hear it even though it sounded so loud in the dark room.

His eyes narrowed on my face in the dark, and he growled at me. "You up in the middle of the night stealin' my food, girl?"

"No, Daddy." I shook my head hard back and forth. Why didn't I take the crackers back to my room before starting to eat them?

"You lyin' now, too?" He reached down and unbuckled his belt. The clanking of the metal buckle was so loud in the quiet, dark room. I heard the leather, my heart racing faster as it slid past each loop of his jeans.

"Please, Daddy! I was so hungry!" I whimpered, as he took both ends of his freed belt and held them in one of his giant hands. "It was only one cracker! I'll put them back! See?" I shoved the pack of crackers back onto the shelf. I was hoping that he would let me go back to bed. It was just one cracker, and I was so hungry. But while my back was turned, I felt the first slap of the leather against my back. My thin nightgown did nothing to protect my skin.

I really wish I had taken those crackers to my room.

JULIETTE - AGE 10

I LAY BACK on my bed watching a long-legged spider spin a web around the bug it just caught. The web that was hanging from the corner in my bedroom looked as tattered and dirty as everything else.

I just finished my homework and was listening to the kids playing next door. They sounded like they were having fun. I didn't know what they were doing, and I didn't feel like watching from my window.

I was thinking about what Mary had said today when she cornered me on the playground during recess. She told me about a conversation she had overheard her parents having the night before. Apparently, Mary's grandfather was a doctor when my daddy was a boy. He had been really sick, and, even though he got better, the illness made him infertile. I had to look up the word later, but Mary had already known what it meant. My daddy wasn't able to have any children.

Mary made sure that I understood that my mother had an affair (another word I had looked up later), and that was how she got pregnant with me.

I had been sitting with my back to my favorite tree, reading a scary story. It was about a woman who had really bad things happening to her. Eventually, she found out that she was cursed because of a necklace that she had bought at a yard sale. When she realized that having the necklace made her cursed with all those bad things, she destroyed the necklace, and the curse was lifted.

The story made me smile because it gave me hope. Maybe I was cursed, too. Maybe, if I was cursed, the bad things that happened to me all the time would stop if I could break it, just like in the story.

Maybe, I could find out what was wrong with me. Maybe it was my eye. Daddy always called me a demon spawn. He would stare at my eye while he punished me. I hated my eye. I didn't know why one of my eyes was black and the other green. Everyone who looked at me either flinched, looked sad, or sometimes they would act scared.

"Hey, freak, did you hear me? Your daddy isn't even your daddy. Your momma was a whore. No one even knows who your real dad is. He's probably a freak, just like you." She glared at me, making her pretty features twisted and mean. All the other kids that had gathered around for the show all snickered and laughed.

I just sat there and looked up at her with a smile on my face. She didn't know it, but she gave me a gift I never thought I'd receive. My daddy wasn't my real father.

JULIETTE - AGE 17

I HAD JUST FINISHED CLEANING the dishes and putting them away when I heard the front door open and slam shut. I closed my eyes. My not-father, Jeff, was home.

When he walked into the kitchen, I put a big smile on my face, hoping that he wasn't in a mean mood today.

"Dinner is ready. I'll make you a plate," I told him in a cheerful voice. We never sat at the table that sat neglected in the small dining room area just off the kitchen. Jeff always ate the meals that I cooked in his recliner in front of the television, while he drank several cans of beer before finally falling asleep in his chair. Sometimes he actually made it to his bedroom.

My smile faltered when I turned back around, his dinner plate in my hands. He was already drunk. He was standing just a few feet from me, and I could smell the alcohol on his breath.

"If you want to go sit down, I'll bring you a beer so you can relax." I'd learned over the years to do whatever it took to make him happy, even if he got meaner when he drank. Usually, it was enough to keep him from coming after me with his belt or fists. If I didn't argue or give him what he wanted without being asked, he'd leave me alone.

He continued to stand there, though and stared at me. No, not me - my eye. The black one that he hated so much. The hate that was ever present rolled off him in waves. He narrowed his bloodshot eyes and took a step forward.

Before I could step back or throw up a hand to protect myself, his fist landed on my cheekbone. The pain radiated through my skull, causing flashes of light to flicker behind my closed eyes. The plate of food I had been holding went flying and crashed to the ground, and I brought up both hands to cover my face while I waited for the pain to dim.

He rarely ever hit my face. His favorite place to hit me was my stomach or, when he used his belt, my back. I think he tried to be careful so he wouldn't get in trouble with the authorities if some well-meaning teacher reported visible bruises. But this time, he didn't try to hide anything. And with the swelling I could already feel it was going to be a nasty bruise.

The next hit wasn't a surprise, but it did take the breath out of me. I doubled over, letting go of my face to grab my stomach. The little bit of food I ate from the dinner I cooked him threatened to come back up.

He took advantage of my open face and landed another blow to the same cheek, sending me flying backward and landing with a hard thump. The pain from my hip hitting the hard tile floor couldn't compete with the throbbing pain from my cheek. He had never broken a bone before, always careful not to leave visible bruises, permanent injury, or any injury that might warrant a visit to the hospital. But I was almost certain that my cheekbone was broken.

I rolled onto my back from the kick that he landed on my stomach while I lay there still gasping for breath. I didn't have time to try to curl back into a ball before he was on me, straddling my hips. He took both my hands in his and transferred them to one of his hands. My tear filled eyes caught on what he was holding in his newly freed hand, and a tremor of absolute terror shot through me.

The blade he held was the switchblade he always carried in his back pocket. I knew it was sharp because he'd sit in front of the tv at least once a week and slowly, methodically, sharpen it with a whetstone and oils. I'd seen him shave a small patch of hair on his arm more than once.

"Demon spawn!" He spit into my face, the saliva landing on my bruised cheek. "I hate this eye." He mumbled to himself. "Should have plucked it out of you when you were just born, then I wouldn't have had to look at your demon father's face all these years."

He looked at my other eye. "You shouldn't have green eyes, either. Julia had blue eyes. Your face, it's all his." His hand holding the knife shook with his rage. "He raped her, you know. I know that you know that I am not your father. I kept you after my Julia died because she asked me to. While she laid there dying after giving birth to you," he sneered. "She begged me to name you after her and to take care of you as if you were my own," he laughed an ugly sound.

He dragged the tip of the blade over my eyelid while I squeezed my eyes shut, hot tears wetting the hair at the side of my head. The sting from the cut scared me so bad, I wet myself while lying there on the kitchen tile.

"After she died, I named you Juliette instead of Julia. I couldn't bring myself to give you her name after you killed her." He hung his head for a second. "But I couldn't help but name you something I thought she'd like." He raised his head again, and his glare intensified. "But after spending more than a day with you, I knew I could never treat you like you were my own."

"P-please," I whimpered, not sure what, exactly, I was begging for. My life? To be let go? For him to end my torment once and for all?

When he dug the knife into my cheekbone just under my black eye, I screamed while he laughed.

"Time to get rid of that eye, now." His putrid breath, the pain that was still radiating in my stomach, the new pain of feeling that blade dig deep into my flesh, had vomit rising too fast to stop it.

I jerked my hands from his grasp and shoved with all my might, throwing him off of me just in time to turn my head and puke all over the floor. I watched in morbid fascination with one eye as my vomit mixed with the urine and blood that fell in a steady flow from my cut skin. I felt the knife slide through my skin as I jerked up. When I gently probed with the tips of my fingers, I gasped with pain when I brushed against the open wound. My fingers came away covered in blood.

I couldn't see through the swelling from that eye, and I was too scared to check to see if my eyeball was even still there or not.

I looked over at Jeff, finally realizing he hadn't attacked me again. He was lying against the cabinets, blood pooling around his head. I didn't know if he was dead or not, but I had no intention of waiting around for him to attack me again.

I stumbled to my feet, slipping in the mess on the floor, and left a bloody trail of drips, footprints, and handprints along the walls to the front door. I struggled to get it open for a minute, whimpering in distress, needing to get outside and away from the man who had the nerve to call me a demon. He was the monster in this story, not me. Maybe he was my curse, and getting away from him would free me.

CHAPTER
ONE

I RAN the brush slowly through Mabel's long silver hair, being careful to avoid yanking on any tangles that might have developed from rubbing against her pillow all day.

I had many favorite residents at the nursing facility I worked at as a CNA. Most of the residents were sweet and kind. Just a few were ornery just for the sake of being ornery. And a couple were shameless flirts. The flirts were harmless, of course. Comments were often made with not-so-subtle innuendos, and sometimes there were physical "flirtations". Samuel liked to pinch bottoms, while Gabriel liked to try to occasionally reach up a scrub top.

It was no secret, though, that I loved my job. I loved caring for my residents. As a CNA, my job was basically to help in daily activities such as assisting with baths, helping to feed them if necessary, light cleaning, and taking vitals. The jobs that required more than the community college training I was able to afford when I left the group home after high school, went to the actual nurses.

One of the nurses, Melissa, was like a carbon copy of Mary from elementary school. I had been so glad to be rid of that girl. Her dad was offered a job in another state, so they moved just before middle school. Once she moved away, most of the bullying stopped. I stayed to myself, made myself as invisible as I could, and most of the other kids let me be.

High school was over before I knew it since I spent most of my time studying, and when I didn't have any school assignments, I read. The librarian let me spend all my free time in the library, and since it was high school, I was often one of the only ones there. She also supplied me with apples and crackers. I never knew if she was aware that the snacks she provided while I was studying or just reading at one of her tables was the only food I ate some days, but I was extremely grateful for her thoughtfulness.

When I lived at the girl's group home for the few months I was there after leaving Jeff bleeding on our kitchen floor, I ate more than I had probably eaten in my whole previous seventeen years. The damage had already been done, though. I was small in both height and stature. I was only five-feet even and barely weighed one-hundred pounds. I didn't get my period until I had been at the group home and on a steady, nutritious diet for a couple of months due to malnutrition.

The group home was actually very nice. The other girls that lived there were mostly friendly. Several of us were in a similar situation. We had been in abusive homes with our parents. A couple of the girls chose to stay private and didn't speak to anyone at all. I was one of those silent ones until Judy, the house mother, lured me out. She was also the one that helped me figure out my future.

I had an ugly scar that healed well, but due to the location and how deep it had been left, the skin puckered, and my lower eyelid pulled slightly down. Judy knew how bothered I was by the scar, and taught me how to dab concealer on to help it blend into the surrounding skin. She also gave me a pair of non-prescription glasses that helped conceal it even more. But what I appreciated the most were the contact lenses. Since there was no way to make my black eye the lighter green color of my normal eye, she got me lenses that were a deep brown. I wore them daily, along with the glasses. I wasn't even able to tell I had different colored eyes when I wore them.

"Juliette, darling." Mabel tapped my knee with her soft fingertips. "It's 4 o'clock."

"Oh my goodness. Thank you, Mabel." I stood up and placed her hairbrush into her nightstand drawer. "Do you want me to help you into your bed?"

"No, thank you, dear." Mabel smiled at me and waved her hand toward the small television that was on the dresser at the foot of her bed. "I'm going to sit here a while longer and watch my shows. You go on now. Make sure everything is how it's supposed to be."

I bent down and placed a kiss on her papery cheek. "I'll be back in a little bit."

She patted my cheek and told me in her sweet voice, "I know you will, dear. Now, shoo!" She waved her hand toward the door this time.

I smiled at her again. Yes, I had a lot of favorite residents, but Mabel had been my favorite since the first day I came to work at this nursing facility almost three years ago.

I hurried down the corridor and turned the corner to the next one that would lead me to the first resident room. At 4 o'clock, Melissa, the current bane of my existence, doled out the medications that each person needed. Unfortunately, Melissa was horrible at her job. No one knew she often got the pills mixed up because I always went behind her and double-checked the medications before anyone took them. Luckily, Melissa and I always worked the same shifts, so I could be sure that it was sorted properly. On our days off, I was assured that the nurse working always got the medication deliveries correct.

I passed room three on my way to room one and saw Melissa placing the tiny paper cups with the pills inside them on the trays of the shared room. Some rooms had double occupancy, while others that could afford it had private rooms, like Mabel. I entered room one and checked the cups. I had been double-checking the medicines for so long that I could tell by sight if the pills were correct or not. I swapped the cups out and gave the correct ones to the right patients.

After I made sure they had plenty of fresh water and had swallowed their pills, I went into the rest of the rooms. The single occupancy rooms weren't in danger of receiving the incorrect medications, thank goodness, because the cups were labeled for the room numbers. There was only the danger of giving the wrong ones to the shared rooms.

I made the rounds to take vitals on the ones that needed monitoring and wrote notes in their charts. I also wrote notes for myself in the small notebook I kept in my scrub top. Some residents needed fresh bedding sooner than what was typically required, and some needed baths. Thomas, in room six, was developing a bedsore that was going to need to be treated right away and was required to be reported to Melissa.

I was just finishing up bathing one of my patients when I felt a tugging in my belly. It was a feeling I had started getting right after I started working there. It always filled me with a bit of dread and sadness.

I quickly finished helping the patient back into their bed and went down the hall as quickly as possible without running. I had been written up before, and I didn't want to lose this job. Melissa was always watching for ways to reprimand me. Luckily, she couldn't actually fire me since she was just a lead nurse and not the one in charge. Luckily, our admin loved me, so even though Melissa often reported to Tracey that I had broken a rule, Tracey always threw the report out and reminded me to be careful.

I followed the feeling in my gut and went into the room before coming to a complete stop and almost dropped to my knees.

"No. No, no, no, no. Mabel!"

I swiftly moved over to her bedside and shoved the rolling table away with her untouched dinner tray still sitting on it. From past experience, I knew that once that feeling took hold of me, there was no changing the outcome. My patient was going to die.

I sat on the edge of her bed and took her limp hand in mine. Her skin was so soft. She had that thin, papery skin that the elderly got over time, but hers were softer than most. Mabel used her skin care products religiously. She was always telling me that beauty faded before you knew it, and it was important to take care of your beauty early on so it would last much longer. I wouldn't say I ignored her advice, but I was skeptical that it was advice that I actually needed. I knew I wasn't beautiful with my hideous scar, so there was hardly a need to maintain my skin.

"Oh, Mabel," I whispered, and fought to hold back my tears. Mabel was taking her last breaths. Her little chest was barely moving with each inhale and exhale. Her face was pale, and her hand was cold in mine. Technically, I was supposed to call the nurse, who would then call in emergency services, but I knew there was nothing that could be done. It was Mabel's time. I wasn't ready to let her go, but nothing stopped death when it came for you.

I squeezed my eyes shut and took a deep breath before putting my forehead on her sweet, smelling cheek. "Go in peace, sweet, sweet Mabel," I whispered into her ear. I let the tear that escaped my eye roll down my cheek as I felt her chest go still.

The tugging feeling in my gut dissipated as soon as she was gone.

AFTER I REPORTED her death to Melissa, I spent the rest of my shift fighting back tears. I couldn't show them to the other residents. I had to be strong for them. I knew I would spend the rest of the night crying over the loss of such a wonderful friend once I finally got home. My only regret was that I hadn't known her longer.

I comforted several residents that had been close to Mabel. One of the men, Jonathan, was virtually inconsolable and his grief nearly did me in. We sat together long past my shift ended and comforted each other by telling our favorite stories about Mabel. We laughed and held hands for hours. Jonathan rubbed his eyes, the deep grooves in his face marking the years of sun and laughter suddenly scrunched up, and his shoulders began shaking.

I wrapped my arms as well as I could around the large man, gently rocked Jonathan back and forth, and rubbed his back while he got his grief out. I knew they had been close, but I never realized he loved her as deeply as he had. His tears told me he was sad, while his shaking shoulders told me he was devastated. But his complete loss of composure for a man with such a prideful nature told me he was utterly heartbroken.

"She never had children. Did you know that?" I nodded because, yes, I did know that. "When she was very young, younger than she should have been, honestly, her parents forced her into a pre-arranged marriage. That's the way so many rich folks have done it for ages," his voice got stronger the more he spoke, as if taking comfort and strength in talking about Mabel's life.

"The man she was married to was not a good man. He could be very violent. Mabel didn't want to bring a child into that kind of life. When her husband had finally passed, her parents had already been dead for some time. She inherited quite a bit of wealth from her parents and her husband, but it was too late for her to have children. Since she didn't have anyone to share her wealth with, she created a charity that provided shelter for abused women and children."

My breath hitched. "What was the name of the shelter?"

"Well..." He looked at me and smiled. "Each shelter has a different name, but the charity that they are all funded by is called Lost Dove."

It was my turn to speak, and I did so with only a whisper while I tried to hold in my tears. "When I was seventeen, I was attacked by my father," I laughed bitterly. "Well, not my father. He was thrilled to point that out after making my life as miserable as he could, instead of walking away when my mother died."

"He knew he wasn't the father?"

I nodded my head. "Yes. I found out when I was ten," I rolled my eyes at that lovely memory, "that he had been sick when he was a kid, making him sterile. I think he may have been more okay with having me in his life if my mother hadn't died while giving birth to me. I honestly don't know. He hated me quite a bit."

"Is that when you got that?" He gestured to my left eye, the one with the deep, puckered scar that pulled the flesh of my lower eyelid down. I hovered my hand there for a moment as if I could cover it up and make it disappear. Instead, I tucked my hand down under my thigh.

"Yes. He said my eyes must be from my birth father and was drunk enough to think it was a good idea to cut it out of me. That's when I managed to get away by kicking him off of me. I ran out the front door while he was passed out from hitting his head on the cabinet. I ran down the road and didn't stop until I reached an intersection and was nearly hit by a car. A passerby held on to me until a police unit arrived. I had been hysterical and looked like I had been mauled by a wild animal. They took me to the hospital to get stitched up. While there, my father arrived with his own cut that needed tending from hitting his head on the cabinet.

"He almost had them convinced to send me back home with him, but a woman wearing a dove pendant on her scrubs made a phone call. An emergency order was made to put me in a group home. In the end, my father ended up going to jail for four years." I looked down at my lap and whispered, "He got out last month with some time served and good behavior counting toward his total even though he didn't even go to jail until I was already eighteen. He hasn't tried to contact me, though. So that's good."

"You found out what the dove pendants meant, I suppose?"

"Yeah, the house mother was very kind and made sure we all knew how lucky we were. I learned from her that a rather extensive network of women kept their eyes out for the abused, and did everything they could to get them away from their abuser."

He smiled broadly. "Our Mabel was an amazing woman. I guarantee she made sure that the Lost Dove charity will be taken care of and will survive for some time to come." I felt my heart lurch at the thought of the charity not being able to continue to save girls like me.

"I hope so," I murmured.

"Chin up, sweetheart!" Jonathan chucked me under the chin and then stood up before picking up the cane that he didn't really need, but enjoyed having anyway. "You get home safe now, you hear me?" I nodded and stood up as well, and as I was walking toward the front entrance, I heard him call my name, so I turned my head back to look at him. He wasn't as slumped over and devastated as he had been a couple of hours ago. I could still see the shadows of grief in his eyes, though.

"Thank you, Juliette."

I nodded and called out to the elderly gentleman who had been Mabel's beau for going on twenty years, "Any time!" I waved and walked out the door.

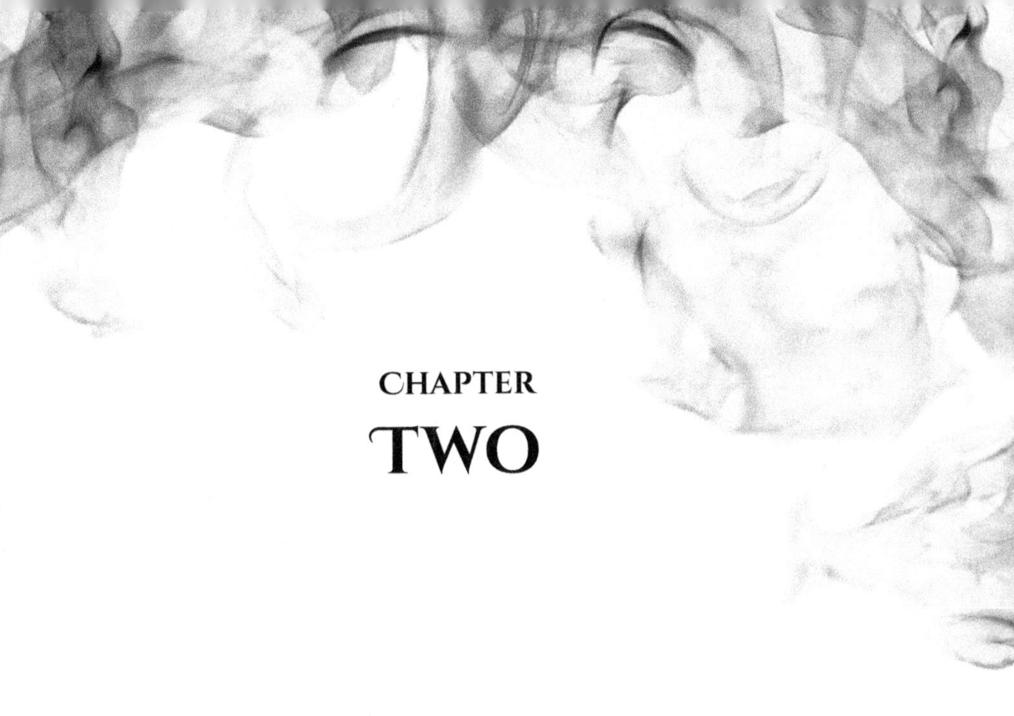

CHAPTER
TWO

JULIETTE

It was late, and I was running out of time. The last bus of the night was about to leave the stop that was a block down the road. I started running and waved frantically at the bus driver. He stopped abruptly and swung the door open for me.

"You're pretty late getting off work, Juliette."

"I know, John. It was a busy day at work today." I bent down and kissed his dark cheek. "Thank you so much for stopping for me. You saved me from wasting money on a cab."

John's deep voice rumbled out, "Any time, little lady. Now, you go sit down and take a load off so I can get you home."

I waved at the big man and walked to my usual seat. I always sat in the first row of double seats facing the front of the bus. The seats at the very front of the bus faced the inside toward each other. I didn't like them because all the stopping and starting made me sway too much and made me nauseous.

At the next stop, a woman holding a baby in one hand and the hand of a tiny girl in the other climbed onto the bus, and gave John a small smile while the little girl held up her mother's bus pass. John passed the little girl a piece of candy with a wink, and the little girl giggled and held up the candy so her mother could see, while the mother nodded and smiled adoringly down at her child.

They sat in the row on the opposite side of the bus from me, facing the inside of the aisle, right behind the driver's seat. The mother placed her arm around the little girl, while she happily unwrapped the piece of butterscotch candy and popped it in her mouth.

For the next few miles, I watched as the mother, wearing a waitress uniform, and was tired and worn out looking, smiled at her children and listened attentively as the little girl spoke to her about her day.

I often thought about my mother. I wondered what she might have been like. The picture I once had of her showed me that she was a petite, beautiful woman. And though her hair was blond, it wasn't the white-blond shade that mine was.

As I watched the mother nuzzle the top of her infant's head, I wondered if she would have loved me, if she would have kept me safe, if Jeff might have been a nicer person.

I wished so many times over the years that I still had that picture of my mother. When a social worker had gone to my home to pack up what few things I had worth keeping, it had been while I was in the hospital. When I woke up the next day with a patch over my left eye and bandages wrapped around my rib cage, a small bag of my belongings was sitting in the chair by my bed. I never got to tell anyone about the picture hidden in the tear in my mattress. When I asked to return to the house to retrieve it a few days later, I was told Jeff had destroyed everything that was left in my room when he was released on bail.

As I watched the tiny girl with little black ringlets, I wondered if I would ever have a little girl of my own. I pictured a sweet-faced pixie with straight white-blonde hair smiling up at me while sucking on a sugary piece of candy that a kind, giant of a man gave her. I allowed myself to wish for my own kind, giant man that would wrap his big, strong arms around the both of us, keeping us safe from the evils of the world.

My dreams abruptly ended when I heard John call out to me. "Here's your stop, girl. Now you get home safe, you hear me?"

I walked back to the front of the bus and brushed another kiss on John's rough cheek. "Thank you, John," I whispered, and didn't glance back at the small family huddled together on the bench behind me as I made my way down the steep steps of the bus, wrapped my cardigan close around me, and turned toward my apartment building a block away.

I waved to the couple that was leaving the building as they held the door open for me. The apartment building wasn't the best, but it was nicer than the first one I lived in when I first moved out of the group home. I put most of my paycheck into the nicest, safest building I could afford. It was tall and brick, with four two-bedroom units on each floor. I lived on the fourth floor and was lucky to have nice neighbors that were quiet but friendly.

When I stepped off the elevator, I all but dragged my feet down the short corridor to the door marked 4C. The long, emotional day was catching up to me quickly. I needed my bed more than I wanted a long, hot soak in the bathtub I usually indulged in. I was hungry, but too tired to drag myself to the small kitchen for anything. Usually, I didn't allow myself to go hungry. The past taught me that hunger hurt, and I tried to avoid that at all costs, but my body and mind were too weary to eat.

I dropped my bag on the small sofa, shrugged off my cardigan, and dropped it onto the floral duvet on my full-sized bed when I made it to my bedroom. I pulled off my scrubs. While waiting for the water in the shower to heat up, I stood at the sink, carefully removing my contacts and placing them in fresh solution, carefully avoiding looking at my eyes.

I took a cotton ball from the shelf above the toilet and poured a small amount of makeup remover on it. I gently scrubbed the thick, special, expensive concealer that covered my scars. The one above my eyelid was thin and straight, a pink line that I was assured would fade into a white, almost invisible line over time.

The scar below my eye was a different matter. Over the last four-and-a-half-years, it hadn't faded. It was still a dark pink. Against my pale skin, it stood out darkly and was highly visible. It was slightly puckered, and pulled my lower eyelid down in the center, making my eye look grotesque with the whites so exposed. With the thick black frames of my glasses, the concealer, and, of course, the contacts, the effects of the scar weren't as noticeable. Only sometimes would someone look a little too close and remark on it. I tried to not let anyone that close.

Once I threw away the cotton ball and brushed my teeth, I took my hair down from its confining bun and ran my fingernails over my scalp, silently apologizing for the torture I had placed on it once again. I ran my fingers down through the waist-length white blonde hair. I finally climbed into the bathtub and pulled the shower curtain closed.

I let the steaming water rain over me, tilted my face to the ceiling, and waited for the soothing heat to melt the knots in my stiff muscles.

And there, beneath the gentle spray, I cried.

I WAS PUTTING my cardigan and bag into my locker the following morning, when I saw someone lean against the locker next to mine out of the corner of my eye. I glanced over and smiled at Emmy.

Esmerelda worked part time and seemed to be a nice person. I didn't have much to do with her since we didn't work together often, but when we did work together, she seemed competent and treated the residents with respect. That definitely could not be said for many of the other people I worked with.

"I heard about Mabel. I'm so sorry, girl. I know you were pretty close." She raised her hand to her hair and fluffed up her short bob. "A few of us thought it would be nice to go out for drinks tonight. Kind of celebrate her life, you know? Everyone really liked Mabel and wanted to toast to her."

I started shaking my head. I wasn't the going out and drinking kind. I was the stay inside and read a book with a hot tea kind of girl.

"No, you can't say no this time, Jules. You always say no. You never hang out with any of us. You barely even talk to us. If you want to lose the few people that even like you, you have to show you care about them, too."

I flinched. I knew I wasn't liked by many. I was too introverted, too withdrawn, and always turned down the invitation to hang out. I didn't eat with my coworkers either. I preferred to be alone after so much of my life was spent avoiding bullies. But I didn't like hearing that the few people who liked me would give up on me. I didn't want to isolate myself, really. I just didn't trust people's motives.

"Look, I know that you and Melissa don't get along." I looked down at my sensible nursing shoes, avoiding her direct stare while she continued, "but this isn't about her. Like I said, we all liked Mabel, and since you were closest to her, we thought it would be nice if you joined." She leaned closer. "But, trust me, girl, if you refuse to come out with us, it's going to show everyone that you don't care. About Mabel or the rest of us. It's only one night...for now. So, what do you say?" She smiled at me with a lopsided smirk.

I wanted to shake my head. I wanted to say 'no thank you, another time'. I wanted to plead with her not to give up on me. But then I remembered my daydreaming on the bus last night. Would I ever have that? A child and a big, strong man to protect us from the rest of the world? It would never be a possibility if I didn't take a chance. Leaving my apartment for a couple of hours to hang out with my coworkers was a small step that I could take.

I tilted my head at her. "You said tonight? I don't have anything to change into here, and I really don't think I have anything nice at home either."

She waved her hand dismissively. "No biggie, I have a couple of changes of clothes in my locker. I'm always forgetting to take it all home with me. I'm sure we can put together something for you to wear."

I looked at her dubiously. She was around five-foot-eight and probably had fifty pounds more than I did on her gorgeous, curvy body. I looked like a twelve-year-old boy next to her. A short twelve-year-old boy. My boobs were practically nonexistent, my hips barely wider than my waistline. I wore a size one. She probably wore a size twelve. Her boobs alone wouldn't fit into one of my shirts, but she thought I could wear something of hers?

She laughed at the look on my face. "Trust me, Jules, I've got you covered. Are you going to come out with us?" I took a deep breath and nodded. Nothing ventured, nothing gained, right? She squealed and clapped her hands. "Yay! We'll meet back here at the end of shift and get ready, okay? Nothing big or fancy or crazy, just drinking." She took off out of the locker room.

"Emmy!" I called out. "I don't drink."

I heard Emmy laugh as she went to work.

CHAPTER

THREE

JULIETTE

I GROANED while I twisted my torso, one hand on my back, the other reaching as far as I could to get the deepest stretch possible. Then I did it in the opposite direction. My back ached. My feet ached. But most of my aching was settled in my heart.

It had been a long day. The residents were understandably subdued in their mourning. I spent a lot of time consoling the elderly friends of the deeply loved Mabel. Though it warmed me inside to know that she was such a well loved and respected woman.

I thought about sneaking out and making my way home so I could strip out of my dirty scrubs and have a nice long soak in my admittedly cramped bathtub. I had no desire to go to any club. Now or ever. The thought of being in a crowded club with so many strangers, all staring at me like I was an oddity or a freak, just didn't appeal to me in the least.

I had to get to my locker, where my purse was. If I had my keys on me, I might have just escaped out the front door before anyone could be the wiser. I poked my head in the door and immediately spotted Esmerelda. She was standing in front of my locker, leaning against it, with her arms crossed and a smirk on her face. I could see she was holding clothing in her hand, and I inwardly cringed. I was busted. She was never going to allow me to get away with escaping this. I sighed and did my best to square up my shoulders and appear brave.

"I'm so glad you're done! I was about to go hunt you down and pull you away by your hair like my mama would have done," she laughed at me and started tugging on my scrub top. "Come on, come on, let's get this off so I can get you dressed to go! The others are going to leave in a minute and save a place for us in line."

I helped her remove my top and scrunched my shoulders, trying to conceal my small chest from her view. She slapped my hands down. "Now stop that! There is nothing wrong with your body. Everyone is made different, and girl, plenty of guys would love to have a petite, small thing like you to take care of. It would make them feel manly."

I wasn't interested in making a man feel manly. But I was pretty shy about my body. I had always been small, and as a woman, I felt even more inadequate than when I had been standing in the gym locker room in high school when all the other girls would flaunt themselves and preen in the mirrors while side-eyeing me and snickering behind their hands.

Emmy took my shoulders and pushed them back, making me stand up straighter. "See! Look at you! Your boobs are small, but they are perfectly round and perky. At least they aren't overly large like mine. I bet when mine are sagging to my knees, yours will still be firm and where they are supposed to be," she laughed again, and then shook out the clothes she had been holding. "Okay, so I have this sweater from a couple of weeks ago. It's one of those that is long and goes below my butt. I bet on you it goes to at least your thighs, maybe even down to your knees." She shoved the deep burgundy colored, soft, knit sweater at me and bent down to rifle through a pile of stuff on the bench in front of us. "I have a belt if we need to take it in and a pair of tights that shouldn't be too baggy."

Somehow she managed to get me completely dressed without me looking like a hobo or like I was a little girl playing in her big sister's clothes. The sweater was oversized and hung off one shoulder no matter how many times I tried to yank it back up, but it didn't look bad. Unfortunately, I had to take my bra off since the white cotton strap looked ridiculous with my exposed shoulder.

We debated on the belt since it didn't really fit, but with it slung loosely around my hips, it kept the sweater from looking like a tent on me. The black belt worked well with the burgundy sweater that really did look like a dress on me since it fell nearly to my knees. She changed her mind on the tights, though, since they were too baggy and the sweater was long enough, reaching to just an inch above my knees. My black ballet flats finished off the look.

"I wish you would take your hair down, but overall you look amazing. I've never seen you out of your scrubs before." She nudged me with her elbow as we cleaned up our discarded clothing, stuffing them into the lockers, and prepared to head out. "Do you have to wear those glasses? I bet you'd look great in contacts. Those big frames hide so much of your face."

"I have to wear the glasses," I mumbled. I couldn't tell her why or show her what I was hiding. "My hair is really long, and if I take it down, it will look weird from being rolled up in a bun all day."

"I guess I can see that." She took another look, tilted her head as she studied me, and finally shrugged. "I guess I'll leave you alone for now. I can tell you are already uncomfortable enough right now. But one day, I'd love to do your hair and makeup." She smiled at me and took my hand, dragging me out of the locker room and toward the exit, both of us waving to the head night nurse.

She pulled out her phone and checked it when it dinged at her. "Our ride's here!" We walked up to a small sedan, and she smiled brightly at the driver. "Thanks!" The Lyft driver nodded politely, but didn't say anything as he pulled away from the curb and started off toward the business district, where several restaurants and clubs opened after the offices started closing each night. It was a popular place for young business people to relax and unwind after a long day behind a desk, in a courtroom, or wherever their particular work had them slaving away all day.

I felt eyes on me and looked up to see the driver staring at me through his rearview mirror while we were stopped at a red light. He smiled at me, and I shivered. I didn't like the look of interest in his eyes or that he was so blatantly checking me out. I rubbed my hands on my thighs and looked out the window, ignoring him for the rest of the drive.

When we pulled up in front of a building that had a huge line outside and a large double front door with a dark red sign that read Brimstone, Emmy started bouncing in her seat, clearly excited to get the night started. She threw open her door and told the guy, "Thanks for the ride! I'll be sure to leave you a good review."

He winked at me in the rearview mirror and said, "Be sure to share my information with your friend. I'd love to give her a ride anytime."

I quickly got out and slammed the door shut, so thankful to finally be away from his creepy stare. I looked at the long line of people and cringed. The women were all wearing outfits that looked like they were going to a fancy nightclub. Dresses were short and shiny. Hair was well-groomed, and faces were made up like every YouTube tutorial I had ever seen. They all looked amazing and beautiful and like they belonged. Sure, there were a few that wore jeans instead of dresses, but they made up for it by wearing cute tops. Even Emmy looked great, fitting in with her jeans and tank top that had sequins all over it.

"They are over there." She pointed to the group of girls that was made up of our co-workers. There were a couple of guys with them that I hadn't seen before, and I wondered if they had met them in line or if they were invited to come along. We walked over to them, and Emmy glared at a couple of girls back in line who were making grumbling sounds about us cutting in line until they quieted down. I hunched in my shoulders, embarrassed.

"Maybe we should go back to the end of the line," I whispered to Emmy.

"Nah, they'll leave us alone. Just ignore them."

Everyone shouted hello, and a round of hugs was handed out to Emmy. I was surprised when I received hugs as well, and was shocked when Melissa even gave me a small one-armed hug.

"The line will start moving pretty quickly here in just a few minutes. The doors officially open at 9pm."

"Just wait until you see this place, Jules. It's amazing inside. It is all black, everything. The floors, ceiling, and walls are completely black. There are red lights along the walls and lights at the bars, but the only colors in the place are red and black. The dance floor is in the middle. You have to step down into it, which I think is really cool because you can sit along the edge of the dance floor and look down into it like you are sitting on a balcony." Emmy was obviously a huge fan of the place, and I had to admit that her excitement was making me interested in seeing this place for myself.

"The drinks are a little bit overpriced, in my opinion," said one of the guys that were standing with us.

Melissa snickered and looked at the guy with disdain. "Please. You only say that because you're too cheap and don't want to buy any girl you're interested in more than a cheap drink."

He flushed red at her words. "I'm not cheap. I just think ten-dollars for a mixed drink is too much when I could buy almost an entire bottle for that much."

Melissa snorted and turned her back on him. "I wouldn't waste my time on a guy that can't even shell out a little bit of money to impress a girl."

I felt bad for the guy because ten-dollars did seem kind of expensive for a drink. Seeing all the people in line and calculating how many each one would drink, I imagined the owner made more than enough money to lower the cost by a dollar or two. But then again, businesses took a lot of money to run and employees to pay. What did I know? I could barely afford to pay my rent since I chose to stay in an apartment that was higher than my finances say I should be able to afford. All for the feeling of security. It was worth it.

The line finally began to move just as I had been wondering if the doors would ever open. I was so tired, and my feet hurt from working all day. The ballet flats I wore weren't nearly as supportive as my nursing shoes. I got jostled around a bit as we slowly made our way forward. I had my ID out, and a twenty-dollar bill ready for the cover charge as Emmy had instructed me to do.

After our group made it past the bouncer and I was the last one of the group, I had to stop longer than they did as the bouncer took a long look at my ID, then me, and back to my ID again and again. I was small, and he obviously had trouble believing that I was legally old enough to enter a bar.

I had no problem if he wanted to stop me from entering. Honestly, I would have loved to hail a cab and make my way home, but the huge guy finally handed back my ID and told me to go ahead inside. Disappointed, I finally walked through the large open door and gaped at the room in front of me. The place looked gigantic. The dark interior was just light enough from the red wall sconces and the bouncing lights to make out the room.

Emmy was right. Everything was red and black, from the floors to the ceiling. However, my favorite part about the place was the symbols that glowed red all around the walls. They almost seemed like words, but if they were, they were of a language I had never seen before. They almost looked ancient.

The first area we were standing in from just inside the entrance wasn't completely removed from the rest of the club, but it had partial walls that separated it from where I could clearly see the dance floor area. The partial walls helped cut down on some of the loud music that I was sure would be overwhelming once we got closer to the speakers that looked to be arranged facing the center of the room. Small tables were set up in this entry room. I supposed it was so people could sit and have conversations without having to strain to yell at each other.

Even though the whole place was intimidating me a bit, I still found myself somewhat eager to explore and see what else this club had to offer. I had never been in a place such as this, had never even been in a regular bar, let alone a dance club, so this was a new experience. Even though I was extremely shy and withdrawn by nature, I was also very curious. It was just difficult for me to let myself go enough to satisfy that curiosity.

I felt a tug on my hand and glanced over to see Emmy trying to drag me over to the bar that already had a crowd of people yelling out orders to the bartenders. "Come on, we need to get our drink on and find a seat before the place gets crowded."

"This isn't crowded?" I asked, looking around at all the bodies.

She laughed and said, "Just wait. In an hour, you won't even be able to move without having to squeeze past a sweaty body."

"That doesn't sound very fun," I mumbled. She just ignored me and kept pulling me toward the bar and squeezed us in between two guys wearing button-down dress shirts. One had his tie still in place, looking cool and calm. The other had his top two buttons undone and a cocky grin on his face. I looked away quickly when the cocky guy saw me looking at him. I didn't intend to show any interest and definitely didn't want to make eye contact.

"Hey!" Emmy gave the bartender a big smile. "Can we get two sex on the beaches?" The big guy wearing a tight black t-shirt with long, shaggy blonde hair smiled, showing off one dimple in his left cheek.

"Sure thing, sweetheart." He turned to grab two glasses, and I saw the words STAFF in bold red across the back of his shirt.

Emmy turned to me and said, "Okay, this is how this works. We should have had this conversation already, but I forgot who I was dealing with." I frowned. "Never take a drink from a stranger. Ever. Never walk off with a stranger, either, unless you are going to the dance floor and will be in sight of the group you came with. Never go home with anyone without your friends knowing who you are going home with."

I shook my head. None of that sounded like anything I would do anyway. I was happy to find a seat and just watch people for the next hour before finally being able to make my excuses and going home.

"It's okay, I know the place is out of your norm, but I will make sure you have fun. Next time we go out, you will know what's happening and will be so much more relaxed. Trust me!"

I didn't know about that. I was just ready to get this over with. The bartender came back over with a couple of tall glasses filled with orange and pink liquid with a cherry floating on top.

"That's twenty-dollars." I reached down to my purse, but Emmy already had two twenties lying on the gleaming black bar top.

"The rest is yours, handsome." Emmy winked and handed me a glass before retaking my hand and spinning me around to lead me back over to our group of co-workers. They were all chatting loudly. Their excitement was palpable as they sipped their drinks and stared around the room at all the guys while several guys were grouped up and staring back. It was like watching a mating dance. It kind of reminded me of the one dance I went to in middle school where all the guys stood on one side of the gym while the girls grouped together, sipping punch and giggling while looking at the boys from under their lashes. I thought adults might have grown up some, but I guessed not.

CHAPTER
FOUR

JULIETTE

ONCE WE CAME BACK TOGETHER as a group, Melissa took the lead and started walking through the archway and into the main part of the dance club. I was right; the sound of the music got so loud once we were through that it would make having a conversation nearly impossible. She led us around the outside of the dance floor, which was one huge sunken square surrounded by high walls. There were ledges along the outside of the walls with barstools facing the inside. The whole thing was enclosed with open doorways and steps leading down. It sort of reminded me of a pool.

There was an open walkway all the way around the area between the barstools for people watching and small tables with clusters of chairs around them. Further back from the large dance floor with the glittering black surface and glowing red lights illuminating the edge around the base was a larger seating area with many more tables where larger groups could sit.

I looked up and spotted the DJ booth on the second floor overlooking the entire dance area. There was a set of stairs to the left of the room with a tall, imposing man standing at the base of the stairs, his arms folded across his chest. Obviously a bouncer. He seemed to be guarding the stairs. I assumed that it was a VIP area. I followed the stairs with my eyes and saw that the upstairs area had a balcony that ran along the length of the room and ended at the wall where the DJ was located. I could just make out a few tables and what looked like couches in semi-circles with low tables in front of them. It looked much more relaxing than this giant room with the crush of bodies surrounding me. Was it going to get even busier here? That had to be some kind of fire hazard.

We finally made it past the dance floor and to a table with four chairs, but the girls were already swiping chairs from the neighboring tables to make room for each of us to sit down. I gingerly sat on the black wooden chair and placed my purse on the ground by my feet, not seeing how I'd be able to put it on the table in front of me since everyone's glasses were taking up most of the small top.

I was facing the dance floor even though I couldn't see it due to the walls surrounding it, but it didn't look like anyone was currently on it. I assumed people would want to start drinking first before they made fools of themselves. I looked at my glass that I was still holding dubiously. It looked appetizing enough, but I had never had any kind of alcohol before.

I absentmindedly scratched at my inner wrist and decided what the hell and gingerly took a sip through the tiny red straw. I had no idea why the straw was so small. It seemed a bit ridiculous. I was surprised that the drink was actually sweet and refreshing. It mainly tasted of orange juice, but had a hint of other fruit flavors, and under all that was a bite of something that had me wrinkling my nose. It didn't really taste bad, but it was definitely nothing I had ever tasted before. I shrugged my shoulders, took a longer pull through the ridiculous straw, and hummed to myself at the flavor again. It was definitely growing on me.

My belly started to get warm, and I could almost feel the tension beginning to leave my stiff shoulders. I took another sip and looked up when I heard laughter.

Emmy was smiling at me, and a couple of the other girls had big grins. Melissa had a smirk on her red painted lips. "Oh my god! Don't tell me this is the first time you've ever had alcohol?" Melissa threw back her head and laughed. "Oh, this is priceless!"

Emmy glared at her. "Don't be a bitch, Melissa. Not all of us were stealing mommy's vodka out of the liquor cabinet when we were twelve."

Melissa just waved her hand. "Oh, relax, Em. I'm just having a bit of fun. Isn't that why we're all here tonight?"

"Actually, I thought it was supposed to be about remembering Mabel," I half shouted, to be heard over the pounding bass.

"Wouldn't Mabel want us to have fun in her honor? I'm sure the old lady got up to all kinds of fun in her time. So we're just doing it for her now." Melissa saluted with her tiny glass, threw her head back, and swallowed the whole thing in one go before picking up a wedge of lime and sucking it into her mouth. I didn't think getting drunk and yelling out a conversation in a bar crowded with strangers really qualified as honoring a wonderful woman, but I couldn't argue the matter here.

I decided to ignore Melissa for the rest of the night and took another sip of my drink. I looked around and saw a few people stepping down into the dance area and, I wished that I could see what they were doing there. I had never danced before, not even at school, so I was really curious as to what people did inside a dance club when they weren't drinking and shouting at each other.

I held my cool glass to my wrist, which was feeling rather warm and itchy. The cold condensation soothed it while my belly got warmer and my head felt lighter.

I looked over toward the stairs where movement had caught the corner of my eye and sucked in a breath. A man stood next to the bouncer that was guarding the stairs. He was dressed in solid black from the neck down. His shirt was buttoned fully, and the fabric had a sheen that almost glowed under the dim red lighting above his head. He was as tall as the huge man that had been guarding the stairs. I didn't know where that would place him in height, but it was most definitely taller than the average man.

He wasn't as brawny as the bouncer, but he was still broad through the chest, and his arms were snug inside his shirt sleeves without stressing the material. His shirt was tucked in smoothly against his abdomen, showing how flat and very trim it was. His thighs were thick in his suit pants and indicated that the lower half of his body was just as fit as the upper half.

I drug my eyes slowly back up his body, over his chest, past his throat with an Adam's apple that moved while he spoke, over the square chin with a hint of five o'clock shadow, and got stuck on his lips. As I watched his lips move, I admired the fullness. I couldn't see detail of the shape, nor could I tell what he was saying, but I was fascinated by the way they moved and was startled to feel my breasts tingle. They had never done that before.

I quickly looked away and met the smug eyes of Melissa.

She shook her head at me and gave me a pitying smile. She didn't say anything. Likely she didn't want to be reprimanded again by Esmerelda, who seemed to have appointed herself my guardian for the night. But I could see a hint of malice in her eyes.

She picked up her next tiny glass and shot it back, the same as she had done with the others I saw her with, and sucked on the lime.

"Ladies!" she shouted, as she stood and smoothed her sequined red dress down her thighs. "I'm going to go get the man I've been working on for the last few months."

One of the girls, Lisa, squealed and looked around wildly, nearly falling off her chair. "He's here? That man is F - I - double N - E fine!"

Emmy pushed her shoulder and almost sent her to the floor. "There is only one N in fine, you goof." Lisa shrugged her shoulders and giggled.

"It doesn't matter. The man deserves an extra N."

Nancy, another day nurse, looked up quickly. "He's here? Oh

man, I am so jealous! Please don't be mad that I daydream about your man, Melissa. A girl would have to be dead to not appreciate that hunk of man meat."

Melissa tilted her head. "As long as you bitches don't do more than dream." Then, she looked at me. "I don't share." She sauntered away.

I watched as she went and leaned over to Emmy. "Who is he?" I asked in her ear, so I wasn't screaming my ignorance to the whole group.

"Girl, that man over there is the owner of this club." She shook her head. "Melissa is going to crash and burn, and it's going to be ugly."

"Why do you say that?" I watched as she approached the two men and saw I was right. Melissa was a tall woman at around five-foot-eight, but she was wearing tall heels, so she had to be standing at close to five-foot-eleven and the men still towered over her by several inches. My breath hitched as I watched her reach her hand out, and as he took her hand in his, I felt a small, but sharp pain in my chest.

"He is never seen with a woman. I've heard he may be gay, but that might just be the women he's turned down talking."

I relaxed my tight grip on my glass when he released her hand after just a brief second, but I couldn't look away as they spoke. They were standing very close, which I supposed would be expected since it was so difficult to hear above the music, but it bothered me more than I could rationally explain. It must be jealousy over the first guy that my body, or mind, had ever been interested in. But, of course, I was interested. I looked around and saw every woman in the area was also looking right at him. He was the perfect male specimen. Designed to entice a woman on a biological level to mate and procreate. He was obviously rich, strong, and powerful.

As I watched the man and Melissa have their conversation, I noticed as he tilted his head that his hair seemed to be pitch black. A black so dark that it blended in with the shadows. No. That wasn't right. They seemed to absorb the shadows. It was the strangest thing I had ever seen. I looked down at my glass and saw it was empty. Maybe I was drunk, and that was making me see things.

I looked over to Emmy, about to tell her I wanted to go get another drink, when a server came to the table with a tray laden with more glasses. Apparently, someone had already ordered another round of drinks. I reached down for my purse, determined this time to pay my share. I had a ten-dollar bill out and was laying it on the server's tray before anyone else could. I quickly snatched up my glass and took a strong pull from the little straw that I was beginning to think was actually quite cute and let my eyes settle back over on the owner.

He had his hand on Melissa's shoulder. The large masculine hand dwarfed her thin shoulder and made her look delicate. I had to look away and blink my eyes a few times to rid myself of the wetness that suddenly flooded them. It was ridiculous. My eyes were probably just overly dry from wearing my contacts much longer than I usually did. I had re-wetting drops in my purse, but I didn't want to embarrass myself by using them in the middle of this club. Besides, no one knew I wore contacts. I wore fake glasses so I could pretend I had normal eyes. It would make me even weirder if they knew I was wearing both contacts and glasses at the same time.

The thought sobered me right up. Well, maybe not literally. I was actually feeling so much warmer and looser now than I ever remembered being before. But emotionally, I sobered. I was a freak. I had these freaky eyes that scared people and ugly scars that made people cringe. Melissa was talking to a man I had never met before, and she had every right to lay claim to him. Finders keepers.

I huffed into my drink and was shocked to see the rest of my second glass was gone. And looked down at the table in front of me, where Emmy had just pushed one of those tiny glasses that Melissa had been drinking from. Intrigued, I picked it up with my forefinger and thumb and started to sniff the pale yellow liquid but bumped my nose into Emmy's hand instead.

I looked over at her to see her grinning at me. "You don't want to smell that." She took a tiny salt shaker I hadn't noticed sitting in the middle of the table, hidden by the multiple empty glasses coated in sugary substances, each with the cute little red straws in them. I grimaced as she licked the back of her hand because, eww...germs. "Okay, what you want to do is, lick your hand, then take the salt and sprinkle it there, so it sticks. Or you can use any other body part," she winked, "and when you're ready, lick the salt off." I watched as she poured salt over the spot she licked and picked up the small glass in front of her. "Lick, pour, lick, shoot, and suck."

I watched with an open mouth as she did just that. She licked the salt off her hand, tossed the entire contents of the glass in her mouth, grimaced, then stuck a lime into her mouth and sucked on it much the same as Melissa had done earlier.

"But...why?" I asked, dumbfounded.

She laughed loudly, throwing her head back, making her big, brown curls shake. "Because it's fun! Now your turn."

I looked at my glass, and the shaker of salt dubiously and slowly lifted the back of my hand up, mentally calculating how long it had been since I last washed my hands and if it had come into contact with anything since then. Since I couldn't think of anything, I squeezed my eyes shut, licked a small area, then jumped when I felt it get cold and opened my eyes to see that Emmy was pouring a generous amount of salt over the wet spot. I took a deep breath and licked the salt, wrinkling my nose at the flavor. Then, before I lost my nerve, I tossed the drink into my mouth and swallowed. I nearly choked at the horrendous taste. It was utterly awful.

Emmy shoved the lime into my mouth as I was gasping for breath. I started sucking on the lime furiously, grateful that it helped dull the flavor.

"What was that?" I gasped

"That, my little innocent, was tequila! It's the best way to get hammered quickly or just get a buzz on so you can start enjoying your night."

I didn't see how something like that would help anyone enjoy anything.

I picked up my glass and sucked through the straw again, but only got air. I frowned into the glass as if I was going to see something in there, as if my straw had betrayed me, but there was nothing but ice and a cherry down at the very bottom. I shrugged my shoulders and turned the glass up to my mouth to grab a piece of ice. I needed to cool down. My belly was past feeling warm now, and my head was swimming just a bit. I chewed on the ice I managed to capture with my lips and rubbed my forehead with the back of my hand, feeling the granules of salt rub roughly against my skin. Apparently, I didn't lick it all off.

I wiped my forehead with my fingertips to brush off any clinging crystals and then decided the ice would help cool me off, so I put the glass to my face. It felt so good. I looked around, but noticed our table was mostly empty with just me and Emmy.

"Where'd everybody go?" My voice didn't sound right. It was deeper than usual, and I was talking much slower than I normally did. I had to blink a couple of times to bring Emmy into focus and then shook my head to help clear it when her image wobbled.

"They went to go dance." She stood up, grabbed my glass out of my hand, and set it on the table. I giggled as I watched the straw spin around. *What a cute little straw.* I was tugged out of my chair and stumbled over my two feet as I staggered to an upright position. "Oh my god. Are you hammered already? I know you are small, but Jesus. That can't be normal." She started pulling me along, and I followed close behind her, turning my body sideways to fit between all the people that were absolutely everywhere. They weren't kidding; the place might as well have been empty when we first came in. It was wall to wall now.

The smells of the people were overwhelming my senses. There were cologne and perfume smells, all battling for dominance and body odor that wasn't quite hidden. Some people really needed to start using a different kind of deodorant because whatever they had currently was not doing the job properly.

I stumbled a bit and almost fell on my ass when my shoe slipped over the edge of one of the stairs as Emmy pulled me into the dance pit. I looked around through bleary eyes at the bodies jumping, twisting, and writhing all around me. Emmy let go of my hand, and I panicked for a second before I realized that she had pulled me into the center of the group of girls we had come with. Everyone had their arms raised and were swaying their bodies, laughing and smiling. I couldn't hear what everyone was saying, but they looked like they were happy and having a lot of fun.

I raised my arms like they were and slowly swayed my body back and forth, not fast or graceful, but it was still fun, I supposed. The music felt like it was running up my body through my feet and vibrating into my chest. I closed my eyes and just felt the rhythm. It was an interesting experience. Having my eyes closed seemed to help my swaying, and I felt myself smile.

I felt hands on either side of my waist and a large body pressed against my back. I knew that couldn't be Emmy. Why would she press up against me like that? I opened my eyes and saw one of the girls smirk at me and looked to my right to see Emmy glaring at the person behind me. She pulled on my shoulder, hauling me over to her other side. I heard her yell, "She's not interested, bub." She flicked her fingers at the person. "Shoo, go find someone else to manhandle."

I looked at the person and saw it was a young guy with blond hair and a polo shirt with dark wash jeans. He looked irritated at Emmy and then looked at me. He mouthed something at me and held out his hand. I shook my head quickly, closing my eyes when the movement made my head spin, and opened them back up to see the guy look disappointed, and then shrug his lean shoulders before turning around and moving up behind another girl a few feet away.

I stayed with the girls through a couple of songs before I got too thirsty and hot to stay on the dance floor any longer. I tapped

Emmy's shoulder and pointed back toward our table, and waved my hand at my face to let her know I wanted to go back and sit down. She nodded her head, looked at one of the other girls, and hitched her thumb in the direction of the table before turning back toward me, once again taking the lead, pulling me behind her.

CHAPTER
FIVE

JULIETTE

ONCE WE WERE BACK in our seats, I leaned over, careful not to lean so far that I would slide out of my seat, and yelled at Emmy. "Thanks for watching out for me, Emmy. I didn't know you were such a great person. I feel awful that I hadn't made friends with you before, but you are a really great person!"

Emmy frowned at me and made me frown back. "What?" I asked, afraid that I had said something wrong.

"It's just that I know I got you really drunk, and I feel bad. I had no idea you were such a lightweight." I could see her sigh deeply, and she placed her hand over mine on the table and leaned in close so that I could hear her. "Jules, you are a great person, too. I always knew that. That's why I pushed so hard for you to come out tonight, but now I am worried I made a mistake."

I jerked my head back, hurt. I didn't like that she thought hanging out with me was a bad thing.

"No, no, no. I don't mean that it was a mistake to be friends. I just mean that this environment was a mistake. You obviously are so far out of your element that it isn't even funny. We should have gone to a diner or something and had a quiet dinner. This," she waved her hand encompassing the entire dance club, "was a bad idea. I look at you and see that now. You and I will be great friends," she squeezed my hand, "but a great friend would know not to put someone so far out of their comfort zone."

I teared up and started rapidly blinking my eyes. Other than the residents at the nursing home that I had gotten close with, I hadn't found many friends. None really. It was my fault since I kept myself so well guarded, afraid to be bullied, that I didn't let myself open to the possibility of a real friend.

"I think I have to use the restroom," I shouted at her.

She nodded her head. "Yeah, that's a good idea. Then we can get out of here and go somewhere to have coffee and wind down from all this, yeah?"

I nodded back at her, and we stood, retrieving our purses from the floor as we did so. Emmy led the way past the bar in the very back of the room between our table and the dance floor, and entered a short hallway with red lights leading the way toward doors marked Male and Female. There was a short line, so we both leaned our backs against the wall.

I thought my head would have stopped spinning once we weren't being blasted by such loud music any more, but it seemed like the spinning was just getting more intense. When I closed my eyes, it made the sensation worse, so I popped them back open and stared at the ceiling, admiring how the red glowed over the darkness.

The whole place was amazing, and I decided that I loved the club's atmosphere. Even the frantic energy of the people was intriguing. It was almost like the club itself was feeding off the energy that the patrons put out. I wondered if such a thing was possible. It seemed rather fanciful, I supposed.

The line slowly shuffled along until we finally made it to the door. The inside of the bathroom was so much brighter than the rest of the club, though the lights were, thankfully, dimmer than they would be at an average establishment. The brighter lights made it easy for the women lining the sink area to reapply makeup that they had sweated off while dancing and rubbing up against their partners. I saw women reapplying lipstick and powder. One was even rubbing the corners of her eyes and reapplying eyeliner.

I entered the next available stall and carefully sank down onto the toilet seat. Squatting was just beyond my current capabilities. I promised myself a hot shower with lots of soap as soon as I got home and managed to relieve my bladder without falling onto the floor. I eyed the floor and admired how pretty it was with the silver sparkles inside the black. If I squinted my eyes, I could imagine I was looking at a galaxy out in outer space.

I carefully wiped and flushed with the toe of my shoe, only wavering a little bit as I tried to keep my balance before opening the shiny black stall door. I waited patiently for one of the grooming women to make space so I could wash my hands. I met Emmy at the sink, and she smiled at me.

"Ready to head out of here?"

"Yes, but, honestly, I wouldn't mind coming back sometime. I actually did have a lot of fun."

"Maybe not so many drinks, though?"

I giggled. "I'm pretty sure I only had the two and that little one you made me drink with the salt."

"Ah, yeah. The shot of tequila is probably what did you in. Do you think you can make it without throwing up?"

I hadn't felt like throwing up until she said something, but after that, I started feeling my stomach swirling. I placed my head over my stomach. "I don't know."

"Yeah, let's get you out of here before it gets worse. I promise that the fresh air will make you feel a lot better."

I nodded, my head feeling loose and wobbly, as we dried our hands and turned to leave when my eye on caught a bright red dress.

"Melissa."

She was leaning into the corner of the large bathroom,

attempting to hide her face. She looked up when she heard me say her name. Her face twisted into a scowl so fierce, I almost stepped back. Her makeup was smudged under her eyes, and her cheeks were blotchy. It was obvious that she had been crying.

Emmy walked over to her. "What's wrong? Did something happen?"

Melissa straightened her shoulders. "I'm fine. Just had a small fight with my boyfriend."

Her boyfriend? The boss? I frowned at the twisting in my gut that didn't feel the same as the churning nausea from the drinks. I didn't like the thought of her with that man. It felt wrong. It felt like it shouldn't be her with him. Touching him.

"Really, Melissa? Since when have you and the club owner been dating?" Emmy scoffed.

"We've been seeing each other for weeks." She lifted her chin.

"Seeing each other? Melissa, the only way you've been 'seeing' him is by seeing him across a crowded room."

Melissa snarled. "You know nothing!"

She stomped past Emmy and checked me with her elbow, knocking me into the wall. My head bounced against the wall making stars dance behind my eyelids. I started to slide down when my knees buckled, but Emmy kept me from falling.

"Hey! Watch what you're doing, you psychotic bitch!"

Melissa whirled back around. "Did you just call me a bitch?"

"No," Emmy taunted. "I called you a *psychotic* bitch."

I blinked in surprise at the venom in her tone. Melissa was known for her nastiness, but Emmy was always so sweet and happy. I was in shock that she could be so angry.

"Go ahead, coddle the little freak. Should have known the bitch couldn't even take one tiny bump," she sniggered, while looking at me.

I cringed at being called a freak. It had been a really long time since anyone had called me that. I thought I had stopped it from happening once I started wearing the contacts.

"It was more than a little bump, Melissa! You made her bang her head into the wall."

"Whatever," she huffed in annoyance, now that several women had started paying attention. I looked around and saw the bathroom had become packed with women wanting to see what the fighting was about. One thing I have learned over the years, people loved to gather around to watch someone get tormented. "I'm out of here!"

She spun on her tall red heels and shouldered her way through the crowd, before throwing open the door and storming out. Emmy turned to me.

"Are you okay?"

I sighed in exhausted frustration. "Yeah. I just want to go home." She grimaced and led me out of the bathroom while some of the women were openly staring, some of them talking loudly about the fight.

We left the hallway and walked back over to the table where the girls had sat back down to tell them we were leaving.

"Awww, why do you have to go, Emmy? We hardly got any time together!"

"Yeah, Emmy, why do you have to go?" We spun around to see Melissa standing behind us. I thought she had left, but apparently, she was just getting ready for round two. "Do you have to get the little baby home since it's past her bedtime?" She pouted at me. "Are you too overwhelmed and can't handle being around all the adults, *freak*?"

There were several gasps behind us since Melissa had yelled her comments loud enough for everyone to hear.

"Melissa!" the shocked outburst came from behind me, but I didn't know which one of the girls it was.

She looked at the rest of the girls behind me. "What? You all know it's true. You all say the same things about her that I do. At least I am honest. I don't pretend to be her friend to her face, and then talk about how weird she is to everyone else when she's not around." She looked at Emmy. "Right, Esmeralda?"

My heart sank, and I looked over at Emmy. When I saw the guilty look on her face, I felt my cheeks start to burn, and tears filled my eyes. I didn't want to cry in front of these people. I didn't want to show them how much of a baby I really was. I started backing up and jerked my arm back when Emmy reached her hand out to me.

"Jules..." I shook my head and kept backing up, still blinking rapidly to stop the tears from falling.

"Whoa, darlin'. I am more than willing if you want to fall into my arms," a deep voice spoke from behind me, as I stumbled backward and collided with a solid form. Hands went to my waist and slid around me, holding me tightly. My arms were pinned to my sides, my purse dangling from one hand. I couldn't move to get away. All I could do was wiggle my body. "Shhh, sweetheart. I won't hurt you, but I can definitely take care of you." His breath tickled my neck as his face sank into my neck.

I felt his tongue lap at my skin and shivered in revulsion. He must have thought it was from pleasure, though, because he rubbed against my backside. "That's it, baby. We can have a lot of fun together. Why don't we find a quiet corner and get to know each other?"

Emmy stepped forward. "She doesn't want you, you idiot! She wants to get away! Let her go!"

"Really?" he drawled. "Why don't we ask her?" He put his mouth right at my ear and said, "What do you think, sweetheart? You want to come with me and let me show you how much fun we can have together?"

I whimpered and shook my head, but fought back against the panicked feeling. I could smell the alcohol lacing his breath. I didn't really think he would hurt me or force the issue. Instead, I had a feeling he was being overly amorous without realizing I just wasn't interested.

Emmy stormed up to him and started really laying into him when he finally let me go and raised his hands.

"Okay, okay, calm down. I didn't mean any harm. I just thought the little thing would be interested. Why else would a girl come to a meat market like this?" He started backing away.

A meat market? I guess that would be an apt description of a place where so many seemed bent on finding a partner for the night.

"Well, she's not! Maybe you won't put your hands on a woman without her permission next time!" Even in the dim lighting, I could see how red her face was. I looked over at the group and saw they had a bunch of different emotions. A couple were shocked at what was happening. But Melissa was smirking right at me.

Suddenly, the air felt like it was charging, like the moment before a powerful storm started pounding rain and lightning began striking the earth. The bouncer from the stairs was striding over, likely to see what the commotion was, and the man, the owner that Melissa had declared her boyfriend, was right behind him.

It wasn't the bouncer that spoke first, but the owner. "Someone want to explain what is going on over here?"

His voice was deep and had a slight menacing growl to it that caused all the fine hairs on my arms to stand up. His voice had a faint accent that I couldn't place, but was likely European of some kind. He scanned the faces of the group, making a short stop on Melissa, who stood up straighter and ran her fingers through her hair. When they met mine, I felt those lightning strikes hit me right in the center of my chest. I grabbed my wrist and furiously started rubbing at the ache I suddenly felt there. His eyes dropped to my hands, and his jaw hardened until the muscle there jumped with the tension.

Melissa stepped forward and raised her hand to place it on his arm, but he stepped back from her and turned his glare on her. She took a quick step back and pouted. He shook his head and looked back at me.

"Are you okay?" His voice, though much softer, was no less menacing than before. The full weight of his stare on me made those lightning strikes worse, and the tension gathering in my chest made it hard to breathe. I tried to make my head nod, but my neck muscles suddenly felt stiff and loose all at the same time. My head wanted to loll around due to the dizzy feeling flooding my brain, but I couldn't make my muscles move. I couldn't catch my breath, and my vision was growing dimmer as the edges of my eyesight got darker and darker. The last thing I knew before I passed out was hearing the boss curse viciously and lunge for me as I fell.

CHAPTER

SIX

VAREK

"FUCK!" I let out a growl, as I watched my fated mate start to crumble to the floor. I jumped forward to catch her tiny body and cradled her to my chest.

I had been feeling off all night, which was why I was in the club instead of behind my desk doing paperwork or watching the monitors. My brand had started tingling a couple of hours ago, and while I was standing in the club eyeing the partiers, the feeling had intensified to give me a strong urge to scratch at the skin there.

I had gotten distracted by the human woman who had, once again, cornered me, trying to make a play. A few weeks ago, when she had first shown her interest, I told her that I didn't return her interest, but she was persistent. Any time I spent in the club, which wasn't often, she had been there as if lying in wait. Earlier, when she tried to press closer to my body, I placed my hand on her shoulder to keep her from touching me. But unfortunately, she wasn't getting the hint and was starting to become a problem. I was talking to Rake

63

about banning her permanently when the commotion caught our attention.

We saw the group of women that the persistent human had been with, and just past them, to a woman shouting at a human male. He had been holding someone, but she was too small to see over the crowds of people. When I got closer to the group, I could feel the brand lighting up my insides, telling me my mate was nearby. I looked around to see if I could spot her, but didn't get the feeling that I had found her yet. Then I laid my eyes on the small woman that the human male had, luckily for him, released and stepped back from.

When we made eye contact, everything within my body lit up. I had only allowed myself a few moments over the last twenty-one years to imagine what my mate would be like. I hadn't wanted to dwell on it, not wanting to be disappointed if she didn't match the vision that I had created. Not that I was particularly eager. I thought I could have continued going the way I had been without ever meeting my mate. I certainly would never have envisioned this frail woman I was now holding.

When I saw her, the first thing I noticed was her size. She would only come up to my chest. I realized I could never be rough with her, or I could do real damage. Next, I noticed her face was nearly completely hidden by overly large black framed glasses. I could tell the lenses were nothing but clear glass, and they weren't to help her see better. I had to find out what she was hiding or hiding *from*. I could see her eyes through those clear lenses, but something was wrong. They were a dark brown but didn't quite look right.

I pulled her body closer to me. She had become overwhelmed by the overload of sensation that crashed through her system when coming face-to-face with her mate. It was a very real possibility that she didn't know anything about the demon world. I could sense she was human, but she was also more. She was likely one of the stories we occasionally encountered of a demon impregnating a human female and abandoning her, not realizing that he had fathered a child.

I turned to face the group of women and saw one tall brunette staring at my mate anxiously.

"Sir, I will take her home if you could call us a car. She had a little too much to drink tonight, and I think she became overwhelmed by that guy."

I growled deep in my chest. "What guy?"

Her eyes got big, and she stammered out, "I don't know. He had grabbed her, but when I told him to let her go, he finally did. He left as you were coming over here."

I knew now who she was speaking of. So, it was my mate that he was holding and I couldn't see. I glanced around through the crowded room to see if I could spot him. I turned to Rake. "Find him!" He nodded sharply at me and immediately moved through the people. He knew I wouldn't be able to settle my rage until I dealt with the male that had laid hands on my mate.

I turned back to the woman that was wringing her hands. "You don't need to take her. I will make sure she is alright." I turned to walk through the club to take her to my penthouse at the top of the building we were currently standing in. She gasped behind me and stammered out a denial, but I didn't stop to listen. I was striding through the entry room when I had to quickly stop as someone jumped in front of me.

"What are you doing?" the human that had been practically stalking me for weeks screeched at me. "You can't take her!"

"I already have." I stepped around her, but she stopped me again, stomping her foot in rage.

"I have been right here, trying to get your attention. You kept brushing me off, and now you're taking the little freak? Just call her a cab and send her home. You don't need to take care of her."

I leaned forward, carefully working to keep my eyes from bleeding to black. "I have repeatedly told you that I don't want anything to do with you or your little delusion that you are special. But, unfortunately, you haven't seemed to be able to get the message through your obtuse little skull, so let me make this as clear to you as

I can. You. Are. Banned. From. My. Club." I allowed the menace to coat my words. "And you will never talk about her that way again. *Am I perfectly clear?*"

Her face was red enough to be seen in the darkened club and she opened her mouth as if she were going to argue. She swallowed hard, clamped her mouth shut and nodded, but her eyes were narrowed and held a wealth of defiance. She would continue to be a problem, but she still would not be allowed back inside the building. I needed to find out what her relationship was with my mate because she seemed unstable and a possible threat to her safety.

Once again, I stepped around her, nearly to the demon entrance and my personal quarters, when I was stopped once again. I growled and spun around to glare at the human, but realized it was the brunette from earlier. She seemed to actually be concerned for the welfare of my mate, so I tried to have patience as she stuttered out her reason for stopping me.

"S-sir, her p-purse!"

I nodded my thanks, took it from her without releasing my mate's legs, and strode away. I nodded to the guard at the entrance to The Tower as he opened the door for me. My long strides ate up the ground quickly, entered my office, walked through it, and out through the back door to the elevator that only had one stop.

Once the elevator doors opened, I entered the expansive open space of my apartment lounge. I strode past the black leather sectional and fireplace and down the hall to the master bedroom. No one but myself and my housekeeper had been in this room for decades. I gently laid her down on the red comforter and carefully removed her glasses, placing them on the nightstand. I then pulled off her tiny shoes and wondered at how small her feet were compared to mine.

I needed to learn this woman's secrets. I needed to understand why she hid behind those ugly frames, and I needed to know why she had a deep scar marring the skin below her left eye. Her features were delicate, her skin pale and smooth. Her oversized sweater dress hid much of her body from me. I didn't know the shape of her body. I didn't know how large or small her breasts were, though, considering the rest of her, she was likely on the small side.

In the past, I'd had all shapes, sizes, and colors. Both in human as well as Other. I had little reason to turn one down. I hadn't been indiscriminate, and many extremely beautiful women had tried to entice me to their bed. I learned to be wary of many. Unfortunately, too many women, human, demon, or otherwise, were too power hungry to trust, so I hadn't allowed myself to be caught in any woman's web. Looking down at this woman, I wondered, would I have been so drawn to her if she hadn't been my mate? Was it possible I would have allowed her to wrap me in her web?

I looked over at her purse, which I had dropped at the foot of the bed, and opened it, needing some clues as to who fate had decided to give me. Inside I found her wallet, a set of keys, and an ID on a lanyard that declared her a CNA. Her name was Juliette. I tasted the name on my tongue as I tried out the feel of it on my lips. The picture of her looked much as she looked now. The same hair pulled back in a tight bun on the back of her head. Same large frames covering much of her face. She was hiding herself, that was clear.

I put the ID aside and opened her wallet. She didn't have a driver's license or any credit cards. She had one debit card and a state ID. There was thirty-two dollars in cash in small bills inside a pocket. And that was it. I looked at her state ID and saw it was nearly identical to her work one. It listed her address as an apartment building that had decent security on the lower end of the scale but definitely not in the poorer neighborhoods.

Her height was listed as five-foot-one. I shook my head. I was more than a foot taller than her, nearly a foot and a half. I could break her easily. But, looking at her lying so still in front of me, I knew I needed to be the one to protect her. I didn't know if it was from the mating pull or simply from looking at her frailness and knowing how easily she could be hurt physically.

I placed everything back into her bag and set the bag next to her glasses on the nightstand. I stood over her for several minutes, just taking in her features and what I could see of her body. I walked out the door and to the linen closet down the hall and retrieved a small, soft blanket. I didn't want her to get cold, but I also didn't want to disturb her by pulling the blanket out from underneath her body. I laid it over her, covering her from her neck to past her toes.

I walked over to the wall-length windows and looked out over the city that I had called home for more than one-hundred years. I helped build and grow this city. It had been a small, yet busy town once. With the right hints in the right ears, the city built what it needed to grow and thrive. Many demons had followed me to this place just as they had to the other cities, states, and countries over the thousands of years I ruled on this Earth.

I didn't have any memories of being in hell. I didn't know why I had been banished to Earth or if it had even been a punishment. I just knew that entering any portals I had come across was impossible, including the portal in the basement. My club is what allowed the demons to come and go, to enjoy their time on Earth, to stay indefinitely if they desired. But if they stayed, they followed my rules. Rules meant to keep both humans and demons safe.

I caught the reflection of my mate in the window and wondered again at fate's plan for us. Why her? What would be the reason that someone so fragile was placed in my path? I couldn't turn my back on her no matter the reason, even if I wanted to keep her safe. I looked down at my wrist, where the brand had been barely visible for twenty-one years. It was now a bright red, and I had no doubt that Juliette's was as well.

My little broken doll was trapped with the big bad monster with no way of escaping. If only I had the confidence that I wouldn't break her any more than she already was. I frowned as I continued staring sightlessly out of the window. She was an enigma, and I needed to solve the puzzle.

CHAPTER
SEVEN

I GROANED as my head pounded. I didn't remember ever having a headache quite like this before. My eyelids felt swollen, and my mouth felt disgusting. My tongue felt like I need to scrape it clean.

I stretched out my body and almost groaned again, but in bliss, as I reveled in the most luxurious bed I had ever laid on. I had splurged on my mattress when I got my own place to live. I had spent too long on that horrible, dirty mattress with springs waiting to slice into my skin, so I bought the best mattress I could afford the first chance I got. Granted, it wasn't much, but it was still so much better than the mattress from my childhood home. The beds at the group home weren't bad, but they weren't high above a concrete slab, either.

This bed, though, was heaven. My eyes popped open. Why would my bed feel so luxurious? Where was I? I gazed around quickly and saw the red, white, and black room. The walls were white, but the bed I was lying on and the rest of the furniture was black. The bedding was red, matching the pictures hanging on the walls. The artwork was abstract and almost brutal in the slashes and splatters of black and red paint.

I swung my legs over the side of the bed and brushed my shaking hand over the top of my head, feeling the bun at the back of my head that had come loose and was barely hanging on. My heart was pounding in fear, and my breath was coming fast in and out of my lungs, making my chest burn.

I looked around wildly, not seeing anything familiar. The room was huge, and the decor was luxurious, but the fact that I had no idea where I was made me see it as a scary place from a nightmare. Thoughts of being kidnapped, raped, and tortured had me wanting to run screaming from the place, but at the same time, I wanted to curl into a ball on the bed. Maybe pretend I was safe at home in my apartment.

My eyes landed on the table beside the bed, where I saw my glasses and my purse, and a relieved gust of breath left me. I reached for it, and when I dragged my bag over, I accidentally knocked over a glass of water and noticed the two white pills that were lying next to it, now soaking in the spilled water. I ignored the mess and frantically searched my purse, looking for my cell phone. I let out a relieved sigh when my fingers wrapped around the cheap plastic and pulled it to me, flipping it open. My relief was quickly squashed, and I cried out in frustration to see that the battery was dead.

I threw the phone down onto my purse and stood up, wobbling a bit as my legs took a moment to accept my weight. I took a few steps forward and then turned in a circle. Everything was clean and fresh. It looked like it was cleaned daily, the carpet freshly vacuumed, and the furniture dusted and polished. I noticed several different doors and moved to the closest one, pulling down on the lever and swinging it open to discover an extremely large closet.

The closet had a center island and a bench. Rails held suits in all black, each looking similar and very expensive. Open shelves held neatly stacked t-shirts, sweat pants, denim pants, and anything else that a man would possibly need in a closet. Everything was all black.

I backed out of the closet, closing the door as I went, and turned toward another door a few feet from the man's closet and opened it to discover a very similar closet that was completely empty, not even a mote of dust.

I turned to another door that was cracked open and pushed it wide. It was the bathroom. A bathroom that I thought only existed in magazines. The white tile floor was gleaming, and the black marble countertops were spotlessly clean. A gigantic black tub had jets surrounding the inside, and the double sinks had wide black spouts hanging over the basins.

The shower was the largest I had ever seen. I didn't know they could get so large, and I didn't understand why one would need to be. The front of it was a massive glass wall so clear it was nearly invisible. A person would have to scrub it down daily in order to maintain that sort of complete cleanliness.

I turned to the mirrored wall above the sinks and stared at my reflection. My eyes were huge on my face. I looked like I was in shock, and I felt like it. My face was paler than normal, my hair was a mess, and my eyes were bloodshot from being irritated from wearing my contacts all night. My eyes felt scratchy and sticky. I desperately needed to wash my face. I looked over the gleaming countertop and saw the small basket in the middle between the sinks that had neatly arranged washcloths rolled up.

They were all in black, white, and red. It was definitely a color scheme that was carried through the suite. It made me think of the club, and I wondered if I was still at the same location. But why would I be? The last thing I remembered was a fuzzy recollection of a man holding me when I didn't want him to. I remembered feeling scared and seeing Esmerelda screaming at the man to let me go. Then the tall, angry looking bouncer was storming over toward the commotion we had been causing.

The other girls had been standing back, watching. I frowned. They hadn't come to my aid, had they? A man was accosting me, but they stood back and let Emmy handle the situation. Melissa was there, too, but she was standing with her arms crossed over her chest, her hip jutting out, and a smirk on her face. She had been enjoying my discomfort.

Then Melissa's eyes had gone wide, and she had stood up straighter. A look of disbelief had crossed her face. What had she been looking at?

I took one of the rolled-up wash clothes from the basket, hesitant to mess up the display, but I needed to wash my face. I looked through a few of the drawers to find they were mostly bare. There was no medicine cabinet where people would usually stash things like toothpaste and facial wash, so if there was any in this bathroom, it had to be in one of the drawers.

I moved over to the other sink, opened the top drawer, and saw a neat arrangement of male paraphernalia. A razor, a small bowl with what looked like soap in it, a large brush but with a short, stubby handle. A comb. They were all arranged on top of a microfiber cloth. Obviously, it was to protect the drawer from messes. I didn't think it really mattered, though. Whoever cleaned the place was very good about keeping it spotless. I would think even a dust mote would be too frightened to want to land on a surface.

I stood there staring at the arrangement of a man's shaving kit. Finally, I reached out with a shaking hand toward the tube of tooth-paste lying next to a toothbrush. I wouldn't touch the toothbrush. I didn't want to touch the paste either, but I felt disgusting and wanted to clean my mouth. I took a tiny bit and used my finger to scrub at my teeth and tongue. I rinsed and spit and then did the whole process over again.

I carefully replaced the tube exactly where it had been and started opening other drawers, but I came up empty. There was no face wash. I turned the water to hot and was surprised at how fast the water changed. In my experience, the water took ages to warm up. I ran the washcloth under the scalding water and immediately turned the temperature down a hair. I wanted to clean my face, not melt it off. I wiped at my face with the cloth and held the towel to my eyes for a few moments. I needed to take my contacts out, but without a case or solution, I would have to throw them away, and they were my last pair.

I sighed and lowered the towel. And then I gasped, a scream getting lodged in my throat. A man was standing in the bathroom in front of the other sink. He had his hand placed on the counter and was leaning against the marble, staring at me. He was the owner of the club. I had seen him last night, but I hadn't seen him well. Here in the bright light of the bathroom, I had no words to describe what his presence did to me. His appearance was more handsome than I had initially thought. Handsome wasn't the right word for him, though.

He was magnificent. He was masculine, the type of masculinity that all men would strive for. There was an air about him that screamed alpha. Supreme confidence ran through every cell in his body. I was immediately intimidated and started trembling.

I opened my mouth to speak, to ask him why he was here, to ask why I was here, but no words would come out. I did manage an embarrassing squeak, though. He didn't smirk at me or laugh at my timidness. He didn't look angry that I was in his space. He didn't give anything away with his stare, and it was making me even more uncomfortable. I swallowed hard. I took everything within me, all my inner strength and backbone, to hold his stare instead of running past him and out the door.

"Contacts," he murmured.

I wrinkled my forehead. "Huh?"

"I knew something was wrong with your eyes last night and couldn't figure out what it was, but looking at you now, I can see what it was that was bothering me." He ran his eyes over my face. You don't need glasses either, do you?"

Realizing that I didn't have my glasses on, I put my fingertips to the scar under my left eye.

"Don't do that," his voice was still low, still just a soft murmur. I wondered if he was trying to calm me or keep me from freaking out more than I already was. "You don't have to cover up from me."

"Why?" I whispered.

"You have no idea who you are, do you?" his deep voice almost sounded like a purr, and I realized it really was calming me. I would never have guessed that a man so tall and powerful would be able to relax me in such a tense situation. Especially, since it seemed like he was the one that put me there to begin with.

I let my hand lower, wishing I had my glasses with me, needing that armor I had grown accustomed to relying on. "Why am I here?" I couldn't bring my voice above a whisper yet.

He ignored me and reached into the back pocket of his black jeans. His movements caused the long sleeve Henley style shirt with the top two buttons unbuttoned to stretch across his chest, showing off the defined pectoral muscles there.

He pressed a couple of buttons and placed the phone to his ear. "Talon, can you send someone to the closest drug store and pick up some contact solution and a case." He spoke to me then and asked, "Is there anything else you need from the store?"

I opened and closed my mouth a couple of times, probably looking like an idiot, before finally saying, "A toothbrush and face wash?"

He nodded at me approvingly and relayed the request to the Talon person he had on the line. He pushed his finger against the screen, slid the phone back into his back pocket, and crossed his arms over his chest, this time making the sleeves of his shirt pull across his arm muscles.

We continued to stare at each other, no words passing between us. I couldn't pull my eyes from his face. The deep scruff on his face looked like it had been at least twenty-four hours since he had shaved. The hair on his cheeks was black, precisely the same shade as the thick, wavy hair on his head. It was styled in a way that looked like he spent little effort on it. Just combed it each day and then spent the rest of the time running his fingers through it to push it out of the way.

It didn't look long enough to pull back in a ponytail or man bun, but it was definitely longer than the average businessman would have. There was one wave that seemed to stay over his forehead, just above his right eye. I wondered if that lock of hair irritated him, and if left alone, would it make it into his eye? I also noticed that there was something strange about his hair.

I had thought last night that my eyes were playing tricks on me. His hair had looked like it was absorbing the shadows he had been standing in. Here, in the bright light of his bathroom, his hair wasn't absorbing shadows, but it did seem to have a different quality than any other person I had seen. It wasn't shiny under the lights. It also wasn't dull like someone's hair might get if they were sick or malnourished. It was difficult to wrap my mind around. It was so unique.

His bright, deep green eyes continued to hold my gaze, and I felt like he was somehow reading my soul. I had the fanciful thought that by the time he was satisfied, he would know every secret I had. His eyes were not unkind, but they had no warmth either.

I tried to ask another question, hoping to get some insight. "Can you tell me where I am?" I heard the tremor in my voice. I was ashamed that I was showing him how weak I truly was. I didn't know why it was important that I prove that I had strength inside of me, but it was an insistent voice inside of me that I felt I needed to heed.

"You are in my penthouse."

"Where, exactly, is your penthouse located?"

One side of his mouth tilted up ever so slightly, so slightly that it was barely noticeable.

"You are above my club, Brimstone. What do you remember from last night?"

"I remember a guy being too handsy and my friend..." I shook my head when the memory of being told that Emmy had also talked about how strange I was came back to me. "The group I was with yelled at him to let me go. One of the bouncers came up to the group, and... that's all I can really remember."

"Hmmm." He rubbed the stubble on his jaw, and a slight rasping sound filled the room. Then, I noticed what looked like a tattoo on the inside of his wrist when his sleeve pulled back slightly with his movements. The design was very familiar. It was a bright, red color. As I looked at it, he became very still, letting me stare.

It hit me why it looked so familiar.

All my life, I'd had a mark on my inner wrist. It grew with me, keeping its shape even as my skin would have grown and stretched. It was hardly noticeable. Really, no one had ever noticed it. Except, I knew it was there. As a part of me, I had grown to secretly love it. I would rub it when I was upset, bringing me peace and calmness. It had been itching last night. I remember that now.

With effort, I tore my gaze from his mark and looked down at mine. It was the same shade of red that his was. The markings were easier to read now that they weren't the same color as my skin. The markings that were always just the tiniest bit raised looked more pronounced. The symbols that I had no idea what they meant stood out against the paleness of my skin.

I rubbed my fingertips over the markings. They didn't smudge or fade. Instead, they looked like a tattoo that had been etched onto my skin for years, instead of just a few hours. I looked back up at him. "What is this? What does it mean?"

He just stared at me as if he were working out a puzzle. I looked back down, and instead of trying to rub the marks off, I gently traced the lines with a fingertip. The markings were strange, unlike anything I'd seen before. And then I remembered seeing similar markings on the walls of the club. I had thought they were just interesting wall art to add to the atmosphere of the club, but now I sense that they held a deeper meaning.

I looked back up to him to see his eyes were on my skin, tracing the lines with his eyes as I traced them with my finger. "They are words, aren't they?"

He gave one brief nod, but didn't allow any more than that. They were important, I could tell. That we had the same marks on our wrists seemed equally important. Until last night, they had been the color of my flesh. Now, they were bold and seemed somehow meaningful. He didn't seem inclined to explain, so I forced myself to drop the subject.

A chime came from his phone, and I watched as he fished it out from his back pocket once again. He glanced briefly at it before replacing it and said, "Stay here." He turned and quickly left the room, his stride like a graceful predator's.

I stared at the doorway he had disappeared through and waited. I needed answers, and I knew I would only be able to get them from him. I was in a stranger's home with matching strange symbols on our wrists. Yet, somehow, he didn't seem like a stranger. Instead, my soul seemed drawn to him even as my mind whirled.

CHAPTER

EIGHT

JULIETTE

It wasn't long before he returned with a plastic shopping bag, and I watched as he reached in and withdrew several items.

First was a toothbrush, and then were several bottles of creams. Apparently, whoever did the shopping didn't know what to get, so they just grabbed several different kinds. I was relieved to see the brand that I usually used. There were also a couple of moisturizers, and lastly, he withdrew a box that held a bottle of contact solution.

The man continued to just stand there as he watched me looking at the array of care products now littering his black marble countertops.

"Are you going to watch me?" I asked nervously.

He didn't say anything as he held his pose of crossed arms and leaned against the sink. I mentally shrugged my shoulders at his non-answer and reached for the toothbrush. However, his hand stopped me when he reached out for it before I could touch it, and I watched as he deftly opened the packaging before handing it to me.

I opened the drawer that held the toothpaste I had previously used and gave him an apologetic look for revealing that I had snooped earlier and used his stuff. I quickly applied a small amount of the paste to my new red toothbrush and tried to ignore him as I brushed quickly. When I was done, I ran my tongue over my now smooth, fresh teeth, grateful to start feeling human again. A hand was in front of my face, and I looked at it to see a bottle of facial cleanser. It wasn't my usual brand. It was one that I had wanted to try, but it was always too expensive for my meager budget. I took it gratefully and turned the water on to a little less hot than I had the first time I had the hot water on.

I lathered my face and wiped off the cleanser with the washcloth I had used previously and then saw him holding out a tub of moisturizer. I gave a small smile of thanks before unscrewing the top and dipping two fingers inside, gathering enough to smooth over my face. When I was done, I wasn't surprised to see him holding the bottle of contact solution and the case that came standard in the box.

I looked up at him, wanting to say that I didn't want to take my contacts out no matter how desperately I needed to remove them from my aching eyes, but his stare told me that he wouldn't accept a no from me.

I shakily took the bottle from him and hesitated another minute, trying to gain courage. I didn't ever let anyone see my eyes. They had been the bane of my existence, the reason for so many people to hate me. Finally, I looked at him and felt my eyes fill up with tears.

He cocked his head to the side, studying me.

"Remove them."

"Please?" I asked quietly, hoping he would relent if he saw my despair, but his stare wouldn't let me get away with ignoring his demand.

I took another shaky breath, opened both lids to the contact case, and squeezed the bottle of solution until both sides were full. I then squeezed some over my fingers to clean them before reaching first for my right eye and removing the dark brown contact. I looked at him through the mirror to see him staring at my eye. He showed no outward sign of surprise, but I could sense that it was there.

I squeezed my eyes shut and finally opened them and slowly, mechanically, pinched the contact from my left eye and placed it inside the remaining open top of the case. I didn't look up, letting my eyelashes obscure my irises.

He placed a long finger under my chin and lifted my face up to meet his. I stubbornly kept my eyes downcast, delaying the inevitable. He just stood there and waited silently for me to shore up my courage.

After what felt like an eternity, but also brief seconds, I finally lifted my eyes and let him see me. With my face washed, the scar was highly visible, the still red scar marring my natural porcelain skin while pulling the lower lid down. The scar above my eye wasn't that bad, but still, it was there. My black iris was by far the worst part of everything. I took a deep, steadying breath and looked at his face as he studied mine.

He didn't say anything for the longest time. I braced myself for the ridicule, the flinch, and for the handsome man to look disgusted.

He did none of those things.

He, instead, traced the worst of the scars and said in a deceptively calm voice, "How did you get this scar?"

I tried to look back down, but he wouldn't let me.

"Tell me!" he demanded, his voice still soft, but with anger lacing every word.

I swallowed hard. I could see that the anger wasn't directed at me, but seeing his rage at all, it was frightening. I could sense that this man was probably the scariest person I would ever meet. I had thought my not-father was the most terrifying man alive once, but now I knew how wrong I was.

With a shaking voice barely above a whisper, I answered him, "It was the man that raised me."

The atmosphere in the room turned hot, heat radiating from inside him, scalding my skin without physically burning me.

"Explain."

I took a ragged breath. "He hated my eye. He said I was a demon. He said that my real father was a demon that raped my mother and impregnated her. He hated looking at me. One day, a few years ago, he came home drunk and attacked me with a knife. He was going to cut my eye out." A tear slipped down my cheek and swept over the finger he still held pressed lightly to my scar.

The heat in the room turned up even hotter at my words. His face remained stoic, but in his deep green eyes that were the color of emeralds, the same shade as my own right eye, I saw fury burning. As I watched, the green bled to a black so deep and bottomless I felt like I would fall into them and never find my way out. Inside those dark depths, I saw torment and suffering. I saw pain and death. I saw that he would be the one to cause it.

I drew in a deep breath as I watched them change back to green slowly, as if he were conducting a battle within himself to control his anger. It was fascinating and scary. Fascinating because, when his eyes had bled to black, they looked exactly like my left eye. I doubted my eye held that world of pain and suffering in it, though.

"Where is he?" his voice was still low and deep. He had yet to raise his voice or show any emotion other than anger, and the brief moment of surprise when he realized that our eyes were eerily similar.

"He got out of prison a few months ago. I haven't seen or heard from him."

"Do you know where he is right now?"

I shook my head. "No. I have tried for years to forget everything he had done to me. When I think about it, I end up having terrible nightmares, so I do my best to forget that he even existed."

The nightmares were brutal. I was always shaky and sweaty when I woke up after one of them. It always felt like it was happening all over again.

I didn't say anything, but I could see his intentions.

"I really don't care what happens to him, truly. But I don't want anyone else to suffer because of him. You would go to prison for hurting him. He's just not worth it."

He just hummed low in his throat, a tone of disagreement. He finally stepped back and gestured toward the door. "Come, let's go eat, and we can talk about what's going on."

My stomach let out a loud grumble at the mention of food. I placed a hand over my abdomen and gave him a sheepish look. "Food would be great," I whispered, and exited the bathroom in front of him.

I stood in the bedroom, unsure of where to go. He walked to the door I hadn't tried opening earlier and pulled the lever before, gesturing to me to lead the way. I did, and I walked down the hallway without knowing where I was supposed to go. I figured he would tell me if I was going in the wrong direction, but considering his bedroom was at the end of the hallway, it didn't seem likely that I would get lost.

The hallway ended at a set of gleaming black stairs which I took while holding on to the banister. The flooring looked slick with its shininess, and I didn't want to slip. There didn't seem to be a danger of that, though. As shiny and smooth as the flooring looked, it didn't feel slippery.

At the bottom of the stairs, I waited for him to direct me again, but he took the lead this time. I followed him past a sunken living room with a black leather sectional couch and a low, black coffee table over a deep red rug. They were facing a black gas fireplace. The floor-to-ceiling windows flooded the room with natural lighting, and I could see the tops of buildings in the distance.

We walked into a large dining area and up to a bar with tall, black stools. He stopped at one of the stools and pulled it out for me to climb onto. I did so awkwardly. I was still wearing the sweater from the night before and didn't want to accidentally flash him my panties. Once I was settled, he walked around the island, entering the kitchen.

He pulled open the refrigerator and took out a package of bacon and a carton of eggs. He set the packages down on the counter that was very similar to his bathroom countertop. Then he walked over to the sink and washed his hands before taking out a skillet from inside a cabinet. I watched as he quickly and efficiently fried up some bacon and then set it aside to drain on top of a plate with a paper towel on it.

When he was done scrambling several eggs, he plated up the food and set one in front of me. I glanced at the food and then up at him. Finally, I took my fork and dived into the fluffy eggs.

"I will never be able to eat all this," I said, as I shoved the forkful in my mouth. I groaned at the flavor. I didn't know if it was because I hadn't eaten anything since the sandwich I ate for lunch yesterday afternoon, or if the eggs were really just that good, but I managed to eat nearly all of the food he placed in front of me.

He watched as I ate, an approving look on his face. I noticed he wasn't eating much, his focus on me instead of his food. When I set down my fork and leaned back, he seemed to snap out of his trance, walked back over to the refrigerator, and pulled out a large pitcher of orange juice. He filled a glass and slid it in front of me.

"Thank you. The food was delicious." I gave him a small, grateful smile and took a sip of the orange juice, reveling in the icy sweetness. It was probably the best breakfast I'd had in years.

When I had downed the last of the drink, he stood up and took my dishes, placing them in the sink. Then, he returned to my side of the island and held out his hand. I hesitated for a moment before slowly putting my hand in his much larger one. The contrast between our sizes, skin tones, and evident strength was fascinating.

My heart jumped and sped up at the feeling that coursed through my hand and up my arm. It was like a buzz of static electricity, making the fine hairs on my arm stand on end, giving me goose-bumps. I held in a shiver and clenched my teeth. I knew whatever was happening was significant. Whatever my body was going through was directly related to touching this man.

I bent my head back, looking at the man. He was so incredibly tall I couldn't help but feel intimidated by our differences in height. Everything about him was in direct opposition to me. He was tall where I was short, even for a woman. He had black hair that seemed to absorb the light around him, as peculiar as that was. I had white hair, the blonde without a single hint of gold to warm it. Silver could be seen when I was in the sun, but it was basically pure white.

He was so confident and had a natural aura of authority. I was a timid little mouse, beat down by years of abuse and mistreatment by others. But there was something about him that was like a magnet to me. I looked at him, really looked at him. He was bold and intimidating. I had a feeling that he could end someone's life as easily as saying 'hello'. And though I knew these things somehow deep within me - I wasn't scared of him. Oh, I was definitely cautious. But my fight or flight instincts didn't tell me to run. Instead, I felt like I should curl up by his side and let him be my champion. He would protect me from anyone that would wish me harm. How I knew this was a mystery since the man had barely spoken a few words, hadn't smiled, nor had he told me why I was even in his home, to begin with.

After staring down at me long enough to make me start to fidget, he finally gave my hand a slight tug, leading me down two steps into the sunken living room. He indicated that I should sit on one end of the black leather sectional while he sat next to me, angling his body with one knee bent on the seat and his arm resting over the back of the couch. I had his full attention, and I wasn't sure if I should run out of the door screaming or snuggle closer and close the space between us.

"We have much to discuss," he began, in his lightly accented voice. The low roughness of it pleasing my senses. "You were not raised in our world, so you have no idea what I am to you, nor do you understand the significance of the symbols we both share."

I looked down at the markings on my wrist, again marveling how it had still been flesh colored just yesterday and nearly impossible to see.

He rubbed his hand against his jaw. It was the first sign that he wasn't entirely confident that I had seen him make since he appeared in the bathroom with me. "I apologize," he said, in his gravelly voice. "I am not sure where to begin. I'm sure the whole of it will be confusing and unbelievable."

I nodded my head at him because, yes, I had no idea what he was going to say, but it was already difficult to believe what was happening.

I watched as his eyes danced between mine, taking his time as if mesmerized by the differences in my irises.

"You said that your father..."

"Not my father!" I didn't hesitate to interject.

"...not your father." He inclined his head, acknowledging that I didn't want to be claimed by Jeff. "Had accused you of being created by a demon with your mother." I nodded my head. "He was right."

I inhaled quickly, causing me to choke on my own saliva. He calmly and patiently waited for me to settle.

"Would you like something to drink?"

I shook my head and then nodded. I didn't really need anything to drink, but I needed something to do. Even if it was just holding a glass. He rose from his seat and returned quickly with a glass that I assumed was wine. I started to shake my head at the offering since my only experience with alcohol was last night when I drank too much and was having trouble remembering all the details.

He continued to hold the wine glass. "You don't have to drink it, but you might need a sip or two to help calm your nerves."

I hesitantly took it and stared down at the light pink liquid.

"It's a sweet wine, something that should go down easy should you need it."

I nodded and waited for him to resituate himself on the couch where he had been before.

"Like I said, your biological father must have been a demon. It's not unusual for demons to seduce human females into sex. It is not uncommon, even, for those dalliances to result in procreation. Most of the time, however, the demon-human hybrid never learns that they have demon blood running through them. Very few are actually able to tap into their demon side.

"Some have physical differences, what humans would call abnormalities." I raised my hand, remembering I wasn't wearing my contacts, so used to never being around people without them. I almost felt naked, definitely felt exposed and vulnerable. He took my hand and lowered it until it lay between us and left his hand there, gently rubbing over my knuckles.

"Some have power that humans never have. There are those that think they are witches because they are able to tap into a source of magic that some demons possess. Depending on the breed of demon that conceived the child, there could be multitudes of things that differentiate the hybrid from a typical human. But humans tend to ignore what they can't explain.

"Demons are a race of people that are from the realm of the Underworld. Unlike what Christian religions teach, demons are not evil. Demons are just different. We have been hiding our true identities from humans since time began. We quickly discovered that humans hurt and hate what they fear. We may be stronger physically, and some have magical powers, but humans outnumber us one-thousand to one. If we were to be discovered in this modern age, humans would either cage us as monsters or try to eradicate us altogether.

"As the oldest living demon in this realm, I am responsible for policing our kind. I make the rules, and they follow them. If they don't, they get punished."

I could only sit and blink. My mind was whirling with all he had told me so far, which wasn't much, but was probably the most important information in this conversation. I took a sip of the wine and closed my eyes at the flavor. It was sweet, as he said, and had a subtle fruitiness to it, somewhat like strawberries. I could also feel my stomach get warm, not unlike how it had after the drink Emmy had ordered for me last night.

He cleared his throat, and I looked back up. He looked as stoic as ever, but I could see just a hint of unease in the tightness of his jaw.

"What the symbols on our wrists indicate is that we are unmated fated."

"Fated?" I asked, confused.

"All demons have a fated mate. When one is born, the elder one is struck with a burning sensation as the brand appears on their skin, the baby is also marked, but I assume no one notices it, or if they do, it might be considered a strange birthmark. Sometimes a demon finds its mate after just a few decades. Others might wait centuries. Or longer. Fated mates are considered a gift. They are impossible to resist, and many fall deeply in love because their fated was designed especially for them by the fates. So even though they don't know each other, they are irrevocably drawn together and find themselves very happy. Most of them, anyway."

I took another sip. "Most of them?" I whispered. I didn't know anything about being a fated mate until now, and I wasn't sure what I thought of it, of being tied to this extremely alpha male. But at the thought of rejection, I felt my eyes sting with tears, and my heart started to race.

He nodded his head, his eyes not missing my reaction.

"There have been a few instances where a demon was already in a relationship with another when their fated was born. A demon cannot become aroused by another once their fated is out in the world, and won't be able to enjoy sex for females or have sex at all for males. If they were already in a relationship and were suddenly given the possibility of a mate, they could become very resentful."

It made me sad to think of two people being in love and then being told by fate 'too bad'. "Do they have a choice to cut ties with their fated? It doesn't seem fair that they have to give up someone they love for someone they are forced to be with because of fate."

"There is only one way to cut ties, as you say." His thumb stroked my hand again, and his fingers tightened slightly around mine. "One of the fated pair must die."

CHAPTER
NINE

JULIETTE

THERE WAS nothing for me to do but stare.

Did he intend to kill me so he could be done with the mating? I was twenty-one-years-old, which, if what he was saying was true, then he had been celibate for twenty-one-years. A sexy, virile man was denied sex because of me? How could he not resent me?

An inner part of me, the small, greedy part, was delighted that he hadn't had a woman in so long.

He tilted his head to the side and studied me. "You are pleased."

I widened my eyes. How did he know that? How could he read my emotions so well when I could barely read his expressions?

He chuckled softly. The sound flowed over me and heated me in a way the alcohol never could. "No, I have not even thought about another woman since you were born." His intense look grew even more so when he added, "I don't intend to ignore the mating."

My chest was rising and falling quickly. I was overwhelmed, but I was also fascinated.

"You don't know me. I don't know you. What if the fates got it wrong?" I asked softly.

"I have been alive since the first humans roamed this realm, Juliette. I have learned to trust my instincts. I also see something in you that intrigues me. I don't know what it is yet, but it calls to me."

I latched on to the only safe topic at hand. "How do you know my name?"

His lip ticked up just slightly, noticing my change of subject and allowing it. "I looked through your wallet."

I wanted to be miffed, and I was, at his audacity, but all the rest of the stuff being thrown at me today seemed to make his invasion much less important.

"Can I ask what your name is? I was told last night by the girls I was with that you are the owner of Brimstone. But no one mentioned your name."

"My name is Varek."

"Just Varek? You don't have a last name?

"I do not. I don't know my beginnings. I assume that I was born in hell like most full-blooded demons, but I have no knowledge of ever actually having lived there."

"How do you file information with the government without a full legal name?"

"I use an alias and change it periodically through the years so as to not raise suspicions. It was much easier a few hundred years ago, even one-hundred years ago. With modern technology, the government is able to keep track better, and they don't play around when they want their share of the rewards when taxes come due."

I sat there contemplating what he had told me. He didn't know his origins, so that meant he didn't know his parentage. Demons were from hell, but he didn't remember ever being there. His age was beyond comprehension.

"You said there are different breeds of demons. Do you know what breed you are?"

He took his hand away from mine for a brief moment, just long enough to put a finger under the stem of my wineglass and tilt it up toward my mouth. "Drink."

Assuming he thought I needed liquid courage, I took a long drink of the wine and swallowed nervously, coughing lightly at the slight burn.

"I am not actually sure what my breed is. No one has ever told me if they knew. I am more powerful than any demon I have ever come across." He smirked at me, and as I watched, his eyes bled to black like they had done in the bathroom. Dense black swirled around his head and back and settled into a semi-solid form. He was now sporting a set of horns that curled up from the sides of his head and twisted before pointing up toward the ceiling. Wings that wisped with tendrils of black smokey shadows had a solid, yet seemingly insubstantial form. They were fascinating, and I wanted to stroke them so badly that my fingers twitched. I wanted to know if they felt real or if my fingers would slide through them as if they weren't there at all.

A slight movement caught my eye, and when I looked toward the movement, I gasped. A thin black tail flicked back and forth like a cat that was being playful...or preparing to attack. The tail was exactly the same as the horns and wings. I looked back up to the horns, amazed that I could see details in the shadows, like the way they had grooves that spiraled around from the base all the way to the tips. The wings didn't look feathery, but they also didn't appear leathery either.

I felt a touch on the side of my leg and glanced down to see the tail with the angular end flick back and forth against my leg just below my knee. I watched in fascination as it stopped flicking and started rubbing. The sensation was strange. I could feel it, and it was hotter than the air in the room, but the touch was lighter than expected, like being swiped by a soft, warm feather. I watched as the tail wrapped around my calf, before releasing its hold and slid past my knee and up my thigh. Then, it started to slide up the hem of the sweater dress I was still wearing. I slapped my hand down over the sweater to keep the invader from exploring depths that no one had ever seen other than myself before.

I never felt the tail under my hand. It seemed to evaporate, and wisps of shadows curled out and dissipated before the tail reformed and stroked the top of my hand. I slowly turned my hand over, hoping it wouldn't disappear again. It stroked the inside of my palm, and I slowly closed my hand around it. It felt solid-ish. I had a sensation of holding something solid, but I also knew that if I were to tighten my hand, it would just vanish again if it felt like it. I gave a testing squeeze and was delighted that it held form.

I heard a rumble of sound and looked up at Varek. He looked amused, but there was something more in his black eyes. A heat that hadn't been there a minute ago, and it grew warmer as we stared at each other. I was startled when I felt the tail wiggle in my fist. I released my hold and then softly petted the shadows in apology. I heard a low growl and turned back to Varek once again. He looked hungry and almost feral. I swallowed, understanding. He wanted me because he hadn't had sex in twenty-one years. I was his fated mate and his only option to get laid.

"So..." I swallowed roughly, my throat tight. "We are mates then? You don't plan to kill me to get rid of me?"

"No, we are not mates."

The pain that flared inside of me took me by surprise. I recognized it as heartbreak even though I had never been in love before. I didn't love this man, but knowing he was supposed to be mine but wasn't...it hurt, and I wanted to get away from him so he couldn't see the pain he had caused.

I quickly sat the nearly empty wine glass on the low coffee table in front of us and stood, swaying just a bit as I took my full weight on my wobbly knees. "Excuse me, I need to use the restroom," I mumbled, as I quickly turned to head toward the hallway. There had to be a bathroom nearby for guests. If I couldn't find one, I would just go back to the master bath. I needed to go back to the bedroom anyway so I could grab my glasses, contacts, and purse.

Oh, and my shoes. I needed to get away. It was time to go back home.

I opened the first door I came to and found a linen closet arranged neatly with all black towels of various sizes along with toilet paper and cleansers. The next door was on the opposite side and was a large bedroom in nearly solid white with gray accents. Very monochromatic. Somehow, it was elegant and not boring. I closed the door and tried the next one. I finally located the bathroom with a gorgeous clear sink bowl on a white pedestal and a large chrome spout. I locked the door behind me and sat down on the closed toilet lid.

I put my heels on the edge of the toilet seat, wrapped my arms around my knees, and buried my head in my legs. Why was I so upset? What was I even upset about? I felt irrational and over-whelmed. I thought through the conversation. He said we were fated mates. He had been waiting for me for twenty-one years. But when I asked, he said we weren't mates. Did he want to get rid of me? He said no. I was so confused and distraught. I shouldn't be feeling so much emotion over a man I had known for less than twenty-four hours.

He was attractive in a way that seemed unbelievable. A face and body like his should be posted on billboards or tv screens. Maybe it was just the concept of such a man belonging solely to me. Perhaps, the thought of such a powerful man in front of me, protecting me, was the most appealing. *But he said we weren't mates.*

I was going around and around in my head and getting nowhere. I needed to escape and be surrounded by my belongings. I needed sleep even more than I needed answers.

I dropped my feet to the floor, went to the sink to wash my hands, and took a few deep breaths. Then, when I was ready to face the world again, I cracked open the door and peeked out. I didn't see Varek, so I crept down the hall and up the stairs as quickly and quietly as possible. I was surprised to find my belongings in a neat pile at the end of the bed.

"I know you need to get away, and I will allow that for now. But we still have much, much more to discuss, Juliette."

I glanced over, startled at the sound of his voice, and saw him staring out the floor-to-ceiling windows. I didn't say anything, just slid my feet into my ballet flats, stuffed the plastic grocery bag into my large purse, and slid the strap over my head.

I looked at Varek for a long moment. I knew he was looking at me in the reflection of the glass, our eyes looking right at each other. Finally, I broke eye contact and nodded my head before turning and leaving the room. As I entered the entryway, the elevator doors opened, and a tall man with blonde hair took a half step out and gestured for me to enter the elevator.

"I'm Talon, the head of security. Varek has asked me to make sure you get home safe."

I nodded at the tall, handsome man and said, "Thank you, I appreciate it. Will you call me a cab?"

He shook his head. "I will drive you home and escort you to your door."

"That's unnecessary," I protested, not wanting to make the man go out of his way. "I'm sure you have more important things to do."

"Ma'am, nothing is more important than doing what my boss tells me to do."

"I guess that's true," I sighed and stepped out of the elevator once the doors opened, and he gestured for me to proceed with him. We found ourselves in an underground parking garage below Brimstone that I didn't even know was there. "Well, this is convenient," I said, as I looked around. The space wasn't overly large. It seemed only big enough to hold about twenty vehicles, so It was definitely a private garage. There were several spaces open, but there were also several spaces full with all manner of luxury vehicles.

He led me over to a large SUV with deeply tinted windows. The paint was, of course, black, and it was shiny as if it had been just waxed earlier today. He opened the back door for me, and I awkwardly climbed inside, carefully keeping my thighs covered as well as I could. I buckled my seatbelt, lay my head back against the seat, and closed my eyes with a heavy sigh.

Talon never spoke again, and I found myself lulled into a light sleep as the vehicle drove me toward my apartment building on the other side of the city.

I felt a light touch on my shoulder and opened my eyes. "I fell asleep." It was a statement of the obvious.

He nodded his head. "Yes, you were out for nearly twenty minutes."

I covered my mouth and let out a huge yawn. I blinked my eyes several times to clear the moisture from them before reaching down to unbuckle myself.

"Thanks," I mumbled, as he helped me climb down by holding on to my elbow.

He inclined his head in acknowledgment and shut the door before hitting the lock button on the driver's door handle.

We both headed inside my apartment building, and he patiently waited while I fished around in my purse, pushing aside the shopping bag until my fingers wrapped around my keys. I unlocked my mailbox in the lobby and withdrew the small stack of mail. I quickly scanned through and saw that there was one utility bill and one credit card application, with the rest being nothing but junk mail. I dropped all but the bill into the recycling bin and walked toward the elevator.

"You really shouldn't throw away mail like that. It needs to be shredded so people can't try to steal your identity."

I looked over at Talon as we stood across from each other in the elevator. I pressed my finger to the number four button. "Talon, I have no credit for anyone to try to ruin. I am twenty-one-years-old with no credit cards, and the only place I've rented is this one. I'd be surprised if someone did manage to use my name to get credit."

"That may be, but if it did happen, you would be fighting for years to convince debt collectors and credit bureaus that it wasn't you. And if you try to get another job or a new apartment in the future, you could be turned down because of it."

I inclined my head. "I guess I just figured that since I don't make very much, no one would be very concerned with using my name."

As the doors opened, Talon poked his head out first and scanned left then right before standing back and allowing me to exit. "You'd be surprised," he said.

We walked to my door, and he held out his hand for my key. Instead of arguing at the unnecessary need for him to unlock my door when I was perfectly capable, I just held up the correct key for him to take.

"What are the rest of these keys for?" he asked, while he slipped the key easily into the lock and turned.

"One is for my mailbox, one is for the door to my apartment, and one is for the lobby. The doors stay locked after 10:00pm."

He nodded his head. "That's good. Not perfect since it isn't secured during the day, but it could be worse. Not sure the boss would allow you to stay here if it were unsecured all night."

I raised an eyebrow and stood in the middle of my living room floor while he took the few steps necessary to scan my kitchen, and then in the other direction to scan my bathroom and bedroom. I waited until he was back with me by the front door before asking, "Allow me?"

"The boss will want to ensure you are always safe. Of course, a guard will be posted here regardless, but it will make him feel slightly better to hear about the locking doors at night."

I shook my head. "But why would he care?"

He looked confused, a wrinkle between his eyes. "I thought you were aware of the situation?" he asked carefully.

"The situation where he said we weren't mates when I asked him?" I huffed in annoyance.

"Well, you aren't mates yet," he replied, and pointed at my wrist where the red tattoo-like brand was. "You aren't fully mated until the brand turns dark red. Right now, you are fated, but have not consummated the bond. Not yet mates."

I blinked down at the mark. Is that all Varek meant when he said we weren't mates? That we just weren't mates...yet? "I have a lot to learn," I mumbled, still looking at the mark.

"Yes, you do. But don't worry. Varek is very patient. A male who has lived as long as he, has learned how to wait for what he wants. He will teach you and help you adapt to your new world."

I blinked up at him, absorbing his words and allowing them to comfort me. I never expected this day to happen last night when I joined the group at the club. Never in my life would I have expected to find out that I truly was made from a demon like my not-father had accused me of all my life. Never had I thought that maybe, just maybe, it might be the best thing that ever happened to me.

"Thank you for the ride, Talon." I reached out my hand to shake his. He grasped my fingers, gently squeezing.

"You're welcome, Juliette. I promise that everything will work out how it's supposed to."

"I just may hold you to that promise, Talon."

He grinned and left. It wasn't until I had closed and locked the door and was undressed in the bathroom that I had thought to ask...who was going to be guarding me and how?

CHAPTER

TEN

JULIETTE

WHEN I WOKE UP NEXT, it was to my own stiff mattress and rough sheets. It's strange to know now that I was missing out on such luxuries as a plush mattress and bedding so incredibly lush and soft. I wish I could have enjoyed the shower big enough for at least four people with plenty of elbow room. And where the water heated immediately.

As I stepped into my own bathtub/shower combo that had rust stains I hadn't been able to remove in the years I had lived here, I wondered if I had turned materialistic overnight. If I had one regret from my brief stay at the penthouse apartment, it was that I didn't have a chance to try out that fantastic bathtub.

I washed my long hair twice before adding too much conditioner, as usual, only bumping my elbows against the walls twice. Then, when I was done, after finishing washing my body and shaving almost everything from the neck down, I dried myself off with the small, thin towels that I got last year at an after Thanksgiving sale for a dollar a piece. I was so proud of my find at the time, but now I longed for the plushness of that one washcloth I used yesterday.

While I was applying the smallest amount of high-end moisturizer to my face so I could have it last for the next year, my eyes caught on the marks on my wrist. Varek had called it a mating brand. I thought about what he had said about it turning dark red once we were truly mated, but he didn't explain what it would actually take to become mated. Or what being mated would entail.

I could guess that being mated would be equivalent to being married, which is something I honestly never really gave any thought to. I was aware of my trust issues. It wasn't just men that I was scared of. All people, in general, had shown me that no one was to be trusted. I closed my eyes and hung my head with my hands braced against my sink.

The betrayal of Esmerelda was hitting me harder than it should. I hadn't spent much time with her before the night at the club. Before Friday night, we had only been coworkers who occasionally worked together and talked even less. But the speech she had given me and the attention she had shown me had made me do something that was very rare. I had started to hope.

I didn't blame her, really. Everyone was right. I *was* a freak. But I thought that she was a person that could look past my weirdness and would accept me for who I was. Only a couple of other people showed me that they didn't care. I thought about the house mother at the group home. She was amazing and helped me so much. She saw me, the real me, didn't judge, and didn't allow the other girls to bully me. She taught me how to be more comfortable with myself by hiding my imperfections.

I thought of Mabel and smiled. She never saw me as I really was, but she still showed me that some people were all goodness and light. Her light had shone so brightly, I couldn't help but be drawn to her. A tear slipped down my cheek and dropped into the sink. I will never forget her kindness. Finding out that she dedicated her life to helping others like me, the broken and scared, made me wish for a world where people like her were the true leaders.

I went back into my room and dressed in a comfortable pair of lounge pants and a t-shirt and then spent twenty minutes combing out my hair and applying an oil that would keep it healthy and shiny. No one ever saw my hair down, but that didn't mean I didn't take care of it as much as I could. It was my favorite thing about myself. Unfortunately, it garnered too much attention since it was a strange color. By keeping it up, most people didn't notice it, and therefore, notice me. I liked being invisible. They wouldn't whisper about me or laugh if they didn't see me. Or cringe away.

To be fair, with my contacts and makeup, there weren't really any stares anymore, but old habits die hard.

I gathered my dirty clothes in my laundry basket and grabbed my bag with soap and fabric softener. I made sure to grab a roll of quarters from my dresser drawer before heading toward the living room. I slipped on a hoodie and zipped it up, sliding the hood over my head, and then took my keys from the bowl by the door.

When I opened the door, I backed out, balancing my laundry basket in one hand and closing the door with the other. I slid my key into the lock when I felt my basket sliding out from under my other arm. I glanced over and shrieked. I threw my hands up, causing the basket to go flying in one direction and my keys to go in another.

I quickly turned to run back into my apartment, but the door was already locked. I banged on my door and twisted the knob as if someone was going to open it for me from the inside. Which was impossible since I didn't even own a fish, let alone have a roommate that would let me in. That didn't stop my frantic actions, though.

When I realized I wasn't getting in and a quick look around didn't show me where my keys had gone, I spun around and put my back to the door. The huge man in front of me was too close. There was no way I'd be able to run away from him.

I was panting hard, my heart beating wildly before his words finally penetrated my terror.

"Calm down! Stop screaming. No one is going to hurt you!" The man standing in front of me with his hands held up in the air was the angry looking bouncer from the club, the one that had been guarding the stairs all night and came over with his boss to see what the commotion was when I had been accosted by the drunk guy.

My scream ended in a dying wail that echoed up and down the hallway.

"Thank god," he said, as he put a finger to his ear and wiggled it around like he was trying to get his hearing back.

I could feel my cheeks redden from embarrassment. Talon had told me that someone would be watching my apartment when he dropped me off yesterday. I just hadn't expected someone to be literally at my door.

"What are you doing scaring me like that?" I snapped. I stomped over to my upturned basket and hastily started grabbing clothes and stuffing them back in. I looked around and wanted to crawl into a hole when I saw a pair of my light blue cotton panties draped over the toe of his big black boots. My humiliation took a turn into never wanting to leave my apartment again when he bent down and picked them up with both hands. He held them up, dangling them in all their granny panty glory before I snatched them from his hands and buried them down at the bottom of my basket.

"You could have warned me, you know?" I huffed, and spotting my keys several feet away, stomped over to them and swiped them up. I continued down the hall to the elevator and pushed the button for the car several times.

"It won't actually arrive any quicker by pushing it more than once, you know."

"I know that!" I said, as I pushed it three more times. "When did you get here?" I asked, still facing the elevator doors.

"I just arrived about an hour ago. I relieved the guy who was here overnight."

I turned then, incredulously said, "All night? That's ridiculous!

Nothing ever happens around here. That's why I rent from this building. It has the best security I can afford."

He scoffed and looked back to where we had come before looking back at me with his brow raised. "You just screamed your head off like a pack of hellhounds were about to rip you to pieces, and not one single person looked out their door to check to see if you were okay."

I turned back to the elevator, thankful that the doors had finally opened, and stepped in.

"Maybe they couldn't hear me?" I mumbled.

The joker put his hand to his ear, cupping it. "What was that? You have to speak up. I'm afraid I don't have all my hearing back yet. Are you sure you aren't part banshee?"

I chose to ignore his comment.

"The building is secure. No one would have been able to get in without a key." I lifted my chin smugly. "So there wouldn't have been a reason for anyone to think something bad was happening."

He looked at me incredulously. "You can't be serious?"

Okay, it was kind of a stupid remark. And now that I think about it, I was disappointed that no one thought to check to make sure I was alright.

"Maybe someone called the police?"

"And by the time they arrived, you would have been nothing but an oozing puddle of broken limbs and guts," he pointed out unhelpfully.

I decided to change the subject. "How did you guys get in here anyway? The door stays locked all the time."

He didn't even give me an answer, just an 'are you kidding me right now,' look.

He followed me off the elevator and down the dimly lit hall. The basement didn't have the nice carpeting or painted walls that the apartment floors had. Instead, it was nothing but cinder block walls and cement flooring. Single bulbs dangled from their simple fixtures, and a couple of them blinked on and off. The space had always creeped me out, but it was safe.

"What are all these doors for?"

"They are storage units that some of the residents pay for. A few of the guys ride their bikes to work, so they store them down here instead of in their apartments." I looked back at him. He still looked like he was about to hulk out and shred someone with his bare hands even though he sounded interested, not angry enough to kill. "What's your name?"

"Rake."

"Rake? Like the garden tool?"

Now he looked like he could kill someone. I swallowed hard. "Uh, I mean, I didn't mean to..."

"Yeah, Rake, like the garden tool. You know how many times I've heard that one?"

"I didn't mean to offend you. I know what it's like to be made fun of. I wasn't doing that."

I walked through the open doorway of the laundry room. It had three washers and three dryers, which didn't seem like nearly enough for a building this size, but most of the units had washer and dryer hookups inside, so there weren't actually that many of us that needed to use the ones down here. I had one of the smaller, one-bedroom units, so there wasn't a laundry room inside my apartment.

I walked to my favorite machine, the one that didn't smell like someone had left their week-old gym socks wet in it for a year. I quickly dumped everything in and pulled my detergent from my bag. I dropped two pods in and lowered the lid. I fished my roll of quarters from the bottom of the bag and peeled away the paper so I could fill the greedy machine with several of my hard-earned dollars.

"You know you're supposed to separate those, right? You've got your whites all mixed in with your colors, and your delicates are going to be ruined by being washed with your towels."

I snorted. I turned around and leaned against the washing machine after I turned the dial and hit start. "My entire wardrobe, including everything that is still upstairs, doesn't cost as much as your shoes. Everything I buy, other than my underwear, comes from thrift stores. So, if I ruin a fifty-cent t-shirt, I doubt it would be the disaster of the century. Besides, there are only three machines. I'd have to wait even longer if anyone else was using them before I got here. The sooner I can get done and get out of here, the happier I would be." I pointed to the one at the end of the short row. "Not to mention, that one smells like moldy cheese and popcorn soaked in dog pee, and this one." I tapped the one next to me. "Leaves beautiful brown stains on everything. I may have fifty-cent t-shirts and two-dollar jeans, but I want them to last more than one washing."

He stared at me for a long moment before nodding his head.

"So, what do you do now?"

"Now, I wait. If you leave your clothes unattended, they tend to end up in a soapy pile on the floor."

He grimaced. "I should have brought my book."

This was interesting. "What do you read?" I asked, intrigued.

He shuffled his feet, leaned against a dryer, and peered out the doorway. When he was done fidgeting, he sighed and mumbled.

"What was that?"

He glared at me, his look murderous. I smirked. I was beginning to realize Rake was all bark and no bite. He mumbled again, a little louder.

"Did you say romance?"

He growled. "Yes! I read romance."

My jaw dropped open. "Get out! Really? That's so cool. You don't hear about many guys reading romance, even though you just know that there have to be some out there, right? What's your favorite genre?"

He rolled his eyes and huffed, obviously not wanting to have this conversation, but I thought it was a great way to pass the time.

"You aren't going to let this go are you?"

I grinned. "No way."

He sighed long and loud. "I liked to read paranormal stuff."

"Like demons?" I goaded. "Do you like it when demons find their true love and live happily ever after?"

He growled. "Keep it up, little girl, and I'm going to leave you in this spooky basement all by yourself."

I looked around. "It is pretty spooky, isn't it? One time I couldn't make it down here during the day, and I really needed my scrubs washed for work the next day, so I had to come down here at night. You would think it would look exactly the same as it does any other time, but I swear the creep factor jumped up at least one-hundred percent. Every little sound, creak, and buzz of the light bulbs made me jump. By the time I was done, I literally ran down the hall and almost peed myself waiting for the elevator."

We were both laughing when a shadow entered the doorway.

"Hey, Juliette." Curt from 2B walked in and smiled at me. "I was hoping I would find you here."

I put my head down and made sure my hoodie was covering me fully. "Hey, Curt," I whispered.

He walked to the smelly cheese washer and started putting his gym clothes in before dropping one pod inside. I raised an eyebrow and glanced at Rake. He had a smirk on his face. Yeah, maybe that's why that washer always smelled terrible.

Curt turned around and looked at Rake. "Hey man, are you new to the building? I haven't seen you around here before." He stepped over with his hand outstretched. He was a brave guy. Rake was nearly a foot taller than Curt and had at least fifty-pounds of muscle on him. Not to mention, he always looks like he is having his mug shot taken after offing a bus full of nuns. I would have figured most people have enough self-preservation to stay a decent distance from someone like Rake.

Huh. I realized I was perfectly comfortable with him. Somewhere between scaring me half to death and me teasing him about reading romance, I had grown comfortable with him. I didn't think that I had ever felt so comfortable with anyone else quite so quickly. I wasn't intimidated by him, and he treated me like I was normal.

I pushed up my glasses, a habit I had developed whether they needed to be pushed up or not when I was feeling nervous and froze.

Rake straightened up, suddenly on high alert. I looked at him wide-eyed. I wasn't wearing my glasses, which meant I probably wasn't wearing my contacts either. I definitely didn't put on any concealer over my scars. I was so discombobulated and thinking about the last two days that I just forgot. I stared at Rake. I had been arguing, talking, and laughing with him this whole time. Not once did he look at me strangely. Instead, he treated me like I was completely normal.

I thought of how Varek's eyes had changed from green to black, how he grew horns, wings, and a tail. In light of that, I guessed I wasn't that unusual. I started to smile.

"No!" Rake barked, glaring over at Curt.

I hadn't been paying the slightest bit of attention while I had my minor freak out, so I must have missed quite a bit of conversation. I looked over at Curt, who was standing there with his face turning a concerning shade of red.

"Dude, you can't answer for her," he stammered out.

"I can and I will. The answer is no. If you don't want to accept that, I can make sure you don't have a dick left to use on anyone," his voice was a deep rumble of menace.

"Ummm, hey, guys. What did I miss while I was spacing out?" I tried to diffuse the situation, but I didn't want Curt to see me without my contacts and makeup, so I was careful to keep my head down as much as possible.

"This limp dick over here was asking you out for coffee," Rake spit out. "I told him you were taken, but he doesn't want to take no for an answer from me." He turned and looked at me, his glower still firmly in place. "You want to tell him, or do you want me to set him straight?"

"Uh, nobody needs to be set straight. So stand down, big guy."

Curt must have taken my words as encouragement because he took a step toward me with his hand out. "I knew you weren't with anybody," he said, with a big grin. "I've been watching you for ages and have never seen you with anyone. So, would you like to go out for coffee with me after our clothes are done?"

I took a step back. I didn't want to get closer regardless of the feral noises that were coming from the bodyguard to my right.

"I'm sorry, Curt. I really can't." I was hoping he would leave it at that, but he turned out to be a persistent fucker.

"Aww, c'mon, Juliette!" He was practically whining. It was very unmanly, and even if my brand didn't already have someone earmarked for me, I wouldn't want to go out with him. "I've been biding my time. I see you come and go from work, and you don't do more than say hello. Now you're here, and I just see this opportunity that I've been waiting for. You are laughing and talking to this guy, so I figured you weren't into girls after all."

Umm, what?

"What?" His words took me by surprise enough that I lifted my head and looked at him in shock.

"Whoa! Your eyes are freaky. What happened to your face?" He looked fascinated, like someone who was seeing a cool looking bug up close.

Rake stepped in front of me, and I heard the barely leashed violence leaching out of his voice. "I think you want to leave and return for your clothes after Juliette is done, don't you?"

"Why would I leave my clothes?" He truly sounded confused.

"Juliette said no, and now I am telling you that you need to leave. Do I need to make myself clearer? Because I can stuff your entire body into this machine right here and then toss the whole thing out into the dumpster out back."

"Okay, okay. Wow. Juliette, all you had to do was say no. I won't bother you again." He sidestepped Rake and started moving past me. He began to pause, but kept moving when Rake let out another growl. "FYI, you might want to put your guard dog on a leash before someone calls animal control."

I heard his quick footsteps as he made his way down the long hallway. When I heard the elevator doors swish open and ding shut, I looked at Rake. "Did that really just happen?"

He didn't reply, just shook his head and leaned back against the dryer again.

"They don't bother you, do they?" I asked in a quiet voice, watching his reaction closely.

"Pipsqueaks like that?" he snorted, and shook his head again.

"No. My eyes... and scars," my voice was small and timid. Nobody had completely ignored my defects so completely before. Varek hadn't reacted, really, but he had stared intently at them as if he were memorizing them. Rake had no reaction at all. His lack of reaction had put me at such ease that I had completely forgotten that I wasn't covered.

"Your eyes? Juliette, you are part demon. You should be glad you don't have a forked tongue or a tail coming out of your ass. Your eyes look like a demon's when they are showing themselves. Well, not all demons have black eyes. Some actually have red, some have green or yellow." He shrugged. "We're a diverse bunch. No one can really judge another's appearance, you know?"

"Are you being real with me? Like, really, real? Demons won't care about my eyes?"

"Well, there is always an asshole in the bunch. But, nah, no one will care. You might get looked at twice, but not because they think you are freaky, but because it's cool."

"That's.." I shrugged my shoulders, overwhelmed with relief. "That's just... I don't even have words." I didn't think I would fully believe him until I was around more demons, but he didn't show a single hint of deceit.

I had been struggling with the idea of demons, being the progeny of one, and being mated to one - but if demons were as judgment-free as Rake, I thought I could actually be pretty happy being one of them. Humans never accepted me. Maybe I could find my place with the demons.

CHAPTER
ELEVEN

JULIETTE

On our way back up to my apartment, Rake practically demanded that he carry my basket for me. After the way he scared off Curt, I wasn't too sure I should give in on principle alone, but I let him have it after he started complaining about how women shouldn't have to carry stuff when a big manly male was around to do it for them. I finally got tired of listening to it, so I just stuffed it in his arms so he'd be quiet.

When we reached my floor and stepped off the elevator, I came to a complete stop while Rake kept walking. It was a few feet further when he realized I wasn't with him and turned around.

"What's wrong?"

"You do see the guy standing at my door, right?" I pointed at the guy who was just as big and brawny as Rake, but with long dirty blond dreads pulled back into a ponytail at the back of his head.

"Oh him? That's Talon's brother, King. He's here to take over my watch."

"It's going to take a lot of getting used to, you know. And I really don't think any of this is even remotely necessary. I'm nobody. No one is going to target me."

I was still rambling when I fit my key in the lock, and both guys followed me in, making the space shrink in size. My apartment was already small, but these guys took up so much square footage that there was practically none left.

I took my basket from Rake. "Thanks for keeping me company. I really appreciate it."

"No problem. But if you were to move into The Tower, you wouldn't need a guard on your door. Just saying." He nodded to King and started walking out the door, but he paused with one hand on the knob and one on the door frame. "You know, I was told that you are quiet and a little scared. You didn't seem that way to me." He turned, shutting it firmly behind him.

I stared at the door. He was right. From the very beginning, I was talkative and even shared jokes. My only guess was because he put me off kilter from the first moment we met. He also never treated me like most people did. His personality put me at ease and let me be the real me, the one I kept bottled inside for most of my life. I wondered if I could let this me out more often.

I turned to this new guy and waved awkwardly. "Hi. I'm Juliette."

"I know your name," he huffed.

"I'm really sorry about this. It's not my idea."

He looked at me from the seat he had taken on my small second-hand couch I picked up from a neighbor after they had bought a new one. They were going to set it on the curb when I saw them carry it out of their apartment. I just had to fix the sagging spring problem by putting a piece of wood under the cushion. Not the greatest fix, but at least I didn't sink into the big dent that used to be there.

"I don't mind. No one really minds, just so you know." He shrugged his shoulders.

"Okay, well, I'm just going to go put my laundry away. I don't have much to offer, but I think I have some milk and sweet tea in the refrigerator."

He nodded his head and leaned back, closing his eyes. I didn't have anything else to say, so I took my basket into my room. As I was getting ready to start folding, I felt my phone buzzing in my pocket. The name that showed up on the display was enough to have my heart start racing.

"Hello?" I answered, with as much calmness infused in my voice as I could manage. I was sure that Varek was able to pick up on it though.

"Juliette," his voice was like warm chocolate. It poured through me, relaxing and exciting me all at the same time.

"Varek," I whispered back.

"I wanted to check on you. My men are telling me that you seem relaxed with them around. You aren't intimidated or scared by them, are you? If they are too much for you, they can stay posted outside your door instead of inside with you."

I could practically feel the bricks in the wall I had erected between me and the rest of the world start to crumble. "No, they are fine. I'm not scared of them at all. I'd hate for someone to have to stand in the hall for hours when I have a perfectly comfortable couch and a television."

"They aren't there to relax and watch television, Juliette."

I hummed my agreement and picked up a t-shirt absent-mindedly. As I folded that one and then the next, the silence stretched on. It should have been awkward and uncomfortable, but instead, just having him on the phone where I could hear his breathing and the occasional rustling of papers was comforting.

"Food should be arriving any moment. I hope you like steak."

I hadn't had much of it. Growing up, I never had it and the group home stuck with easy meals that could feed a lot of mouths. I ate a lot of spaghetti there. But the few times that I did have steak in the last couple of years, I loved it. "I do."

"Good." It was like a purr in my ear. Goosebumps danced across my skin.

"Thank you, Varek. Thank you for the dinner, for sending people to watch over me."

"It won't be for much longer." My heart sank. I cleared my throat before trying for a nonchalant tone.

"Oh?"

"This is only temporary, Juliette. I will have you moved into The Tower soon."

"What?" I gasped. "We barely know each other. You are talking about moving in already?"

"We are mates, Juliette. I am not sure if you feel the same pull that I do, but every instinct is telling me that I need to make you mine. I have been told that it would only get worse as time goes by. Fate is going to push us together." I swallowed hard because, yes, I felt the pull. But I was scared to death of making any sudden leaps.

"Can we talk about it?" I whispered.

"Of course. Now, go eat your dinner and get a good night's rest. I will see you soon. Oh, and Juliette?" he called out, just before hanging up. "Be a good girl for me."

"See you soon," I whispered to the dial tone.

I sat there staring at my phone when I heard a knock on my apartment door. I dropped the t-shirt I had been folding before his phone call, and walked back down the short hall to see King standing at my door with a large black gun in his hand. I watched him bend down to look through the peephole before putting the gun in a holster I hadn't noticed earlier and opened the door. The scent of meat and spices wafted from the open doorway.

A young guy in a backward-facing ball cap stood there holding two large sacks of what had to be making that wonderful smell. My stomach clenched, making a rumbling sound that had both men turning to look in my direction. I blushed and ducked my head, turning around to head back to my room. I was hungry, but I needed a few minutes to compose myself after speaking with Varek again.

After finishing my laundry, I returned to the living room to find King with a plate in his lap piled high with steak, potatoes, and no vegetables. He nodded his head toward an empty plate and open containers of all kinds of delicious looking food.

"Eat."

I walked forward slowly. "This is a lot of food." I looked down at all the offerings, licking my lips.

The look he gave me made me think that he thought I was a little slow on the uptake. "I'm a big guy. Pretty sure I could eat twice this much."

I just shook my head a little and sat down on the other end of my small couch, which still put me pretty close to the large man. It made sense that all the guys he employed as guards be huge, but I'd never seen such large men before.

I bent over and picked up my plate and then made my choices after perusing the offerings. I sat back and eyed King's plate. "No vegetables for you?" I questioned, as I speared my fork into a tasty looking green bean.

"I'm a carnivore," was all he said, as he took a healthy bite of mashed potatoes. I raised one eyebrow, and he glared back at me. "What male doesn't love meat and potatoes?"

"Fair enough."

We sat in silence while we ate, him polishing off the rest of the food in the containers once I assured him that I was completely full.

After he cleaned up the mess of containers and I washed our plates and silverware, he produced two smaller containers from the refrigerator that I hadn't known were there. Then, he grabbed the two newly cleaned forks from my drying rack and took them with him back into the living room. I was getting used to his silence. He still looked irritated, but I was beginning to think that was a shared trait amongst the guards.

I followed him back to the couch, sat down, and took the fork and one of the containers. I popped it open and nearly moaned at the rich chocolate smell. A generous slice of triple chocolate cake took up the container, chocolate frosting covering the whole piece. Curls of shaved chocolate decorated the dessert, and little swirls of chocolate dotted the top.

"This looks absolutely amazing! I don't know if I will even be able to eat half of it, though, without getting a stomach ache. Or diabetes."

"Not a problem. Whatever you don't eat, I will."

I looked at him incredulously. "Or...I can save it for tomorrow."

"Boss can send you more tomorrow. No sense in saving it."

"You are not eating my cake!" I declared, as I sunk my fork in and got my first taste of rich, decadent chocolate.

"And if I eat it while you are asleep?"

I must have looked feral when I looked up at him, fork in my mouth.

"Okay, okay, I won't touch your precious cake." He took another bite, grumbling to himself. "Women and their damn desserts."

I hummed in agreement and kept eating. In the end, I didn't even manage to finish a quarter of the slice. It was just too big and too rich. I was still worried about getting a belly ache, but it was so worth every single bite.

I carefully stashed the remaining cake in the crisper drawer under a head of lettuce. I figured the guy didn't like vegetables, so maybe it would be safe there. I stood in the fridge, eyeing it. He would probably be able to sniff it out. I frowned and closed the door. I walked into the living room and eyed him, giving the best glare I could muster. "That cake better still be there the next time I check."

"Female, no one is going to steal your cake. If you want more, all you have to do is ask for it, and the boss will have it here in under an hour." He looked offended. I wasn't sure if he was more offended that I questioned his integrity or that the boss wouldn't meet my needs.

"Sorry. I'm not used to having to share." I looked at the floor and toed my foot at one of the stains on the carpet that I had never been able to remove in the time I had lived here.

His voice was softer. "I get it. I think you'll find that many of us do."

I looked up and saw he wasn't looking at me but at his phone. He looked like he was playing some kind of game on it.

"Umm, okay. Well. I need to get ready for bed since I have to get up for work tomorrow." I started walking toward my room and stopped again. "I'm assuming you won't be here when I get up, so I just want to say thanks for being here. I don't agree that I need bodyguards, but I can't deny that I feel safer with you here. And, uh, the company is nice, too." I didn't wait for a response, just turned toward my room and didn't stop until I closed the door behind me.

My alarm woke me with its annoying shrill as it usually did, and the banging on the wall next to my head came next as it usually did. My neighbor was a night owl, often up late watching loud movies in their bed that was obviously in the same position mine was. It was a daily ritual that they would protest my alarm waking me up while I ignored their TV going until all hours of the morning.

I sat up and scrubbed my hands over my face, and groaned. I had to go to work and face my co-workers. I didn't know what the day would bring, but I could only guess that Melissa would be full of hostility. Esmerelda wouldn't be there today unless someone called out, so at least I wouldn't have to face her and deal with the news I had found out at the club. I looked toward the top of my dresser and saw her sweater neatly folded with the belt wound up on top of it. I would put them in a bag and take them to work to keep in my locker until she came in. I figured we would have to talk about it, but I was glad to be able to put it off until another day.

I slipped from my bed and took a quick shower. I followed my routine of wrapping my hair into a tight bun and then putting in my contacts. I blinked my eyes several times, allowing the disks to slide into place comfortably, and stared into my reflection. The brown contacts did a pretty good job of concealing my natural color, though if someone were to look very, very closely, they would be able to see the left was darker.

Varek had obviously been able to tell. It hadn't taken him long at all to demand that I remove the lenses so he could see my natural color. He hadn't seemed taken aback, maybe a little fascinated, though.

I took my concealing makeup out of the basket and applied it liberally, making sure that the redness of the scar was fully covered. I blended it in with the rest of my face, but I made a point to have the whole scar completely concealed. The makeup always felt thick and heavy, but it was a sacrifice I was willing to make in order to feel okay enough to leave the apartment. I was still in shock that not only had I not worn my contacts and had my hair down all day yesterday, but I hadn't even put on my concealer.

After I had my glasses firmly in place and my scrubs on, I put my lanyard with my ID and keycard over my neck. I took the sweater and belt and opened my door. I walked barefoot into the living room and saw the room was completely empty. It was tidy, and a quick glance at the guest bath with just its simple pedestal sink and commode was dark and empty. I guessed my guard was either outside or I no longer had one. Though, that didn't seem likely with the way Varek seemed prepared to keep me safe until...I didn't know exactly what he was waiting for. Maybe for me to get comfortable with the whole thing?

I walked into my kitchen, took a used grocery bag out of my small pantry, slid Emmy's items inside, and tied a knot on the top. I placed it by the front door just as the knob rattled. I jumped back, startled when another large man stepped inside holding a bag of food and a tray with two cups of steaming coffee. He looked up at me and saw my frightened look, and grimaced.

"Sorry, I didn't mean to scare you. I went downstairs to grab the food while you were in the shower and didn't know you would be done already." He walked the new bag of food into the kitchen and started removing foil-wrapped food from it. "You have breakfast burritos this morning. Potato, egg, sausage, and cheese. Quick, easy, tasty, and will give you enough energy to make it until lunch." He nodded to the cup with a large J written on the side. "Caramel latte. The boss told me to tell you that if you let him know your preferences, he will make sure you get what you want next time."

I crossed my arms over my chest. "The boss wants to know my preferences."

The guy, who I didn't know because he hadn't introduced himself yet, who still looked just as big and intimidating as the rest of them, had already unwrapped one of the giant burritos and was taking a huge bite. He nodded his head and mumbled around a mouthful of food. "He wants to make sure you are taken care of, but he doesn't want to send you something you don't like or can't eat."

"Mmmhmmm." I stood there watching him devour his food. I wanted to protest on principle and refuse 'the boss's' offering of food, but it was impossible for me to ignore any food that was given to me. I snatched up one of the burritos left and unwrapped a corner. The tortilla tasted freshly made, and the potatoes were perfectly crispy on the outside and soft in the middle. The egg, sausage, and cheese were all perfectly balanced. "So good!" I moaned.

The guy nodded at my words and popped the last bite into his mouth. "Georgia is the most amazing cook in the world. Everyone tries to get Georgia to cook for them, but she is very loyal to the boss. She was excited when she found out that he was finally mated and was happy to start cooking for you." He gave me a severe look. "You have to tell Georgia how good her food is and that you love it. Don't insult her, or we will all suffer if she decides to go on a cooking strike. She did that about fifty years ago, and we are all still worried that she might do it again."

"She went on a strike fifty years ago?"

"Yeah, it was the worst five years, ever."

"She went on strike for five years!" My mouth was hanging open in shock, but I couldn't stop eating for long, so I closed it around my burrito and took another bite. "What happened that she stopped cooking?" I asked, around a mouthful of breakfast goodness.

He shrugged his big beefy shoulder and peeled his second burrito out of its foil wrapping. "Not sure. But we think that someone the boss had been dating insulted her food."

My appetite soured for about ten-seconds before I shrugged and took another bite. I wasn't alive fifty years ago. It's not like he cheated on me. I would have to get used to the idea that he had been alive for so much longer than I have.

"I usually take the bus to and from work. Are you going to ride with me, or should we take a cab?" I mentally tallied how much money I had left over after bills and cringed at how many times I'd be able to take a cab. There weren't many.

"The boss would never want you taking public transportation. He sent a car." His phone chimed, and he dug it out of his pocket and looked at it while polishing off his last bite. He threw the second wrapper in the trash. "Car's here if you're ready."

I straightened my shoulders and moved to grab my purse. If Varek wanted to send me a car instead of riding the bus, well, I would just have to thank him later.

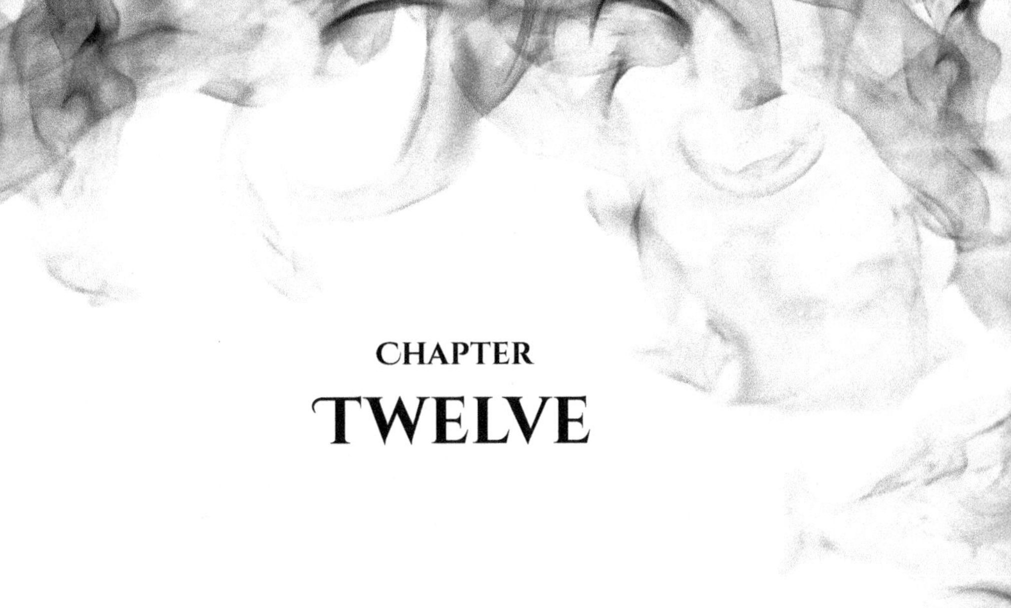

CHAPTER

TWELVE

VAREK

I watched Juliette climb into the back seat of the car I sent for her through the camera posted outside her building.

I wasn't about to take chances with her safety. I had her entire building wired, and guards were posted strategically in the area. She wouldn't know about the cameras or men that were watching her location continuously, but she didn't seem to mind the ones that guarded her more closely. My men were reporting that she had accepted the situation quite easily.

I wanted to allow her time to come to terms with our situation. It was a significant change to the life she thought she was going to live, and I could imagine it was overwhelming. I wanted to make the transition as easy for her as possible, but it had to be quick. I had learned to be patient over the thousands of years, but I wouldn't give her space for long. I anticipated that she would come to me tonight so we could continue the conversation we had started before she left The Tower. Talon had reported that she seemed upset that I had told her we weren't actually mates. I had been speaking as someone that

121

knew how demon mating progressed. It hadn't occurred to me that she would jump to the conclusion that I had meant we weren't mates at all, rather than that we weren't mates *yet*.

I would give her time, but I wouldn't wait long for her to come to terms.

She was not at all what I had expected my mate to be. I hadn't given it much thought toward it over the years, but I hadn't expected someone so...broken.

She was beautiful. There was no denying that. But she had little self-confidence and virtually no self-worth. I would have to make it my top priority to show her that she was so much more than her scars.

I had been surprised to see her eyes. That was something that didn't happen to me often. I was rarely stunned by anything anymore. Seeing that her demon side was so close to the surface was interesting. I needed to find out who her biological father was. I had questions for him that needed answering.

"Boss," the sultry tones of the succubus that was one of my managers and closest friends interrupted my thoughts, as I had been staring out at the empty street for several minutes.

"What can I do for you, Sasha?" I sat back in my leather chair as I watched Sasha stroll in, her hips swaying, always exuding the sexual appeal that all succubi were known for. It was a part of their DNA; impossible to avoid, impossible for them to subdue. Though she prided herself on her breed of demon and was ever willing to seduce, she was not one to attempt to steal a taken man. A few months ago, she had tried to seduce the local vampire king in front of his mate, an act she had been highly embarrassed over, and not just because his mate would have been more than capable of destroying her had I not intervened. She hadn't known that the male was mated at the time and her biological instincts pushed her to use her talents against a male so appealing to any female or male. Since then, she had been more cautious about who she seduced.

"I just wanted to let you know that the alcohol order for Brimstone arrived on time, and everything looked to be in order. I have the usual guys in the club putting it all away in the storage room. The order for the rest of The Tower will arrive later tonight at five."

I looked at my gold watch. I saw it was nearly 9 am. The company we used for deliveries was a new one that I had only hired a few weeks ago after the last company had been less than reliable. There had been several discrepancies in the orders causing difficulties for my businesses. This new one was always prompt and, so far, had impressed me with their service and professionalism. I made a mental note to send a healthy tip to the company. I found that people worked better and stayed loyal when they were happy and well paid.

I looked at the stack of forms and proposals waiting for me on my desk. I had several things to look into that were all business related. I sighed. I had spent the last couple of days moving things around in my schedule, so I could concentrate on spending time with my fated mate. However, there was still much to see to before I could focus solely on educating her on her demon heritage and cementing our bond.

"Thank you, Sasha. I'm glad this company is working out better than the last one. But be sure to let me know if they start showing signs of failing in their contract. I don't want things to deteriorate as they had before needing to fix such a fucking mess again."

I turned back to the monitor one more time before closing the feed. I didn't put cameras on her place of business since there were workers there twenty-four hours a day. It was something I planned to rectify soon, but I had confidence in the men I had guarding her. They were my best soldiers, and many had been with me for centuries.

"Can I ask you about your mate, boss?" She walked over to the couch that I had in the sitting area. My office was a large room, one where I conducted several different types of business. My desk was toward the back, taking up most of the back wall, with twin plush leather chairs in front of it. While that was where I conducted the majority of my business, the sitting area against the other wall was more where I met with closer acquaintances and friends. Sometimes, we discussed important matters, other times, it was where I would sit to relax, unwind and have a drink. I rarely spent any time in either of my clubs. Not that the demon side of the business could merely be called a club.

I turned my chair to look over at the demoness that I had known for over a thousand years. She was like a sister to me, and though we often went separate ways, we continued to cross paths over time. In the last century, when I decided to open up a place where demons could go and openly be what they were without fear, Sasha had agreed to settle in the area and work for me. She enjoyed the challenge of the job and had been doing it well before most human women had begun joining their place in the workforce.

We had never been more than friends. Neither of us felt more than a mutual respect and appreciation for the other's place in the world. Hers was the daughter of a high-ranking general in the Underworld, a job that she had never been interested in. I had never met him because he never left that realm and because I could never enter it. She had left and found she liked it more in the mortal realm.

"What would you like to know?" I looked over at her as she reclined on the leather couch and crossed her legs.

"I hear she is...different."

I nodded my head in the affirmative. "She seems to have had an extremely rough life. She has physical scars from the man that raised her. I imagine the scars she carries inside her are deeply more vast."

Her face tightened in anger. She was never one to tolerate the abuse of women. She had been born into a time when women were nothing more than chattel. Even a demoness had little to no rights back then. So, she had taken to the cause of protecting women from abuse for centuries.

"Was he punished?" she growled

"It is my understanding that the human male spent four years in prison. However, he was released recently for good behavior."

She scoffed. "I will never understand the human justice system. A person could destroy another's life by doing the most horrible things, yet they spend very little time being punished before being set out on the world again. Do you know how many repeat offenders there are? Men who hurt the innocent rarely ever actually learn their lesson. If they were demons, they would have been dealt with in a much more satisfactory manner."

I hummed my agreement. Once I found her tormentor, I would destroy him piece-by-piece. I couldn't allow the man to breathe the same air as my mate, not after he tried to destroy her soul.

"So, is she pretty?"

I turned fully toward her and took her in. Her succubus nature gave her the very best that looks had to offer. Her hair was a deep red, her demon eyes yellow, but would be a brilliant blue with her glamor up. Her face was what almost any man would be willing to commit crimes for. She had been the reason for many battles in the early centuries of swords and armor.

"There is a softness to her, a sweetness that few have ever possessed. She is also small and very delicate. So far, I have only seen her after a night out and then waking up slightly hungover." She had taken it remarkably well, waking up in a strange place.

"She only comes up to my chest. It makes me want to tuck her under my chin and protect her from all the realms," I sighed. "I knew that finding one's mate would change everything, but I had no idea the feelings would be so intense. I have to allow her time to come to terms with her life changing against her will. She has made a life for herself that she seems content with, though she barely earns a livable wage. Her whole existence, from the time she was born until now, has been barely living. She lives in a small apartment that she can hardly afford because she wants to feel safe. And yet, when she found herself afraid of Rake when he had surprised her at her door, not one of her neighbors tried to come to her aide." I suppressed a growl at the memory of what he had related about the incident. "I checked, and not one call had been made to the police. If she had been in real danger, no one would have been there to help her."

"Her father could have turned up at any time to hurt her once he was let out of prison," she seethed.

I shook my head. "She was very adamant that he not be referred to as her father. But, yes. If he wanted to hurt her, he would be able to. I have someone working on finding his location and checking on what he has been up to for the last several months. I can't allow the fucker to live for what he has done to her.

"I also know I won't be able to give her much time before I have her living here under my protection. The place where she works is not a good place for her either. She enjoys it, but the people she works with are not good for her self-worth. They were the same women that came as a group on Friday night. There is one, in particular, that was definitely bad news."

"I heard about this from Rake. He said that the same human woman that had been trying to hang around you for the last few weeks was here again trying to get your attention?"

I wanted to let the weariness take over. Sometimes, I felt every one of my years. I was aware that bonding with my mate would have the effect of erasing the ennui that many of my kind tended to face after such vast amounts of time. It was something that I was looking forward to.

"Yes. The woman has become a problem. Even more so now that I know she is a coworker of my fated and that she doesn't like her. She will cause problems that Juliette does not need to face right now. This change in her circumstances will be more than enough for her without adding more issues from an obsessed stalker that can't take no for an answer. If the bitch finds out that Juliette and I are to be mates, she will likely do something dangerous."

"You can't let your fated stay away from you for long," she warned.

"I am aware. I have no intentions of letting her stay away," I growled, frustrated with the prospect of my fated taking too long to accept me.

"You have a plan for tonight?" she guessed.

"I do."

"No sharing?"

I smiled then. "It is no secret. I intend to start wooing her."

She threw her head back and laughed.

"I am so glad I could entertain you," I said wryly.

"Can I be invited to dinner?" she asked, while wiping a stray tear from her eye.

I snorted and steepled my fingers together while giving her a droll look. "I'm thinking a private dinner would be more appropriate for the time being."

"Well, can I take the place of one of the guys as her guard at least?"

"Would I be able to tell you no, and you actually listen to me?"

Her grin was both evil and enchanting. "What do you think?"

I think that if these two women became friends that my life would be vastly more interesting. I wasn't sure if that was a good thing or not.

THIRTEEN

JULIETTE

THE DAY WAS PRETTY MUCH the same as any other day that I spent at work. There were bodies to wash, hair to brush, spills to clean, faces to shave, and food to be fed. It was never monotonous, though. Even though each day was similar, it was never precisely the same.

What was most different this day, though, were my coworkers' reactions. They all wanted to know what I did after the club Friday night. They had all seen Varek carry me out in his arms. The word had spread to nearly everyone under the roof of the nursing home. Even the residents were asking questions about the large, handsome man. Melissa, on the other hand, was glaring holes through my scrubs. If she had a knife, I had a feeling I would have been sliced into a million pieces by noon.

At 4 o'clock, when it was time for meds, there were even more mess-ups than usual. Medicine cups were placed in the wrong rooms, which usually never happened. I didn't know if she was being careless on purpose, or if she was so blinded by her anger and hatred of me that she couldn't concentrate on the important task in front of her. Luckily, I was able to get the right medicines to the correct residents without any horrible mishaps.

When I was leaving for the night, exhausted and stressed from the day, and climbing into the black car with Rake holding my door open, I felt eyes on me. I looked around, but didn't see anything of concern until I glanced back at the building. Melissa was standing at the glass doors, not hiding a look of hatred burning in her eyes. I felt a cold hand of dread squeeze my chest as a shiver ran up and down my spine.

"You need to stay away from that woman," Rake muttered, as he followed my gaze.

"You don't need to tell me twice," I whispered, as he shut the door and cut off the view from the glass doors.

Rake's palm slapped the tops of his thighs as we both settled into our seats, and the car began to move. "I have great news!"

His tone was overly bright and cheerful and immediately made me wary. "I'm afraid to ask."

He let out a chuckle. "It's nothing bad. In fact, you will probably enjoy yourself quite a bit."

"You sound like you are trying too hard to convince me of something before you even tell me what it is." I looked at him pointedly. "Just tell me what is going on."

"Juliette, I promise it's not bad. Varek wants you to have dinner with him tonight. He has instructed that we bring you to join him at a restaurant tonight."

My hands started trembling. Whether it was in trepidation or excitement, I wasn't entirely certain. When he noticed the tremor in my hands as I tried to fold them together, he gave me a sympathetic smile. "Being mated to a demon is not a horrible thing, Juliette. Demons are highly possessive, and since they can't even become aroused by another, cheating is virtually unheard of. A demon won't be unfaithful to their mate. Unlike humans who treat their spouses like they are disposable, demons mate for life."

"I'm not really afraid," I whispered. I wasn't. I was surprised to find myself intrigued and almost eager. Knowing that Varek would be committed to me and never stray, knowing that someone would stay with me forever, was a prospect that I had never thought I'd have.

"Look, Varek is an intense male. He is the leader of all demons on the earth's realm, so he has to be strong and sometimes vicious. But he is also patient and understanding." He awkwardly patted my shoulder. "He will be good to you."

I nodded my head. I had already sensed that from him. He was definitely intense, but I could tell that he wasn't going to be violent toward me though he was capable of extreme violence. I didn't know how I could be so sure of that unless it was just from all the times I had spent around hateful people who wanted to hurt me. No, Varek would never hurt me.

When we arrived at the apartment, we were met at the door by a stunning, tall redhead. She was the most beautiful woman I had ever seen and, judging by the traffic jam she was causing, the other people on the street thought so as well.

She smiled brightly at me, and I couldn't help the small smile that I returned shyly. Rake walked me up to her and introduced us.

"Juliette, this is Sasha. She's normally Varek's club manager, but she got excited and a little over-eager to meet you." Rake gave her a narrowed look.

She attempted to look innocent, but spoiled it by the smile she wasn't hiding very well. She started bouncing on her toes. "I'm so excited! I get to help you get ready for your date tonight." She clapped her hands, then hooked her arm through mine before she started us toward the apartment entrance. "I brought you a few things you can try on, but you don't have to wear any of them. I just didn't know if you had something to wear to an upscale restaurant or not. I didn't want to make any assumptions one way or another, but Varek wants to spoil you." She leaned down close to my ear and whispered, "I have it on good authority that he wants to woo you."

I tripped over my own feet and would have fallen had she not been holding my arm. "He wants to woo me? Why would he need to do that if we were already fated mates?"

"He knows that this is going to be difficult for you and wants to make it as easy as possible. I think by courting you, he's trying to show you that he is honorable in his intentions. In the demon world, when fated meet, they both know and understand what is happening and most often jump straight into the new relationship immediately since one or both of them have been waiting a very long time. Everyone knows that finding your mate is not exactly rare, but, basically, those that find them are lucky."

"He feels lucky to have me as a mate?" I asked doubtfully.

"Of course, he does! Why wouldn't he?" She looked at me like she didn't understand why I would question it.

I studied her closely. She was more than just beautiful. This close, she exuded a sex appeal that couldn't be matched. She also seemed like a genuinely nice...demon? Why would he be satisfied with me if he had this woman around him?

Sasha sighed. "I am a succubus demon. I can't help the appeal I have. It's a part of me. I can tell you that I have known Varek for centuries, and I love him like a brother. So, you will never have to worry about me trying to get between the two of you. I would never do that to mates, and definitely not Varek."

I shook my head. "No, I wasn't thinking that at all." I hung my head. "I am just worried that he will be disappointed in me." I looked back up at her. "He doesn't really have a choice, does he?"

"Fate doesn't work that way, Juliette. Yes, sometimes fated pairs don't work out, but that is because one in the pair chooses to stay with the one they had already been in a relationship with before they became fated. It's rare, but it does happen. Most of the time, if someone has a chosen and receives the fated mark, they will separate amicably since everyone knows that it isn't anyone's fault..." She stopped and threw her head back, her shiny hair swaying behind her. "Ugh, I feel like I'm explaining this wrong." She looked at me again, studying my face carefully. I flinched, knowing what she was seeing. She spoke softly this time and put her hand on my cheek under the scar that I carefully hide from the world. "Fate doesn't get it wrong, Juliette."

I blinked at her. She looked so earnest, and absolutely no doubt showed on her face. I nodded, and she smiled again.

We got to my apartment door, and Rake unlocked it with a key I didn't remember giving him, and when I entered and saw the garment bags, I looked at Sasha with an eyebrow raised. "Does everyone have a key to my apartment?"

They looked at each other and then back at me. Rake answered as he dropped down on my broken sofa, "Only the ones that need access to it." He leaned back his head and closed his eyes.

Sasha gathered the garment bags and led me to my bedroom. "Come on, you jump in the shower, and I will set your things out." She looked at me from head to toe critically. "I think I have the perfect outfit for you." She laid all the bags on my bed, removed one from the pile, and smiled beautifully at me. When she made a shooing motion at me, I hesitantly sidestepped to the bathroom.

"Do you know where we are going tonight?"

"Yes! You're going to love it!" that was all she said, as she hung the bag on the back of my bedroom door. She then went back for the other bags and opened my closet before beginning the process of hanging them up.

"Ummm...what are you doing?"

She looked at me as I stood on the threshold of my bathroom and then back at the bags I was still gaping at. "Varek wanted to make sure you had several choices. These are all yours now." She tilted her head with a teasing sparkle shining in her eyes. "I think everyone forgot to tell you that mates can be very generous to each other?"

I nodded dumbly. "Yeah." I had been in his penthouse and his club and had seen how extremely wealthy he was, but I guess it hadn't occurred to me that he would spend his money on me.

"It's overwhelming, I'm sure. But, honey, you'll get used to it."

She winked at me, and I blinked dumbly at the gesture that made her appeal ramp up to a thousand. "Now, hurry up and get in that shower! The clock's ticking!"

I turned into the small bathroom, kicked off my pants, and unraveled my hair from its tight bun. After I was fully unclothed, I stepped into the shower that took so long to heat up that I had to get into the habit of turning it on while I was undressing.

I quickly soaped my body and then washed my hair, scrubbing my scalp thoroughly. I left the conditioner in while shaving my legs before going back and rinsing.

Stepping out of the shower, I used one towel to wring as much of the water out of my hair as possible and wrapped the other around my body. I peeked my head out of the bathroom to see Sasha reclining on my bed with her back to my headboard, playing with her phone.

She looked up and smiled. "You're quick. Are you ready?"

I bit my lip, unsure, but feeling the butterflies fluttering around in my stomach. It had only been two and a half days since I had seen Varek, but I was excited to be able to spend more time with him.

"I'm going to step out while you get dressed, and then I will help you with your hair and makeup, okay?" She walked to the closed door and paused with her hand on the knob. "Everything is going to work out perfectly. You'll see." And then she was gone, the door clicking closed softly.

I pulled the towel off my hair and body, hanging both up in the bathroom, and ran a large comb through my hair, getting any tangles out before plugging in my hair dryer. It took a little bit to get it dry enough not to leave wet spots on my new dress, but when I was done, I quickly slipped into a bra and panties and slid the dress up my body.

I looked in the mirror and blushed at what I saw. I had never worn anything so beautiful before. The fabric was silky and shimmered in the light of my bedroom. What had me blushing, though, was the cleavage baring neckline. I tried tugging it up a little bit, but it wasn't going anywhere. It wasn't scandalous, but for someone that stayed covered at all times, it was definitely something I wasn't used to. The deep blue fabric was a beautiful shade of sapphire. I loved it immediately.

I slipped the heels on, thankful they were low heels, and took a few cautious steps around the room, surprised at how comfortable they were and how steady I was in them. Finally, I took a deep breath and opened the door. I called for Sasha, who wasted no time in coming back in. She grinned after walking a circle around me.

"It looks great on you. I knew it!"

"Did you pick this out?"

She chuckled. "Nope, this was all Varek. But when I saw it earlier and then saw you, I knew it would be the perfect choice."

She picked up a case I hadn't noticed and set it on the bed, opening it. Inside were so many makeup products she could have done an entire cheerleading squad.

"I, ummm, need to put more concealer on...over my scars."

"It's not necessary, but if it makes you more comfortable, then go ahead."

I nodded, showing thanks, and went back into the bathroom where my supplies were. She watched as I dabbed concealer over my scars and blended it in carefully.

"Varek said the man that raised you is the one that gave you the scars?"

I stiffened. I tried not to think about that night, or else I was likely to end up having dreadful nightmares. I swallowed thickly. "Yes. He attacked me and was planning on cutting my eye out."

She looked at each of my eyes and frowned. "I don't understand why he would do something like that."

"I have one black eye that he called my demon eye. He said I got it from my birth father, the one that he said raped my mother and got her pregnant. After she died having me, he hated me instantly."

And yet, he still chose to raise me instead of giving me up. So many times throughout my life, I had wondered why he kept me. "I guess he thought that punishing me was his way of punishing the man that took my mother from him."

I turned back to her after finishing. "I am wearing contacts. It keeps people from asking questions or acting weird about it."

"I'm sorry," she said quietly. "I didn't mean to pry."

I shook my head. "You weren't prying. It's okay. One thing I learned from my time around demons these last few days is that they don't care about my strange eyes. Humans are more judgmental. It's been nice."

"You don't want to take your contacts out?"

I shook my head again. "Not tonight. I'm still getting used to this. And if we are going out to dinner, there will be a lot of people looking at us."

"Okay." She smiled gently.

She was quick with my makeup, and I gasped when I looked in the mirror. She made me look beautiful. She had used a light hand, just highlighting and using neutral tones, but it was perfect.

"Thank you," I whispered.

"It wasn't me that made you look beautiful, Juliette. That's all you." She put her brushes away. "Now, I think we should leave your hair down."

My heartbeat quickened, and I ran my fingers through the ends. I was stepping out of my comfort zone in order to wear the dress and leave off my glasses. I wasn't sure I could leave my hair down, too. I stared at my reflection, the subtle makeup, the dark brown eyes, the pale skin tone, and the silvery white hair that fell in a straight sheet to my waist.

I turned to her and nodded. "Okay."

She beamed at me, a proud mother admiring her daughter. I laughed softly, then I gave in to impulse and gave her a quick hug.

"Thank you, Sasha."

"I'm just glad that I have a new friend." She winked and walked me to the door. "Enjoy yourself tonight. Varek is quiet and commanding, but he is a good male. He will be a good mate to you."

I drew in a deep breath and nodded.

FOURTEEN

JULIETTE

When I slid into the back of the SUV that was waiting for me in front of my building, I hadn't expected another person to already be in the backseat.

"Hi," I whispered shyly.

"Juliette," Varek's voice was a deep rumble. "You look lovely."

I ducked my head, feeling self-conscious. I fiddled with the hem of the dress, playing with the edge and then smoothing it back down. I looked at him from under my lashes. He was an amazing sight to see. He was, once again, wearing all black. His black dress shirt was unbuttoned at the throat, and the jacket hung open. My eyes traced over his taut abdomen and thick thighs that were a hair's breadth from mine.

I didn't see his hand move, only felt the gentle pressure he placed under my chin, raising my eyes to meet his.

"Your hair is remarkable. I've never seen anything quite like it before. I'm pleased you left it down."

I swallowed at the compliment. "Thank you. And thank you for the dress. I love it."

His finger left my chin and lightly traced down my neck, over my collarbone, and arm before taking a lock of hair in his fingers. He fanned out the ends and brought it to his nose. My face felt hot as I watched him inhale deeply, and I could have sworn he growled.

We stared at each other for several beats before he let my hair go.

"I have a meeting tomorrow night, but I'd like for you to come to the club on Wednesday. It isn't as busy during the week, so I think it would be a good time for you to be introduced to my employees. It's a perfect opportunity to show you around the club and familiarize you with it."

I tilted my head. "Why do I need to be familiar with your club, Varek?"

"When we are mated, it will belong to you as well."

I felt my face heat again and shook my head emphatically. "I hadn't thought about that. I don't think that is necessary, really."

He was about to reply when the SUV came to a stop, and a valet opened the back door. Varek slid out and held his hand out for me. I placed my hand in his and stared in fascination as my entire hand was swallowed in his much larger one.

I slid out, carefully keeping my dress smoothed down my thighs with my free hand so it wouldn't ride up and flash anyone. When I was solidly on the sidewalk outside a fancy looking restaurant, Varek placed his hand on the small of my back and led me to the door that was being held open by someone wearing a tuxedo. The man nodded to us, acknowledging Varek with a polite and respectful, 'Sir'.

We walked inside, and I was immediately surrounded by sounds of clinking glasses, silverware hitting expensive plates, and hushed conversation. The smells were divine and caused my stomach to clench in hunger.

A maître d' greeted Varek by name and led us to a table toward the middle of the large open room. Each person we passed had their eyes on us. The men nodded respectfully to Varek while the women stared in blatant lust. The few people that looked at me instead of

him stared with undisguised curiosity. I could imagine it was probably a surprise to see that he was finally with someone after being
used to years of him being alone and uninterested in anyone.

Varek ignored them all as we stopped at our table, and he waved
away the maître d' and took my chair himself, gently helping me
scoot my surprisingly comfortable seat in. I felt his fingers linger
along the back of my neck, under my hair, raising goosebumps along
my arms until he trailed them lightly over my shoulder as he walked
around the table.

After he seated himself, Varek ordered a bottle of wine while
picking up my menu and handing it to me. "The place is ostenta-
tious, the patrons even more so, but the food is delicious. Anything
you choose will be perfect."

I nodded and picked up the single-sided menu trimmed in gold.
There weren't many selections, and there weren't any prices. I had
heard of this place from the women at work. They always bragged
when a date took them because it was difficult to get reservations,
and it was the fanciest restaurant in the city. Looking around at the
small round tables with white linen table cloths and small crystal
vases at the center of each table, all with a single perfect red rose, I
could understand why anyone would be excited to come here. It was
impressive. I felt so out of place.

After deciding on a chicken breast plate, I set my menu down and
sat back as the waiter arrived with the bottle of red wine that Varek
had ordered. He declined a taste of it, allowing the man to pour us
both a small amount into the crystal clear wine glasses he had
turned over upright on our table. I watched as the dark liquid
swirled into the glass before settling. After Friday night, I wasn't very
sure about drinking. I hadn't known I would get so drunk with so
few drinks.

"Drink as much or as little as you want, Juliette. You are safe with
me. Always." Varek's deep voice made my whole body shiver, and I
looked at his deep green eyes before reaching out and taking the delicate looking glass, taking a tiny sip.

It was crisp and sweet. Tart at first before settling into a fruity aftertaste. "It's delicious." I knew I sounded surprised. I had heard the nurses talking about how expensive wine tasted disgusting, but this didn't taste bad at all. I took another sip before setting it back down on the table.

Varek gave the waiter our food orders and then took my hand from across the table. At his prolonged silence, I looked up to see him studying me.

"You wore your contacts." It was a statement, an obvious one since I was, indeed, still wearing my contacts. But, nevertheless, I could hear the disappointment lacing his words.

"Yes," I whispered, as I fidgeted with a fork. "I don't feel comfortable out in public without them in."

He nodded his head, the look in his eyes compassionate. "I hope I can help you grow more comfortable in the future, but I do understand."

I smiled gratefully. He was very good at putting me at ease, I had noticed.

We talked about light subjects, ones that most people enjoy while on a first date, and the evening went smoothly. It was nice getting to know him and learning about the club. I was enjoying myself and relaxing after an entire glass of wine, and he seemed comfortable in my presence as well. We were just finishing the last of our delicious dinners when Varek let out a low growl that made my head jerk up. I saw he was looking behind me, his face blank, but his eyes looked murderous.

Someone stepped up to the table next to us. I expected it to be the waiter again to clear our plates, so I was surprised to hear Melissa's voice.

"Well, hello. Fancy meeting you here."

I wanted to roll my eyes at her seductive tone, but settled for bringing my clenched fists into my lap under the table. I glanced up when she didn't start yelling at me and realized she hadn't even noticed that I was sitting there. Her eyes were only on Varek. I looked behind her to see an attractive man looking agitated in a nice suit and tie. I would have been upset, too, if my date had ignored me to talk to another person.

Varek didn't say a word back to her. Instead, he nodded a polite greeting to the man standing behind Melissa and reached across the table, holding out his hand and waiting for me to place my fingers over his, the way he had done when we first sat down. It took Melissa a moment to get flustered that he was ignoring her, and for her to finally notice that he was with someone. I was looking at Varek when I saw his eyes narrow slightly and his jaw get tight.

"Don't," the one word was spoken low, but there was no mistaking the warning in his tone. I looked up to see Melissa staring at our clasped hands, her face turning a deep shade of red. It looked like she was about to explode.

The gentleman tried taking her arm, "Come on, Melissa, they are waiting for us at our table." He turned to Varek. "We are sorry to interrupt your dinner, have a nice evening."

He nodded to me and pulled on Melissa's arm to steer her away from our table, but she dug her heels in and screeched out, "No!"

She placed both palms on our table roughly, leaning in. Her bright red dress gaped open in the front, revealing her red lace bra. She slapped her palms down on the table again, making the wine and water glasses jump along with my heart rate. Seeing her this crazed was making it hard for me to catch my breath, my heart was beating wildly, and my eyes started misting.

Varek looked at me, at my reaction to her rage, and his eyes narrowed while his jaw muscles jumped. He squeezed my hand once and let it go. While he had been watching my reaction, it hadn't gone unnoticed by her. She was screaming about me being a home-wrecking whore and that he was her man. It was obvious that Varek had enough when he began to rise from his chair.

For a brief moment, I clung tightly to his hand, wanting to stay connected to him so he could protect me, but I let it go again when he gave me a subtle nod of reassurance.

He straightened and faced her.

"I don't know who you are or why you believe you have a right to cause this type of disturbance, but if you don't leave right this second, I will destroy you." The last was said so low, that no one other than the three of us could have heard it. The menace in his tone had me flinching back and curling my arms around myself. Varek must have seen that, too, because if I had thought he couldn't look any angrier before, I was wrong. Dead wrong. The fury was blazing off of him, and I noticed tiny wisps of shadows curling around his body.

He was losing control, and he needed to be calmed quickly. I took a deep breath and straightened my shoulders, gathering up all my courage. I reached over and stroked his arm, noticing that it produced an immediate reaction in him. His body froze for a brief second before relaxing again, the wisps of shadows that I hoped nobody else had noticed dissipating.

Melissa reacted to my gesture as well. She screeched again, her default setting to being angry, it seemed, and launched herself at me. Her hand was out, ready to slap me across the face. I cringed and ducked, letting go of Varek's arm to throw my arms up over my head. When the blow didn't come, I slowly lowered my arms, peeking up at Melissa.

She whimpered, her words dying quickly, as Varek held her wrist, tugging back from his hold on her, but his grip was firm. It didn't look like he was hurting her, her fingers weren't red as they might be if he were cutting off her circulation, but his hold was immovable. He leaned in close, whispering in her ear. I saw her sag against his body, the move making jealousy, unlike anything I had ever felt before, knot in my stomach. I wanted to vomit up everything I had just eaten simply from seeing Varek holding another woman, even knowing it wasn't in desire. I tried to will the feeling away, but I knew it wouldn't go, not until they were no longer touching and not until she was out of his life for good.

I saw movement out of the corner of my eye and watched as

Talon walked up to our table, dressed in a suit and tie, looking as if he had been waiting outside and had just been called in to intervene.

"Boss." He nodded to Varek.

"Take her out of here. Keep a closer eye on her and make sure that she doesn't come around me or my fated again," Varek's words were smooth, with his hint of an accent just underneath, but the fury was also there, riding his tone.

"Yes, boss." Talon nodded to me. "Juliette." And then he walked away, holding the arm of Melissa much the same way Varek had, unbreakable but not tight. Her head was hanging, and her shoulders drooped as he led her away. My heart gave a slight tug. I didn't particularly enjoy seeing anyone looking so broken. Yes, she brought this on by acting crazed and attempting to slap me, but seeing her look so shattered was almost heartbreaking.

Varek straightened his cuffs and sat back down, looking much as he had before Melissa had shown up, unruffled from the experience.

"Varek, I have to work with her," I said softly. I couldn't deny that the entire episode had shaken me. I already knew her to be petty and vindictive with how she went out of her way to try to have me written up, and the way she spoke about me and to me. But I had never seen her this way. I also knew, just as he did, that Melissa was fascinated by him. She had convinced herself that they would be together and that he would pick her even though he had never been seen with any woman. Now that Melissa had seen him here, with me, she wouldn't be the same petty woman. She was going to be out for blood. My hands shook as I thought about how difficult, if not downright dangerous, she could make things for me.

"Look at me," he demanded softly.

I looked up at him, studying his deep green eyes, the ones that looked like emeralds cut and polished, the same ones that would turn black as the deepest hole with no end to stop your fall if you were unlucky enough to fall in. It was a facet of him I hadn't gotten to know yet, another part of him that was dangerous...but would never hurt me. On the contrary, he would use that side of himself to protect me at all costs. It was there, easily readable because he allowed me to see it.

"I will never allow her or anyone else to cause you harm. You belong to me, and I protect what is mine."

I swallowed over the thickness in my throat. Here, before me, was probably the most dangerous man I would ever know in my lifetime... and he was mine—my protector.

"I believe you."

He nodded in satisfaction and turned his head to look at a well-dressed man who rushed up to the table, only the slight tightening of his jaw showing that he wasn't pleased with the interruption.

"Sir, I am so sorry about the interruption to your dinner." He straightened the glasses on the table, placing them where they had been before the interruption, as he called it. When he was done, he gripped his hands tightly together. "Please, if there is anything that we can do here at the Trinity to show our deepest apologies..."

"Mr. Greyson, meet my fiancé, Juliette," he cut him off, and reached back to take my hand, causing me to blush at his words. I supposed, in a way, we were engaged. Though, from everything I had learned from Rake and Sasha, being mated was much more than merely being married in the eyes of human law. It was forever, and only death was capable of severing the union.

Mr. Greyson, whom I assumed was either the manager or the owner, slightly bowed in my direction. "My congratulations to you, Varek, sir. I want to offer you our finest desserts as best wishes toward your upcoming nuptials. And as compensation for the trouble here tonight. If I may."

Varek looked at me questioningly. It sounded good. The food had been delicious, the best I had ever eaten, really. But I knew that even though I had not yet looked around the room, all eyes were still on us, and I felt very disconcerted with the attention we had garnered. As perceptive as I was learning he was, Varek turned back to Mr. Greyson. "I think we will take a rain check on your generosity. It was a very trying experience for Juliette, and I believe she would be more comfortable if we left."

Mr. Greyson looked at me again with a frown. "I understand, but I'd hate for the experience here tonight to tarnish your opinion of our restaurant. So, please, allow me to send the dessert home with you. Perhaps you will be able to enjoy it better in the privacy and peacefulness of your own home?"

I smiled and nodded. "That would be very kind of you, Mr. Greyson."

Varek squeezed my hand again in approval.

"I will see to it right away. Please consider your meals on the house for the trouble here tonight."

Varek released my hand and stood up, buttoning his suit jacket and straightening his cuffs. He walked around to the back of my chair and helped me scoot back far enough to stand on shaky knees that still hadn't completely calmed down.

"I wouldn't dream of not paying for our meal, Mr. Greyson. What happened here was at no fault of the establishment." He pulled his wallet from the back pocket of his slacks and withdrew several bills, laying them on the table. "I will undoubtedly bring Juliette back." He glanced down at me as he took my hand and set it gently over his arm. "I believe she enjoyed her meal as much as I did."

I blushed and nodded my head. "Everything was absolutely delicious. I thought the wine was amazing, too."

Both men chuckled, but Mr. Greyson was the one to respond. "Well, it is a good thing you are marrying the owner of the vineyard, ehh?" He winked at me, shook Varek's hand, and left just as our waiter walked up, holding a bag that looked like it had more than just two servings of dessert.

"Thank you for coming to Trinity. I hope we will see you again soon." His tone was slightly nervous, but very respectful.

Varek nodded and led me out of the restaurant. Not once did I look around to see the stares or try to listen to the whispers, many of which were not very subtle.

CHAPTER

FIFTEEN

JULIETTE

IN THE BACK of the luxury SUV, I fidgeted with the clutch that Sasha had insisted I use, instead of the oversized bag I usually had with me at all times. This one was only large enough to hold my phone and keys. I wasn't used to carrying around something so small and nearly left it behind in the restaurant. I had barely remembered to grab it from the table as we were walking away.

I ran my finger over the button flap, opening and closing it, then just running my finger over it again.

"Something is bothering you."

I sighed at the deep, smooth voice that caused shivers to race over my spine. His slight accent was as delicious as the smells that were coming from our bag of desserts.

"Is that what happened with your coworker?"

I looked at him from the side of my eye. "Do you even know what her name is?" It seemed even more insane than her actual behavior. That this woman could have been essentially stalking him for weeks, but he never even learned her name in all that time.

"Juliette, I never had a single reason to learn her name. I never paid her any attention other than to politely tell her I was uninterested. I was hoping the problem would go away on its own as it had in the past with other overeager admirers." He shook his head and ran a large hand through his midnight black hair. "I don't want you to think that I am callous or cruel. I just never spared her a thought when she wasn't right in front of me trying to gain my attention. When that happened, I worked quickly to shut it down."

"I saw you put your hand on her shoulder," I reminded him gently.

"I did?" he sounded surprised.

"Yes, at the club the other night. You were standing by the stairs, and she went over to talk to you. After a few minutes, I saw that you had your hand on her shoulder."

He nodded thoughtfully. "Ah, yes. I remember now. She had leaned in and was attempting to touch me. I had been feeling out of sorts all evening, I didn't know what was happening, but it felt...important. My brand had started feeling itchy, and my skin felt tight over my whole body. It was more than I could bear when she tried to touch me. I put my hand on her shoulder to keep her away." He placed his large palm over my cheek and stroked his thumb over the sensitive skin of my bottom lip. "It wasn't until I saw you, *touched you*, that I finally understood what had been happening with me all night, what had drawn me into the club when I had no plans to go in that evening. It was you. You were waiting for me."

We stared into each other's eyes for what felt like an eternity. I wanted to drown in the bottomless depths of his. His eyes, when black, were a bottomless abyss, but his green ones were no less fathomless. They were ancient and told tales of all his thousands of years. He was an ancient being, and I saw how tired he was, how wearing life had become after such a long time. There were no wrinkles on his skin, no silver hair on his head, but he was old, conceivably the oldest soul on the Earth.

And I knew that I was the only person alive, now or ever, that would be able to breathe new life into him. I desired to be that for him more than anything I had ever wanted before because I knew, to the depths of my soul, that he would be saving me, too.

I leaned forward the few inches that separated our faces and lightly pressed my lips against his. We were still looking into each other's eyes as our lips met for the first time. They stayed open when I pressed a little harder. But my eyelashes started to flutter when I felt his tongue lightly trace the seam of my closed lips. They fell completely when his lips coaxed mine to open, and that tongue swept inside.

His moan was deep and carried a hint of desperation when he reached up and gripped a handful of my hair at the back of my head. He tilted my head to one side, allowing himself deeper access. I felt like I was being consumed whole. Flames were erupting inside my chest and spreading outward to cover my entire body. I wanted to run my hands down my chest to make sure I wasn't actually being consumed by flames, but lost the will to do so when his other hand wrapped around my back and pulled me into him.

I threw my hands against his chest, not to push him away but to brace myself against the fall.

"I will always catch you," he whispered against my lips, before deepening the kiss that I had thought couldn't get any more intense.

I realized I was straddling his lap, and my dress skirt was tucked up around my waist, when I felt his hand slide down to grip the back of my rear end and pull me even closer into him. I could feel his hardness. I could taste the desperation on his tongue. I wanted it, to soothe it, I really did, but my heart was beating erratically, and my breaths were wildly out of control. I was desperately terrified that I was losing myself.

As perceptive as ever, Varek slowed the kiss. His hand went from griping to soothing. The hand in my hair started stroking me, petting me. He was calming me, and he was allowing my heart to settle. It brought tears to my eyes. When our mouths broke apart, he lifted his thumb to catch the tear that fell. He placed that finger into his mouth as his eyes stared into mine.

When he was done tasting my tears, he pulled me close again. This time he was simply offering me the comfort I didn't know I needed. My head lay against his chest, and he continued to soothe me. When I had finally calmed, surrounded by his smell, heat, and touch, he whispered, "It's okay, my jewel. I will always give you what you need. You need patience, and I have plenty of that. I will show you that you will never have a reason to fear or doubt me. I will protect you from the world, and I will also give you the world." I felt him nuzzle and kiss the top of my head.

I closed my eyes and sighed in contentment. Truly happy for the first time in my life.

I hadn't realized I was drifting off until I felt the vehicle come to a stop and the engine turned off. I reluctantly sat up and looked out of the car window. When I saw we were sitting outside my apartment building, I sighed and pulled away, sliding my leg off his lap. I didn't want to leave his warmth. He was comforting, and somehow, in such a short amount of time, I had begun to rely on him.

Once I was situated with my dress at an appropriate place on my legs, Varek pulled on the door handle and slid out, holding his hand out for me to follow. I started to slide out, but remembered, again, about my small clutch and looked around for it until I saw it lying on the floorboard. It must have fallen after being jostled by our make-out session. My face heated at the memory.

Once I was standing next to Varek, I turned to Talon, who was standing against the passenger door, either to stand guard over the vehicle or just to wait for Varek to return after walking up. "Thanks for the ride and the help with Melissa, Talon." He nodded his head at me, tipping up the corner of his lips. "Umm, can I ask..." I glanced over at Varek quickly, hoping that I would be able to get an answer from them both. "What did you do with her tonight?"

"I had one of the other guards take her home. I also made sure she understood the situation by pressing the understanding on her that both you and the boss here are off-limits. I also made sure she understood that she would no longer be working with you at the nursing home."

I straightened my back. What? "But..."

Before I could even get another word in, I was cut off by Varek, him turning and lifting my head to meet his eyes with a hand placed on my cheek. "Juliette, there is no way I would allow that woman to remain around you. I cannot guarantee that my men would be able to keep you safe while you are in that building. There were just too many possibilities of things that she could do to you when they weren't able to stay near." His thumb rubbed over my bottom lip again, his eyes on his thumb, watching where his own lips had been just a short time ago. His eyes darkened. They met mine again, and I watched as wisps of shadows spread out around him. "Baby, I need you safe. I wouldn't be able to function if anything were to happen to you. I would destroy every soul in this realm to get to you if you were in danger."

My heart rate sped up as I listened to the earnestness in his voice. I didn't know what he meant exactly, but I was certain that I didn't want to put him in the position to be affected by my being hurt. At the same time, I didn't want to see him hurt either. I nodded. "I understand. I just don't understand how you would be able to force her to quit?" He rubbed the back of my neck, showing his understanding that craning my head back to look at him due to our height differences wouldn't feel good after a while.

"I have a lot of power in this city. It is not difficult to make sure her nursing license is pulled or to make phone calls to have her fired," I gasped. I didn't know if it was wise for anyone to have that kind of power. "But," he gently squeezed my neck, "Talon tried to simply persuade her to see reason before resorting to those extremes," I sighed in relief. I didn't want to see her lose her license just because she was jealous and lost a man she never actually had in the first place.

"But, understand me right now, Juliette, if that woman causes any trouble after the warning she received tonight, I will not be lenient. She gets one chance. If she disregards that chance, I will destroy her. Tell me you understand. I don't want you thinking of me as a monster should I have to deal with her," his words were like steel, and his eyes were fierce. There was no way to misunderstand how serious he was about what would happen if Melissa caused any trouble.

I nodded my head. "I-I understand, Varek."

His eyes studied me carefully, searching for any hint that he had scared me. But I wasn't scared of him. Wary, sure, anyone would be a fool not to be cautious of someone as ancient and powerful as he was. But he didn't scare me. Not the way my stepfather had.

He nodded, satisfied, and leaned forward to place a small kiss against my closed lips. "Come one, let's go up, get tucked safely into your bed." He led me into my building, up through the elevator, and finally, to my door while his hand stayed grasping my neck gently, but firmly the entire time. By the time we both walked into my living room, where Sasha was reclined back on the couch reading a book on an e-reader, I had grown accustomed to the weight, was comforted by its presence there, and mourned the loss of it when he let me go.

He nodded to Sasha, who smiled broadly at the sight of us both and swung her legs to the floor, setting her tablet on the coffee table. But she didn't say anything, just watched us together with her hands clasped and between her thighs.

Varek turned to me. "Don't forget, tomorrow night we are going to the club so I can introduce you to everyone. I want you to be comfortable there." He lowered his head after he received my nod and placed a soft kiss against my lips. It wasn't passionate like the one we shared in the car, but it held no less meaning to me.

After he left, I locked the door and turned around, leaning my back against the wood, and waited for Sasha to speak.

CHAPTER
SIXTEEN

JULIETTE

I HAD EXPECTED THERE to be a lot of drama at work. At the very least, I had expected Melissa to show up even more irate than she had been at the restaurant. Maybe the other employees at the nursing home would be angry that I had inadvertently gotten her fired-she was very popular after all. But none of that happened. Instead, it was strange how everyone went about their day as if Melissa wasn't missing.

The nurse who replaced Melissa was a part-timer who usually worked the weekends, but apparently had agreed to come in to work the weekday shift until the head nurse could hire someone new. Since we worked opposite shifts, we didn't really know each other at all. However, I was glad to find out she was efficient and thoroughly checked her work, something Melissa had never done. If I had been able to work with this woman every day instead of Melissa, life would have been much easier and less stressful.

It wasn't long before the end of the day came, and still with no questions or comments. I had to appreciate it for the gift it was and also feel a bit sad for Melissa that it seemed no one missed her even though she had worked there before I had.

Talon held the back door to the SUV for me and offered a hand to help boost me up into the seat. What was new? I was small, so I needed a boost to do a lot of things that most people took for granted.

Once we were on our way, Talon spoke. "Are you ready to head to the club tonight?"

I thought about that for a minute. I didn't have the greatest experience the last time, but I had enjoyed the frenetic energy that had been pumping through the place. I thought it might have been much more exciting and fun if I had been with Varek and maybe even my guards. I bet Sasha would give us a completely different type of girl's night out than the previous experience.

"I guess I'm looking forward to it. I'm a little nervous meeting everyone, but, yeah, I think I'm okay with going to the club."

He nodded and focused on the road, looking like he wanted to say something else, and either couldn't find the words or was worried about letting them out. I wanted to tell him to spill it already but ended up nervously fiddling with the hem of my scrub top.

I was startled enough to jump when Talon finally interrupted the silence. "He has a lot more businesses than just the club, you know."

I had my hand resting over my racing heart. "Does he?"

I could see Talon's eyes crinkled ever so slightly in the corners, telling me that he was enjoying that he had startled me so thoroughly. I primly crossed my hand over the top of the other and cleared my throat.

"I would imagine someone as old and powerful as he is would have a great many businesses."

"He does. Some are just investments. He is a silent partner in dozens of businesses that asked for a loan. Once the initial loan is paid off, he usually will sell his shares back to the owner. A few he has kept in his own portfolio if they are successful enough. But his personal businesses that take most of his time are his club...and the other clubs."

I scrunched my forehead, my brows pulling together in confusion. "Varek has more than one club? Are they in other cities?"

"Well, actually, now that you say it like that, yeah. Varek has multiple clubs in most major cities in the US and in several major locations throughout the world. But I'm not talking about the human clubs. I'm talking about the real reason for clubs like Brimstone."

I had a feeling that I might know where this was going. With the way the word 'human' got thrown around, I was beginning to understand that demons either needed to or wanted to keep themselves separate from humans.

"Do the demons have a separate club from the human one?"

"That's exactly right. You haven't really seen them, but demons don't generally look like humans. Sure, some are pretty close that they would probably get away with passing for a human even without their glamor. But the majority of demons look a whole lot different. So Varek created a place for demons to feel comfortable being themselves without the glamor. No humans are allowed since demons wouldn't feel comfortable if a human acted scared or if they were afraid the human would report them."

I sat back, disappointed. "Oh. I guess that means I won't be able to go in either."

"Actually, you'd be wrong."

"Really? I would be allowed in the demon clubs?"

He shook his head and looked at me through the rearview mirror while we were stopped at a red light. I could see the apartment building just ahead. "You keep forgetting that you are part demon."

I bit my lip. Oh yeah, that.

"But even if you weren't part demon, you would still be allowed simply because you are Varek's mate."

"Demons can have a full-blooded human for a mate?"

It was his turn to look confused. "Well, no, now that you mention it, there are no demon/human mates. Hybrids...yes. But I have never heard of a full-blooded human being mated to a demon."

"So, what kinds of clubs are just for demons?" I asked, eager to learn more about the world I had unexpectedly found myself immersed in.

"That's part of what he is planning to show you tonight. He asked me to warn you, so you weren't caught off guard when you show up later."

He stopped talking, and it didn't look like he was going to say anything else.

"Wait. That's it? You drop that on me, but you aren't going to elaborate any more than that?" I asked incredulously.

He chuckled from the front seat. "Yep, that's it. He asked me to give you a heads up, and I did. The rest is up to him."

"Well, now my mind is just spinning in a hundred different directions, wondering what more there could be. Clubs just for demons? Where? The place isn't big enough for another club." Now that he had told me about it, I couldn't stop wondering. I guess I found out something new about myself tonight. I didn't do well with secrets. Who knew?

We pulled up in front of my building and waited in the backseat for Talon to open my door as he'd asked before he had exited from his door. I saw him look around before finally opening my door. I looked up at him when I got out and was standing there on the sidewalk. "Is that really necessary?"

"Juliette, the boss would decimate the city, and me along with it, if I allowed any danger to come to you. So, it's better safe than sorry, don't you think?" He waved his hand in front of me to lead the way.

"I can understand self-preservation. I just don't know why there would even be a reason to worry. I mean, Melissa is angry, but I can't imagine she'd be a major threat."

"It's not just her. Being the leader of beings that most humans would consider an abomination poses a threat to your safety if his true identity got out." He held the door open for me and waited while I checked my mail. It was all junk mail except what looked like a greeting card. "Besides all that, he is a powerful man in the business world. I doubt there are many enemies there, but Varek would never take any chances. So, it's better to go along with it."

We were riding up in the elevator when my curiosity got the better of me, and I slid my finger underneath the sealed flap. The envelope had no return address and only had my address with no name. I hoped it wasn't a birthday card for a neighbor's kid.

I was sliding the card out of the envelope when we were stepping off the elevator and started heading to my door. Talon turned back once he was at my door and realized I wasn't still walking with him. Instead, I was standing in the middle of the hallway holding a blank card. It had nothing on the outside at all. When I opened it to see if there was anything on the inside, I gasped.

Talon strode back to me quickly, took the card from my shaking hands, and cursed under his breath. Inside was a message that said-

I FOUND YOU...

THE WORST THING about the message wasn't the words themselves, but that they were written in blood. It was smeared across the card as if the person who wrote it had blood on their hands. They wrote the words with the tip of their finger dipped in blood.

I looked up at Talon, "It's him, isn't it?"

He didn't answer. He just glared at the card and held his hand out. I handed over the envelope with a shaky hand. I took several deep breaths and tried to calm my racing heart.

"Why else would I have gotten that? It has to be him."

"It could be another demon, maybe. This would have been the best way to gain Varek's attention," he growled the words. Clearly, the message had gotten to him, too.

We quickly entered my apartment. I stood by the door as he

made a quick sweep of the place, checking for any intruders. When he came back, he was still angry. "You need to pack a bag. It's not safe for you here." I watched as he pulled out his phone, hit a few buttons, and then held it to his ear.

I nodded numbly and walked into my bedroom, wondering if being mated to such an important man...male was worth it. Then I thought of the gentle way he was with me, the way he treated me, and how he had kissed me. I didn't know if he was worth it, yet, but it was worth trying. Besides, this was probably all my mess, and he had nothing to do with it.

I pulled out a duffle bag from the back of my closet and started putting my work clothes into it before picking out a couple of pairs of jeans and tops. I figured I wouldn't have to stay away forever, and I would be able to come back for more later. I stuck my head out the bedroom door. "Hey, Talon?" I heard him talking in low tones still by the door. When he paused his conversation, I asked, "is it okay if I take a shower and change now? Or, should I wait until we get to the penthouse?"

I waited for him to relay the question to who I assumed was Varek. When he answered, telling me I could change here and to take my time, I relaxed muscles I hadn't even realized were still tense. If he wasn't concerned enough to hurry me out of the apartment, then there must not be any imminent danger. I shut the door and walked to my closet to pick out an outfit for the club this evening. I remembered what most of the women were wearing and shook my head. I didn't want to look frumpy, but there was no way I would be able to dress like that and feel comfortable.

I settled on one of the dresses that Sasha had brought over. It was a simple little black dress that wasn't too short for my comfort. It looked long enough to come to my knees, and the shoulder straps were wide with the bodice in a straight line across the top. Hopefully, it wouldn't make my small chest look any smaller than it already was.

I took a quick shower and then blew the wetness out of my hair without completely drying it. While I stood in front of the mirror putting on my makeup, I contemplated my eyes. I wanted to feel comfortable enough to go out with Varek without the need for my contacts. I wanted to show him I could be brave enough to be in public without them. I looked away from my eyes and kept applying the concealer and powder.

When I was putting on a light eyeshadow, I kept my gaze off my eye color. When I started applying a thin coat of mascara, I growled at myself and threw the tube in the sink. I leaned against the basin with my palms pressed hard against the porcelain. I ranted in my head, calling myself a hundred different names, thinking myself an idiot for caring, and thinking myself a coward for being scared. Then, with a shuddering breath and misty eyes, I finally looked up into the mirror again. I stared and stared.

And then, with trembling fingers, I reached up and pinched first the right lens from my eye, revealing the brilliant green. It was almost exactly the same shade as Varek's. After a few more long seconds, I reached over to my left eye and pinched the lens from that one. A deep black iris stared back at me. There was not a hint of color and nothing to differentiate the iris from the pupil. It was solid black. A tear fell from that eye. With it came all the heartbreak. Hate from who I had thought was my father. Taunting from children I had gone to school with—the flinches from strangers.

I held my hand over the toilet, dropped the two dark brown lenses into the bowl, and watched as they floated down to the bottom of the water. And then I pushed the handle down, watching as the water swirled them around quickly before they disappeared from sight.

I looked back up into the mirror. This is who I was. I wasn't "normal". I was half demon, and I was the fated mate to the king of demons. I needed to be brave and strong, and I needed to face my own fears. The demons I had been around had already shown me that they were more accepting than any human had ever been. They were my family, and I would accept them for who they were, too.

I took a tissue and wiped the tears from my face carefully, trying to preserve my makeup, and swiped a little more powder over my cheeks to even them out. When I was done, I gathered my supplies together and placed them in an overnight bag I'd had for ages, but hadn't had a reason to use, then I walked it into the bedroom and placed it into the still open duffle bag. I zipped the bag and slid into the black, low heeled sling-back shoes that Sasha had suggested I wear with the dress.

I picked up the duffel and my purse and carried them both to the living room, where Talon was waiting patiently. He stood from the couch, walked around the table, and stopped in front of me. He stared down at my face, his eyes dancing back and forth between mine for several seconds. I lifted my chin higher. He nodded twice with a smile and then held out his hand for the duffle, took my keys, and escorted me out of the building and into the back of the luxury SUV that my fated mate owned and drove us across town to the building that held my future.

CHAPTER
SEVENTEEN

I WATCHED as the G-series SUV pulled up to the curb and stood back as Talon stepped out of the driver's side, and walked around to the back passenger door. My fated was inside and waiting for me.

After the news of her receiving an anonymous card in the mail with such an ominous message, I didn't think it would be possible to let her leave The Tower again. I knew it would be a fight since she loved her job working as a nursing assistant at the nursing home, but her safety was worth more. I had acknowledged to myself earlier that she might be angry, but I'd rather see her safe and not talk to me than for her to not be talking to me because she was dead.

She was so fragile. I saw her delicate bone structure, so easily damaged, as she climbed down from the height of the vehicle. A height that I took for granted as I had no problems stepping in or out —same as any of my men. But her small stature made her look like a child that needed a boost from an adoring parent.

She turned to face me, and I caught my breath at the vision before me that was decidedly un-childlike.

She was stunning.

Her hair was down, the lights from the street lamps nearby casting a glow that made the silvery white strands of her hair look like moonbeams. Her alabaster skin held an ethereal quality that made me think that she might be a goddess sent to this realm to either save me or drown me in my own destruction.

Her form was slight, but for all her thin, waif-like form, she was, without a doubt, a woman. The curves were not pronounced, but sinewy and seductive. She moved with grace and poise as she walked toward me. Her smile had dimmed as she stepped closer, and I realized that I had not greeted her, nor had I shown her any of the appreciation I had been thinking.

I stepped forward to meet her in the middle and wrapped one arm around her hips, just under her ass, and the other, I held under her hair at the nape of her neck. Nothing in this world could have stopped me from plundering her mouth deep with my own as I lifted her. Our height differences were dramatic, but I would find the best, most enjoyable ways to circumvent any difficulties. There was no need to cause either of us discomfort trying to reach the other when she was small enough for me to simply pick her up and bring her to my height.

She sighed into my mouth, and her arms wrapped tightly around my shoulders. I felt one of her hands delve into my hair, holding on as tightly to me as I was to her.

The thing with fated mates was, though the fates knew their job well, it was never a guarantee that the fated couple would find the other appealing in either looks or personality. It was never a foregone conclusion that the pairing would work out perfectly. Most of the time, of course, the fated pair would be to each other's liking. At the very least, they would grow to care about each other deeply. Occasionally though, the fates made a match so perfect that the fated pair would be combustible, lighting the world on fire with their passion. Those around them would admire the rightness of the pairing and tell future generations of the chance of getting such a perfect match. They became legends and what every young teen dreamt about when wondering what their fated would be like.

This was beyond even that.

I had seen those fated. The rosy cheeks of the couple as they got to know each other, eager to join and begin their extraordinary life together. The deep, simmering passion threatened to pull them under and not let them up for days until it was slaked enough to allow a few hours apart without causing pain from the separation.

What I felt at this moment for my Juliette went beyond a simple lust or passion. Days would never be enough to calm the raging inferno that danced between the two of us.

I broke my mouth from hers and rested our foreheads together, our breaths the only thing between us. I looked into her mismatched eyes and saw myself reflected in them.

"Hi," she whispered shyly.

I threw my head back and laughed, something I hadn't done in so long that I couldn't even remember when it last was. I grinned at her, placed a small kiss on the tip of her little nose, and turned to enter the club.

I carried her past the waiting line of gawking club patrons and the bouncers that were stationed at the doorway. I didn't set her down until I reached the first bar closest to the entrance. I set her on the stool at the end and took a half step back. She looked flushed but happy. Her eyes shone brightly under the dim lighting. I ran my thumb over the curve of her cheek, just under where I knew her scar to be.

"You are well?" There were many things I wanted to ask her, but first and foremost, I needed to know that seeing the note from her mailbox had not harmed her in any way. She understood exactly what I was asking because she answered me without hesitation.

"Yes. It startled me, and it wasn't fun getting such a scary note, but I am okay. I promise," her voice was soft and melodic, but sincere.

I nodded. "You have brought your things for an extended stay?" I knew my voice was gruff with expectation, but I could not allow her back to her apartment. Her location had been compromised, and I would not be able to protect her there as well as I would be able to in The Tower. If she demanded she return home to stay, then she would have to make room for both me *and* my guard.

"I brought a duffle bag. Talon said he would bring it up." She ran her fingers through my hair. It felt like she was trying to smooth down the strands that she'd disturbed while I had kissed her out front. But, little did she know, I didn't mind the signs of possession she left on me. I took both her hands in mine and kissed the tips of her fingers.

"Good. Now, would you like a glass of wine or maybe a mixed cocktail before I start showing you around?"

She tilted her head in thought for a moment, as she looked at the bar with its many bottles of alcohol on display and the wine glasses hanging from the top of the bar.

"The wine we had at dinner was delicious. I hadn't expected it to taste so good. But the drink I had here last Friday was pretty good, too."

I turned her head back to face me, hating the brief time I lost her eyes on me. "We have an eternity for you to experiment with every type of wine or cocktail. Why don't I have Vin surprise you with something? If you don't like it, then we can have someone from the next bar try to make you something you might like?" She smiled and nodded, agreeing to my suggestion. I turned to Vin, who was standing, waiting patiently behind the bar without standing overly close that he would interfere with our private moment. "Can you make something that Juliette might like?" He grinned, winked at my fated, and immediately turned to issue a low bow of apology in response to my warning snarl.

I felt Juliette's hand on my forearm, gently stroking, and looked down to see the tell-tell wisps of shadows belying my rage and loss of control.

"It's okay, Varek. He didn't mean anything," her voice was full of concern, and I hated that I had caused her any worry. We both turned to look at Vin when his voice reached us.

"No worries, Miss Juliette. I forgot how territorial newly mated demons could be. Varek would know that I meant nothing by it, but in his current...condition, reasoning wouldn't really be high on his list of capabilities right now."

"Oh, but, we... we're not...we haven't..." she trailed off, and looked at me with wide eyes. As if she were just now realizing that my possessiveness would only get much worse.

"Oh, wow." Vin looked at me and grimaced. "Damn, boss. How about I spread the word to let people know to be careful?"

I growled and picked up Juliette's drink so she wouldn't have to carry it, and took her hand in the other, helping her down from the stool. "How about you concentrate on the job I pay you for?" I tilted my head toward the door that had just opened to allow the clubbers to enter and begin their long night of drinking and revelry.

Vin grinned, showing that he had been with me long enough to know that I wasn't actually angry at him, and leaned forward on the bar. "It was nice meeting you, Juliette. We'll talk more soon, and I'll tell you all kinds of tales about the big man." Then he turned toward the group of women that shimmied up to the bar, giggling and talking loudly over the music that the DJ had just turned up with the opening of the club's business night.

I placed my arm around Juliette's shoulder and walked her away from the group of women and their stares. Leading her toward the VIP stairs, we bypassed several demons that had joined the crowd to have harmless fun among the humans. Many demons had lived their entire lives with humans, were raised as such, and had no problem living as one of them. That was a significant reason for the two parts of The Tower. Demons would remain my main priority when it came to the clubs. I looked over at Juliette, who watched with wide eyes at the couple dancing provocatively on the otherwise empty dance floor. *She was now my top priority in* all *ways,* I corrected myself.

We stopped at the base of the staircase. Rake stood at his usual post, arms clasped behind his back, legs spread slightly apart. It was a ready pose, one that would have him prepared to engage any threat that arose in a swift and deadly manner.

"Hi, Rake," Juliette's sweet voice could barely be heard over the noise of the music, but Rake smiled down at her in greeting, even though they had only seen each other a short time ago. Rake was a male that was ordinarily quiet and serious. There was a reason he had been second in command of security for as long as he had. But it seemed Juliette's natural sweetness had worked her magic on my stoic friend, the same as she had done to everyone else that knew her.

"Juliette." He smiled at her, then gave a brief nod toward me. "Boss."

I held out my hand, and we clasped forearms firmly before he moved the velvet rope away from us and retook his position as soon as we started moving up the stairs. At the top, I led Juliette over to the bar against the back wall of the VIP area. It was set up the same as the other bars in the club. It was fully stocked and had a demon as the head bartender. I employed several humans, but they were all in support positions, servers, bartenders, and cleaning crew. The more essential positions such as staff leads, security, and managers were always demon only positions. The fewer humans that could possibly learn our secrets, the better.

The bartenders in the VIP lounge were always demons since only demons could even access the lounge.

I introduced her to the staff and carefully watched to make sure they were treating her with the respect she was due, and was satisfied to see they took her seriously as my fated. Once we were mated, all that I had would be hers, including this club. If anyone didn't realize that, then they were idiots and would find themselves quickly out of a job, and possibly a life.

I continued to lead her around the club. We headed back downstairs after a brief conversation with the DJ and toward the last bar along the back wall. The entire time we spoke with the staff, she smiled, her eyes shining with happiness. She looked relaxed, and I had a feeling something important had happened for her tonight. It wasn't lost on me that she looked completely different from what she had when we first met. In such a short time, she had blossomed. Her hair was down, and her contacts were gone. She was gaining confidence, and it was beautiful to witness.

We were walking toward the front of the club to get to the door that led to my office and the rest of The Tower, when Juliette was yanked to a stop next to me. I wheeled around with a snarl on my lips, ready to destroy any man, woman, or demon who thought to touch my female. However, I froze when I saw the blade glinting in the low red lights of my club. The blade that was currently being held to the throat of my fated.

There was no holding back my rage. I felt it swelling inside, consuming me from the inside and spreading out. The floor below my feet began to tremor ever so slightly. My vision changed to see only in shades of gray, the lines so sharp I could see each strand of Juliette's hair that was being pulled back in the fist of the woman that had been nothing but a problem for weeks.

It was time to end her.

CHAPTER
EIGHTEEN

I HAD BEEN HAVING such a fun time with Varek. He had led me from the front to the back, to the VIP area, introducing me to each of his employees and explaining things along the way. As a result, I now knew much more about running a dance club than I ever thought possible to know. And I enjoyed every single minute of it.

We were heading toward the door that he said would lead to the offices and to what else he wanted to show me, when a sharp pain jerked me to a quick stop, tearing a shocked cry from me and pulling my hand from Varek's in the process. It took me several seconds to realize that someone had grabbed and yanked me by my hair. It had been a very long time since anyone had pulled my hair, and I found that I didn't miss it at all.

I stood there in front of Varek, reaching up to grab the hand that was holding my hair when I saw the danger in Varek's eyes. I watched as the iris' bled to black, and even though it was very dark in the place, I could just make out wisps of shadows start to drift lazily around his body. I widened my eyes. He couldn't lose control of his demon in the club. I didn't want him to get into any kind of trouble, or have trouble coming to him if the wrong person saw him in his demon form. What would the human authorities do?

I felt a prick and a sting against my neck and then a warm trickle tickling my skin as it slid down. I swallowed hard at the look in Varek's eyes. If he looked enraged before, he looked homicidal now. With my swallow, whatever had cut me dug in even deeper. I could swear that I literally felt vibrations from his anger as his eyes never left the bead of blood as it continued to slowly roll down past my collarbone.

I then watched him raise his eyes to mine once the bead of blood disappeared under the neckline of my dress. His eyes went to the right, to the person that was holding me. I watched as he raised his arm and held his hand out. My eyes widened, and my heart almost started beating as loud as the music at seeing tendrils of something white float toward his hand.

I looked around wildly for help, trying to see if anyone that he had introduced me to was nearby and if they were noticing what was happening. But unfortunately, I couldn't move my head without causing what must have been a knife to dig deeper into my skin.

The person behind me finally spoke, and I couldn't say I was very surprised by who it was or what they had to say.

"I told you that you were mine. I refuse to let this little tramp take you away from me," Melissa snarled.

I almost rolled my eyes. It was like a cliché. *The woman that wants somebody that already wants or has someone else.* Next, she would do the line, 'If I can't have you, nobody can'. Except, it wasn't Varek that she was planning to kill. It was me.

I looked from his eyes that were still black, that deep abyss black that made me feel like I could sink down and never return to the surface, back down to his hand. It was still outstretched, and the tendrils of something were streaming quicker into his hand. I didn't know what he was doing, but I could feel that it was dangerous. It was a power that no one should be allowed to have. My skin felt clammy, and I had to swallow back the scream of terror threatening to crawl out of my chest.

It wasn't until I felt the hold on my hair loosen and the knife at my throat fall away that I realized that whatever he had been doing had weakened Melissa. I didn't necessarily think it was a bad thing that he gained control of her, but I also was terrified to learn what he was actually doing.

I took a hesitant step forward on trembling knees and felt both her hands fall away. I slowly took the last two steps over to Varek's side, watching his pure hatred for this woman play over his features. When I turned to look at her, I saw that Talon and Rake were both standing at her back. They each had a hand under her arms, holding her up. When I got my first good look at her, I gasped, my hands flying to my mouth in horror. She looked as if she had aged decades. Her loose skin had a gray pallor, and her face was full of deep wrinkles. She looked like a marionette doll as the guards kept her from just falling to the floor in a heap of skin and bones, and her head bobbed around on her neck.

I turned to Varek and frantically grabbed his outstretched arm. "Varek, you have to stop! You're killing her." He gave no sign of acknowledgment of my frantic cries. He didn't even blink those deep black eyes. He simply stared at her and held that hand out as the tendrils left her chest and flowed into his palm. I glanced around worriedly and saw that no one was paying any attention. We were in a loose circle. Sasha and King had joined us, closing off any view from outside the circle. Humans couldn't see that a demon was among them, killing one of their kind.

I stepped in front of Varek, put my hand over his, and stared up at him imploringly with tears slipping down my cheeks. "Varek, please stop," I said it quietly, but I had no doubts that he could hear me just fine. My hand over his did nothing to stop the flow, and his gaze stayed locked onto hers over my head. All he did was jerk his hand and pull harder. Suddenly, I could feel that same tug in my chest that I always felt right before someone in the nursing home died. It was the feeling of a soul leaving a body, a sign that a person was truly dying.

I placed my hands on his chest and lifted up on my toes as high as I could. I was still too short to reach his face, but I was close enough to gain his attention if he would just look away from Melissa and see me.

"Varek, please listen to me. Don't do this. Please don't take her life," I sobbed. "I can't live with her death on my conscience.

He finally broke eye contact and looked down at me incredulously. He blinked as if he were coming out of a trance. "You can't expect me to allow this woman to live after she hurt you." His voice was rough and deep, as if he were holding back a growl. He glanced down and watched the blood still oozing from the cut. He clenched his jaw so tight I was afraid he would end up hurting himself. I lifted my hand to cover the wound, hoping that it would help him dial back the anger if he couldn't see my blood.

"It's not that bad. Varek, please," I begged, "I'm not really hurt. You stopped her before she could do any more. Now please, please let her go." I closed my hand over his again, and he stared at me with furious eyes before closing his with a low growl that rumbled from deep in his chest. I felt him close his fist and heard a soft gasp of pain behind me. It was the first sound I'd heard from Melissa since this had begun.

I turned to see Talon and Rake holding her slumped body. They looked nearly as angry as Varek did.

"Get her out of here," he snarled. "Make sure she understands the next time she even looks at Juliette again, it will be her death."

They both nodded tersely and carried her between the two of them to the entrance. A few humans looked over but went about their partying. They probably assumed that she was just another patron that drank too much and was being escorted to a cab by the bouncers. But I could see that she wasn't merely drunk. Her skin was sallow, and her hair was limp and dull. Just another few minutes, and her whole body would have been lifeless.

Varek turned my head, his eyes were green again, but they were still angry. I swallowed hard. "Don't ever stop me from trying to protect you." His snarl should have made me pee myself, but I knew deep down that I was the one person in this world safe from harm when it came to him.

I shook my head. "I don't want you to stop protecting me. I just don't want you to kill someone for me."

He clenched his jaw tight. "She would have killed you without a second thought. You think I would have been able to watch her draw your blood and not destroy her?" his words were filled with menace.

I ran my fingers lightly over his jaw, wishing I could make his teeth unclench. "I understand, I do. I just don't want another death weighing on my soul." I whispered.

He picked me up the same way he had done when I first arrived outside the club. "Your soul is the purest soul I have ever seen, Juliette. There is nothing marring its beauty. It's as pure and selfless as you are."

He walked to the door next to the bar and kept striding forward without slowing as a guard opened it for him. As the door closed behind us, the sounds from inside the club abruptly cut off, and blissful silence greeted us. My ears were slightly ringing in the absence of all that noise.

He continued to carry me forward down a long hallway, past several doors, and down to the end. Another guard was standing at that door, and he, too, opened the door for us. I looked around and saw we were in a very large office with a beautiful wooden desk taking up the majority of the space at one end and a seating area to one side of the room, across from a wall of windows. He walked me through the office and another doorway to a small space with just one elevator and another door.

He pressed his thumb against a scanner, and within seconds the doors slid open to reveal a sleek, modern elevator with mirrors on all sides. He pushed the top button marked P, and I felt the car swiftly moving us. I looked at the mirror behind Varek and saw how he was dwarfing my body. I couldn't even see myself other than my face. I looked up and saw he was staring at me, too. Our eyes met in the mirrors, and I saw the anger he had been carrying slowly morph into a look that was a different type of frightening. He looked hungry. He looked like he wanted to devour me whole.

The thought made me restless. I felt the need to squirm in his hold, but I resisted the urge, never wanting to be put down. How could I want someone so dangerous when I had been around a dangerous man my whole life? A dangerous man had nearly destroyed me. I knew that this male would never hurt me, but he would devour me, though. He would consume every part of me until I was nothing left but *his*. It was there in his eyes.

The doors open silently, with no ding to indicate that we had arrived at our desired floor. I could see through the mirror that we had landed at Varek's penthouse. The familiar black and white decor was already beginning to feel more like home than any I had ever felt before. He carried me into the apartment, stepped into the sunken living room, and sat on the plush black leather couch facing the fireplace. The new position caused my legs to widen and my knees to slide next to his hips. The skirt of my dress slid up my thighs until I was straddling him, and my black lace panties were exposed. The new position put me in direct face-to-face contact. I stared into his breathtaking face and watched his eyes shine with that same hunger he had shown while we were still downstairs.

I also realized that this was the first time that we were truly alone since the first day I woke up in this very apartment. Not much had changed in the few short days since we had met, yet absolutely nothing was the same.

The atmosphere in the room morphed, charged with heat and electricity. My skin warmed, and I felt a drop of sweat slowly start to roll down my spine as my breathing grew shallow. I suddenly only had one thought on my mind, and it was that I wanted him to kiss me with a desperation I had never felt before for anything in my life.

More than I had ever hungered for food, even more than I had ever wished for my mother.

He was all I saw, all I needed.

The moment his lips touched mine, I moaned while a storm raged around us. I sizzled with heat as lightning danced along my skin. The sparks of electricity ignited my core, and I fell deeper into the demon that fate had decreed was mine.

He took my mouth in a surprisingly gentle kiss, his tongue playing softly across my lips. But I didn't want slow. Instead, I wanted to be consumed by him and the promise of sinful pleasure I saw in his eyes. He had been showing me what he was capable of in small doses since we met. It was past time for him to engulf me in his flames.

I opened my mouth to allow him entry. He took full advantage and then kept going. If I thought he had kissed me before, I was beyond wrong. His kiss wasn't gentle any longer. It wasn't meant to seduce, it was meant to take, to claim.

He pulled my hair tight against my scalp as he grasped it in both fists. The pain only added to the pleasure, a pleasure so profound I thought that I would surely end up nothing but ashes by the time he was done with me. He was dominant, and he was hungry. His growls had shivers rolling across my skin and making the fine hairs on my body stand on end.

It was decadent and wicked.

I gasped when I felt something stroking my bare thigh and opened my eyes to see that he had fully transformed into his demon self, the glamor he always wore completely gone. I realized that what I felt was his tail. I leaned back, breaking the kiss and taking much needed deep breaths. I looked at his horns, at the thick black shadow that looked insubstantial, but I knew it would feel solid beneath my touch. With the appearance of his horns, wings, and tail came a spicy burnt scent. He smelled like burnt cinnamon, just a hint of it, and it wrapped around my senses, making me even more drunk on him.

I felt his tail move further up my thigh and brush against the wet gusset of my panties. It was a place I had never had anyone touch before. It was intimate and forbidden to anyone else. To him, though, it was as much his as it was mine.

I arched my back as he stroked, pressing harder against me. I had no idea it was possible to feel this way. I gasped when I felt the shadowy tail slip underneath my panties and stroke my bare skin. I bucked into his hold and then cried out when I felt the cool air touch the bare skin of my breasts. I hadn't even noticed that he had removed a hand from my hair and was lowering the bodice of my dress, exposing my breasts to his hungry gaze.

His tail set me on fire, and his burning hot mouth fanned the flames.

I clenched the lapels of his suit jacket into my fists and held on while my back arched, and I screamed out a release that I had never felt before and desperately hoped to feel again. I finally slumped down, my body buzzing with aftershocks and my mind turning hazy with each pulse of my core.

I was barely aware of being lifted and carried. I felt myself being laid on the softest mattress I could imagine. I smiled softly when I felt my fated mate remove my shoes and then slide my dress down the rest of my body. I hummed contentedly when I felt the bed dip next to me and snuggled in as close as I could when I felt his arms gather me to his side and his nose nuzzle against my hair.

I was lost to the world when the last thing I heard was, "Sleep, my beautiful jewel. I will keep you safe...always."

CHAPTER
NINETEEN

JULIETTE

I woke to an empty bed, the sheets next to me long gone cold. I sat up slowly, holding the red sheet to my chest and looked around the familiar room. It was clear that I was alone, no sound came from the entire master suite and I couldn't hear anything coming from beyond the door. There was no telling when Varek left or if he was even still in the apartment.

I slid to the edge of the mattress and swung my feet down to the surprisingly warm floor. I left the sheet behind and padded into the bathroom on bare feet and wearing nothing but my panties. I made quick work of using the toilet and washing my face with the cream that Varek had stocked his bathroom with. A quick perusal of the drawers showed me that not only had he stocked me up with facial cleanser, but any other necessity he thought I would need and then some. It was very much the opposite of what it had been like my first time waking here, I didn't have to use his toothpaste this time. Instead, there was a pristine toothbrush waiting for me.

After I washed, brushed, and moisturized, I went back into the bedroom and into his closet. I needed to find something to wear until I could figure out what Talon had done with my duffle bag. I came to an abrupt stop when I opened the closet door to discover my clothes hanging on one side of the giant closet, and my empty duffle folded neatly and sitting on the top shelf over the pitifully small amount of clothing hanging on the rod.

I took a pair of jeans and a simple t-shirt down from their hangers and dressed quickly after finding my bras and panties in one of the drawers. I looked around to see if I could locate a laundry basket for my dirty panties, but didn't see anything. I walked back into the bathroom to see if I had missed one in there, but I couldn't find anything in there either. I didn't want to leave my dirty underwear laying on the floor, so I just stood there at a loss as to what to do next.

I jumped when the door opened and turned expecting to see Varek, but instead, was startled to see an older looking woman wearing khaki slacks and a dark blue polo. She appeared to be in her early forties or not much older. But there was something in her eyes that showed age and maturity though. I had the distinct impression that this woman was much older than her appearance suggested. I was beginning to understand that it was impossible to judge a demon's true age.

We both stood there facing each other, her holding a basket for laundry with a few pieces thrown in as if she were walking through the large apartment finding scraps of cloth that may have needed washing. And then there was me. I stood there awkwardly holding a pair of used panties.

She started shaking her head and her facial expression morphed from one of shock at finding me in Varek's bedroom unexpectedly, to one of anger. I guessed that she hadn't received the memo yet that Varek had a new fated and that I was now living with him. At least, I assumed that this is what I was doing. I wasn't quite sure and didn't want to make too many assumptions. I mean, obviously we would be living together at some point, likely sooner rather than later, but I didn't quite know yet if our current arrangements were permanent. It seemed that Varek and I would need to have a conversation, and soon.

"No, no ,no. You don't belong here!" She started marching over toward me, dropping her basket on the floor and reaching both hands out to grab me. I was surprised to see she looked so determined. And very angry. Her broken English was thick with a Mediterranean accent. "No, Master Varek, he doesn't want no woman in his home." She grabbed my arm holding the panties with both her hands and started dragging me toward the door. Her grip was surprisingly strong and it felt like the small bones in my wrist were being ground together making me gasp in pain.

I tried pulling back against her forceful tugging, but she just became angrier and kept dragging me down the hallway. As we got closer and closer to the front door I tried to tell her she was mistaken, but she wouldn't listen.

"Please, you have to believe me! Varek brought me here!"

"No! Master Varek doesn't want a woman in his home!" her words were sharp and kept cutting me off. "I take you to guard, they will punish you. Will get rid of you."

She pulled me to the elevator and let go of my arm with one of her hands so she could press the button. I took that opportunity to jerk my other hand away from her and tried to run away to the kitchen. I didn't know what I should do. I didn't know where my phone was. Maybe I should just go with her. All the guards knew who I was and would make sure she knew I was with Varek.

Though she was being forceful, the last thing I would ever want is for this woman to get into any trouble. I realized that she was just doing her job and, in a way, I was grateful that she was trying to protect Varek and his home from women that might manage to find their way inside uninvited. I could just picture Melissa attempting something like that. Though I doubt she would have just run away from the woman. I could picture her being pretty violent. This woman could have been easily hurt trying to protect Varek's home.

The thought made me stop and turn back to face her, holding my hands up, trying to ward her off.

"Please. I need you to listen to me. Varek and I..." I started to plead again but she cut me off once more with a swipe of her hand cutting through the air as if cutting off my words.

"No! I take you to guard." She reached for my arm again. This time I didn't fight her. I nodded meekly and followed her back to the elevator where the doors still stood open. I walked in with her and stood there, head bowed, my hair hanging tangled from our struggle, while she continued to hold my arm. Her grip hadn't lightened any, if anything, it had tightened, probably to prevent me from being able to pull away again, so my bones were feeling rather bruised. I tugged at my sleeve under her hand and murmured quietly, hoping she wouldn't think I was trying to escape again. I just wanted her to let up on her painful grip.

"Please, can you loosen your grip? My wrist is hurting since you are so strong."

She looked down at where her hand was holding on to me and lifted my wrist up before glaring at me. "You no move." Her command was harsh. She hadn't liked me putting up a fight to get away from her earlier while she was doing what she believed to be her duty. I nodded at her and stayed perfectly still.

She pushed the sleeve of my shirt up my wrist and revealed the deep redness there that was already showing signs of bruising. I knew from experience that it would be much worse later. My skin had always bruised easily though, it was a curse to have such pale skin, I supposed. That and the sensitivity to the sun. I would turn as red as a cooked lobster if I spent more than a few minutes in the sun without protection.

She clucked her tongue at the damage and said, "You should not fight me." I didn't want to point out that she had already been crushing my bones from the moment she grabbed onto me in the bedroom. I stayed silent as she inspected my wrist and then heard her gasp as she turned my hand over to inspect the damage to the inside of my arm. "You mate." It wasn't a question. She met my eyes then, looking down at me with wide eyes. She looked at the marks again and then back to me. "Master Varek?" I nodded slowly, as I watched her naturally tan skin pale as the blood drained right before my eyes. Then she dropped my wrist as if it had burned her.

She closed her eyes and when she opened them she smiled a small, anxious, smile. "I'm very sorry."

"I know. You didn't know. You didn't know anyone was supposed to be there. That is not your fault. It's good that you try to protect Varek's home." I smiled back trying to make her feel better. "Just saying though, I could have been a bad person and if I had any weapons I might have been able to hurt you or even kill you, you probably should call a guard for help."

She laughed then, an eerie sounding cackle. "I don't need a guard." I watched in fascination as her face morphed from the pretty, older woman she appeared to be into something from a nightmare. Her face looked almost mummified, everything about her looked old and past the point of rotting. Her eyes were dried out, her teeth brown and broken. She held up a hand that was mostly bone, missing patches of dried skin, with thick yellowed nails sharpened to lethal points.

I swallowed nervously.

Suddenly, I felt the elevator swiftly lowering. We had been standing there, the woman having gotten distracted by inspecting my wrist instead of pushing the button. Someone was calling the elevator. I blinked at the housekeeper.

"I protect myself, always. No one hurt," she sounded proud of herself, her voice raspy, sounding painfully dry and gravelly, though she didn't seem to be in any discomfort.

I nodded my head. She was obviously a type of demon, though I had no idea what kind. She must have sensed my confusion, and slight terror that couldn't be hidden. Her teeth clicked and rattled before she opened her mouth again, her jaw dropping much further than a normal human would be capable of. It was both frightening and fascinating.

"I what you call Banshee." The word seemed to hover in the air for several seconds. Her eyes jumped over my shoulder. Way over my shoulder. Then she shrank back into the corner of the elevator. I would have wondered what could cause such a reaction in a creature that looked like she could out scare just about anyone, but when she moved into the corner I saw the reflection of Varek behind me. Only he wasn't his human self.

He had changed into his demonic form. Large, black onyx horns curved up toward the ceiling and wickedly sharp. Shadowed wings were held widely out behind him, blocking out all view from the room beyond the elevator. They were as long as he was tall, from the top of his head and brushing the floor at his feet. If he weren't holding them out in a display of fury, they would be dragging along the ground.

Dense black shadows wove all around his body while his fathomless black eyes pierced through the warmth of the elevator and focused on the woman huddled into the corner, head bowed in respect. Her form swiftly changed back into the woman she had been before and I quickly jumped in front of her, my hands raised to defend her against any attack Varek thought needed to happen to defend me.

"Varek! Wait! She wasn't hurting me! She was just showing me what type of demon she is."

His solid black eyes studied me a moment before finally starting to relax, his huge wings folding back against his body. Then his eyes zeroed in on my wrist. The bruising was revealed by the shirt sleeve that had slipped down my arm while I was trying to block his attention from her.

"Shit," I muttered, as I quickly pulled the sleeve down, covering my hand. I stared into his furious black eyes, trying to catch my breath as the temperature dropped another few degrees. How a demon from hell managed to make things so *cold* instead of the heat

I would have expected, I didn't understand. But so far, I was learning that nothing in this world was as it seemed. "I can explain..."

"You are hurt," his normally deep voice was nothing, but a growl and the menace that had been rolling off of him in waves since the moment the elevator doors opened seemed to grow in volume until I was all but choking on it. I could hear the woman whimper in the corner. She was whispering "sorry" over and over, occasionally slipping into a language I couldn't identify. Her guilty pleas weren't helping me convince Varek that she hadn't really been trying to hurt me.

I quickly thought of how I could calm him down before things escalated worse and dismissed the idea of getting closer to him like I had done before. Instead, I turned around and went to the woman cowering in the corner. She was scared of his wrath when she had done nothing wrong. She only tried to remove who she thought was a woman that had invaded Varek's personal space. I wouldn't allow her to be punished and I couldn't stand to see her scared for another moment.

I put my arms around and whispered, "It will be okay, I promise." When she did nothing but whimper, I turned my head and glared at my fated mate.

"You can stop now!" I snapped at him in frustration. "She was only doing her job and you should be proud of her! Not glaring at her like you are about to rip her head off at any second!" My words had her burrowing deeper into my arms and had a snicker coming from someone I couldn't see standing behind Varek.

Varek lifted one dark eyebrow and slightly tilted his head. He watched me with a look that I couldn't quite decipher, before easing back some of his aggression. The small space in the elevator noticeably raised several degrees as he folded his arms over his chest and relaxed his wings once again.

"Explain."

I sighed and looked down at the woman that was huddled, crouched low on the floor in a protective ball, and whispered to her,

"It's okay now, come on." I helped her to stand and faced Varek again. "I want to go back up and sit down, first. I don't think I want to have this conversation in the elevator." I reached out with a slight tremble to my hand, to push the button, giving him the choice to either step on with us or stay out in his office.

He stepped onto the elevator and quickly allowed his wings, horns, and tail to dissipate, the wisps of black shadows disappearing before my eyes. As soon as he entered he had me in his arms and placed a soft kiss on my lips. I smiled, immediately calmed by his touch. I glanced over at the woman and saw that she was smiling softly, too.

"What's this?" I looked around Varek's large chest and felt my face flame as Rake bent over and picked up the scrap of fabric from the floor that I knew to be my panties. I groaned and snatched them out of his hands before he could hold them up for everyone to see.

"Seriously? Why me?" I mumbled, as I buried my face into Varek's warm chest.

"You need to stop dropping your panties all over the place, Jewels," Rake's words were immediately cut off, with what sounded suspiciously like a hand hitting upside a head. I refused to lift my face from the comfort and security of Varek's chest.

Once the elevator doors opened up into the foyer of the penthouse, we all filed out and headed to the sunken living room and each took a seat on the comfortable leather furniture. Varek tugged my hand, causing me to lose my balance and fall into the side of his body. He reached over my thighs and pulled my legs flush against his. He grunted his satisfaction at how we were situated once not an inch of space was left between our bodies.

Everyone sat quietly for a moment before I sighed and began speaking.

"I was just finished getting dressed and was looking around for a place to put my...erm...dirty clothes when..." I looked at the woman. "I am so sorry, I don't know your name?"

"Amara, miss."

I nodded. "Amara came into the room. She saw me there and immediately told me I wasn't allowed to be there and started to pull me out of the apartment. I struggled and tried to explain, but she was determined to protect your home, Varek." I smiled at her. "You were doing your job, Amara, you did nothing wrong and I'm sorry that Varek," I turned to him and gave a little glare, "didn't tell you that I was here or that he has a fated now."

Varek inclined his head. "It was an oversight that will not happen again. I will make sure all my staff are aware that you live here now and are to treat you with the same respect that I am." I was glad when he turned to Amara. "Thank you for doing your job. It was my fault that you didn't know my fated was here. Going forward, you can address any concerns with her regarding the care of our penthouse."

His words left me shocked. "Varek, I don't think..." He cut off my protest, continuing speaking to Amara.

"Make sure you consult with her about menus and any other needs. Check with her regarding scheduling."

I tried again. "Varek, I'm not sure that I..." This time, I drifted off when Varek's bright green gaze met mine.

"You are the lady of the house now, Juliette. I have several businesses to run and I would like you to be in charge of our home." He lifted an eyebrow. "Do you not want to?"

I dropped my eyes to my lap while I fidgeted in my seat, running my fingers over the hem of my shirt. "It's a big responsibility. What if I mess it up?" My voice was small and quiet. It was obvious to anyone in the room that I was intimidated, which was ridiculous because it wasn't as if he'd just declared me as CEO of his businesses. He wanted me to help plan dinners and make shopping lists. I wasn't even required to do it all on my own.

Varek placed a finger under my chin and lifted my eyes back to his. "Amara will help you and guide you. If you have concerns you can come to me or call at any time, day or night. Are you okay with this?"

I studied his face for a long minute looking for the truth. He believed in me, wanted me to be the lady of the house. He wanted me to belong.

I nodded.

Life was moving forward at a pace nearly too fast for me to keep up with. But every time I started to feel overwhelmed by what was changing or what was expected of me, Varek was always right there, making sure I knew that I wasn't alone.

CHAPTER
TWENTY

VAREK

I HATED BEING CALLED AWAY from my fated's sleeping side.

Too early this morning, I had received a call from Talon and Sasha, both demanding that I see something important.

I had three dead demons in The Tower.

Months ago, it had been brought to my attention that a new designer drug had been brought into my building that was designed especially to work for demons. For a race that found it difficult to get drunk or high, it was something I was finding difficult to control. But now, it was turning into something much deadlier than just a drug that causes euphoria for my demons. What most don't seem to realize is that we are such a diverse race that there could not possibly be a one size fits all. What would be relatively safe for one, could cause massive hemorrhaging in another.

I spent the few hours since I left the warmth of my bed, and the enticing woman lying in it, questioning employees and figuring out what to do with the bodies. They had died inside my building, but hadn't all been in one club. One had been found in the bathroom of the casino. One, a female, had been lying in a bed in one of the private rooms of the sex club. And the other male had been sitting in one of the spectator boxes of the fighting arena. Three different places, and each of them had been alone at the time. Only the one at the casino had been caught on video having taken the red pill.

In the months that we had been investigating, we still weren't any closer to finding out who was bringing in the pills. But now, we were seeing that they had a much deadlier consequence than we had previously been told by my scientists that had studied it. The drugs were designed to cause feelings of heightened euphoria, but the side effects were dangerous to most and now, obviously, deadly to some. Severe dehydration was the most common. Brain bleeds, as what was responsible for these demon's deaths, were less so but infinitely more dangerous. So, it was imperative that we find who was responsible for bringing these into The Tower and put a stop to it. I would be teaching them a lesson they would be unable to recover from.

So, after dealing with a potential threat against all demons in my building, I wasn't in the best of moods. Hitting the elevator button, eagerness to get back to my fated with the hope that she was still in our bed had died a sudden death, when I saw Amara in her banshee demoness form standing over my Juliette. With her claws poised to attack, it had immediately set off every protective nerve in my body.

I hadn't stopped to think about Amara being one of my most trusted employees or that I had known her for over fifty years. All I saw through the black haze of fury was the need to end the life of anyone who would threaten my fated mate.

But my mate had stepped in, again, to stop me from destroying someone that threatened her. I was still too keyed up to fully appreciate that she prevented me from ending one of my most trusted employees, one of the few I actually considered a friend.

I pulled her as close to me as possible without setting her directly on my lap. I would have done so had I not wanted to prove to Juliette that I had some self-control, even if it had been held back by a fraying string.

Now that Juliette had agreed to be the lady of the house, which basically meant she would be living with me for the rest of eternity, I could finally relax, even if I wouldn't be entirely at peace until we completed our bond.

Rake nodded his head at the two of us, and told me he was going to go back down to the security office to help Talon try to make more sense of the drugs. Amara told us she would finish up her cleaning duties after she apologized to Juliette profusely and begged me for my forgiveness again. I waved her off, thanking her for being diligent and reminding her that Juliette was the only woman other than herself or Sasha that would ever be permitted in our home.

"Come with me." I pulled Juliette to stand with me. "It's time to show you The Tower."

She didn't say a word, just looked confused as she followed along with me toward the elevator after hurriedly running back to our room to slip on a pair of shoes.

We rode quietly down and left through my office and into the long corridor that led to the entrance of The Tower.

"Where are we going?" Her curiosity had finally gotten the better of her as I opened the large door similar to the one leading into Brimstone. She looked around at the small room that was nothing but a bank of elevators.

Two of the elevators went to each level of entertainment. The third one led to the apartments for the Guards that lived full time inside the building. There were a handful of guest rooms for those that traveled far to meet with me for one reason or another. I often had demon leaders from other cities across the world come for meetings to discuss plans for the clubs they were in charge of. Mostly, those rooms sat empty, though. Much of our business was able to be conducted via video chat. Modern technology has made everyone's lives easier. One-hundred years ago, it would have taken weeks, if not months, to travel. Even just correspondence had taken too long in some cases.

"This is where your lessons begin when it comes to my businesses and how things are run."

"I don't really think that's necessary. I mean, I am a CNA and have no idea how you would even run a business. Can't you just tell me the gist of it?" She tucked a strand of white-blond hair behind her ear. I had noticed it seemed to be a nervous habit.

"I won't bore you with the details of each business, but the same way I took you around Brimstone last night, I need to show you around to each place to introduce you and make sure you know where everything is."

She shrugged one shoulder and looked up into my face. "If you think it is necessary, then, of course, I will tag along with you." She smiled that small, sweet smile of hers. Her plump lips tilted a little at the corners, causing her cheeks to crease slightly where dimples would have been if she had them.

We stepped onto the elevator, and I pressed the button for the first of my demonic clubs.

"This part of the building we simply refer to as The Tower." I waved to the buttons on the keypad. "As you can see, each button is marked for each floor and what they represent. This first floor is the casino."

We stepped off, and, like the previous night, I showed her around the floor, introducing her to the manager and staff. Several of the patrons called out a greeting, and a few wanted to stop and talk, but I cut each of them short with a thanks and a reminder to make an appointment for a meeting if they had something important to discuss.

Juliette was getting a lot of attention. There were several curious looks, and I was surprised to see that there were a few hostile looks thrown her way. It was well known that I had been waiting for my mate for years. So, it should have been no surprise for anyone to see her walking by my side. No woman, demon, nor human had graced my side in over two decades. So the females here should have been accepting, not hostile. I made a mental note of the ones that seemed angry at her presence.

"This whole place looks amazing with all the black tables and light fixtures everywhere. I see you carried your color theme in here, too." She grinned up at me, her eyes twinkling in amusement at me.

"Black and red are very demonic colors," I stated.

She nodded her head sagely. "Oh yes, nothing speaks more than the bowels of hell than black and red."

I squeezed her side and watched, fascinated, as she squirmed and giggled. It was not a sound I had heard from her until now. She had been quiet and reserved since I first met her. Her rough life had left her in a constant state of stress and worry. I felt my heart beat just a little bit harder at the knowledge that she was comfortable enough with me to let down her shields. I vowed to hear that sound come from her every day for the rest of eternity.

Her eyes were large, bouncing from table to table as the patrons played their choice of games of chance. "Would you like to play a game?" I waved to the room in general that held multiple tables, each with either cards or dice being either shuffled or thrown. "I could teach you how to play blackjack. It's an excellent game for someone to learn from."

She paused before looking up at me with hesitation. "I don't think I'm ready for that. Maybe you could bring me back sometime, and I could watch you play for a while until I get a feel for it?" I studied her, trying to see if she really wanted to play or if she was genuinely intimidated by the thought of playing. I was beginning to understand that Juliette had not had much interaction with others and had likely never been included in most activities as a child.

I gave her hand a gentle squeeze. "Of course. Would you like to see the next floor?"

She smiled gratefully. I decided then that I would invite my guards to our home for a game of poker. She had made friends with them quickly, and they all seemed to have a mutual affection for one another. Instead of it bothering me like I would have assumed, I was grateful that it gave her more people in her life. It was time to show her that she was welcomed and that she was a part of a group and not still standing on the outside, looking in at the fun.

"I'd love to. Where are we going next?"

I led her back the way we had come.

"The next stop is the dance club."

"Ooh! Is it anything like the one downstairs?" She paused and then looked down at herself. "Varek, I'm not really dressed for this."

"*Amica mea*, you could wear anything and be the loveliest of all creatures around you. We are only walking through. If you see a floor you would like to explore better at another time, then that's what we will do."

She stayed silent, not contradicting me though I could see her struggling with my words. One day she will have the confidence to see herself the way I do, the way I have since the first moment I lay eyes on her. I will see that her spirit is brought back to life.

We stood in silence as the lift took us swiftly to the next floor. As she took a step forward, I held her back once the doors slid open with a slight tug on our joined hands.

"I should warn you that demons are much different than humans. What you saw in the casino was very tame as most gamblers care little about entertainment beyond the chips in front of them and what they hope to win in the next round. These next floors will show you the more base nature of demons. We tend to be crea-tures of a perverse nature and enjoy our carnal pleasures. I need you to know what happens in each of the businesses as a new owner, but." I cupped her cheek to make sure she knew I would understand her reaction. She hasn't been a part of the demonic world, and it would likely be a shock to her. "If you feel uncomfortable or want to leave anytime, just tell me."

She swallowed hard and hesitated only for a fraction of a second before nodding her head. It was easy to read the trepidation my words caused, but it was better to warn her before thrusting her into my world without warning.

"Good." I leaned down and placed a gentle kiss on her lips, wanting to linger, but knew that I was running out of self-control quickly. The mating brand was pushing me to claim her, to finish the bond, and I was becoming just as impatient. If I allowed myself more of what we had done together the night before, I wasn't certain I'd be able to hold back. Until she was ready, I would be patient even if my patience was fraying quicker than I would have expected.

I reached out and opened the door to the dance club, immediately letting the intense beat of the heavy music wash over us. I watched her face instead of looking at what I knew she would see inside my demon's playground.

CHAPTER
TWENTY-ONE

JULIETTE

I wasn't quite sure what to expect after the warning Varek gave me, but I didn't know if I was ever going to get the picture of a giant demon with tentacles fondling six demonesses at once out of my head. I would be replaying the image in my mind for days to come, trying to figure out where, exactly, all those limbs were roving.

Then there was the demon that was nothing but bones, completely naked, but somehow drinking a beer. But the beer stayed inside...somewhere.

"Varek?" I called over the loud thumping beat of the music that I'd never heard before.

His answer was laced with humor. "Yes, Juliette?"

"Where is that beer going?" I asked, still not taking my eyes off the floor that I expected to flood at any moment.

"That is a Gashadokuro demon. He will never spill a drop of his liquor, trust me."

He pulled me by the hand and led me over toward the bar, pressing through the crowd of demons of every shape, size, and color. I couldn't take my eyes off the view as the bodies writhed and swayed. There were acts going on that I was guessing would never be allowed in any human club. Not even the most risqué clubs would allow someone with spider legs to crawl up another person's body, and… nope, not going to keep watching that one.

I looked over the bar to the bartender and was surprised to see someone who looked mostly human other than the gray skin, pointy ears, and fangs that indented his bottom lip. I watched as Varek spoke to him, then gestured toward me. I assumed he was introducing me, so I lifted my free hand and gave a shy wave. I was startled when a woman ran up to us and threw her arms around me. She had the brightest red hair and yellow eyes that nearly glowed in the darkness. It took me a second to realize I was looking at Sasha.

"Hi!" I smiled and hugged her back. "I thought you were gorgeous as a human but wow! I can't believe how breathtaking you are."

She rolled her eyes and threw her hair over her shoulder. "It's the succubus allure."

"Well, that may be true, but you're still beautiful." I looked around and saw many of the creatures staring at her with longing and started to understand. "That must get tiring, I bet."

She reached for a glass of glowing green liquid that the bartender slid in front of us and drank it down in one long swallow. She gasped out a breath and did a small shiver before wiping her ruby red lips that matched her hair perfectly with a finger tipped in a long fingernail that could only be described as a talon. "You have no idea." She frowned and looked over her shoulder, then dismissed her many admirers. "I have trust issues. I never know if someone is attracted to me or my allure." She shrugged, attempting to play it off, but I could sense the self-doubt and how cynical she was when it came to her attractiveness. I couldn't do anything but give her a weak smile and an awkward pat on the arm.

She threw her head back and laughed. "It's okay, Jewels. Don't feel sorry for me. I might not like it, but one day my fated will come along, and then this," she waved toward the onlookers that looked ready to drop to her feet and beg for her attention, "will finally stop."

"Really?"

She sighed. "Mostly. Having a fated changes a lot. Mostly, my allure will be solely for my one. Those most susceptible could still be pulled in," she grimaced.

Varek turned to me. "Geralt will make sure the word is spread that you are to be treated just as they would myself. Of course, Sasha has already begun to tell her crew, but she mostly manages the human club downstairs and isn't up here as often."

"Yep! I was just up here doing my rounds when I saw you guys step in." She nudged me with a grin. "Kinda crazy, right?"

I looked around again and took in the different creatures with their otherworldly colors and builds that I had only seen in books on mythology. "Yeah, it's a little crazy. I never knew this world existed." I winced when I saw a demon with a mouth that reached from ear to ear and was full of what looked like razor sharp teeth leaned into it's dance partner and looked to be taking a bite of their neck. I would have asked Varek to intervene, but the partner seemed to be enjoying it.

"Are you ready to go?" Varek whispered in my ear, and I couldn't suppress the shiver that ghosted along my skin with his warm breath.

"Yes," I practically moaned, and then blushed furiously. He chuckled darkly and kissed my neck softly before placing his hand on my waist to guide me back toward the entrance.

"Bye, Sasha!" I called out with a wave, as we weaved our way back through the bodies.

Once we were back in the elevator and I could finally take a full breath again, I leaned my head against his arm. I hadn't realized until now how safe I felt with him. In a crowded room full of what most people would consider monsters, I was never once frightened for my safety. It was a revelation that I hadn't expected.

"Are you okay?" His deep voice startled me from my musings. I glanced up at him, craning my head back to really get a good look at his face.

"Thank you," I whispered, and leaned up as far as I could on my tiptoes and kissed his chin.

His chest rumbled with pleasure. He wrapped his arms around my lower back, lifting me an inch further, allowing our lips to meet, and spoke against my lips, his sexy accent making me want to make my own pleasure sounds. "For what, *Amica mea*?"

I rubbed my nose against his chest as he settled me back on my feet, his slight scent of burnt cinnamon something I was beginning to crave. I just shook my head instead of answering him and asked my own question. "What does that mean, what you called me? You've said it a couple of times now."

He grunted at my non-answer. "I'll tell you when you're ready."

I looked back up at him. With my cheek to his chest, all I could see was the underside of his chin, and grinned.

The doors opened up, interrupting our moment, and I started to step back, but he tightened his arms around me, not allowing our bodies to separate. I felt him lean down to sniff my hair, much the same as I had done his chest, and then kissed me there. I closed my eyes and gave a little sigh of contentment. I hadn't expected this kind of closeness, had never felt this with another human being in my life. But, of course, he wasn't human. He was a demon, as was I, and we were fated to be together. Someone or something had declared us mates somewhere in the vast stretch of the universe. I didn't think they got it wrong. Not at all.

A clearing throat caught our attention, ending our moment. Again, I tried to step away, but the only distance that Varek would allow me was to turn at his side so I could see who was standing in front of us.

"Sir, I hadn't expected you this evening. And not with such a delectable morsel." He looked me up and down, oblivious to Varek's stiffening posture or the menace that began to fairly ooze off him in waves. "It's been so long since you've brought a play partner up here.

May I ask if you are planning to share?" He licked his lips, his dark gray skin seeming to ripple as he continued to stare at me.

I just knew Varek was about to commit the kind of violence that couldn't be undone, so I snapped a finger making the demon startle and narrow his eyes at me.

"Hey, buddy! Learn how to read a room, huh?" I held up my wrist, clearly showing the mate mark.

He started a low growl but caught sight of my wrist, then sharply jerked his eyes to Varek and cut it off abruptly, swallowing hard. He finally noticed that Varek had completely demoned out, his wings spread wide, and his tail wrapped around my leg possessively. I smelled something faintly sour, the scent making my nose twitch.

He dropped to his knees and bowed his head, beginning to stammer out apologies so fast I could barely make out his words.

"I beg your forgiveness, my Lord. I had no idea. Please accept my humble apologies. I never would insult you or your beautiful mate. I was so overcome with her beauty and charm I couldn't help myself from wanting to taste her delectable thighs..."

"Seriously!" I snapped. "I can only stop him from killing you once. After that, you're on your own!"

He glanced up and saw that his words were only making things worse and nodded so fast that if he were human, he would have given himself brain damage from rattling it around in his skull so hard.

"Yes, yes, please forgive me, my Lord, Lady. I am so very sorry. My mouth runs away with me when I am nervous." He lowered his forehead until it touched the ground. "As much as I would want to suck every inch of your mate's body, I would never," he wheezed out, and I sighed.

"Varek?" I looked back up at him and was relieved to see the corner of his mouth tilt up in amusement, though his eyes were still shooting killing vibes. But it seemed that the immediate danger was over.

He let out a snarl but looked back down at me, pulling me closer still with his tail and taking my wrist with the mark, giving it a lick and a kiss. It wasn't the time to be getting any kind of turned on, but I couldn't help the need that blasted through me at the feel of his tongue against my skin. I shivered, making his lips curl against my wrist.

"Yuri, get up and go back to your post before I rip your head off," Varek sighed, and pulled me past the groveling demon still lying prostrate on the floor.

"Yes, sir, thank you for not ripping my head off, sir." He scrambled up to his feet and gave a wave as we walked past a tall counter and toward a black door. "Have fun fucking your mate, sir! Will you be allowing viewers?" His hopeful question had Varek pausing in his stride, but then he shook his head and put his hand on the large brass door handle.

"No, Yuri. Never!"

As we walked through the door, I could hear Yuri wistfully say, "What a shame."

When the door closed behind us, I was on the verge of laughing. Until I realized what we had walked into.

Bodies were everywhere. It was not like they had been at the dance club when they had been mostly just writhing and mimicking sex. No, in this room, there was no pretend. No preludes or warming themselves up for the act of fucking. They were literally fucking. Everywhere.

I looked up and saw a cage swinging above the crowd where there seemed to be at least three bodies, and what they were doing to each other was definitely the cause of the swaying cage.

I gulped, my eyes wide. "That's secure up there, right?"

I continued to look around, my eyes catching on various acts, some I had heard about from the more raunchy talk at work in the breakroom, others I had no words for. I tilted my head as I watched one couple on a short stage in front of the crowd, trying to understand what I was seeing and how someone could get their foot to do that.

I glanced back at Varek once I realized that he hadn't responded to me and caught him watching me with a grin on his face. My face heated as I went from curiously scrutinizing what I was seeing, to realizing that I was literally standing in a sex dungeon. I used my free hand to cover my face and mumbled, "Oh my god," into my palm. My only defense was that the acts were just not...normal. It didn't even hit me, not really, that they were all having sex out in the open.

"This is a giant orgy. You walked me into a giant orgy with no warning." I turned to him and smacked his arm. "Varek!"

I heard several gasps that were concerning until Varek threw back his head and laughed a deep rumbling laugh that made me catch my breath as I watched. I wasn't the only one fascinated by the sight. I was vaguely aware of much of the activity in front and above, us stopping, and more gasps were heard, but I couldn't tear my eyes away from the beautiful sight.

"I apologize, my Jewel. I honestly forgot to warn you with all the commotion with Yuri." He wiped his eyes. "But it was worth seeing your reaction."

He took my hand and walked me around and through the bodies, heading toward a hallway I hadn't noticed. He ignored the whispers and the demons that were calling out his name. As we walked, I felt more than one hand, tail, or tentacle tentatively brush against me.

He stopped once we cleared the bodies and stepped into the long hallway, turning to look at me. "Would you like to see the private rooms?"

TWENTY-TWO

JULIETTE

I SWALLOWED hard at the intense look on Varek's face and couldn't stop myself from nodding at his question. I was apprehensive and entirely out of my element, but I was ready to step out of my comfort zone in order to explore my place in Varek's life. I could sense that he would give me forever if I needed it, but it wasn't necessary. With him by my side, I just knew that I could be a stronger, more confident version of myself that I had never allowed before out of fear. I was tired of being afraid.

Hand-in-hand, we walked down the hall slowly as he began to explain to me that not all demons wanted to be part of the mass orgy that was so popular. The mated pairs would never allow another to touch what was theirs. But that didn't mean there weren't mated couples that didn't enjoy having someone watch.

The rooms we passed all had windows for viewing, many of them black. Some of them were clear and what was happening in those rooms was enough to make my cheeks burn. But there was one that had an opaque tint to it that I couldn't resist glancing in. Inside I saw two bodies together, obviously engaged in the sensual act of making love, and that's what it appeared to be, making love. It was impossible to see much, but it was so much more erotic than any of the public acts I had seen so far, either in the public room or in the private rooms that welcomed voyeurs.

I hadn't realized that my breath had sped up or that my heart had begun pounding in my chest until I felt the gentle touch of Varek's hand graze against my neck, softly smoothing my hair back with his knuckles as the fingertips lightly rubbed against my skin. Goosebumps dotted my arms with his touch and made my breath catch and hold.

"*Amica mea,*" his deep voice rumbled quietly against my ear, and his lips ghosted over the flesh there. The words that I didn't understand, and wasn't yet ready to know the meaning of, held a whisper of need and a wealth of promise. I knew what he was asking without him saying the words. As I watched the silhouettes of the bodies moving together on the bed, I knew what I wanted and hadn't been willing to attempt before I met this man, this demon. I wanted him to touch me like that. I wanted to feel him worship me the way the larger body was worshiping his partner.

I tore my gaze away from the view in front of me and turned to face my fated mate. As I did, his hand slid around the back of my neck and tightened just enough to let me know that he was there, that he was going to demand my attention. My eyelids fluttered as I made myself look from his broad chest up into his deep green eyes that would always remind me of brilliant emeralds. Eyes that didn't look fathomless and indifferent to the world around him as they usually did. Right then, his eyes were full of promise for our future, a future I desperately wanted to be a part of, to belong to this one male for the rest of eternity because no one else was him. No one else would ever compare.

"Varek," I breathed.

It was all that needed to be said. Everything I was feeling, everything I had ever dreamed of, but was too timid to admit, was there in my eyes. In one swift move, he lifted me, his arm going under my ass and the other staying along my back, never losing his grip on the back of my neck. I wrapped my legs around his waist and felt the proof of his desire, hot and hard against me.

He brought our mouths together and kissed me in a way that he hadn't before. I thought our kisses were passionate and emotional before, but I was wrong. The kiss he gave me at that moment was enough to make me fear losing myself completely and, at the same time, know that he would always be there to find me.

I felt myself being carried swiftly through our mouths never left each other's. The air changed and became still. It was my only indication that we had left the hallway and entered a room. The sound cut off abruptly, the music and the moans from the party happening in the main area immediately ending, leaving us with only the sounds of our breaths and the movements of our lips.

He pushed me up against the door, pressing his large body against mine, dwarfing me and making me feel even more delicate. It was a feeling I reveled in. I would never have thought I'd feel comfortable being so vulnerable, but I trusted him with every fiber of my being. This male that could destroy anyone would never cause me a moment of distress.

He tore his mouth away from mine, making me whimper at the loss. His hand on my neck tightened further, tilting my head so I had no choice but to look him in the eyes.

"*Amica mea*, you must be sure. I will claim you, mate you, make you mine for all eternity if you don't tell me to stop right now. I will wait forever for you until you are ready for my mark to be branded on your flesh," his chest vibrated against mine as he growled out the words. "But if you say yes right now, you will get every inch of me. My heart, my soul, and my cock will be yours. Do you want that?"

I swallowed hard at the intensity with which he was staring at me. "Varek." I stopped and swallowed past the lump in my throat, and blinked my eyes rapidly to quell the tears that were forming due to the feelings that were threatening to overwhelm me. "I want nothing more."

At my words, he growled fiercely, causing my core to tighten and my blood to heat. I felt the heat spread throughout my body until it coalesced in my center, where we were pressed together tightly. His rock hard cock gave a jerk, making me want to rub against it until it did it again.

His mouth descended again, taking my mouth in a brutal kiss that took my breath away. But they didn't stay against mine for long before they left my lips and started a trail down my neck, his tongue swiping at the delicate flesh there, and I had the most intense desire to feel him sink his teeth there. I didn't know where the impulse came from. It was just something I felt as instinct would be right.

When he reached the neck of my shirt and could not go any lower, he growled in frustration, lifting his head to glare at the offending material. He then set me on my feet, letting me lean my body against the door so I wouldn't collapse on my weak knees, and put both of his hands on the neck of my shirt. Before I could blink, he had the material ripped down the center, leaving me with only the delicate pale pink lace bra covering my small breasts.

I watched as his eyes changed from green to black, the darkness completely overtaking any color. I stared, entranced as his wings unfurled and lifted behind his back, blocking out the low light in the room we were in. Wisps of shadows drifted off of him and began to twirl around me, brushing across my arms and smoothing across my cheeks as if the shadows wanted to have every part of me, too.

I gasped when he dropped to his knees in front of me, his head reaching my breasts, his horns curling right by my face. Fascinated, I reached out with trembling fingers and ran the tips lightly over the obsidian surface. His groan of pleasure at my touch made me bolder until I wrapped my small fingers around the horn, pleased that it felt solid under my grasp. Then, when I felt the heat of his mouth engulf the entirety of my right breast, I tightened my hold reflexively.

He rumbled out his pleasure as he tightened his lips around my nipple, sucking hard, making me squeal at the unfamiliar pleasure and pain. I didn't know if I wanted to pull him away or tell him never to stop. I felt twin pricks against my skin, looked down to see what had caused the sensation, and gasped to see that he had fangs. I had never noticed them before in the times that I had seen him in his demon form. Seeing them now made my core pulse with desire.

There was another ripping sound, and I felt my bra drop down my arms to my elbows, but I didn't want to let go of the anchor his horns had become in order to shed the last of my upper clothing. Then I felt the wet heat of his tongue directly on my breast, and my knees buckled. I would have fallen if it weren't for the steady grip of his large hands holding my bottom.

He left my breasts then, licked a path down my chest, and made his way to the waistband of my jeans, again growling at the barrier keeping him from his destination. He didn't rip them, though. Instead, this time he took one of his hands from my ass and tugged roughly on the button and then the zipper before taking both hands and yanking them roughly down my thighs, taking my panties with them in one swift motion. It was then only my hands on his horns that kept me from crumpling to the floor.

As soon as my pants were down to my calves, he picked me back up and carried me over to the bed, gently setting me on the edge of the mattress that was covered in a smooth black sheet. I let go of his horns, placed my palms flat on the bed behind me, and watched as he sat back on his heels. I took each foot and carefully pulled off my flats before pulling the denim off my legs completely. Once I was free, he reverently kissed each of my ankles and began a path up each leg, taking his time to kiss and lick each inch of his journey.

When he kissed both of my hip bones and then inhaled deeply at my core, I collapsed on the bed, my hands no longer able to hold me up. I blinked up at the dim light above the bed, hazily noticing the beauty of the chandelier hanging there, the crystals refracting the low lighting and making patterns against the ceiling. I lost the view when my eyes fluttered closed at the first feel of his tongue as it swiped up through my folds.

The feeling was indescribable. The pleasure was nothing I could have ever imagined, and my back bowed with such intense pleasure when I felt him wrap his lips around my clit and sucked. My hands gripped the sheets and fisted tightly.

"Varek!"

His answering growl to my scream caused even more wetness to drip from me, which he greedily lapped up. He plunged his tongue deep inside me, and I shattered. My screams reverberated around the room as he brought me to a climax so intense, I didn't know if I would survive it.

I didn't know how long I lay there panting, but when he lifted my limp body and placed me further into the center of the bed, I felt his naked body slide against mine. I somehow found the strength to lift my arms and wrap them around his back, spreading my fingers wide and reveling in the strength I felt there. His muscles bunched and moved as he fit himself between my open legs, his hips settling against mine.

He looked deep into my eyes as he moved his hips back, and I felt the thick hardness of his cock slide against my wetness. We both moaned at the sensation as he glided back and forth, the long length of him becoming coated in me.

I felt something glide smoothly against my leg and then wrap securely around my thigh. His tail gripped me, lifted my leg up, and spread me open. His cock notched against my opening, and then carefully, he started to push forward.

I winced at the intrusion. He was so much larger than I had allowed myself to imagine. Though I couldn't see him, I knew that he was bigger than I would ever be able to take comfortably my first time. He paused, then he lowered his head to kiss me deeply before continuing to push forward in a steady glide.

I screamed into our kiss, and he swallowed down the sound of my pain as he finally hit the end of me. I broke from his lips and threw my head back, squeezing my eyes shut, and panted.

"*Amica mea*, you have taken all of me. Your body was made for me and mine for yours." He lifted his torso, taking his palms from my cheeks, and placed them on the bed next to my head. "Open your beautiful eyes and look at us together."

I did what he commanded, curiosity warring with my hesitation at seeing what had felt like he tore me open with. My neck muscles felt weak, but I managed to lift my head enough to glance down the length of my body and caught my breath at the erotic sight.

Varek's cock was sliding in and out of my channel, his thickness shiny with my wetness. Large veins were easily visible, and as he slid back in, I could swear I was able to feel each one as they rubbed against my inner walls. It was enough to have me clinch violently around him. His loud curse only added to my pleasure, letting me know that he was as affected by me as I was by him.

"That's it, my jewel, squeeze my cock." His tail let go of my leg and slithered up until it was at the place where we were joined and then ran over my clit, putting just the right amount of pressure to send me over the edge.

As my walls spasmed and more wetness ran out of me between our bodies, Varek thrust savagely, much more than I ever thought I would have been able to take, making my release feel like it was going to shatter me into such small fragments that I would never be the same again.

Once I came down from the most incredible orgasm that I didn't even know was possible, I collapsed back onto the bed, sweaty and breathing erratically, only to have Varek pull out of me completely. Then, with a snarl, he flipped my limp body onto my front, and his tail hauled me up to my knees.

"Now it's my turn," he growled softly into my ear, before plunging deeply back inside.

CHAPTER
TWENTY-THREE

NEVER. Never in all my existence had I felt the kind of soul shattering pleasure as I felt while fucking my mate. I had always heard that making love to one's mate was a pleasure unlike any other in the universe. I had never discounted the stories, but feeling was definitely believing.

As I thrust back into my mate's scorching heat, I closed my eyes, relishing in the perfection. When I was finally able to reopen my eyes, I took in her beauty and couldn't help but admire the strength that was her. Others might look at my mate and see someone small and frail, but I knew differently. She was never a victim, she was a survivor. But more than that, she was a fighter. Anyone that came from what she did would have had to be.

I ran my hand over the softness of the flesh on her back and smoothed her tangled hair to the side, allowing me a view of her enticing neck. My fangs throbbed in a way they had never before, and suddenly all I could picture in my mind was what it would feel like to sink my fangs into her as my cock flooded her with my essence, sealing us forever as one. I wanted that more than I had ever wanted anything in my existence. It was a dilemma, though, because, at the same time, I never wanted this perfect moment to end.

I sat back on my heels and watched as my thick cock plunged in and out of her impossibly tight cunt and allowed my shadows to come out and play. Thick shadows wrapped around her torso and began plucking at her nipples as I held tight to her waist, my thumbs pressed into the base of her spine. I allowed the shadows to roam over her body, leaving no inch of her unexplored. Then, when I felt myself coming to the end of my patience, knowing that I wouldn't be able to hold on much longer, I had the shadows assault her breasts and clit, relentlessly pinching and pulling.

As I felt her walls tighten further to the point of causing me delicious pain, I pulled her back up to meet my chest and growled, "Come now, mate! Fall with me!" The tingles charged up my spine causing an explosion unlike anything I'd ever known. I threw back my head and roared, shaking the foundation of the building we were in before I struck deep, sending my fangs into her flesh.

My vision went black, her screams deafening me as we both fell into the abyss of pleasure together. The burning of my wrist was nothing but a faint echo, unable to override the ecstasy of filling my mate with my essence for the first time. Under everything, the pain, the pleasure, was the rightness of forever clicking into place.

I pulled her body closer to me as I fell to the side, not wanting to separate from her, even knowing that this was now our future. It seemed I wasn't alone in my desire to stay connected as she snuggled as deep into my body as she could. I wrapped my arms around her, relishing the trembles that still racked her body.

We continued to lay there long after our breathing calmed. My cock that had only partially softened was still lodged inside her warm channel as I ran my hands soothingly up and down her body, everywhere I could reach. As small as she was, there weren't many places I couldn't touch.

For the first time ever, I felt a sense of calm. Of somehow being content instead of being in a constant state of restless or listlessness, never in between. I had grown so accustomed to being unsettled, that I hadn't realized how bad it had gotten until this moment as I lay with my mate, utterly content as if my soul had finally found peace. I was finally whole.

Juliette's breathing had deepened as she fell slowly into sleep, and I didn't want to disturb her, but I knew she'd be much more comfortable in our own bed. No one would dare disturb us in here, but it wasn't home. So I was quite startled when she sat bolt upright, clutched her chest, looked around frantically, and jumped out of the bed before I could think of stopping her.

She was frantically yanking on her pants while widely looking on the floor until she spotted the shirt that I had torn from her body. She held it up and grimaced as she saw the ruined garment, then threw it back to the floor. She spotted mine instead. She grabbed it from the floor where I had dropped it carelessly, then yanked the black shirt over her head and watched as it fell to her knees. It wasn't until she headed for the locked door that I finally shook myself out of my confusion at her behavior and rolled off the bed, stalking toward her.

I grabbed her shoulder just as she managed to yank the door open and pulled her around to face me before she could run out of the room. "Juliette, what is the matter?"

She looked anxious as she looked up into my eyes, her own were watery and full of sorrow. "I need to go, Varek. It's calling me."

"What's calling you?" I asked in bewilderment. Her phone hadn't rang, and she hadn't even looked for it, just started pulling on her clothes. "Juliette, talk to me!"

"I can't. I don't have time!"

With a surprising amount of force, she pulled out of my hands, and before I managed to reach for her again, she ran down the hall-way. With a curse, I grabbed my pants from the floor, yanking them on as I wondered about her strange behavior. I had just taken her virginity and mated her roughly, biting into her neck like an animal to seal our bond. I thought she had been with me the entire way, but now I was beginning to worry that I had been too rough, or that she had discovered that she wasn't ready after all, having just been caught up in the moment of lust as we toured the sex club.

"Fuck!" I growled, as I flung the door open so hard that the wood along the hinges splintered, not that I gave a good fuck at the moment. I had a mate to chase down. If I had to throw her over my shoulder and carry her to our bed, I would. I would chain her there until she was convinced that mating me was the best fucking thing that had ever happened to her, god damnit.

I stormed down the hallway, letting our new bond guide me to her location, and was shocked to find that she hadn't run straight to the elevator, but was instead inside another of the private rooms. I snarled viciously at the thought of someone finding her alone and forcing her inside with them. She had a fierceness lurking inside of her that I wanted to coax out, but she wasn't there yet. Anyone could easily overpower her.

I put on a burst of speed at the disturbing images running through my mind, and when I came to the room she was in, I slammed my fist against the door, once again causing the wood to splinter. The roar died in my throat as I caught sight of my mate kneeling on the floor, her hand on the chest of Yuri. He was laying still as death, his breaths were shallow, and his heartbeat was so faint, I could barely hear it. He was also bleeding profusely from his ears.

But what surprised me the most was seeing her entire body glowing faintly, her hands the brightest part of her.

I stood in shock as I watched her whisper to the demon, and as his last breath faded away, she dropped her head. I took a step forward and dropped to my knees beside her, placing my hand on her back. She was warm to the touch, much warmer than any human should be, but it quickly lowered until I could believe I had simply imagined the heat she was radiating.

"Juliette?" I knew what I saw. She didn't have to explain it to me. I also now knew who her father was. No other had the ability that she had just exhibited.

A sniffle from the bed caught my attention. I stood up and took in the naked demon reclining back on the bed, her face white, but her slitted pupils were blown. She was high as fuck. Ignoring her for now, I glanced around the room until I caught sight of the small, clear plastic bag of pills and stalked over to them.

"What's that?" Juliette's tired voice called from her position on the floor.

"This," I held the bag up as the demon on the bed cringed away, "is a drug that was recently brought into my building. Unfortunately, we haven't been able to discover the source to put a stop to it since there's no way in fuck I would ever allow this shit in The Tower."

The demon whimpered and lowered her head.

I sighed and pulled my phone from my back pocket, glad that I had swiped it off the ground when I grabbed my pants. I dialed Talon and raked a frustrated hand through my hair as I explained that he needed to get a couple of his men to come take care of the scene.

I walked back over to Juliette and held my hand down for her to take. Her smile wavered as she looked up at me and took my hand. She looked exhausted. It seemed that guiding souls was a taxing process.

As we walked down the hallway, she stumbled once, and I quickly picked her up, ignoring her weak protests. "You are exhausted, mate. I would never allow you to carry your burdens alone."

"I'm not so much tired as I am sad," she sighed, as she gave up quickly and leaned her head on my shoulder. "It breaks my heart every time a soul leaves."

"Why?" I questioned. "Every soul has an ending. To be escorted to their destination by someone as caring as yourself would make the journey a peaceful one, instead of the frightening one that most receive. You are doing something wonderful for them."

"I never thought of it that way," she whispered.

I ignored the gasps of shock as I walked through the lobby of the club and carried my mate into the elevator. We were both undressed, me more so than her, neither one of us wearing shoes. I would have to ask Talon to bring our belongings to the penthouse later.

"You should. You should also be proud of what you do. Bringing peace to those in their final moments and showing them the right path to their final destination is a kindness."

"How did you know what I was doing?"

"I could see it. You were beautiful, glowing like an angel of mercy, your love warming the room."

"Really?"

I stepped out of the elevator and carried her to our bedroom, gently setting her on the bed. I began removing her jeans again, though much less roughly than I had the first time. I reached up and smoothed the hair from her eyes. "I take souls, too, as you have seen. Though the way I do it is not nearly as gentle as you. I don't guide them. When I remove a soul, I simply will them away, and they are cast to the Underworld. Generally, the souls I take are being punished. They would only be heading to one place."

"Yuri died from a drug overdose?"

I sighed in frustration. "Not necessarily. We are finding that the drugs aren't always safe. We have had three previous deaths in The Tower due to this drug. Unfortunately, we are no closer to finding who is responsible for the spread than we were when we first discovered it."

"His soul was pure." A tear fell from her clear green eye, making it shine like an emerald with the wetness.

"Yuri was a good man. I couldn't even make myself want to actually hurt him when he was being such an idiot."

She giggled, making my heart feel lighter hearing the soft sound. "He was silly. I wish I could have known him." She sobered, the smile falling from her lips as quick as it came.

"You would have liked him." I kissed the top of her head and tucked her into the bed.

"You aren't joining me?" she asked with a yawn.

"I want nothing more than to slide into this bed with you, but I have to talk to Talon about what happened."

She nodded her head and reached up to stroke my jaw. "I understand." I placed my hand over hers and slid it to my mouth, kissing her palm.

"Sleep well, *Amica mea*. I will be back before you miss me."

She closed her eyes and sighed. Her voice was barely audible as she said, "I already do."

CHAPTER

TWENTY-FOUR

VAREK

I STRODE into my office after calling Talon to meet with me once he had the body taken care of and seeing to Yuri's partner. I was angry enough to hurt something or someone. Somebody had infiltrated my Tower and was killing my demons while I was sitting around with my dick in my hand, instead of ripping their head off. What made tonight even worse was that they had ruined a perfect moment with my mate. I should be by her side at this moment. Better yet, I should be buried inside of her again.

I wrenched open my desk drawer, conscious enough to take care not to damage the wood like I had down downstairs, and pulled the file from my drawer and set it on my desktop. It was pitifully small. We had such little information to go on up to now, but this time we had something we hadn't had before—a witness.

With any luck, Yuri's partner would have a name for us, even if it was just the person that sold her the drugs. We needed the manufacturer, but I'd be happy to find the supplier. If I were incredibly lucky, they would be the same person.

After flipping through the file as I had done a hundred times before while learning nothing new, I slammed the folder closed and spun my chair around to look out the large window that took up most of the wall of my office. Since it was street level, it didn't have the magnificent view of the city my penthouse did, but I wasn't seeing the view anyway.

There were always fires to put out when it came to running so many businesses, especially when dealing with demons that held little value in human morals and rules. But recently, there have been many more issues that have been demanding my attention with little to no resolutions.

That bitch that had tried to hurt my mate. She would have killed Juliette in front of me if given a chance. But, thanks to my mate's interference, she still wasn't taken care of. Not really. It frustrated me that Juliette had refused to allow me to take her life, but she was new to our ways. She wouldn't understand for a while, yet that it was a world of kill or be killed. And ending our enemies before they could end us. Her heart was too soft. Honestly, I never wanted her to change. Though I could not allow her to stop me from taking a life every time it was deserved, and a woman trying to take the life of my mate most definitely warranted death.

So did her father. That was another problem that hadn't seen a resolution. I had my men scouring the city, certain that he wouldn't go far. A man like him would never be content to let the woman he saw as the cause of his wife's death live on in peace. He had already reached out to her with that note in her mailbox. I was determined to intercept him before he could manage to get to her again. And when I found him, I wouldn't be merciful. I didn't know everything that he had done to her as a child, but just looking at her, it was obvious that he was worse than a monster. He had tormented her relentlessly until she was just a shell of herself. I intended to pull her out of that shell and allow her to become the person she was meant to be.

A knock on my door followed by its opening shook me out of my musings. I spun around in my chair to see Sasha standing there with a somber look on her face.

"Is it true?"

I nodded and watched as she swallowed hard and looked at the floor. "Fuck!" she mumbled, as she walked over to the liquor cabinet, pulled down a bottle of my best Irish whisky, and poured a shot before throwing it back with a slight grimace.

I stood up and walked over to her as she leaned heavily on her palms that were braced against the counter of the small liquor bar. I reached across her and grabbed a second glass. Then I carried the bottle of whiskey over to the sitting area, placing the second glass on the low coffee table between the chairs and the small leather sofa.

"Come, sit down." I poured both of us a full glass. Then I leaned back into my favorite chair and stared into the dark amber liquid before taking a healthy sip.

"Fuck, Varek! Fuck!" She stomped over to the couch and sat down. "I'm so fucking pissed!" She swiped a tear away from her cheek angrily and then picked up her glass with a trembling hand. "We have to stop these guys. This can't go on. It could happen to anyone next. Hell, it could even happen to you!"

"I doubt that would happen, Sasha. Neither you, I, nor Talon have ever taken recreational drugs."

She stared at me incredulously. "You honestly think that it has to be taken willingly? All anyone would have to do is drop it into your drink, and you'd be bleeding out of your ears in minutes."

I grunted. It wasn't something to which I had given much credence, though I couldn't deny the thought had crossed my mind. "The drug seems too unpredictable. Either the batches were messed up, or the drug affected different breeds of demons worse than others."

"Or," she leaned forward, her stare intent, "they are practicing to get the dose right."

I shook my head. "It may be plausible that's what they are doing, but it just doesn't seem practical. If someone had manufactured a drug specifically to kill me, it wouldn't make any sense to practice on other demons. They aren't the same breed as me. No one knows what breed I am, not even me."

She rolled her eyes. "I already told you what you are."

I swallowed down the rest of my drink and sat the heavy crystal on the table. "Unfortunately, I now have proof that you are wrong."

"What?"

"I am not related to Charon in any way, and I am not a Ferryman."

She raised a bright red eyebrow and said, "Oh? Do tell. How could you possibly know that, and how else could you explain what you can do?"

"Juliette ferried Yuri's soul this evening."

I had never seen Sasha lost for words before. She swallowed the last of her whiskey, and slammed the glass down onto the table between us before leaning forward with her hands on her knees.

"What the fuck, Varek! What the absolute fuck?" She threw herself back in the seat and stared at the ceiling. "Are you sure?"

"I watched her do it with my own eyes, Sasha. She's Charon's daughter."

She blinked slowly at the ceiling for a few seconds. "I didn't think he ever left the Underworld."

I leaned forward and grabbed the bottle, filling both of our glasses back up before setting the bottle down next to them. After nudging the filled glass toward Sasha, I picked mine up and lifted it to the light, admiring the dark amber color. "I have never met him, but I've been told stories."

At that, she started laughing so hard that she began to leak tears from her yellow eyes. "Oh, man. He's going to kill you for taking his little girl."

I growled at the thought of anyone trying to come between my mate and me. "He could try."

"Oh no, you don't understand. I met the guy once before coming here. He's an asshole. But more than that, he always wanted children, but was never able to. I wonder why he went after Juliette's mother?"

"I have no earthly idea, but if you think he'd be angry at me, you could imagine what he'd do to the human that tortured, starved, and physically scarred her."

Sasha gave a visible shudder and took a sip of the whiskey. "Oh yeah, that guy is totally fucked."

I sighed heavily. "We still haven't been able to locate him."

"Maybe he's dead in a ditch somewhere?" she sounded hopeful, but I shook my head.

"I seriously doubt that. My instincts tell me that he's been waiting for her and plans to pay her a visit. I want guards around her every time she even thinks about leaving The Tower. As much as I want to draw him out, I don't want her being used as bait. I never want her to have to lay eyes on him again."

She nodded. "Yeah, we can definitely do that. She's been through enough shit." She grinned then. "So, what do you plan to do about Charon?"

I glared at her, which she ignored as she had been doing for centuries. "I'm not convinced he needs to know."

"If he comes back to the mortal realm, he's going to feel her essence immediately once he crosses the portal."

"That could be a thousand years from now."

"Perhaps."

"Don't patronize me."

She just laughed. We both turned to the door as it opened and watched as Talon stepped through carrying a bag which I assumed was mine and Juliette's belongings. He glanced at where we were sitting and immediately headed over to the liquor cabinet. He set the bag down, grabbed a third glass from the shelf, and then walked over to us to sit down in the other armchair with a heavy sigh. He leaned forward to grab the bottle. As he did, he dropped the small baggie with the remaining pills onto the table.

"It was definitely the same drug that killed Yuri. His partner,

Stephanie, is locked in one of the visitor suites with a guard outside the door until she sobers up. With any luck, she will be able to tell us where they came from."

I nodded. "That was my thoughts as well."

"How's Jewels?"

"Sleeping peacefully, I hope."

Sasha was quick to let him know who her father was, and Talon had much the same reaction as she had.

"Holy shit," he breathed.

"Indeed," I replied dryly.

"Well, how does it feel to have one of the kings of the Underworld as your father-in-law?" He grinned as Sasha started laughing again.

"Laugh it up, fuckers."

All it did was make them laugh harder.

I stood up with my glass, draining it of the last of my aged whiskey, and carried it over to the cabinet. I bent down to pick up the bag with our shoes and Juliette's undergarments. "Thanks for taking care of Yuri, Talon. Have you contacted his kin?"

He shook his head. "His mother went back to the Underworld a few decades ago. In order to let her know, someone will have to take the trip."

Sasha jumped up and brought her glass over to join mine for the cleaning staff to take care of in the morning. "Not it!" She shook her head. "You know I liked Yuri, as weird as he was, but nothing can make me go back there."

Talon sighed. "I'll do it. I can leave in a few minutes. Hopefully, I can be back by dinner time tomorrow."

I nodded. "Good. His mother needs to know. Let her also know that we are doing everything we can to find out who killed him, and they will suffer. Greatly."

"Will do."

"I'm going to join my mate and make sure she sleeps well through the night."

I turned to walk through my private doorway and waved when Sasha called out her congratulations on our mating becoming formal.

Once I made it back to the penthouse, I stripped out of my pants and took a quick shower. My cock was already hard again, being this close to my mate, but I ignored it other than to give it a couple of strokes with my soapy palm. I wanted the chance to sink back into her perfection, but I wanted her to rest even more. Tomorrow morning was soon enough to become reacquainted with her little body. I had plans for her.

CHAPTER

TWENTY-FIVE

JULIETTE

I woke up to the most incredible feeling running through my body. Every nerve ending was on fire, and I didn't know if I wanted to pull Varek up from between my legs and demand he enter me or hold him down there until he finished. Or I finished, rather.

"Varek!" I called out as my legs started trembling, and then it was too late for choices or decisions. I was coming hard, my back bowing off the bed. As I lay there trying to learn how to breathe normally again, I felt him wipe his mouth on my inner thigh, the long night of hair growth on his cheeks rubbing against my sensitized skin, making me shiver. He placed a gentle kiss on my clit and then made his way up my body, trailing kisses as he went.

I moaned as he reached my nipples and yelped when he nipped first one and then the other.

"Good morning, *Amica mea*. Did you sleep well?"

"Yes!" I breathed out, as he lapped the sting away with his talented tongue.

"Good."

Then he took me by the hips and flipped me over, much the same as he had done last night.

"Scoot up. Grab onto the headboard."

I did as he said. I walked on my trembling knees until my torso was against the cool wood. I grabbed onto the intricately carved wooden posts and watched over my shoulder as he reached over to the side table for what looked like silk ropes. Shivers of anticipation shook me as I waited patiently while he tied first one hand and then the other to the headboard.

"Varek?"

"Shhh, baby. I will never hurt you." He nuzzled into the back of my neck after swiping my hair to fall over my shoulder to cover my right breast.

"I know that," I whispered. My wrist caught my attention, or rather the dark red brand that was now there did. "I-did you bite me last night?"

He paused and then leaned over to first kiss my wrist, where the brand stood out boldly, and then kissed my neck where I only vaguely remembered feeling him sink his teeth. I recalled a brief moment of intense pain after the bite that was mostly painless.

He brought his own wrist up and placed his larger hand over mine to fully engulf my fist, where I was already holding on tightly to the wood. His brand was identical to mine. There was something about seeing us together and knowing that we were forever connected that settled something inside of me. I hadn't realized I had started crying until the sight of our brands began to blur.

"*Amica mea*. Are you alright?"

"I am," I sniffled, and wiped my cheeks on first one arm and then the other before turning my face to give him a watery smile. "I'm perfect. Varek, I belong to you."

He kissed my lips softly. "And I belong to you, baby."

No one had ever wanted me before. I was hated, mocked, ridiculed, and physically hurt by others all my life. Now I had someone that wanted me, truly wanted me. It gave me pause.

"Varek?" I called softly, as he pulled back and ran his hands up my sides and to my front to pluck at my nipples. I shivered in delight, but even the pleasure couldn't turn off the question that had suddenly flooded my brain.

"Yes, *Amica mea*?" he asked between kisses.

"Do you only want me because I was your fated? Would you have ever looked at me twice if I weren't meant by fate to be yours?"

His movements abruptly stopped. Suddenly, the air heated around me. Dark wisps of shadows began to swirl around my body, and the light in the room became dim as his wings extended and then curled around me, completely enveloping me. I felt like I was being cocooned and had never felt safer. But was it fate, or was it, love? Did it really matter when he was clearly happy for us to be together? I felt like I should be satisfied with what destiny provided for us, but that little girl that longed to be held and truly loved by someone couldn't help but wonder.

"Have you figured out what *Amica mea* means yet?" he finally spoke, asking me casually about the strange words I had never heard before but that he had started calling me days ago. I shook my head.

He wrapped his arm around my hip, reached for my clit, and began rubbing around it in light, gentle circles. I couldn't stop myself from rotating my hips, trying to catch that elusive finger and bring it where I desperately needed it. But instead, I felt a small sting directly on my clit as his fingers came down in a light slap.

"Behave, *Amica mea*."

The sting faded, and heat rushed in to take its place. I felt my wetness grow until it began to roll in a thin line down my inner thigh.

"It's Latin," he said, as he resumed his circling, making my whole body quiver with need.

I felt him adjust behind me until I felt the heat of his cock glide through the wetness between my legs. His tail circled around my hips and then suddenly jerked, making my rear end jut out, the silk ties pulling on my wrists to keep them in place. It was all too much but not enough. Not nearly enough.

His cock stopped gliding and stopped directly at my entrance before making a painfully slow push inside me. He slid in one inch at a time until finally, his hips were flush with my ass, and the head of his cock was kissing my cervix. I swallowed thickly in anticipation of his hard thrusts, but all he did was pull back out just as slowly as he had when he entered. Again, he slid back in after coming to a stop with just the head of his cock still lodged inside.

"You are so very beautiful. You take me so well. You make me want to do filthy things to you as I worship every inch of your body."

He slid back in, torturing me with his slowness. This time when he was as far in as possible, he stopped. He then leaned over my much smaller body and nipped at where he had bitten me the night before, forever marking me as his.

"*Amica*, or *amare*," he growled, as his hands tightened almost painfully on my hips, "means love."

He pulled out until he couldn't pull out any further without leaving me altogether. And then, with a growl, he slammed into me. "And *mea* means MINE."

I screamed as the unexpected orgasm rocked through me. I flew apart into a million pieces, tethered only by this demon that was mine as much as I was his. He began a fast pace as he pounded into my body, his dark shadows circling and rubbing against me everywhere.

He continued to growl as his pace never faltered. "I knew you as soon as I saw you. The only regret I have when it comes to you, mate, is that I didn't try to find you sooner."

The tip of his tail slid over from its hold on my hips to start rubbing on my clit in tight circles. The shadows circled my nipples until they were holding them tightly. Once again, Varek's mouth hovered over my shoulder, where his deep voice sounded in my ear.

"Come for me, *Amica mea*." And then he struck, sinking those fangs deep into my flesh.

I threw back my head to rest against his shoulder as I completely shattered, my scream of ecstasy caught in the cocoon of his black wings. As my body shook, I could feel every pulse of his cock as he poured himself into me.

By the time I came back to myself, Varek had me untied and lifted my limp body from the bed. He carried me into the bathroom and straight into the shower. He never said a word as he held me close and carefully washed every inch he could reach.

"You can set me down," I whispered, as I lifted my still trembling fingers to his cheek. He briefly closed his eyes at the contact, but then shook his head as he continued on with his task. With one hand, he washed my hair, rinsed it, then applied nearly half a bottle of conditioner to it. He gently ran his fingers through the strands, ensuring that no knots or tangles were left. Once he was satisfied, he used the handheld shower sprayer to rinse my hair clean.

The whole time he was silent.

I admired his strength. I was small, but an ordinary human man wouldn't have been able to cradle me for so long as if I weighed practically nothing. He was no ordinary man, and I was more than certain by now that he was no ordinary demon. Even being the king of demons on earth didn't automatically make him the biggest or the strongest. He was already so much more. I had no doubt that he would be able to defeat anyone, no matter how much larger, in battle.

"I'm sorry," I whispered, finally breaking the silence between us. "I didn't mean to doubt you."

"Juliette," he sighed, placing his forehead against mine. "Fate decides things for us every day. But we have the ability to walk away from those things. Most mates choose to stay together, yes, but some choose not to. It comes at a great price, but it is still a choice. If I didn't want you, I would have walked away, and you would have never seen me again. I am powerful enough that I could have done it without the type of sacrifice that most end up making."

"They kill their fated."

"Yes," he said matter of factly. "That was never an option. I would never have killed you even if I didn't want you. The truth is, the moment I saw you, I knew you were different. I knew you were someone I wanted to have in my life. As I got to know you, you became someone I would kill for, to protect, and to avenge." He slid my body around until he had me straddling his hips with my legs wrapped around him. "Fate may be a fickle bitch, but she knows what she is doing, *Amica mea.*"

I cupped his cheeks with both of my hands and looked into his beautiful emerald eyes. "I love you, too, my demon king." I watched as his eyes slid closed, and he breathed deeply through his nose. When he opened them again, they had bled to black.

"My love," he growled in English for the first time, and with an adjustment of his hips, he slid inside me again. By the time we had both come, me with a scream and him with a shout, he needed to wash my body again.

CHAPTER

TWENTY-SIX

JULIETTE

I WALKED with Varek into the suite that was typically reserved for VIP visitors to The Tower. I clung to his hand as we entered, squeezing when I saw the distraught woman, a demoness, sitting in a chair looking devastated. She was slumped, curled into herself, a full cup of coffee sitting in front of her untouched. Glancing over toward the dinette, I could see a plate of food, also untouched.

I hadn't even noticed her in the room last night. My only focus had been on Yuri as his soul called to me. Seeing her slumped in the chair, now looking so defeated, my heart went out to her. I had no idea how close the two of them were, but it was obvious that she was in a terrible place in her head.

She glanced up as we walked in, trailed by Sasha, and her face crumpled. She slid from the chair, kneeling on the floor, and bent over so far that her forehead nearly touched her knees.

"Lord Varek, I am so sorry," her voice was ragged. When she looked up, I could see lines of fatigue and sorrow etched on her face.

She looked like she hadn't slept for a week, and her red-rimmed eyes were watery from tears.

"Stephanie," Varek said, in a firm but soft tone, "please get up."

She nodded weakly and stood back up stiffly, wiping her cheek with the back of her hand.

"I need you to help us find out who is doing this, Stephanie. I need you to tell me where you got the pills from."

"I want to help you," she sighed, and looked down at her fingers. "I thought that it would be a good time, you know? I had heard about the effects. Euphoria? It sounded great. I didn't know it was killing demons until after it killed Yuri. He swallowed one, we both did, and then we started to mess around. It was amazing, the feeling of floating while at the same time my body just got super warm, and then it felt like I was in the middle of the greatest orgasm of my life."

She stopped and rubbed both of her hands over her face. She gave a short, bitter laugh. "While I was laying there floating, Yuri was dying. I didn't even notice at first. We had been kissing, and then he just...pulled away. I was too far gone to realize why, though. Once I could see he was in trouble, I couldn't even make myself open my mouth to say anything. He started bleeding." She shuddered and put her hands behind her neck, pulling down and groaning while rocking her body. "I noticed the blood coming from his nose first. In my mind, I was thinking, how weird, but then there was blood coming from the corner of his mouth."

Her hands moved from the back of her neck to clutch at her hair, grabbing fistfuls of it and yanking as the three of us stood there and watched, unable to comfort her.

"When he collapsed, that's when I finally knew that something was seriously wrong. Inside my head, I was screaming...but I couldn't do anything," she finished, with her voice low and full of pain. She looked up at me and stared, transfixed. "And then you ran into the room, didn't even look around, just dropped to your knees next to him. I didn't know what you were doing, but I could feel the warmth coming from you even through the fog I was in."

"I was trying to help him," I whispered.

She shook her head. "No, you were guiding his soul. At first, I thought you were a reaper, but it wasn't the same. They just tell a soul that it's time to go when someone's time comes. No, you guided his soul," her voice was quiet, in awe as she looked at me with wide eyes.

Varek stepped forward, capturing her attention and taking it away from me. "I need to know where you got those pills."

She looked at Varek with wide, frightened eyes and swallowed hard. She was unable to look away though it was obvious that she didn't like having Varek's full attention on her. I hadn't realized how much power he commanded over the other demons when I had first met him, but the more I saw him interact with others, it was clear that he was the one in command, the leader of all those before him. And they both feared and respected him.

Stephanie finally whispered, her head hanging low. "I got them from a vampire."

My gasp and Sasha's swearing were loud in the room, while Varek didn't make a sound. His only outward sign of emotion was the tightening of his jaw and the slight narrowing of his eyes.

"Who? I need a name, a description at the very least," his voice was even, but there was an undertone of malice that caused the fine hairs on my arms to stand on end.

"His name is Johnson. I don't know if that is his first name or his last. He's about average height with fairly long brown hair. He has a silver ring in his eyebrow." She looked down in thought as she twisted her fingers in her lap. "I can't think of anything else that stands out about him." Finally, she looked up with a pleading look in her eyes.

"How did you get a hold of him?"

Her face crumpled again, and her hands were trembling when she reached into her back pocket and produced a card, holding it out to Varek. She visibly shrank back when he stepped forward and took it from him. She didn't relax again until Varek had stepped back once more.

In a sad voice, she whispered, "Yuri suggested we get the pills to make the night more exciting. Because he had to work, I offered to meet the dealer." She nodded her chin toward the card that Varek was looking at. "He agreed and gave me that card so I could arrange the pick-up." She started crying, her tears turning into sobs. "Yuri is the one that gave me the money for the drugs."

Varek lowered the card and looked at Stephanie for a moment as she cried into her hands. He then stepped forward again, crouched next to the chair, and placed his hand on the female's shaking shoulder. He spoke quietly, his deep voice only a rumble of words that I couldn't quite make out. I watched as Stephanie took a deep breath in, then nodded. Finally, Varek stood up and turned to the rest of us.

"Let's go. I have a phone call to make."

I WASN'T sure what to expect when I was told I'd be meeting a vampire king. I hadn't even known vampires existed until a few hours ago. I was learning more about this new life every day, and I was getting the feeling that I hadn't even scratched the surface yet of what all was truly out there in this world that humans were blissfully unaware of. That was probably a very good thing. Knowing humans, they would likely bomb the entire world, damning themselves while trying to get rid of supernatural beings that had been around long before they even blinked into existence.

Varek's office wasn't large enough for the entire group to gather in, so we were actually having the meeting in the penthouse. Our sitting room was full of both demons and vampires, of which I couldn't help but study closely.

Crispin was as tall as Varek and held the same commanding presence. It was easy to see why these two males were at the top of their lines for power and demanded the respect they both deserved and earned. I glanced over to the woman that was standing by his side. She was beautiful, taller than me, though most people were. She was physically one of the most incredible women I had ever met. She had a strength that just screamed that she was something extra. Though I had been told she was a Hunter in addition to being a vampire, I wasn't one-hundred percent sure I quite understood what that meant. But it was easy to see that they made a perfect pair.

I looked up at Varek by my side as we sat on the loveseat together. He had introduced me proudly as his mate, and the other couple had smiled warmly with congratulations. But seeing them so evenly matched, I couldn't help but wonder if I was going to cause more harm than good for Varek. I wouldn't be able to fight at his side if needed. He would always need to protect me.

As if hearing my thoughts, Varek reached over and took my hand without breaking conversation. He gave it a gentle squeeze of reassurance and then set our joined hands on his thigh. My heart gave a little tremor. I loved this demon so much and so quickly. I didn't want to even think about what my life would be without him in it. He was the first person ever to see me and accept me for who I was. He looked beyond the scars and brokenness.

But that wasn't entirely true, was it? His guards had all accepted me quite easily when they were first introduced to me at my apartment. Not one of them had judged me for my appearance. I had never felt like a freak around them. I would continue to remind myself that I wasn't what I was raised to believe. It was getting easier, and one day I was sure the self-doubts would finally stop for good.

"With the description your demon gave, it was easy to figure out and locate the vampire responsible for selling the drugs." Crispin's words brought me back into the conversation. "He wasn't someone I was aware of being a troublemaker until I started asking around. When my Regional told me that he had been warned more than once about his behavior," he sat back in his seat and crossed an ankle over a knee. "Let's just say, that Regional now understands what it means to be within my notice. I don't take it well when I learn that my vampires are out causing trouble, especially for other species. That looks bad as a whole for vampires, but it undoubtedly looks bad on me. I wasn't pleased."

He nodded his head to a tall, dark man that was standing by the door. "Jared, would you mind letting them know we are ready to speak with the prisoner?"

The other man nodded once and then slipped quietly out the door. Crispin set his foot back down and leaned forward toward Varek, his hands clasped between his knees. "As your friend, I am going to allow you to decide this vampire's punishment. Normally, I would say that since he is one of mine, I will take care of it. But this-" He shook his head and glanced at his mate before looking back at Varek. Then, for some reason, he looked at me as well, as if he were including each of us in this huge decision he had made. "I can imagine what you must be feeling. I would be angry beyond belief. His actions caused the deaths of innocent demons."

Varek inclined his head. "He did. Most of them I did not know personally. One, however, worked directly for me in one of my clubs. He was a good male and liked by everyone. His death was hard."

Crispin nodded again and said, "For that reason, I am giving you the full authority and responsibility for his punishment, for you to serve however you see fit. Personally, I would torture him and then let him burn in the sun for a while before starting over again. At least once for each life he was responsible for taking." He shrugged, taking a sip from the glass of whiskey that Varek had served him when we had all sat down. "But that's just me."

"I will keep your suggestion under advisement. I do appreciate the gift I know it to be."

"Well, I am proud to call you friend, though we haven't known each other long. Perhaps, our mates would like to get together as well, get to know each other?" He glanced down at Ivy.

Ivy smiled over at me, and for some reason, I felt the need to hide from all the attention. "I would love to spend time with you. Us girls will have lots to talk about, I'm sure." She winked at me, and I couldn't help the small smile. "Jared's mate could come along with us, too. She's new to this world, too, and could use a little education."

"Jared?" I asked, and looked around at the two other men that stood as guards for Crispin, though they weren't on alert, simply sitting at the island in the kitchen having a quiet conversation and drinking beers. Obviously, these vampires were at ease around Varek and his demons. It made me feel good inside to know that even another dangerous species of supernatural creature liked and trusted my mate enough to let their guards down.

"He's the one that stepped outside. You'll like his mate, she's a human, too." She cocked her head and studied me. I had to stop myself from fidgeting, to keep myself from pulling my long white blonde hair over my face to hide my eyes like I used to do as a little girl. "But, you aren't really human, are you?"

I looked up at Varek and shrugged before looking back at her. "No, not really. My birth father was a demon. So, I guess that makes me a half-breed."

"Hmmm, I don't know. There's something about you I can't put my finger on." She shrugged and threw her hands up. "What do I know? I'm also pretty new to this world, and this is only my second time meeting demons."

A commotion at the door stopped the rest of the conversation and speculation.

CHAPTER
TWENTY-SEVEN

VAREK

A VAMPIRE in jeans and a t-shirt was led in by the same man that had been guarding the door. He was nothing special, no one I would have looked twice at while on the street. He was average in every way. Perfect for use as a drug dealer, I supposed.

He was walked over to the sunken living room we were in, stepped down, and then made to kneel in front of the seating area. As I studied him, I thought of the many ways I wanted to punish him. The darkness was roiling inside of me. This vampire needed to be punished severely. I couldn't just take his soul and be done with it. Crispin's suggestions held merit, and I would give serious consideration toward them. Before he could be punished, though, I needed information.

"Who gave you the drugs?" It was the one and only question I needed answering from him.

He lifted his head, and, though there was fear swimming in their depths, he sneered his refusal to answer. He turned his head to look at Crispin instead.

"Demons?" His one-word response was full of hate and preju-dice. The many different species often had battles over the centuries due to territory, mostly, but in the modern years, those had become almost nonexistent. I raised one eyebrow.

Crispin cocked his head and studied the man on his knees. "Interesting," he murmured.

No one said anything for long moments as he just kneeled there until the silence began to get to him, and he began to squirm uncom-fortably.

He lifted his chin defiantly. "They take over territories and rule them like they are better than everyone else just because they live longer. In reality, they are just monsters with glamor." He nodded his chin toward my Juliette. "I bet that one is a freak, too. She probably has-" his words died off, as he began to choke.

My tendrils of shadows were wrapped tightly around his neck, cutting off his air supply and the nasty words he was beginning to say about my mate. I watched as his face turned red, then purple, and only tightened further as the blood vessels in his eyes began to burst.

A hand placed on my arm brought me back to the present, and I looked down at my mate. Her delicate features looked worried. I hated seeing anything but a smile on her lips.

"Effective, but possibly slightly excessive," Crispin's quiet words had me looking back over, and I noticed the man had passed out.

"Fuck," I sighed, and let my shadows dissipate. "Sasha," I called out.

"I'm coming, boss." She sashayed from the dining table where she was sitting with Rake and looked over the vampire that was now lying on his side. "He's still alive, barely." She looked up at me with a grin. "Someone should have warned him about your triggers, eh?" Then, she called out, "Can someone fetch a glass of water?"

I couldn't argue with that. I had nearly killed in a blind rage without getting a single drop of information first.

While she was kneeling over the vampire, I noticed Ivy tensing.

She had her hands clasped in fists on her legs and was glaring down at her lap. Sasha must have noticed as well, because she glanced over at her and cleared her throat nervously. It wasn't an action that I had seen Sasha do very often over the centuries I had known her.

"Hey, ummm, Ivy?" she cleared her throat again, and gave a small smile when Ivy looked up at her with a glare. "I know I didn't make a good impression the last time we met. All I can do is give you an excuse. I was hungry. Starving, really, and I didn't even give myself any time to see that the man that was coming through the door was mated or not interested. But, really, it could have been literally anybody." She glanced over at Crispin, "No offense."

He chuckled and grabbed one of Ivy's hands, uncurling the fist still there. "None taken."

Juliette's quiet, melodic voice spoke up from beside me, making me look back down at her, not wanting to miss a word. "You were starving?"

"Uh, yeah." She looked back at Ivy. "I hate it, you know? Being a succubus? So many demons, everyone, really, tend to fixate on me because of my allure. Do you have any idea how many stalkers I've killed over the years?" She shook her head. "Anyway, I was on a hunger strike, and it got to be too much." She looked earnestly at Ivy. "I'm sorry."

We all watched as Ivy's face softened, then she smiled at Sasha as she knelt there beside the vampire. "Forgiven. Maybe you can come to our girl's night and tell us all about it over wine?"

"I'd love that." Sasha's smile was illuminating, and it was easy to see the effect that she had on the non-mated males in the room. Of course, she had never done anything for me since I had always thought of her as a little sister, but it was impossible to deny that she had a succubus allure.

"Here you go." Once the tension had broken, Rake handed over the water she had asked for, and she took the glass.

She paused and looked over at me with a grimace. I sighed and nodded my head. I would have to call in the witch I had on staff to clean whatever mess was made from tonight. He was lying on one of my antique carpets.

Sasha slowly poured the water over his face until he started to sputter and finally jerked awake. She lifted his head up by his hair and kept lifting until he was back on his knees. Once he opened his bloodshot eyes and had stopped coughing, she snarled in his face, nose to nose. "Yuri was my friend, you fucking lowlife asshole." Then she punched him in the dick. While he squeaked in pain, but couldn't move due to her grip on him, she growled in the most ominous voice I'd ever heard her use. "I'm going to make sure I'm there for every second of torture that my king deals out to you. And when you're finally dead? I'm going to toast your demise to my friend that you killed." Then she dropped his head and stood up, kicking him in the process.

I looked at her, taking a sip of my whiskey. "Are you done?"

She nodded once and stepped back. She looked under control, but there was undeniable tension running through her. I imagined that it wouldn't go away until those responsible were dead.

"Alright," I began, focusing back on the coward kneeling on the now wet, priceless rug. He kept side-eyeing Sasha as if she were a snake that was going to strike out at him at any second. She was deadly, but he was missing the most dangerous demon in the room. How he could forget what I had already done to him was a mystery. "You have a hatred for demons. I don't care why. The one and only thing I want to come out of your mouth next is who do you work for?"

He clamped his lips together, and Crispin and I both sighed. The vampire king looked over at me with a shake of his head. "Why do they always play it the hard way first?"

"Perhaps, we aren't scary enough?" I asked thoughtfully.

"Hmmm, I'll have to work on that."

As the Hunter and my Juliette giggled beside us, the man on the floor became visibly more flustered, shifting his weight and bouncing his eyes back and forth between Crispin and me.

Ivy spoke up, "I could use my gift on him?"

"That's much appreciated, Hunter. However, I think a few of us will enjoy forcing the answers out of him. But I will gladly accept it if he continues to remain stubborn," I thanked her.

Finally, I allowed the tendrils of my shadows to slither out along the floor until they reached his knees before they started crawling upwards. He eyed it like it was a snake ready to bite him, but he still stayed stubbornly silent. With a heavy sigh, I finally called out Sasha's name.

Immediately, the man shrunk away from her before she even took a step toward him.

"It was a human!"

We all froze as he began to babble on about how he was approached and offered the job by a guy in a black suit. "I don't know who he is. I just know that he isn't the one in charge because he's mentioned 'the boss' a few times, as in 'the boss wants to know if you can get more into Brimstone'. "

"How do you get in contact with this human?"

"I don't. He contacts me."

"How?" I demanded. I clenched and unclenched my fist, and my fingers were practically tingling with the urge to rip this vampire's soul out in the most painful way possible.

"They gave me a burner phone with no numbers in it. I was to wait until I was contacted, and the number always came up blocked," he whimpered, when Sasha shifted beside him. "That's it, that's everything!"

"Where's the phone now?" I asked, my tone deceptively soft while I could feel the anger roiled inside me.

He hung his head, shoulders slumping. "I trashed it when I heard you were looking for me."

"Were you able to warn them before you got rid of it?"

He whispered, "Yes." His answer had me yanking hard to keep my shadows at bay.

I nodded to Sasha. She and Rake gathered the crying vampire, each taking an arm, and led him out of the penthouse. As I stared at the wet spot on my rug, many possibilities ran through my mind. They could have others working for them distributing the drugs throughout my territory. He might have been the only one, but they might recruit someone else to take his place. What was the goal? Why target the demons? Why would a human use a vampire? How did a human know of vampires and demons?

"It looks like we now have more questions than answers," Crispin sighed, then stood up. "I'm sorry, friend. I will do what I can on my end to make sure that none of my people are involved any more than this one was. We will figure this out."

I stood up as well, Juliette following behind me. "Thank you. I appreciate what you've done and your offer of assistance."

We shook hands, and the women exchanged goodnights and phone numbers as they headed toward the door. Ivy paused before leaving and turned back to face me.

"Please make sure Sasha knows, no hard feelings?"

I bowed my head. "I'm sure she knows, but I will pass on the sentiments."

She grinned. "Good. Also, I thought Crispin could be pretty badass. But that thing you can do with the shadows while you just sit there cool as a cucumber?" She shook her head. "That was pretty neat. Bye, Juliette! I'll call soon!" With that, everyone left the apartment. Juliette and I stared at each other in the sudden quiet. We stood there for a moment before I took her hand.

"Come, *Amica mea*, let's go shower. I know you insist on going back to work tomorrow. I want you to have a good night's rest, and it's late already."

I led her down the hall and into the bathroom. I turned the water on in the shower and turned to my beautiful mate as she blinked up at me with her unique eyes. Her brilliant green one and her onyx one, black as the deepest shadows. They were as mesmerizing as the rest of her, and all I could focus on at that moment was getting her naked, so I could worship her, devour her, and show her how much I craved and loved her.

I stripped her quickly, but took my time treasuring her body, starting with her long, thick hair, paying particular attention to her scalp as she closed her eyes and moaned while I messaged the suds into the strands of her hair.

Once I had her shampooed, conditioned, and thoroughly rinsed, I washed every precious inch of her, but denied her when she attempted to repay the favor.

"No, mate, not this time."

By the time I was satisfied that I had done an adequate job cleaning her, I was on the edge of madness from wanting. I was beyond waiting any longer, so I lifted her in my arms and slowly impaled her on my stiff cock until we were flush together. I closed my eyes, relishing the feeling of being enveloped in my mate's heat. Once I was sure that I had my control back and wouldn't spill inside of her immediately, I began to lift her on and off of me with my hands grasping her tiny waist. She threw her head back and hung on to my shoulders while her desperate cries rang out around us.

When her tight warmth began pulsating around me, I pushed her up against the wall and pounded into her with several hard thrusts. Her screams of pleasure, as well as her cunt squeezing me, and pulsing rhythmically with her release, were more than I could take. I roughly ground my cock into her while burying my face into her neck. Finally, my release flooded her, pouring out the last of my tension for the day.

I was satiated, and my mate was almost asleep on her feet as I dried her and got her ready for bed. I set the alarm on her phone and lay it on her bedside table. When I turned the light off and gathered her close in my arms, I kissed her cheek and sighed with such a deep contentment.

"Thank you for finding me," I whispered into her hair.

But always in the back of my mind, I knew there was a danger out there that had no name and no way to trace.

CHAPTER
TWENTY-EIGHT

VAREK

I sᴀᴛ in my office doing paperwork that was necessary for running so many businesses. I had managers for each individual club in The Tower, but ultimately, I had stacks of paperwork to get through each month. I also would need to hire another demon to run the sex club. Yuri had been great for the position with his outgoing personality and completely nonjudgmental way. He didn't care what a demon's kinks were and was often up for trying a new one himself.

He would be a difficult, if not impossible one, to replace.

As I sat there checking numbers and going over lists, there was a knock at my door. I glanced at the clock and saw it was only 10 am. Juliette had been at work for a few hours already, but it would be several more before I would be able to lay eyes on her again.

"Enter," I called out, and glanced back up when I heard several footsteps enter my office.

A demoness, who I assumed to be Yuri's mother as she bore a striking resemblance to the male, followed behind a grim looking

251

Talon. As he stepped forward and then to the side, he revealed a tall man with white-blond hair and green eyes. Fuck.

Yuri's mother walked forward angrily. "Where is my son?"

I looked over to Talon and waited as he helpfully supplied her name.

"Lord Varek." He bowed, showing me the respect this woman had not. However, I would excuse her as she was a grieving mother and had a right to be upset. "Ardat is Yuri's mother and wished to come to see his body. She wishes to take him back to the Underworld for a proper burial."

I inclined my head. "That is understandable, Ardat. I will have someone take you to him immediately. Please accept my condolences. I wish to let you know that I do have the one responsible in my possession, and he will be met with slow and tortuous justice."

I watched as she deflated in front of me. Her shoulders slumped and curled in as her body bowed forward. She no longer looked like an angry avenging angel and more like the grieving mother she truly was.

"Yes, thank you, Lord Varek. My apologies."

I stood and walked around the desk to face her directly. "None are needed, Ardat. Please know, Yuri was a valued employee of mine, but he was also loved by many here. Few that met him didn't immediately love his charm and vivaciousness. It was impossible to be irritated by him, even though he had no filter on his mouth most of the time."

She gave a watery laugh and looked up at me through her tears. "He is exactly like his father. Thank you, I will remember your words always."

I gave her hand a gentle squeeze and allowed Rake, who was standing at the door prior to Talon's arrival, to lead her away.

I sighed as I watched her go and then focused all my attention on the man before me.

"Charon."

"Varek," he responded in kind. "I hear you've violated my daughter."

I sighed again and shook my head. I walked over to the liquor cabinet and took out three glasses along with a bottle of scotch. I waved toward the sitting area. "Let's do this in comfort, shall we?"

Once we were each settled in and had a glass of one of my finest bottles of scotch, I stared at my mate's father. I knew he would have plenty to say, and I would permit him to express his piece before I gave him mine.

"I want my daughter in the Underworld with me where she belongs."

I tilted my head and studied him.

"You realize that she is half human, correct? A trip to the Underworld could kill her. That is, if she could even pass through the portal."

"She's my daughter. Of course, she'd be able to pass." He lifted his chin and sniffed in disdain.

"What makes you so sure?" I toyed with the crystal cut of my glass as it sat on my armchair, the liquid in it untouched.

"A king of the Underworld would only produce the strongest of demons. She may appear only to be a half-breed, but she is more demon than most common one's ever are."

"And the fact that she is my bonded fated mate?"

"Irrelevant."

"Is it?" I murmured, finally taking a large swallow, not wanting this male to see the emotions that were swimming just under the surface of my skin, pushing to be let loose. This was my mate's biological father. Though she didn't know him, had never met him, and still was unaware of who, and what, she was, I couldn't destroy him. Only for her. "You are aware that I am unable to pass through the portal? That you taking her there would take her away from me?"

"I fail to see how that is my problem."

I had enough. "I have no idea what it's like in the Underworld, but here on the earth realm, mates are sacred. Therefore, no one, and

I do mean NO ONE, is permitted to come between a male and his mate. I don't care who you are to her. I will rip you limb from limb if you attempt to take my mate from me."

My voice was deadly calm, but my form had completely transformed, my voice having gone as dark as my eyes. I sat there watching him with deadly intent if he continued to threaten my bond with Juliette.

He studied me with a blank expression for so long, that I nearly gave into the temptation pounding through my veins, imagining the rending and tearing of his flesh when he slowly smiled. His smile was so similar to Juliette's that it stunned me into reversing my demon form.

"Yes. You will do well. I couldn't have asked for better for my daughter."

Talon and I looked at each other in wary confusion.

"What? You were testing me?"

He sighed and finally picked up his glass, studied the liquid inside it, and took a tentative sip before swallowing the contents in one gulp. "That's not bad. Not as good as we have in the Underworld, but not bad," he sighed and looked at me. "I have tried for thousands upon thousands of years to have even one child with no success. I never knew why. Eventually, it simply became a need to prove that I could. Now I find out that I succeeded and then never got to see her grow up. So, I have to at least ensure that she is taken care of properly now that she is a fully grown woman. And that means making sure her mate is worthy."

"No offense, Charon, but she could have used you long before now. Why did you never return to check to see if your seed took?"

"I suppose I just figured it hadn't. Gods, I don't even remember who her mother was. This is terrible of me, and I know that my daughter will likely be disgusted with me when she finds that out, but it's the truth."

"The man that raised her treated her like shit on his shoe."

He stiffened, and the air around us got noticeably warmer. "What?"

I sighed. "Look, I will tell you what I know, as she still hasn't told me all of it. But I need you to not destroy my building," the warning in my tone was unmistakable.

"I make no promises," his tone was deadly, and I supposed that was the best I was going to get.

"He beat her, starved her, made her believe she was worthless, and often called her a freak. She has your hair."

He smiled at that, a proud, fatherly smile.

"She also has your green eyes. One of them. The other is solid black. Her demon side is strong like you said. But that proof of being a demon that no one from our world would think twice of caused her endless pain and ridicule from the humans she was raised around." I sat back in my chair. "As I said, she could have used you."

"Where is this man now?" he asked, as the floor gave slight tremors beneath my feet.

"Unknown. I have been searching for him. What I am about to tell you next is worse than what I've already said. I need you to remain calm. Talon, pour him another drink."

"Talon, don't bother," he barked out.

I rubbed a frustrated hand over my face and mumbled, "Maybe we should do this outside or in another building." I could just envision the business that I built for the last two-hundred years falling to rubble as my mate's father found out about her scar. "He's been in prison for almost four years, recently let out on good behavior."

"And why was he in prison?"

"He attacked her one night when she was seventeen. He finally decided that he was done looking at the demon eye, as he called it. Fairly apt, wouldn't you say?"

"Quite. But not at all appropriate to joke about," he growled.

I growled right back. "I don't find any of this a joking matter. My mate was left to suffer as a little girl and was nearly murdered by the man who lost his wife in childbirth, and decided to blame her death on an innocent baby. He tried to cut her motherfucking eye out, Charon!" It was my turn to make the building shake, but this time it was much more violent than he had, the light fixture above us swaying and the bottles in the liquor cabinet clinking together.

"Shit," he said, sounding defeated as he rubbed a hand over his brow. "Okay. And you haven't found him?"

"No. I have feelers out everywhere."

"You are certain that he will be near?"

"Absolutely. A man that obsessed will not let her go easily. He will want to finish what he started four years ago. Plus, she received a note in her mailbox that seemed to have come from him."

"And where is she now?"

I tapped my fingers in agitation. I didn't want her to, but she insisted she loved her job and refused to quit. "She's a CNA at a nursing facility for the elderly in town. She's at work right now."

He started laughing, making me glare at him. "A king of the Underworld is letting his mate work for others?"

I froze in my seat. I met Talon's eyes, and he shook his head, the same look of confusion that I had on his face.

"You still don't know who you are? I guess I assumed that the ward he placed on your memories would have weakened enough to be broken by now. It's been so long."

"What. Ward," I gritted, from between my teeth.

"Lucifer was terrified of you. He believed that you would be able to defeat him as the ruler of the Underworld one day and become not just a king but *the* king. Your power to take souls scared him enough that he cast you out of the Underworld and barred you from reentering. But, before he did that, he placed a ward on your memories. I'm assuming you remember nothing from your time before earth?"

"None," I ground out, my jaw popping from how hard I was clenching my teeth.

"Well, isn't that something?"

He stood up and clapped his hands. "Enough chatting! I wish to see my daughter."

I stood up with fists clenched to keep them from shaking. I needed to see Juliette as well. I had a feeling she was the only one that would be able to calm the storm that had begun raging inside of me at this news I had just learned.

"Wait!" Talon said, as we headed toward my office door. "If he's a king of the Underworld, who, exactly, is he?"

Charon turned around and gave me a wink before clapping his hand on Talon's shoulder, making him stumble.

"He's Death."

CHAPTER

TWENTY-NINE

JULIETTE

It felt like I hadn't been to work in weeks, even though it had only been a couple of days. So much had changed in such a short time that I felt like a different person. I walked around the building, doing my same duties, and talking to the same people, but it felt foreign. I felt like I didn't belong in this world anymore. Not in the human world.

Before I had left for work, I had pleaded with Varek to have someone get me a new pair of contacts. I had explained that no one would accept the new me. I was too used to being a freak to the humans as I grew up, and I didn't want that, not from the elderly friends I had made. It would break my heart to have even one of them turn away from me in disgust. He had finally reluctantly relented and ordered someone to buy me a replacement pair of contacts.

"Knock, knock, Mr. Meyers. Are you ready for your bath?" I tapped softly on the door and stepped into the room to see Mr. Meyers watching a game show on his television. He looked up at me from his reclining position on the bed and gave me a bright, tooth-less smile.

"Well, there's my favorite girl!"

"Hi, Frank. How was your weekend?" I asked, as I walked around his room, tidying up as I went.

"Boring as ever. You know I never looked forward to Mondays until you started working here."

"You always say the sweetest things. It's bound to go to a girl's head one of these days." I poured him a fresh cup of water, replaced his straw, and then put the basin in the sink to start running hot water. He would only receive a sponge bath today, but tomorrow would be the full shower experience.

While I was getting my supplies together, he asked me the same question he'd been asking me nearly every day for the last couple of years. "Have you found yourself a beau yet?"

I was sure I was bright red as I cleared my throat. "Actually, I did."

"Well, then! That's great news, great news! You be sure to bring him around soon so your honorary grandfather can give him the stamp of approval!"

"That's a great idea, Frank. I'd love to bring him in and let you meet him."

"Is he good to you?"

I thought of how protective he was and how he held me close to him, the look in his eyes when I caught him staring at me. The look that he never tried to hide or pretend wasn't there. "He's the best."

I grabbed the small basin full of warm water and carried it care-fully across the room, setting it down on his rolling table until a loud scream sounded from down the hall. And then someone shouted my name. I jerked at the sudden commotion, causing some of the water to splash over the rim of the basin and onto the table. I stared down at the water, my mind trapped in what to do. I needed to clean the water up, but I also needed to see what was happening. For some reason, a sense of dread had taken over and squeezed my heart.

My name being screamed again jarred me from my trance, and I looked up at Mr. Meyers, who looked just as confused as I was. "You better hurry up and see what all that commotion is about, missy. The person's liable to wake up Gladys from her afternoon nap, and you know how she gets when her nap is disturbed."

I nodded and gave a distracted smile in thanks before slipping out of the room and hurrying down the corridor, following the sounds of yelling. I found myself in the front lobby along with most of the rest of the staff.

"Wha..." I started to ask, but everyone seemed to step back at once, parting the way for me to see exactly what was causing the disturbance.

An elderly woman was standing there. Her gray hair was long and stringy, missing in patches, allowing a view of her shiny pink scalp. Her face was deeply lined and sagging into distinct jowls, and the skin around her eyes was so droopy that I could see the underside of her inner eyelid.

She was also hunched over, her body so frail that she looked like she was nothing but skin and bones. She raised a gnarled finger with a yellowed fingernail and pointed directly at me.

"You!"

"Melissa?"

At my whispered question, everyone surrounding us gasped and turned their heads back to really look at the woman that was standing in the lobby of the nursing home. If any other elderly person had walked in, it would have been assumed that they were looking at the place as a possible future home. But Melissa wasn't there for that.

I took a tentative step forward and held my hands out placatingly. "Melissa, is there anything I can do to help you?"

She hissed in anger. "Help me? Help me?" She stabbed at her bony chest with her yellowed fingernail. "You did this to me!" she screamed.

I shook my head. "No, I-"

"Yes, you did!" Spittle was flying out of her mouth as she screamed, showing off a mouth that was missing several teeth. "You took everything from me! The man I was in love with, the future I had planned…" She took two handfuls of her brittle gray hair and pulled it in front of her face so she could see it for herself. "Now look at me!" she wailed.

I vaguely heard the whispers and gasps of disbelief around us. All I could do was stand there in shock as pain tore through me. I did do that to her. Maybe not directly, but it happened because Varek was defending me. He was so angry that she had tried to kill me that he nearly took her life instead. Looking at her now, I almost wondered if it would have been better to allow him to finish than to leave her like this. She had been a thirty year old beautiful woman in the prime of her life. Now she looked like what you'd expect to see in a child's storybook about a witch. The only thing she was missing was a hooked nose and a giant mole.

A hysterical laugh began to bubble out of me at the thought. I clamped both of my hands over my mouth to hold it in, but it was impossible. It burst out of me, and everyone turned to stare at me in horror as if I had grown three heads.

"Juliette!" the head nurse snapped at me.

"I-I'm so-sorry! I c-can't help it!" I continued to laugh hysterically, grabbing my ribs as they began to ache.

"I'm going to kill you!" Melissa screeched at me, trying to come toward me.

Somehow, her words helped snap me out of my hysterics, and I took several deep breaths while wiping away tears, noticing that I was wiping away the foundation caked under my eye. "Really, Melissa?" I asked, shaking my head at her in disbelief. "You're going to kill me? Are you forgetting that you already tried to kill me? That's exactly how you ended up the way you are right now."

"You stupid, little…"

"What's going on here?" My guard for the day walked in, finally noticing that there was something going on inside the lobby. Varek wasn't going to be happy if he found out that Melissa managed to not only slip past him but that she also caused a fuss at my work.

"That's Melissa," I pointed at her, and he immediately stiffened. He walked over to her and grabbed her arm in a grip strong enough to make her cry out in pain.

"Hey!" Several of the staff protested, but stepped back when he glared at them.

"Juliette, a word." I lowered my head at the head nurse's demand and nodded as everyone watched while my guard dragged Melissa from the building as she continued to screech profanities at me.

I heard someone ask if they should call the police, and the head nurse snapped that she would take care of it. She turned to me once we were several feet away.

"I have no idea what that," she pointed behind us, "was all about. It's hard to believe that person was Melissa. Things like that just aren't...possible." She seemed to be floundering for words as she looked back toward the exit doors and then turned back to me. She straightened her shoulders and lifted her chin. "But we can't have these kinds of disturbances in this nursing facility. So, I want you to gather your things and leave. Immediately. You are no longer an employee here."

I nodded weakly. "Can I say goodbye?"

"No."

There was no further discussion. Instead, she turned on her heel, walked back to the group, and began ushering them back to their duties. My shoulders were slumped, and I felt defeated as I walked into the breakroom to grab my bag. I hesitated a minute, but exited out of the backdoor that I rarely used. I didn't want to see what the guard was doing with Melissa. I didn't want to know what Varek had in store for her next.

After glancing at my watch to check the time, I walked to the bus stop. If I were right, a bus would be coming along in about five minutes. I had been meaning to go by my apartment to check on things and gather a few items that I wanted to keep. Most of what I owned were thrift store buys that were cheap and convenient when I rented my apartment for the first time and needed things to stock it with. I had no desire to keep any of it, other than a few pictures and knick-knacks I had received from the woman at the group home. She had given me my first gift, and I wanted to make sure it was okay. And I needed space to think.

I nodded to the bus driver, one I didn't know, as I fished out the change needed for the bus fare and then walked back to the middle of the bus, swaying, holding on to the seats as the bus continued on its journey. There were only a couple of other passengers on the bus, and no one seemed to be paying attention to me as I took my seat.

As I sat there looking out the window, I caught my reflection. My hair was in its tight bun, and my glasses were covering a large majority of my face. I sighed and took them off. I then reached up and began pulling the pins out of my hair, letting it fall free. I didn't belong in the human world anymore. Varek was right. But I was going to miss my patients.

I swiped a tear away. I then fished around in my purse until I found my kit with the contact case and a small bottle of solution. He had just bought these contacts for me. Though, I doubted I'd ever wear them again, I didn't want to waste them, so I squirted the solution into the little cups before plucking each contact from my eyes and dropping them carefully into the holders. Then, making sure they were nice and tight, I tucked everything away again.

When my stop arrived, I pulled the cord and waited for the bus to come to a complete stop before standing up and exiting out the open back door. The bus left with a hiss of air and continued on its route as I walked to my apartment building, used my key to enter, and then stopped to check my mail in the lobby. I was almost surprised to see I had very little mail waiting for me. It felt like it had been weeks, months since I had moved into The Tower, but in reality, it had been very little time. Just enough time for my entire life to change.

I dropped the junk mail in the recycling bin and stuffed the few articles of mail that looked remotely important in my bag, and pressed the button for my floor. I felt so tired all of a sudden. I just wanted to get a glass of water and take a nap.

The hallway was quiet when the elevator doors opened. As I walked through the corridor, I could only hear faint sounds coming from the other apartments, indistinguishable sounds of the television or a baby crying.

When I put my key in the door and turned, my mind was too caught up in what had happened earlier that I wasn't paying attention. I hadn't noticed that the door was already unlocked. So, when I stepped inside, I didn't notice right away that there was the smell of cigarette smoke hanging in the air. It wasn't until the blow to the back of my head that caused me to fall to my knees and my keys to go flying out of my hand, that I understood that I had made a terrible mistake.

CHAPTER
THIRTY

JULIETTE

"Hello, daughter."

I whimpered when I heard the words that tumbled around in my head like a distant echo as my brain struggled to catch up.

A foot to my ribs rolled me over. It wasn't a kick, but it was still hard enough to make me catch my breath. I blinked rapidly to bring my sight back into focus. The man standing above me holding the bat I kept by the door for security I'd hoped to never need grinned a wide, yellow-toothed grin.

He didn't look the same as he had four years ago. Back then, his eyes were always bloodshot, and his cheeks were always red from the alcohol he consumed on a daily basis. As soon as he got home from work, he would pick up a bottle. Whether it was beer or something stronger, he was always drinking something that would make him forget that his wife was dead and that he had been left behind with a child that wasn't his.

Now, he looked clean, and his eyes were clear from the years he spent in prison, unable to drink anything. He also looked bigger, stronger. He must have utilized the workout equipment that prisons supplied because he had never had muscles before. The beer belly he had always sported was gone. In its place was a firm and toned body. One that scared me beyond belief.

I thought I had been scared of this man before when I was a little girl, but now, looking up at him, it was like my monster had stepped out of my memories and had grown ten times in size. I started crying.

"I've been waiting for you." He squatted down next to me as I flinched away from him. He cocked his head to the side. "Where have you been?"

I couldn't speak. I just shook my head frantically before finally blurting out the only thing I could. "Please!"

He tsked me. "Oh, little girl, do you think I have any mercy for you? I have done nothing but dream of this moment for four years. Well, actually, twenty-one years, really. But, honestly, I don't know how I managed to hold off for as long as I did."

He stood back up and glared while looming over me with pure malice in his eyes. "It doesn't matter where you've been. Do you know what I see when I look at you?"

I squeezed my eyes shut and prayed to whatever god was out there listening, hoping for some kind of miracle that help would arrive. I should never have come here. Not by myself. Why didn't I think of the danger? I had known he was out of prison, but I naively thought that he was done with me when he hadn't surfaced already. But then, I remembered the note and had the despairing thought that I should have taken it more seriously. I should have known it was him.

I nodded because I did know what he thought of me.

He kicked me suddenly in my side, and I screamed in agony. I felt a sickening crack that I hadn't felt in years but would never be able to forget. "No!" he yelled. "You could never know what it's like, the torture of seeing your wife's murderer every day. Of looking into her, fucking...ugly...eyes, and seeing the monster that created her." With his words, he kicked me repeatedly until I had curled into a ball and sobbed. I used my hands to protect my head but couldn't save my back or shoulders from the agonizing pain.

"But finally." It felt as if he were ripping the hair from my scalp as he took a large handful of my hair and pulled me to my feet. "I have you here, and I will avenge my wife." I felt a white-hot searing pain as he slowly sank a knife that I hadn't seen him pull out into my abdomen.

"Please," I gasped, "don't."

"Oh, I will." He grinned down at me as he slowly removed the knife, only to move it an inch over and started to sink it back into my stomach. "I will. Over, and over, and over." He repeated the move several more times until the world around me began to grow dark. Each plunge of the blade made my body jerk, the pain unbearable. "I will make it hurt. Like it hurt to look at you every day for seventeen years."

I gasped out, my voice thin and reedy. "I was just...little girl. Not...fault."

"My wife was just a woman married to a man that loved her. Was it her fault?" he snarled, and twisted the knife. I didn't think I had the capacity to feel more pain, but I did.

Suddenly the door burst open, and Varek barreled through along with Sasha, Talon, Rake, and another man I didn't know, but seemed to recognize me. I looked away from his rage filled eyes and concentrated on what vision I had left, blinking slowly, to look at Varek's face. He looked ravaged, angry, and in as much pain as I was.

I tried to lift my hand, to reach out to my fated mate with what little strength I had left, but didn't make it higher than a couple of inches from my side before it fell limply again.

My body was jerked roughly as he swung me around to shield his body with mine making me whimper softly. I couldn't manage anything beyond that. I wanted to tell Varek I loved him and that I was sorry. I wanted to tell Sasha thank you for being my first real friend. But all I could do with the last of my strength was work to keep my eyes open. I didn't want to lose any of my final moments of this life looking at the demon that brought me to life.

"I don't know who you all are," the man snarled, bringing the knife to my throat, "but you won't take this from me." Then I felt the cold heat of the blade as it entered the flesh at my throat and slid across. I immediately started choking, and against my will, my eyes slid shut. The tears that fell from my eyes weren't from the pain but from the regret of losing everything I had just gained.

The last thing I knew was hearing the roar of denial.

Varek

I WAS MOVING before the anguished sound had finished leaving my chest. The man that dropped Juliette's lifeless body raised the knife to his own throat, but before he could stab it in, my shadows wrapped around the handle and yanked it away from him, tossing it against a wall somewhere. His surprised yelp turned into shrieks of pain as I tore first one arm and then the other from his body. My shadows held him upright as I used my hands, wings, and tail to slice every inch of his body.

I was only vaguely aware of Charon gathering Juliette's body to his chest, walking over to the blood spattered couch, and sitting down with her cradled in his arms. When I saw a light emanating from his hands, I dropped what was left of the man that had tortured my mate for her entire life and reached out to snatch her from him.

When I hit the ground in the pool that was a mix of Juliette's and the asshole's lifeblood, I raged, realizing that all of my guards were pining me to the floor.

"Let me up! Don't you dare take her from me! Do you hear me, Charon? I will kill you! I will destroy you. Don't you take her from me!"

I struggled to toss my people from me, not caring who they were or how long they had been trusted and by my side. I would destroy anyone that stood between me and my mate.

Charon said nothing to my threats. He just sat there with his eyes closed, his hands glowing. "No!" I thundered, feeling the entire building shake beneath us. My voice broke, and I lowered my head. *"Amica mea."*

~

Juliette

I BLINKED my eyes against the light as I found myself sitting on a cool, metal bench in the middle of a spring meadow. There were flowers all around in every color I could imagine. The gurgling of water caught my attention, and I turned my head to see a fountain just a few feet in front of where I was sitting.

I looked far to my right and saw nothing but a brightness so vivid, I couldn't keep looking at it. When I turned to my left, there was nothing but deep, dark shadows that felt like home because they reminded me of Varek.

"How are you feeling?"

The deep voice beside me had me turning to face him. He was the man that had entered my apartment with Varek. He was blond, the same shade as my own hair, and his eyes were just as vivid green as Varek's. As my one green eye.

"I feel like I know you," I answered instead.

He nodded with a smile. "I am Charon, the Ferryman. I am one of the seven kings of the Underworld. I am also your father."

His words felt right in my heart, and I nodded once in acceptance. I looked down at my body. I was wearing a plain white cotton sundress that was clean of any blood or cuts. "Why don't I feel any pain?"

"I am doing what I can right now to heal you quickly. I'm holding us here, in limbo, I suppose you could call it. Most refer to it as the in-between. You aren't dead, nor are you dying. That demon of yours seems to have forgotten that you are as immortal as he or I am," he chuckled. "It did my father's heart good, though, to see him avenge you so quickly. That male sure does love you."

"Is he alright?" I wanted to be worried, I wanted to be scared, but for some reason, those deep emotions weren't accessible. I assumed it was our location in this strange place. I knew the feelings were there, but all they were at the moment were gentle echoes, telling me what I should be feeling.

"Hmmm, well, let's just say he will be once he calms down and sees you alive and well for himself."

"And I will be? Alive and well?"

"As you ever were. Your wounds will be healed. There is a possibility that any scars that you used to have will be gone as well."

I raised a steady hand to my left eye and felt there, but there was no puckering, no scar pulling my eyelid lower. I looked back up at my father. "It's gone?"

He nodded. "Here it is. As I said, there is a good possibility that it will also be gone on the mortal plain. These things can be tricky."

I lowered my hand back to my lap and really studied the male before me. He was handsome, tall, and muscular. All very similar to Varek. "Did you rape my mother?"

He sighed and shook his head. "No." He stood up and walked to the fountain. "I rarely come to the earth realm. When I did that night, it was to find a beautiful, lonely, sad woman. Her husband had abused her. She didn't want to leave him, but she was willing to spend one glorious afternoon with me." He looked out over the meadow toward the bright light beyond. "I never saw her again. She made her choices. But I wish I hadn't listened." He let his head hang down. "I am sorry, my daughter. I failed you."

I shook my head. How could I blame my mother for wanting one day to experience happiness in the arms of another man? I had no doubts that her husband was just as vile to her as he was to me. There was no way that a man with that much hate inside of him didn't already have it there before I came along. At the same time, how could I blame the male, my true father, for giving my mother that happiness?

"The only one to blame is that man. Did Varek kill him?"

He chuckled. "If he isn't dead already, he will be soon."

"When will I go back?"

"When you are ready."

"How will I know when that is?"

"Only you can know that, my daughter."

I nodded my head. "Can I see him?"

"Your mate?"

"Yes." He waved me toward the fountain, and I slowly stood from the bench and took careful steps toward the fountain. I didn't know what I would see, and I was hesitant to imagine.

When I reached the edge of the gurgling water, I looked down into the clearest water I had ever seen in my life. As I stared, an image began to ripple across the surface. Slowly, the image came into focus. At first, all I saw was red. It took me several moments to realize that what I was looking at was blood—my blood and the man that raised me.

There were body parts strewn about the room, but my eyes skated over those, not wanting to fully take in the carnage that I knew only Varek could cause. I saw the guards standing back, each of them also covered in red. But my eyes settled on Varek, my mate. He was sitting on the floor, his head bowed, his shoulders shaking in grief.

"Oh, Varek," I murmured. Even in this place of muted feelings, I still felt a pang of sorrow for this male that had shown me what it was like to be cherished.

"Like I said, that male loves you."

CHAPTER
THIRTY-ONE

VAREK

I couldn't hold it in. All the pain at seeing my mate sliced apart, her throat slit before my very eyes. It was too much to bear. I needed to get away. I needed to do...something.

I growled and stood up, ready to stalk out of the apartment, away from the pain.

"Wait!"

"Get out of my way!" I thundered, as Talon stepped in front of the door, barring my way away from here.

"Wait, Varek, listen!" He held his hands up to stop me, and then pointed at the couch where my mate was being held in her father's arms for the first time.

"I don't..." I turned my head at the faint sound, and without thought, without conscious effort, my feet took me toward the couch. A heartbeat, faint but steady. How long had that been there? Has it always been there? Did he not ferry her soul because she wasn't dead?

"Boss." Sasha came to stand by my side. "She's a demon. And your bonded mate. I think..." she let out a shuddering breath. "I think that she's immortal."

"Immortal," I breathed out. Charon kept telling me that she was more than just a half-breed. The daughter of a king. The bonded mate of a king. The Ferryman and Death. If what he suggested were true, she was virtually indestructible. She could never be taken from me ever again.

I closed my eyes. The relief that surged in was so strong, that it nearly overwhelmed me all over again. The rage, the pain, and grief had threatened to tear my very essence apart, but this relief at knowing my mate would forever be safe and by my side? It put me back together.

Charon opened his eyes and smiled sorrowfully. "It's a hell of a way to meet one's offspring for the first time. She will be okay, but she is healing in the in-between. I don't know how long it will take her. Her mind is still new and fragile. She still thinks of herself as a mortal human. Once she comes to terms with who and what she is, she'll come back to you."

He stood up, carefully cradling her small body in his large arms, and gently placed her in mine. He bent down to kiss her bloody fore-head. "I wish you would have left some of that human for me to play with. But I have to admit, your methods are effective."

There was a knock at the door, but I couldn't pull my gaze away from her face. She still looked dead, and it squeezed my heart painfully. I had to continue listening to her heartbeat and remind myself that she was alive.

Talon answered the door, and the witch I kept on retainer for cleaning messes that could only be fixed by magical means walked in carrying a small satchel.

"I hear there needs to be some cleaning done, oh!" She looked around the room, and when I looked at her, she cocked an eyebrow. "I think I might need to double my fee on this one."

"Triple it," I grunted, as I walked to the door.

"What about the body...pieces?" she called out.

"Send them to the ether. I don't give a damn."

I strode down the hall, the guards and Charon following behind me, leaving the witch to do her thing. I didn't care about the mess, the whole apartment building could burn to the ground for all I cared, but I still had to abide by the same rule that I set for all my demons. We couldn't let humans become aware of our existence. Seeing a severed body in Juliette's apartment might not reveal us, but once the authorities hunted down Juliette to question her about the body and the carnage, not to mention her own blood, they would find her at The Tower. It was wise to dispose of all proof now.

Charon kept staring at me as we sat in the car until I finally grunted. "What?"

"You're angry at her."

Yes, I was. I was beyond livid. I wanted to rail at her. I wanted to turn her little ass red for placing herself in a position to be murdered by her psychopathic non-father figure. The one that clearly hated her and had always made it clear that his end game was to destroy her.

"That's between my mate and myself."

He narrowed his eyes at me while I just stared back.

"If you hurt her..."

"I would never hurt her!" I thundered so loudly, that the windows in the vehicles rattled and threatened to shatter. A crack appeared over his shoulder.

"You may not hurt her physically, but emotionally?"

"I will not discuss this with you."

"Then who will you discuss it with?"

"Her, only her! When she wakes up from being gods damned murdered in front of my eyes!"

I watched as the crack spiderwebbed out, nearly filling the whole window.

"Perhaps, it is good that she remains in limbo for a while. It might give your emotions a chance to level out."

I gritted my teeth at the thought of how long she could stay away from me. She was in a place I could not reach her, and I wanted to scream at the universe, at the gods for separating us this way. I wouldn't 'level out' until she opened her eyes for me.

As soon as the car pulled to a stop outside The Tower, I threw open the door and got out, careful not to jostle her body. I strode through the front doors of the closed club, thankful it was still daytime, and there were no humans around to gawk and stare. I was sure we made quite the sight as we were, each of us covered in layers of blood from head to foot. When I killed, I was always careful to make sure I did it in such a way that I would not get any of the blood on me, but I could honestly say I didn't give a fuck as I tore the arms from that human's body. I only wished that I had done it much slower.

I shook my head at an employee that rushed forward when we entered through the main doors, dismissing them, and they stepped back, wringing their hands and glancing down at my mate nervously. I didn't think Juliette had any idea of how quickly she had charmed everyone when she came into my life and became the queen of everything I owned. They tore their eyes from her silent, bloody form and rushed to the warded doors leading to my office and the main entrance to the rest of The Tower. I nodded once in thanks and strode through, heading straight to my office and toward the private elevator to which only a few were allowed access.

"You may have to use one of the visitor's suites upstairs. Someone will show you the way. If you need anything else, there is a number to call. They will supply you with anything you ask for." I left Charon at the elevators and kept walking. I had one purpose in mind at the moment.

As soon as I entered my penthouse, I kicked the door shut behind me. I had ignored all offers of assistance from everyone, needing to see my mate privately. I needed to be alone with her, and I needed to clean her from the filth that covered her.

I went straight to the bathroom and looked around for a place to set her, but there was nowhere I could lay her down, and I wasn't going to lay her on the floor. I went back into the bedroom and carefully lay her on top of the made bed, uncaring that she would be soaking the bedding with her blood. I could replace it easily. I was sure there were plenty more around here, just like the one that I was ruining.

I carefully removed each shoe, dropping it to the carpet, then tugged her pants and the panties that I knew had been pale pink when she dressed this morning. After I slipped the scrub top over her head, I unlatched her bra. The blood had soaked through her clothing and saturated her skin. It looked as if she had taken a bath in it.

I ran my hands over her abdomen, where most of her bleeding had been coming from. I trailed my fingertips over the unmarred skin there and closed my eyes. I hadn't dared to look until now, but I finally allowed my eyes to take in the sight of her neck. A breath shuddered out of me as I took in the smooth, pale skin underneath the flaking bits of dried blood. There wasn't a mark left on her, and the relief nearly took me to my knees.

After I divested myself of my own dirtied clothing, I gathered her back into my arms and walked into the shower, making sure to keep the spray off of her until the temperature was one she preferred. I watched as the red suds swirled along the tiled floor before they disappeared down the drain.

I didn't leave the shower until the water ran clear, washing her several times, marveling over her soft skin and her delicate beauty. Every time the memory of watching her eyes slide closed threatened to enter my mind, I shook it away, determined to see my task through.

Once she was as clean as she had ever been, I stepped out of the running shower and grabbed a towel from the warming rack with one hand, wrapping it around her body so she wouldn't be cold, then grabbed another to wrap around her hair, trying to get it the way she liked, knowing I was failing. Frustrated, I carried her back to the bed.

I vaguely noticed that the bedding had already been changed, the dirtied clothing removed from the pile on the floor, and a pale blue nightgown lay across the foot of the bed. I would have to thank Amara for her thoughtfulness. Once Juliette awoke.

Once I had her dressed, and the tangles brushed out of her hair, I slid her onto the sheets and covered her with a clean blanket. I didn't bother with sleeping attire for myself. I couldn't bring myself to leave her, and I couldn't tear my eyes away from her. I pulled the chair over from the corner of the room and sat. And waited.

A KNOCK at the bedroom door jarred me awake from dreams of seeing Juliette falling to the ground. I didn't want the knocking to disturb her, so I padded to the door and cracked it open.

"Yes, Amara?"

"Sir, I have food for you here. Please eat."

"No, thank you, I'm not hungry."

"But, sir…"

"I'm not hungry," I repeated, not wanting to lose my patience with Amara but wanting to get back to the bedside.

"It's been three days, sir."

"I am aware of how long it's been, Amara. I will eat when she eats."

She bowed her head and backed away with the tray that held no interest for me. I would continue to wait as long as it would take.

"COME BACK TO ME, *Amica mea*. It's time for you to return home."

I had begun talking to her somewhere around the fourth day, attempting to coax her soul to return to her body. But, so far, there hadn't been any sign that she was listening.

I spent much of my time sitting, watching, and waiting. But during that time, I was also angry and getting angrier.

Charon and the others had attempted to see her, but I ignored each of their requests. I allowed no one to enter. Instead, I cared for her myself. I bathed her and dressed her. And cursed her when the pain and anger got to be too much.

"Come back to me, *Amica mea*. I need you."

THIRTY-TWO

JULIETTE

I smiled at a pair of butterflies as they flitted over the wildflowers and giggled when they landed on my arm, only to dart off again when I moved. This place was beautiful and so serene. I had never felt the kind of gentle calmness as I did here. But I felt as if something were missing.

There was a tugging on my heart. It had started slowly, something that I had easily ignored, but then the tugging became more insistent over time. I spent a lot of time staring out across the vast meadow toward the shadows that made me feel as if I wanted to cry.

I knew they reminded me of Varek. I missed him. It hadn't been noticeable at first. It was like a distant memory that I tried to remember, but just kept slipping out of reach. But, just like the insistent tugging, his face kept cropping up, more and more as I spent my time sitting amongst the flowers.

I had no recollection of how long I had been there. I had no hunger, no thirst, no need for bodily functions. I just sat and watched. I thought that, perhaps, I was still healing. I had seen, in the fountain when my father had been here, how ravaged my body had been. It must take a very long time to recover from those types of injuries.

So, I waited.

Charon had said I would know when it was time for me to return, but I still had no idea how I would know that.

There was no nighttime in the meadow, only a peaceful calm filled with butterflies and flowers. Every once in a while, my gaze would be drawn back to the fountain, but I had no desire to see myself lying there bloody and broken. But, mostly, I didn't want to see Varek as he was. That was a pain that almost managed to make it through the calmness. The thought of Varek being brokenhearted and on his knees for me.

I laughed as another pair of butterflies flew around my head, circling up and over. It was during moments like these that I had the fleeting thought that I never wanted to leave. Why would I want to return to a world that had the type of evil in it that had tried to kill me? He had basically succeeded. And then there was Melissa. And the girl from my childhood that had told me that my mother was a whore. Her friend that would take my food, the only food I would be able to eat for the day, and would step on it. That world was awful.

The tugging on my heart gave a sharp jerk, making me gasp. It was the first time I had felt anything other than peace since I woke up here. I stood up from my crossed-legged position and dropped the bits of flowers that I had shredded with my fingers. I frowned down at them. I didn't remember doing that. Then, I felt the tug again and rubbed my sternum. I looked around, seeing the place of light, and then the shadows were still there. The meadow with all the colors of flowers was still there. Nothing had changed. So, what was tugging at me?

I glanced at the fountain again, feeling drawn to it. I didn't want to look, though. Did I? Without thought, my feet began to move, sending me ever closer to that water that had shown me something that I knew, had I full range of my emotions, would break my heart.

Still, I grew closer. Finally, when I reached it, I took a steadying breath and looked down.

It took a few minutes. The water kept rippling, and faint outlines would appear only to disappear, almost as if the scene were shifting too fast for the waters to settle into. If I looked hard enough, I was sure that I could make out a car, a building, a bathroom, a bedroom. One thing that seemed to always be a part of the scene, though, was Varek.

Finally, the waters began to clear, settling as if static from an old television was making way for the picture.

I stared down and took in everything. There was me, my body, laying in the bed I recognized as in the penthouse bedroom. Pulled up next to the bed was the armchair that usually sat in the corner of the room. Sitting in the chair with his head leaning back against the top of the chair was Varek. I gasped at the sight of him. He was naked and appeared to be sleeping, though I didn't understand why he would be sleeping in the chair instead of the bed. But what shocked me the most was his face.

I had never seen him look anything but completely put together. Whether it was in the morning or late at night before bed, he always managed to look ready for anything. Sometimes, he would sport a bit of stubble on his face at the end of the day, but usually, he was clean shaven. But now, he looked like he hadn't shaved in a week, perhaps longer. Had I done that to him? The thought made a wave of sadness wash over me. It was the strongest emotion I had felt since arriving.

I reached out to touch his face, but when my fingers met the surface of the water, the image rippled and then dissipated.

"No!" I frantically stared down at the fountain, willing it to bring back the picture, but all I saw was my own reflection. I reached up to touch the smooth skin under my left eye. I closed my eyes and then reopened them slowly, once again seeing that unblemished eye. It was still black, but the scar was gone. The water rippled, and my heart sped up, thinking that it was going to show me Varek again, but I realized that the rippling in the water was caused by my tears.

I turned around and sat down on the bench I hadn't sat on since my father had told me he was going back. I didn't know how long I sat there, but when a hand reached over and took mine, I looked away from the fountain to see the face that I had looked at every day in an old tattered photograph that I had tucked away, hidden in a hole in my mattress on the floor.

"Mom?"

She just smiled sadly at me and brushed a lock of hair behind my ear. "My beautiful girl. I am so sorry."

I shook my head. "Are you really here?"

"No, not really. I am here because you need me." She tilted her head toward the fountain. "Almost as much as he needs you."

I looked back toward the gurgling fountain and felt a wave of melancholy sweep over me. "I think I miss him."

"Of course, you do. Do you realize how lucky you are to have a mate? They are very rare, you know."

I nodded. I was lucky.

"You need to go back, my darling little girl."

I looked at her with tears in my eyes. "It hurts."

"Oh, sweetheart." She pulled me into her arms as the dam on my emotions began to crumble slowly. "I know it does. You were given one of the worst lives that one could receive. It was a horrible life, and it shaded the world around you into colors of hate and pain. But let me tell you a secret." She pulled back and took my face in both of her hands. "If you go back there, to that world that treated you so badly before? You will find a much different world waiting for you. Your mate will ensure that every day of your very, very long life will know nothing but love and joy. You just have to trust in him. Trust in *you*. But you have to go back."

"My biological father said that your husband used to abuse you."

She smiled sadly. "He did. He was an awful man that I felt trapped with. I wasn't able to see a way out. Or I didn't let myself see it. I was planning to leave him once you were born. I just knew that he would hurt you the way that he had hurt me over the years. I couldn't let that happen."

"But you died. I killed you."

"No! Don't ever say that again! That evil man killed me, not you, never you. The day you were born, he hit me so hard in the stomach that I went into labor. He had been angry my entire pregnancy. It wasn't until that day that he finally told me why. When he said that he was sterile and unable to father children..." She looked off, staring out at an old memory that I couldn't see but was obviously very painful. "I was terrified. I tried to leave. I packed a bag and told him it was for the hospital, but I don't think he believed me. Somehow, he knew I was never going back to him if I walked out of that door. So he hit me, right in my pregnant belly. It caused a placental abruption. I bled out on the table in the operating room before they could repair the damage."

"He always said he loved you."

"In some sick, twisted way, I am sure he did. But love isn't supposed to hurt that way. Does your mate cause you pain, make you sad or scared?"

I was already shaking my head before she finished asking. "No, never! He treats me like a princess."

She smiled and caressed my cheek. "Exactly. Go back to him. It's time."

I wrapped my arms around my mother and cried onto her shoulder as she rubbed my back and whispered softly to me. When I finally opened my eyes again, I was staring at the ceiling of our bedroom.

I suddenly felt everything again. So many emotions flooded me at once that I couldn't breathe. I lay there gasping for breath when Varek suddenly came into my vision, leaning over me. He was the most beautiful and welcoming sight that I burst into tears immediately, completely overwhelmed.

He gathered me into his arms and held me so tight it almost hurt, but I didn't want him to let go. I never wanted him to let go of me again.

We stayed like that for several long moments before he pulled back and took my face in his hands. "Never. Again," he growled, and then slammed his lips on mine, devouring me through his kiss. My gasp of surprise was quickly swallowed, as were my whimpers and moans as he bit and licked at my lips roughly.

He broke away from my mouth and kissed a trail to my ear and then down to my neck, where he bit almost savagely, just shy of breaking the skin. Then, after pausing long enough to suck in the flesh there, he continued down until he reached the neckline of the gown I was dressed in. Then, with a snarl and a glare, he tore the gown down the middle with both of his hands and then spread the halves of the gown open to reveal my nakedness.

"Every day and night, I took care of you without really seeing you. Now, you are back in front of me, all of you, and I am going to remind you that I own you and why you want me to."

My nipple was suddenly in his hot mouth, and my back arched at the sensations that were swirling throughout my entire being. "Varek!" I called out, unsure if I was begging him to stop or if I was begging him to please, *please* keep going.

Within seconds, he had my body tugged to the edge of the mattress from where he was standing, leaning over me. He placed my ankles on top of his shoulders, and in one swift thrust, he was buried to the hilt inside of me.

We both stayed still as we panted for breath, absorbing the feeling of being reconnected after so long apart.

I finally couldn't take it anymore, he needed to move, or I was going to start taking care of myself. I moaned and started to slide my fingers along my abdomen, with my clit being my final destination, but he snapped his eyes up to mine, and I watched as they bled to black, as his entire being morphed from Varek the male to Varek, the demon king.

"Do not move those fingers another inch, *mate.*"

His words were harsh, and even though my eyes immediately began watering and my bottom lip trembled, my pussy pulsed and fluttered. When he began to thrust, there was no finesse, no slow build-up, nor were there softly whispered words of encouragement.

Varek was angry, and the longer that he fucked me, the more that anger began to pour out of him, and he seemed determined to pound it into me. I should have been upset, maybe scared, maybe angry that he was angry at me, but all I had the capacity to feel at the moment was raw bliss. Then a scream tore from my throat as my walls clamped down on him hard. He pounded me through my orgasm until my body collapsed back onto the bed again, boneless.

I didn't expect for him to drop my legs from his shoulders or for him to back away from me.

CHAPTER

THIRTY-THREE

VAREK

I PACED BACK and forth across the floor. My fingernails which had sharpened and darkened into lethal black claws were clenched in my hair. I wanted to shout and curse. I needed Juliette to feel what I felt while I waited every minute, every second for her, not knowing if she would even make it back to me. I wanted to make her feel the despair that had threatened to drown me every one of the nine days that she had been away from me.

I turned to face her and saw her in the same position I had left her in, completely exposed to me in every way, legs spread, the glistening wetness from her release spread over her thighs. Her cunt was bared to me and waiting for my return. I traced a path with my eyes up her body until I reached her face. She had tears spilling down her cheeks but understanding in her eyes.

I turned away again.

I continued to pace. My cock was hard and heavy, throbbing in pain from the release I had denied it. But I knew I wouldn't be able to come, not until I purged this torment inside of me.

I stopped once again and faced her, my chest heaving. She was as beautiful and fragile as ever, though there were changes. The obvious one was that her scar was now gone. It was bittersweet. She hated that scar, and what she thought it represented, while to me, it told a story of survival, of living through hell and coming out the other side.

But, it was in her eyes where the real change was. She had finally found herself. Too bad it had taken her leaving me to do it.

"You left me," my growl reverberated around the room.

She nodded.

"I waited for you, watched over you, and you didn't return to me."

Again, she nodded, the tears making her eyes shine brightly.

"I hate you for that," I choked out the words. Words I didn't know I was going to say, words I didn't realize I was feeling until they came rushing to the surface.

I watched as another tear slipped from her eye, and she sat up, slipping from the bed. Then, she got down on her hands and knees and crawled over to where I was standing in the middle of our room, enraged and still pulsing with fevered lust for her.

"Let me make you love me again," she whispered. Then she took my cock in her small hand and guided it to her mouth.

I threw back my head and growled at the ceiling, my wings flaring back, spread wide behind me, my shadows wrapping around the both of us, lifting her hair, tugging on her breasts, caressing her clit.

She swallowed around my length while she whimpered, the tears now falling down her cheeks for a different reason as I watched her small mouth take as much of my thick cock as it could. Saliva pooled around the corners of her mouth and dripped down her chin to her breasts as she reached down and caressed my scrotum. I ground my jaw, my back teeth aching as I fought to keep from thrusting deeper, giving her more than she could take.

Finally, I could take no more and yanked her mouth from me with my fist in her hair, making her gasp as my cock slid off her hot tongue.

"Enough!"

I easily picked her up and, with little effort, slid her down my length until we were as connected as it was possible to make us. I looked into her eyes as I slid her up and down my cock, using her body as if Juliette were made for me. Because she was.

"I'm so sorry, Varek," her breathless words were choked out of her, as I slammed her body down.

I closed my eyes, cutting off the view of her perfect face, but I couldn't block out the sensations of her kissing my cheeks, chin, and eyes.

"I love you so much."

She ran her fingernails over my arms and shoulders, the slight pain sending shockwaves of lust straight to my cock, making it jerk inside her perfect cunt.

"I missed you, even when I couldn't feel you."

A strangled sound came from my throat, and I longed to shut out the sounds of her words. I walked over to the floor-to-ceiling windows overlooking the city, pressed her body against the glass, and began hammering inside of her harder.

"You were the only thought that kept repeating, reminding me that there was more than the meadow. You kept pulling me back, tethering me to you, until I could finally find my way back on my own." Her jagged words broke me until I couldn't deny it any longer.

I crushed her body to mine and kissed her deeper than I ever had before. I lowered my knees to the floor, cradling her body, then gently laying her down on the soft rug. I ran my hands and eyes over every inch I could reach without separating our bodies.

"I missed you," I choked out.

"I would have come home sooner if I could."

"I could never hate you."

She held my clenched jaws in her hands, blinking at me with nothing but pure love. "I would understand if you do."

I shook my head in denial. "No, I could never hate you. I hate the man who hurt you to the point that you died a human death. I hate that you had to stay in the in-between to heal. I hate that you had to stay so long because that same man had damaged your psyche so badly that it took you days to heal from it when you could have been here, with me."

"I hate that for you, too." I watched as another tear slid from her eye and started to fall into the hair at her temple. I leaned down and licked it away.

"You are mine," I growled, making sure that she was looking directly into my eyes. "From now until forever, we will never be apart. I will tear apart time and space itself if you are kept from me again. Do I make myself clear to you, *Amica mea*?"

"I will be waiting for you if that happens."

I sealed our lips together and then proceeded to show her exactly how a male that found his fated mate made love to her after being separated, and when I finally spilled inside of her with my teeth in her throat and my name on her lips, my heart was settled.

I would never forget what it was like to be separated from Juliette, to have her close to me, but unable to reach her. It would likely be a nightmare I would have to live with for a very long time. But my heart and my mind were settled on the agreement that it was not Juliette's fault. Her mind did what it had to do to protect her, to heal her from a lifetime of pain. With the healing powers of the in-between, she would be much stronger, and her mind would no longer be her weakness. For that, I could only be grateful.

~

FOR THE NEXT TWENTY-FOUR HOURS, the time was only for us. I wanted no interruptions. There was no business important enough to take me away from Juliette's side. Everything would still be waiting for us the same as it had for the last week and a half.

Amara somehow knew and provided us with enough sustenance to last for days, as if she were forcing us to make up for the lack of meals we ate in the previous week.

We were reclining in front of the gas fireplace in the corner of the room, while I hand fed my mate fruit and cheese that I explained what Charon had told me about the Underworld and Lucifer.

"You have no memories at all?"

"None."

"Do you think, my-, Charon is right? That you are able to kill Lucifer?"

I squeezed her gently where my arm was holding her below her ribs. "It's okay if you call him your father, you know. I have a feeling that he would probably like that very much."

She shrugged. "I know, I just…I have to get used to it, I suppose."

I kissed her temple. "Okay. As for your question. No, I don't think I could kill Lucifer. Temporarily take his life? Yes. But I don't believe that an immortal being would truly perish even if I took their soul. At least, not for long. I know that what I do is force a soul to leave a body. An immortal can and will regenerate almost any injury. So, would their soul not eventually find its way back?"

"But what if the body were to be destroyed in the meantime? Like lit on fire? Then there wouldn't be anything left for the soul to return to."

"Hmmm. Very good point. Of the souls I've taken, it was due to a punishment earned. I have never cared whether or not they could return."

"So, hypothetically speaking, were you to take Lucifer, or anyone else's soul that was a true immortal, if someone were to keep their body preserved, basically, just safe from undue harm, then they could theoretically return to their body and be perfectly fine?"

I chuckled. "Yes, Miss Scientist, that's what I'm saying."

"That's a bit of a long shot, though, isn't it? I mean, if you are taking his soul, you are probably in the position to do something to his body, too. So I'm just thinking, I guess I could understand why he would be so frightened of you."

I could only hum in agreement. I had spent so many years on earth, and with entirely no memories of the Underworld, I didn't miss what I didn't know. I was content where I was.

"You know," she said, after a few minutes of silence. "I can't help but wonder if there was a valid reason for his fear. Did you threaten him? Or was he paranoid for no reason? It kind of sucks that he would throw you out of your home without a purpose." She sounded like she was getting agitated on my behalf. I chuckled again and spun her onto her back, quickly making her gasp as I loomed over her.

"*Amica mea*, you worry over nothing important. If you truly want to know, we can ask your father. But, honestly, I bare no ill will toward Lucifer for being banished."

"But...why?" she asked, with her brows deeply furrowed.

I ran my nose over hers and whispered across her lips. "Had I never left the Underworld, I wouldn't have you."

"But, you were here for thousands of years before I came along," her words were breathless, as I traced the seam of her lips with my tongue.

"Don't you know, Juliette? I would wait thousands more as long as you were waiting for me there at the end."

I took her lips in a deep, breath stealing kiss, leaving her panting once I finally broke away and made my way down her slim body, paying attention to her hard little nipples on my way to my destination of her cunt. "A thousand years for one taste of this ripe pussy? Another thousand for the chance to sink my cock into your cunt? Done."

Once she screamed out her release, I had her on her knees, taking my cock deep.

"But, knowing that I no longer have to wait for you? That

instead, you will be by my side for the next several thousand years? It was all worth it."

I rode her hard, knowing that her little body could take each of my thrusts. I used my tail to pleasure what I couldn't reach with my hands and my smoke to stimulate her breasts until she was panting and crying out for me.

I didn't care why I was banished from the Underworld. Instead, I considered having Charon send Lucifer a fucking fruit basket.

THIRTY-FOUR

JULIETTE

When Varek and I left our haven in the penthouse, I was a bundle of nerves. When I had met Charon, it was in a strange situation that felt foreign to me. I didn't have the full capacity of my mind to fully process what meeting him meant. Now, I was dressed for the club in a little black dress and knew I was heading down in the elevator to meet him officially for the first time.

As soon as the doors opened and we stepped into Varek's office, all conversation stopped. The room was filled with people who had been worried about Varek and me and were waiting for us to finally show ourselves. Instead of being scared to face them, I found myself excited and grateful that they cared.

Sasha was the first to rush forward, separating me from Varek's hold around my waist. "Don't ever scare me like that again!" She squeezed me so hard, I felt my ribs protest, but I laughed, hugging her back just as tightly.

"I don't ever plan to!"

Talon and Rake were next, ignoring Varek's scowls and growls of warning, giving me quick hugs. "We were all so worried. But, we are glad that you are okay," Talon said, as he patted me on the head like an annoying big brother.

I just took it all in with a grin, knowing that this was my family and grateful for them and every bit of their concern for Varek and me.

Then I was facing Charon. I swallowed hard and looked up at him, seeing all the similarities between us. "Daughter," he said in a soft voice, and held out his arms, giving me the choice to accept him or not. I paused for several seconds before my instincts took over, and I crashed into his chest and soaked up the feeling of being held by my true father for the first time.

I pulled back and looked back up at him, wanting him to see my sincerity. "Thank you for guiding me."

"I wish I could have done more. Your mate already avenged you before I could lift a finger in that direction, unfortunately," he scowled at Varek, who just stared back blandly. "But, guiding you on your journey to healing, that was my honor."

I swiped away a stray tear as I gave a watery smile. "Thank you."

Varek took that chance to gather me back to his side and gestured to the door. "Shall we?"

We were supposed to be celebrating, but Varek also needed to show his face to the rest of the demons. There had been much talk while he kept himself shut away with my body, and it was time to put rumors to bed. We needed to let the demon world know that I was alive, Varek was sane, and that we were still mates. That, if anything, we were stronger than before the incident.

"We don't need to stay long," he was saying, as we walked down the corridor toward the main entrance. "We can have a drink, talk to a few of the staff, and just generally let the public see that everyone is alive. Unfortunately, in this world, demons are quick to jump to conclusions. When there is a hole in the power structure, there are those who are quick to take advantage. I have to let them see that there is no hole to exploit and that they won't find it easy trying to take my title."

Talon looked serious as he walked to the side and behind Varek, and Sasha had taken up the same position to the side and behind me. It all seemed very formal. "Are we expecting trouble?" I asked. Everyone's behavior was beginning to make me nervous. I knew Varek could take care of anything that came his way, but it all seemed very serious.

"No, *Amica mea*, but it is important not to let them forget who is in charge."

"You." I nodded.

He squeezed my hand as we paused in front of the doors, waiting for the guard to open them so we could pass, the sounds of the club immediately filling the hallway. "No, Juliette. *Us.*"

As soon as we entered through the doorway, we drew attention. We would always attract attention. There was no way not to with the size of the males around me, but it was also their looks. Every female, human, and demon alike, took a steadying breath as they got a good look at them. The men in the club either puffed out their chests in false bravado they only felt with the help of the alcohol they drank or lowered their eyes in deference to the true alpha in the room.

Several staff members that I recognized as demons looked relieved as Varek led our group to a large round table that sat with a reserved sign in the center of it. He helped me into the tall seat and gently pushed the chair in, choosing to stand by my side instead of taking the seat next to me. Then, I felt him run his fingers across my bare shoulders, causing goosebumps to pop up along my flesh and a thrill to run up my thighs. He had fucked me nearly non-stop for the last twenty-four hours, but I was beginning to understand that I would never get enough of him. And, now that I was truly immortal, I would have no trouble taking everything that he could give me.

Without even needing to order, a round of drinks was delivered to our table. The waitress stopped at our side and bowed her head.

"Lord Varek, Lady Juliette. I am pleased to see that you are both well. If there is anything you would like, please, just call for me."

"Thank you, Tilisse."

She bowed her head once again and scurried off.

The music was loud, but I had no trouble hearing when Sasha called out to me, "So, Juliette, since you are no longer working at the nursing home, what do you plan on doing with yourself?"

It was a thought I hadn't allowed myself to think about until now and brought a wave of sadness. I would miss them. I shrugged my shoulders. "I honestly don't know."

"You could come visit the Underworld with me," my father called out, holding up his glass in salute. I giggled at the snarl Varek threw his way.

"She will learn the business and work by my side," he declared.

I raised an eyebrow and turned my head to face him. "I will?"

"Are you not my queen?" he asked.

"Does that mean I have to live in your pocket?" I shot back, as everyone around us snickered. He just grinned down at me and kissed the tip of my nose.

"Why don't you look around at what The Tower has to offer before you make any decisions? Then, you might actually find something that you will enjoy doing."

"Like managing the sex club?" Rake asked, while everyone laughed at Varek's death glare.

"You can be demoted." Rake just held up a hand in surrender and went back to his drink as everyone roared with laughter.

The talk soon turned to the subject of the drugs and the lack of finding who was responsible. Talon had been heading up the investigation through the city. Unfortunately, while no more had come into The Tower, they also had not had any luck locating the one that was responsible.

We were interrupted in our conversation when a guard wearing a black t-shirt and the red lettering BOUNCER across the front came to the table and spoke to Varek.

"Sir, I wasn't sure what to do. There was a human woman asking for you." My back immediately went ramrod straight, my fists clenching against the table. "She was very insistent and causing a scene outside. It's an old woman…"

A cold knot of dread lodged itself into my gut, and I sighed in defeat. As he stepped back, the elderly woman stomped forward, and he frowned down at her before turning back to Varek. "Sorry, Sir, I told her to wait outside. I'm guessing that no one wanted to physically restrain an old woman."

Varek sighed and waved his hand. "That's fine, Chase, thank you."

We all stared at Melissa as she stood before us. I would have thought that she would have accepted her situation by now. Sure, I would be angry that the man I had been obsessed with had essentially stolen my life from me, but what did she think to accomplish by continuing to show up where we were?

"Oh, my gods. You are like a roach that keeps coming around that we just can't seem to squash." Sasha's words of disgust were apparently too low for Melissa's human ears, but they caught Charon's attention. When he asked who it was and Sasha explained to him, he sat up straighter in his chair and turned the full power of his glare on her.

"You've been stalking my daughter?" His words couldn't be mistaken for anything other than menacing, but Melissa barely spared him a glance as she continued to stare between Varek and me, her eyes occasionally pausing on where Varek's hand continued to caress my shoulder.

"Can we speak somewhere quieter?" she yelled over the music.

For looking like a frail old woman, she had made an effort with her appearance. Her hair had been dyed black, helping to add a few years back to her face, but not nearly as much as Varek had stolen from her. She had carefully covered the lines on her face as well as she could, applying makeup artfully, but nothing could bring back her youth. She looked like an eighty-year-old woman that was attempting to look thirty. I tried to conjure up some sympathy for her, but I was coming up short.

Varek sighed and turned to me. "Should we hear her out once and for all? Maybe this will be the end of it. I know you don't want me taking her life, but if she continues to be a nuisance, I will be forced to deal with her permanently."

I knew it wasn't a threat. It was simply a fact that I needed to come to terms with. I closed my eyes and nodded. "Okay, just this once. I don't like her showing up all the time, either."

He turned to the group. "I am going to walk her to the office for a private conversation."

Sasha stood up, "I'm not missing this shit show."

The rest stood up as well, but I kept my eye on Melissa the entire time, not able to let my guard down or trust her after everything she had done so far. I watched as she grew angrier by the minute as she eyed us discussing her. She was like a ticking time bomb, and I was sure she was just as unstable as one. Watching her, I could tell that whatever was running through her mind wasn't going to end well. Whether it be for her or us, we would find out soon.

I tore my eyes away from Melissa's increasingly enraged expression and looked up at Varek when he palmed my cheek, running the pad of his thumb over the crease in my bottom lip. "After this, I think I'm ready to get you alone again." I nodded, because why would I ever say no to an unspoken promise like that?

I took his offered hand and stepped down from the tall chair. With his help, it was much less awkward than it usually was with bar chairs. I generally avoided them altogether because I hated how I had to hop to get into them sometimes.

Once my feet were solidly on the floor, Varek bent to kiss my lips, causing my heart rate to speed up just from the brief contact. When he took my hand and began to lead me with the rest of the group toward the hallway, I once again turned to keep an eye on Melissa and realized that she wasn't following us. She was staring at me with murder in her eyes, and I just knew that she had made a decision.

Lightning fast, she had a gun pulled out and was pointing it straight at my heart. She had a look of resignation on her face. She knew she wasn't going to live past this moment in time, but the hatred simmering there spoke volumes. She didn't care, just as long as she took me with her.

When the shot rang out, I expected to feel a jolt of pain. Even if I knew it wouldn't kill me, I knew it was going to hurt, but I felt nothing as I glanced down at my body. It took me a solid five-seconds to realize that the bullet she had aimed for me hadn't hit her intended target. I looked back up, thinking I would see frustration on her face that she had missed. But instead, I saw Varek in front of me, one knee and hand on the ground holding his body up.

My vision narrowed to one point, making everything else disappear except the woman I was going to make suffer. Rage like nothing I had ever experienced took over every single molecule of my being until I was vibrating with it, seeing nothing but Melissa painted in the color red.

The guards circled around us immediately, blocking the view from the rest of the club. One of them grabbed Melissa's arms roughly, causing the gun to drop to the floor and skitter over to stop against Charon's foot, where he casually leaned down and plucked it up, tucking it into his waistband. Few eyes turned to look at the commotion, the sound of the gunshot being drowned out by the loud music, the sight of Varek on his knees causing more of a stir than anything else.

All of this was happening as if in the distance, something I wasn't a part of, as I kept my eyes locked on Melissa's protesting body. She hadn't intended on shooting my mate, but she did. And she would suffer painfully.

I reached out my hand, and without any conscious thought, I searched for that small golden orb hovering deep in her chest. The same place that seemed to call for me when its host was dying, needing assistance in guiding it to the next plane of existence. Once I found it, I reached in with my fist and squeezed as tight as I could, cutting into my palm with my fingernails but unable to feel anything at the moment except pure wrath that this fucking human piece of shit shot my mate.

Then, with all my might, I yanked.

Her body jerked forward a fraction before slumping in the guard's holds. Dead. I held that golden orb as I watched with satisfaction as the light died in Melissa's eyes. And then I squeezed once more.

Tiny sparks fell from my fingertips as I opened my hand and ran over to where Varek was getting back to his feet, his hand holding his stomach, with blood dripping from between his fingers.

I never looked back as the sparks faded to gray and disappeared before they even hit the floor.

THIRTY-FIVE

VAREK

IT ALWAYS HURTS like a motherfucker when you are shot. It doesn't matter how quickly you heal, it won't stop the pain from any wound that you receive.

My breath caught with a grunt as soon as the slug penetrated my body, the impact and the swift pain taking me to one knee. But I would take a hundred bullets to keep Juliette from ever having to experience any kind of pain.

As soon as I caught my breath, I was going to end the foul woman, and I was going to have strong words with my mate about her ever stopping me from ending anyone ever again. If I had just finished what I had started weeks ago, we wouldn't be dealing with this bullshit right now.

I looked up, ready to take care of the problem as soon as I could stand back up, only to watch as my Juliette pulled the bitch's entire soul from her body in one movement. I watched in awe as she squeezed her already tight fist and had the soul crumbling to nothing.

I staggered to my feet amidst the silence of our group as they all took in the impossible. Juliette ran to me, and I braced for her, knowing it would hurt like hell, but she froze before she could make impact, a slow clapping freezing us both.

A human male wearing an expensive suit stood watching just over the shoulder of one of the guards, amusement in his eyes. I jerked my head at the ones holding Melissa's dead body, gesturing for them to take her away before any other humans noticed. Then, keeping my hand pressed to my abdomen, I turned to the man.

He wasn't the typical club goer, dressed in the suit he was wearing. He looked more like a business type that was heading to a meeting in a boardroom. Or with other kingpins. This was the man we had been searching for. Unfortunately, it seemed as if he found us, instead, and at the moment that my mate took the life of a human.

His obnoxious slow clapping tapered off, and he stood there with a grin on his face once he noticed that he had caught everyone's attention.

"Excellent entertainment," he called out, as the waitress from earlier rushed over with a damp bar towel. I nodded my thanks as I took it and began to wipe the blood from my hand. The pain was already easing and soon would be gone altogether.

I continued to stare pointedly at the man as I lifted my arm to make room for Juliette's body to fit into mine. He sighed deeply as if he were disappointed in my lack of reaction to him.

"You have seconds to tell me why you are here and also why you have targeted my people before I kill you where you stand."

"Uh, uh, uh," he said, his broad smile returned with my threat as if it were nothing but an amusement to him. He held up a cell phone and waved it back and forth. "I wouldn't be so quick to jump to the killing and maiming just yet. You see," he called out, straining to be heard over the loud music, not realizing that we could all hear even his breathing perfectly well. "I just caught that sweet-looking little lady right there killing someone I suspect was a human." He cocked his head mockingly. "I doubt that is something the human authorities would be very pleased to find out about, do you?"

I pulled Juliette's body tighter against me when she stiffened at his words. "Why don't I just kill you anyway and destroy your little phone?" I growled.

"Too bad I already sent it to someone I trust then, isn't it? Such a shame that you won't know who and won't be able to stop them from sending it on after I'm dead." He tucked his phone away into an inner pocket of his suit jacket and then straightened his lapels. "Now, what do you say we conduct business like civilized people?"

I couldn't discount his threat. There was no way I would allow Juliette to be taken away from me by anyone. I ground my teeth together. "Fine, let's talk at the table." I gestured for the guards to back up, and everyone slowly walked back to the seats they had just vacated moments prior.

"Who are you, and what the fuck do you want?"

"How about a drink first?" He waved to the waitress. "Hey, sweetheart, how about a scotch on the rocks? It's in the house, right, Varek, King of the Demons?" She looked at me while wringing her hands but took off at my curt nod.

He waited, drumming his fingertips on the tabletop to the beat of the music until she came back with his drink moments later while we all sat in tense silence, waiting for whatever he had to say. I could see the violence shimmering in Charon's eyes at his daughter being threatened, but he knew as well as I did that this was a delicate situation.

"It's a nice place you have here. A little difficult to discuss private business in, but, well..." He shrugged and took a sip of his drink. "Not bad. I'm going to guess that you have the good stuff in your private office, though, am I right?"

I slammed my fist down on the table, making Juliette jump, and I immediately soothed her with a hand to the back of her neck. "Enough bullshit! Tell me why you are here. But more importantly, tell me why you have been killing demons and using vampires."

He shrugged. "I had assumed a king would be much more civilized. Anyway, why I am here is simple. I know you have been searching for me, and I thought it was finally time to introduce myself. My name is Ivan Strogoni, and this city is mine."

I knew the name. I had just never thought that a Strogoni could be arrogant or idiot enough to make a challenge against me. "You own shit."

My words caused the first flicker of annoyance to cross his features. "My great grandfather built this town, and it is my legacy to run it."

"Wrong. I built this town and allowed your great grandfather to do business in it."

His face turned red. "My great grandfather-"

"Was a good man that knew his place in the world. Humans cannot win against demons. I provided protection for him and his son after him, all the way to your own father. They each knew that they had a good thing here. I didn't get in their way of doing things the human way as long as they stayed away from all things supernatural." I reached down, plucked the bullet from my body as it was finally pushed out, and lay it on the table in front of us. "Why you think that you are the one with the balls to take anything from me is a mystery I do not care to know."

"But, you see, that is exactly what I think because I can. And I will." When his eyes went from the bloody bullet over to Juliette, I growled out a warning that caused his eyes to jump back to mine.

"I will humor you. Do tell me why?"

"I have watched everything since I was old enough to understand. I know that this city is in a prime location and that there is so much more I can do with it. I know much more money can be had here without you standing in my way."

"You think to get rid of me? Do you think you can kill me? And what do you think about the vampires? I doubt the local vampire king would take kindly to your threats either."

His slow smile was enough to make me want to break every

capped tooth in his head. "I have been collecting information for the last thirty years, king of demons. I know all your secrets, yours and the vampires. With the knowledge I have and the pile of evidence I have of your existence, I think you will give me just about anything to keep my mouth shut." He sat back in his high-backed stool and crossed his arms. "I think that I am about to become a very wealthy man. Or wealthier, I suppose," his laugh was obnoxious, but his words had cold fury roiling inside me.

"You want us to pay you for your silence."

"Well, are you ready for the world to know that demons walk the earth?" He shrugged as if we were discussing the fucking weather. "I didn't think that was something you were interested in happening."

I looked across the table to my closest, trusted people. No, I couldn't allow the secret of us to get out. One day it might happen. It might be necessary to come forward. But now? It would destroy lives. Most demons would be able to retreat to the Underworld, but I would never be able to do so. We would be hunted like rats until we were eradicated. I lived through many eras of time when there were persecutions. The Salem witch trials were still very fresh in my mind.

"I see you understand the merit of my proposal. How about we start slow? I will give you time to think about it, and when you are ready, you can call a meeting with the vampire king and me. In the meantime, I will require a bit of...insurance." His gaze landed back on Juliette, and I'd had enough. If he did have evidence that Juliette killed that woman, so be it. I would protect her. There wasn't much that money couldn't buy, including my mate's freedom.

I opened my hand, pulling his soul toward me, but nothing happened. His smug smile told me he knew what I was trying to do. "You see? I have been watching. I know that demons and vampires aren't the only ones inhabiting our fair city." He pointed toward the bar. "Witches live here, too. They are very handy with a spell, don't you think?"

I looked over, scanning the patrons at the bar as they chatted, drank, flirted, and laughed. But one woman was standing there with her hand around an amulet, her lips moving in a silent chant. *This motherfucker hired a witch to bind our abilities.* A stronger witch would be able to counteract her spell, and I just so happened to employ the best one in the city. But even with her, it would take time and preparation to accomplish it. If I wanted him dead, I would have to kill him with my bare hands. Unfortunately, doing so in a crowded club full of humans as witnesses wouldn't easily allow me to buy my freedom.

"You aren't taking my mate," I ground out.

"Oh, but I think I am. But, not to worry, I won't touch her." He looked at Juliette with a smirk and a wink. "Unless, she wants me to."

"Never," she spat out.

"Tsk, tsk, my dear. You and I are going to be spending a lot of time together. We should get along. Unless your demon king here works quickly to get me what I want." He looked back at me pointedly. "The sooner we can come to an agreement, the sooner you can have her back."

"Take me, instead," Sasha spoke up. "You'll have more fun with me."

"You're the succubus, aren't you? Sorry, too bad you can't be allowed to use your allure on me. I would think that would be something enjoyable to try at least once." He winked at her, but turned back to me, dismissing her completely. "Do we have a deal?"

Every atom of my being balked at the thought of leaving my mate with this man. He couldn't be trusted, and she would be defenseless against him. I didn't care what threats he sent my way. I would deal with any consequence. Juliette's soft touch on my arm had me turning to face her. "It might be for the best," she whispered.

"No!"

"Varek, it isn't just us that we have to think about. The other demons-"

"Can return to the Underworld," I ground out through clenched teeth.

"And the vampires? The witches? Where would they go? How would they escape?"

"This is a terrible idea."

"I trust you. I need you to trust me. Call Crispin, tell him about this guy. Figure out a plan. I won't have to be with him long."

"And if he touches you?"

"I can survive anything, remember? But I don't think I will have to," her words were confident, even though her fingers were trembling where they rested on my arm. I covered them with my own.

"I don't agree to this." I held up a hand to stop her protests. "But I understand the dangerous position that not just us, but the entire supernatural community is in." I wanted to lash out in protest at anyone and everyone, but I did understand. "I keep saying that I am never going to let you out of my sight again, but I am giving serious thought to locking you away in the penthouse. Permanently."

Ivan Strogoni stood up and straightened his jacket. Then, with one last swallow of his drink, he finished the scotch, shook his head as if disappointed in the quality, and then held out his hand to Juliette. "If you are ready, my dear?"

I pulled her back. "You are not to touch her. Ever," I growled out a vicious warning, until he dropped his hand and shrugged.

"Fine. Let's go. It's getting late." He walked toward the door without another word where the witch was already waiting for him, her hand still wrapped tightly around her amulet, refusing to meet anyone's eyes.

I stood on the sidewalk as my mate slid into the backseat of a limousine along with the Strogoni male that was playing a game more dangerous than he knew and a witch that had betrayed her own people.

THIRTY-SIX

JULIETTE

As soon as we were settled in the car and it began moving, Ivan worked the knot in his tie loose and reached for a chilled bottle of water from a small refrigerator cleverly disguised in front of us.

"My throat is parched after all that yelling," he grumbled, as he cracked open the lid and took several swallows.

"Demons have excellent hearing. They would have heard you if you spoke normally," the witch mumbled, as she continued to hold tight to her amulet.

He looked at me with one eyebrow raised, but I ignored him in favor of glaring daggers at the witch. "Ah, yes, I remember. I know all your secrets and how to exploit them."

"But is it difficult to remember them all?"

His glare was meant to intimidate, but I couldn't have cared less. "I wouldn't say it's difficult. There are just so many abilities that don't seem possible."

I nodded my chin in the witch's direction. "And her? Are you exploiting her as well?"

Her cheeks reddened as she continued to stare out the window toward the streets as we sped by.

"Marcy? No, she just knows who's side to be on."

"Is that so?" It was her turn to glare at my words, but she said nothing to contradict him.

"How does it feel to know you've betrayed literally everyone in your community?" I asked, but she merely turned back to the window and resumed her chanting.

The rest of the ride was silent until we drove through a large set of iron gates that swung open at our approach. The house was large, lit up like there was a party going on inside, but it wasn't as grand as a man who ruled the city would have owned. I was beginning to see what motivated him the most. Greed wasn't a pretty color on anyone. On him, it was just plain ugly.

Without a word, he walked me up the steps and into the house that was decorated as grandly as I supposed he could afford, likely doing his best to pretend to all of his other rich friends. But it felt like it lacked something after being around Varek in his penthouse with its understated elegance. Likely a soul. But underneath the gleaming gold fixtures, there was a dullness to everything. The rugs were frayed and worn, and the pictures on the walls were hanging in tarnished frames. He was probably hanging on to his wealth by a thread as thin as the curtains.

He took me up the stairs and in through a doorway. The room he deposited me in was bare except for a full-sized bed, a nightstand with no lamp, and a door leading into an ensuite bathroom that, if I had to guess, held nothing but toilet paper.

"You are going to regret every second of this, you know," I said nonchalantly, as I walked over to the bed and sat primly on the edge of the mattress with my hands folded in front of me.

He snickered. "Why? Because your demon king is going to rescue you?"

"Oh, Varek will come. But he won't need to rescue me." He simply shook his head like he thought I was a sad, deluded little girl.

Without another word, he shut the door and locked it, the key sounding loud in the room as it scraped against the tumblers. I looked around at the ceiling, searching for anything that would indicate that a camera might be watching. I wasn't sure since I had no experience, but the small black dot just inside the smoke detector had me guessing that was where the camera was. I made a disgusted face. The camera was facing the bed. I would make sure there was nothing that could ever be seen by those that may be watching.

I walked into the bathroom to search it, and as I thought, there were no supplies, not even a tube of toothpaste. But there were also, thankfully, no cameras. I walked back into the bedroom and dropped onto the bed again, thinking about my options.

He was right, it was late, and I probably wouldn't be disturbed again until morning. Varek was probably already with Crispin, discussing all that had been said. Poor Varek. I could just imagine how crazy he must have been feeling.

I bounced on the mattress, testing its lack of softness. It was nothing like Varek's luxurious bed, but it was also nothing like the mattress that I used to sleep on growing up. I would be fine, and this entire ordeal would be over soon. I just needed to make a plan.

The following day after barely sleeping all night, I was ready for whoever showed up at my door. After scooting along the wall to avoid the camera and making my way to the door, I held the toilet lid in both hands. If anyone was watching, I hoped they would see the steam from the running shower and assume I was taking my time.

I was nearly ready to give up my waiting position, wondering if it had been the hours it felt like. Then, finally, I heard footsteps lightly treading down the hall. When they stopped at the door and I heard the key slide into the lock, my heart sped up as the adrenaline began pumping furiously through me. I wasn't a badass and had never defended myself against anyone successfully before unless I counted Melissa, but I was not a victim. I was going to save myself, no matter what I had to do. I didn't want to have to kill anyone, but I would do what I had to in order to survive, and an entire community of super-natural beings was counting on me.

I raised the porcelain lid high over my head, stiffening my arms against the shakiness. As soon as the person swung the door open and entered, leading with a tray of food held in their arms, I swung down as hard as I could. I stood there with my mouth hanging wide open as I watched Marcy crumble to the carpet, the tray clattering to the ground with the sandwich separating into pieces, making a mess everywhere. My stomach growled in protest.

I grimaced as I saw the blood begin to pool under her head. I stood there staring at the destruction I had caused but jumped into action when I heard a noise from downstairs. I needed to move quickly before anyone came to investigate the noise. I turned over her body, searching for the amulet that I was certain held her binding spell. I knew next to nothing about witches, but I did know that they kept their spells in trinkets and an amulet like she continued to hold the night before was the likeliest bet.

I didn't see it at first and wanted to scream in frustration, but after searching around in her hair, I finally found it twisted around her neck. I yanked, but all it did was pull on her body. The cord was black leather and strong. Unfortunately, it was also just short enough that I couldn't slip it over her head. I blew out a frustrated breath as I stood over her body, trying to figure out what I should try next.

I clutched the amulet in my fingers that had gotten bloody from messing with her hair and head, then I placed my foot on her chest and yanked as hard as I could. Her body lifted for a second before the cord finally snapped, making me stumble back until I fell on my ass.

I jumped up and ran to the bathroom. I dropped the necklace into the toilet bowl and hit the lever, watching anxiously as the water swirled. I held my breath until it finally disappeared from sight. I stood there waiting until the bowl filled back up and then flushed again. I was hoping that the drains would take the necklace down into the sewer and far away from the house until it could hold no more power over anyone.

I closed my eyes and felt inside me, not really knowing how to look for my abilities. But I knew they had to be there somewhere. I just needed to know before I went any further that I would be able to defend myself, or I was truly fucked. I gave up with a defeated sigh when I felt nothing, not a blip, buzz, or bump.

I flushed the toilet once more for good measure, then edged my way along the wall back over to where Marcy was lying and took her hands, pulling her further into the room. She wasn't big, but pulling her dead weight along the carpet wasn't easy. By the time I had her several feet in the room so I could close the door when I left, I was panting with the exertion.

I started to inch my way out of the room but paused and ran back to her body. I hesitated for a second, but finally searched through her pockets until I found a cell phone. It needed a facial scan, so after a couple of tries, then wiping a bit of the blood from her cheeks, I finally had it unlocked.

I sat back on my butt and stared at the unlocked phone. I couldn't call the police, and I didn't have Varek's number memorized. I tried searching for the number to the club, but when it rang, a recording picked up with the hours of operation before hanging up on me. I sat thinking, but I was out of ideas on how to get a hold of Varek. Or anyone else, for that matter. I looked up at the open door, realizing I was losing time. Marcy was likely dead with as much as she had bled, and she hadn't made a sound all the time I had messed with her body. I wasn't going to waste any more time by checking if she had a pulse. At this point, I needed to get the hell out of the room and find any incriminating evidence that the asshole could use against the demons.

I remembered the video Strogoni had taken. After looking through her messages, sure enough, Marcy was the one he had sent the video to. I snorted quietly. It was grainy and dark. You could barely see faces, and when Melissa collapsed, it simply looked like an old woman fainted. There was no glowing light from the orb that was her soul. Apparently, modern technology couldn't pick up that kind of thing.

I stood up and scooped up the keys she had dropped. There were only a few keys on the ring, so they wouldn't be much help, but I kept them just in case. If nothing else, they could be weapons. I tucked the useless phone into my bra and shut the door firmly behind me, locking it even though I doubted Marcy was a threat anymore.

As quietly as I could, I crept down the hall, peeking in doorways to see if there were any visible weapons, but all I saw were vases or lamps. I waited and listened at the top of the stairs, hearing nothing. Finally, with a deep breath and the keys firmly clenched between my fingers, I descended. Once I reached the bottom without hearing anything coming from inside the house, I started worrying my lip with my teeth. I had to find his evidence in case it held something better than a dark five-second video of an old woman fainting.

"If I were an office, where would I be?" I muttered to myself, and headed off in the direction of a hallway off the stairs. The first door on the right was closed, but unlocked. With my breath held, I twisted the knob, thanking the gods that the door opened silently. I cracked the door just wide enough to peek through to see that it was empty and spotted a wide desk in front of a large window overlooking a plain backyard that looked like it needed a lot of help. The hedges were overgrown, and the grass was more weeds than lawn. I also saw that the light was waning, and evening was approaching fast.

I slipped through the door and walked over to the desk, sitting in the large chair, wincing as it creaked with my weight. The top of the desk was mostly bare, with just a phone and a small wooden box that, when I opened it, revealed cigars and a shiny silver lighter.

I looked down at the drawers and pulled open the largest one, glad to see it was unlocked and was indeed a file drawer. A quick scan of the files had my first smile since last night spreading across my face. The files were clearly marked. The kings each had their own file labeled with their names. Several other files were labeled 'demons', 'vampires', 'witches', 'fae'. That one gave me a pause. I hadn't realized that fae were real and apparently in the city.

I sat back and thought about how to destroy the files. Unfortunately, there wasn't a paper shredder to be seen, but it would have been too loud anyway. There was a wood-burning fireplace across the room, but I didn't have a clue how to start a fire in one. Then I spotted the liquor cabinet.

It took me two seconds to come to a decision, then I was out of my seat and heading to where glass bottles of alcohol were lined up in perfect rows. I didn't care which one I used, but with a glare, I took a bottle that was a heavy crystal decanter instead of labeled. It was probably his favorite and likely the most expensive.

I had just finished pouring the strong liquor over the contents of the drawer and had the silver lighter open when the door suddenly opened. Ivan Strogoni and I stared at each other for several seconds before he lunged forward. At the same time, I struck the lighter, letting it fall from my hand, directly into his drawer.

His hand was around my throat just as the lighter caught, and the flames whooshed high into the air next to us. The heat was so intense that I was worried that it might catch my hair on fire, but I couldn't move from his hold.

"What have you done?" he screamed into my face, spittle flying out of his mouth and landing on my cheeks.

All I could do was gurgle my answer as he squeezed even harder. My hand fumbled around, desperately trying to grasp anything. I held up my right hand and tried to call on my ability to do what I had done the night before to Melissa, but I still felt nothing.

He laughed bitterly as he shook me like a ragdoll. "Do you honestly think the witch was the only one with an amulet? You can't use your monster powers on me."

"Maybe not," I rasped around the pressure of his hand on my throat. "But I can still hurt you."

I finally felt the heavy crystal decanter on the tips of my fingers. I wrapped my hand around the neck of the bottle, making sure that my fingers had a firm hold. Then, with the last of my waning strength, I swung with all my might.

The bottle didn't shatter, but it did crack in half as it struck the side of his head. I gasped in air and immediately started coughing as the smoke of the burning desk poured into my lungs. As I struggled to breathe, I watched Strogoni drop to the floor, groaning in pain with the side of his head dripping blood.

I squatted down next to him, still coughing, tears sliding down my cheeks. "I told you I wouldn't need to be saved."

Then I kicked the side of his burning desk and walked away as it collapsed on top of the man as he screamed.

THIRTY-SEVEN

JULIETTE

I walked down the driveway taking in large gulps of the clean air. I still coughed occasionally, but it was already lessening, and I was beginning to find breathing much easier.

Night was falling quickly, and the sun had just finished sinking on the horizon when I saw more than one set of headlights coming through the gate. I turned around to look at the house to see flames coming from inside the open door. If Strogoni had survived the fire, I would be very surprised. The heat had been intense, and my arm felt like it had been scorched while I was fumbling around for the bottle.

I looked down at myself and grimaced. I was filthy with soot and smelled like fire. I also had blood all over my hands and arms from where I had handled Marcy's body. I had killed three people in less than twenty-four hours. I would like to say that I have regrets, but I honestly didn't. There was a pang of regret that I was put into the position to kill, but I didn't regret actually taking the lives that I did.

The car in the front stopped with a jerk and screech of tires, the backdoors opening before it had stopped rocking. I was swallowed up in Varek's arms in the next second and breathed in his scent of burnt cinnamon, trying to erase the smell of ash and burning wood from my lungs.

"*Amica mea?*"

I looked up at him and blinked, so happy to see his face. "Hi," I breathed out.

I heard laughter coming from the other car and looked over to see Crispin standing there with one arm on the top of the vehicle.

"Is there anyone left inside for us to kill, little girl?" he asked with a grin.

I flushed. "I don't think so?"

"My Hunter is going to be so disappointed that she missed this," he chuckled again, pulled out his phone, and started walking toward the house.

"Juliette, are you hurt?" Varek was looking me over, checking for injuries through the film of ash and blood on me.

I raised a hand to my throat, feeling that the pain from being choked was already receding, along with the heat from the burn on my arm. I shook my head and raised my hand to his face, making him look into my eyes. "I'm okay, Varek, I promise."

He closed his eyes and breathed deep, while I just stayed quiet and let him have his moment. Then, a few minutes later, another vehicle pulled in. Ivy got out and rushed over to me, and Varek reluctantly let me go but kept one arm around my waist. I doubted he would let me move away from him for quite some time. He had warned me, though.

"Juliette! I jumped in the car as soon as the sun went down and got here as soon as I could in case you needed more help." She hugged me tightly before pulling me back and looking me over, much the same as Varek had. "You look great for someone that was kidnapped, held hostage, and made her own escape." She looked up at the house and to where Crispin was walking back, then back to me. "You probably want a shower and a change of clothes. No offense, but you look like you slaughtered a couple of people and then lit them on fire."

A bubble of hysterical laughter threatened to escape, and I had to pinch my lips together to keep it in before my new friend thought I was psychotic. I nodded my thanks. "I really would love to get cleaned up."

"Then would you mind if we visited in a couple of hours? I really need to hear your story."

I gave a small laugh at her eagerness and looked to Varek. "Is that okay with you?"

He grunted and pulled me closer to his body. "Make it three hours, and I'll have them lead you straight to the penthouse. I don't want my mate around the general public for a while."

"I get it." Ivy smiled and gave a small wave before walking to Crispin, who waited a few feet away.

Varek led me to the car door and opened it. Just before I slid inside, Crispin called out to me. "While we are still here, is there any type of evidence on the supernatural that still needs to be destroyed?"

I looked back at the house that was now fully engulfed in flame, the fire licking at the roof through the broken windows, and shook my head. "Not unless he has a fireproof safe in there. All the information seemed to be in his desk."

"Excellent. You did well." He tipped his head in a slight bow, and Varek grunted.

"Thank you," I whispered, and climbed into the car.

As soon as we were situated and the driver turned the car around to head back to The Tower, Varek pulled me onto his lap. "I hate the position that you were put in."

I cupped his jaw, rubbing over the stubble there. Whenever he worried about me, it seemed that he let his meticulous grooming go. "I know."

He stared into my eyes, his green fading to black and back to green again. "I am so fucking proud of you, *Amica mea.*"

Tears immediately filled my eyes. I had held firm the entire time I was in that house, but a few words from my mate and I was done. I put my face in his neck and sobbed. All the fear, the worry, and the guilt bombarded me at once, and I cried as his big hands held me tight.

"My brave girl. You did so good. I love you, Juliette."

His words just made me cry harder. All my life, I had needed those words. All my life, I had craved a strong shoulder to cry on. Varek had given me everything I could ever want with a few simple words.

Once we arrived at the club entrance, I wiped my face as well as I could and cringed at the mess I had made of his shirt. For once, he wasn't wearing a suit, but the black button-down he was wearing was wet and had gray streaks of soot on it. He looked down at what I saw and shrugged. "Don't worry about it, *Amica mea*. I'd let you cry on every shirt I own just to have you in my arms. Now let's get you upstairs." I tried to pretend that his words didn't have my heart fluttering in my chest, but I was sure I failed miserably.

As soon as he had me out of the car, he gathered me close and kissed my head, leading me past the early arrivals waiting in line. I didn't bother looking over, I knew I would see-shock, envy, and even some hate. After dealing with Melissa, I had no interest in engaging with any woman who might have a crush on my mate.

He led me straight through the still empty club that was due to open at any second and up to our home. As soon as I was stripped of my clothes, he carried them away, probably to order someone to burn them. By the time he returned, I was already under the shower and had my hair lathered up, eager to get rid of any lingering smell. Plus, there was a small, vain part of me that wanted to see if there was any damage done to my long hair. I may be able to heal, but I doubted that ability went toward regrowing singed hair.

He walked into the shower with me, his hands going straight to the body wash. I moaned loudly as his big hands glided over each inch of skin. He took his time washing me, and I knew he was using the opportunity to assure himself that I wasn't damaged. He spent extra time at my throat, where the marks had been fading when he had driven up and were long gone by now.

Once he was fully satisfied that I was clean, he helped me rinse and then got out first to have a towel ready to wrap around me.

"You're going to spoil me," I murmured, as he knelt down to dry my legs. He looked up at me, his emerald eyes shining.

"I plan to spoil you every day for the rest of eternity." He swiped the towel over my abdomen. "You and our children."

"You want to have children with me?" I didn't know why the thought of having his children, of being a mother, the type of mother that I longed to have when I was a little girl lying curled up in the dark, had never entered my thoughts. But, once they did, they sank in, taking root. "I want that, too," I whispered.

"One day, *Amica mea*, we will have a whole house full of children. As many as you want. We will buy a real house with a yard and lots of room to play. But for now." He kissed my belly and stood, towering over me once again, and I craned my neck back to look at him as he picked up my brush from the counter. "For now, I want to spend time with just you. I want to get to know everything about you, know your hopes and dreams, and I want to help you fulfill them all. If you want to travel, we can do that. If you want to learn how to paint, we can turn one of the rooms into a studio. I just want you to do what you want most while we grow our bond stronger every day."

"That sounds perfect."

After he brushed my hair, he lifted me into his arms and carried me to the bed. "Now, I am going to show you with my body how very proud I am of you."

His wings unfolded from his back, and he arched over me, his large body blocking out the light from the ceiling.

"That sounds perfect, too," I whispered.

His tail wrapped around my thigh and yanked, pulling me to the edge of the bed, where he immediately sank to his knees. His hands tipped in lethal black claws and pushed my thighs open until they burned with the stretch. He didn't hold anything back, using his tongue, teeth, fingers, and even his tail to send me into a climax so fast, and hard I didn't know if it was possible to ever recover from.

He didn't push me back up the bed, he just stood and lifted both of my legs, kissing each ankle before placing them together on one of his shoulders. He didn't need hands to guide himself into my waiting opening. He found it easily and notched himself there before sliding in with one slow thrust of his hips. His eyes never left mine as he lifted my hips with his hands.

His movements stayed slow and steady until I was a writhing mess of need. I needed him. I needed all of him. "Varek!" I called out and moaned. "Please, stop holding back!"

He growled and leaned forward, sucking one of my small breasts into his mouth. "I never hold back from you, mate. Sometimes, I will give you a hard and fast fuck." He demonstrated by punching his hips forward, making me squeal. "Sometimes, it will be slow and steady. But I never hold back."

He stood back up and continued his slow pace making me want to bite him. "I like slow," I panted, "But right now? I need to feel your power. Show me what you can do, Varek. Give me your strength."

"You want my strength?" He smiled a slow, wicked smile.

I swallowed at the sight of him, his black wings extended, his horns curled back in sharp points, his shadows dancing around his body. He was magnificent. And all mine. Forever.

"Yes," I breathed.

Then he gave me exactly what I asked for. And an hour later, when we joined our friends in the sunken living room, my legs were still shaky from the gift he had given that was all of him.

EPILOGUE

FIVE YEARS LATER

We were having a bar-b-que. It was something I never thought I'd say to anyone. The king of demons on earth was hosting a bar-b-que at his mansion in the hills.

I stepped to the side as the little dhampir ran past my legs, giggling as she ran from a sentinel. I watched as the two ran from the house and out into the backyard that had a ten-foot stone wall around it. There was a pool to the side with a black iron fence for protection against any little precocious child from getting to the unsafe waters alone.

The patio was large with a sitting area and an outdoor fireplace, lights strung up all around it, making the entire space look like an inviting place to sit, relax, and have a drink with friends.

I had never dreamed of being here. Then one day, I felt a brand appear on my skin. Twenty-one years later, I met the mate that I never thought I wanted. Of course, there were a lot of things I never thought I'd want. It hadn't taken me long to realize what a fool I'd been.

I caught sight of my mate, my wife, and felt my lips tip up into a smile. She was the reason for everything I did now. Then, my eyes dropped to her large, round belly, and I felt a pang in my chest that was half fear, half dread, and all excitement. Her and our first little one. That's what all this was for.

We had five years together. We traveled, and we experienced many things together. We grew as close as a mated pair could possibly be. And now it was time for our next adventure together.

I let the running of The Tower go to Talon. He was always my closest friend and the one I trusted most to do what was right for the demons on the earth realm. He may not be a king, but I made sure he was respected as if he were.

Sasha didn't want to leave Juliette and insisted that we would need a guard. So she traveled with us and was Juliette's maid of honor at our wedding three years ago. It wasn't something that we needed to do. Our mate bond was stronger than any paper could ever compare to, but my mate had been human first, and I wanted to honor that. Of course, seeing how men hit on her everywhere we went didn't help my growing agitation. Having that symbol wrapped around her finger went a long way toward warding off any advances that might have otherwise been thrown her way.

I stepped from the house and walked across the patio to where my mate was sitting, laughing with Sasha and Talon, along with the vampire Counselor and his mate. They had come for a visit from the island where they now resided since their daughter was vulnerable until she came of age. I thought of my own little one and grunted, thinking living on a protected island where my child would always be safe from the rest of the world didn't seem like such a bad idea.

I sat next to Juliette, wrapped an arm around her shoulders, and felt her melt into me. Crispin smiled and nodded, lifting his bottle of beer in a toast.

"Nice backyard, I like it. Very safe."

"Thank you, Counselor. I hear your home on the island is pretty safe, as well."

Ivy grinned as she followed her daughter's giggling form while she laughed and dodged the sentinel again in their game of tag. "It's the best. I'm sure if you wanted to come for a visit, we could get that approved." She poked her mate in the side. "Right, Counselor Crispin."

He merely nodded, "Of course. It shouldn't be hard to get approval for a couple of demons to visit a private, vampire only island. I know people."

She laughed and kissed his cheek.

Juliette sighed, and I looked down at her. "Is everything okay? Is it the baby?"

She smiled and shook her head. "No, the baby is fine, Varek. I'm just happy."

I kissed her head and smiled. "Good."

THE END

AFTERWORD

I appreciate each and every one of you! I hope you enjoyed Varek and Juliette's story. I enjoyed writing this one so much. Varek was such an amazing character. His love for Juliette was so easy for me to envision and I hope that came across on the pages. Juliette's journey to self-discovery was a long one, but I am happy for who she turned out to be.

As always, I welcome feedback. If there is something you find that needs correcting, I'd love to hear about. Please feel free to contact me at My Email.
Please join my Facebook group for giveaways, and sneak peeks into what I might currently be working on. RSullins Book Group
If you enjoyed the story, please consider leaving a review!

Acknowledgments

There are two amazing women that I need to say thank you to.
Clare, thank you for everything you do. For all the laughs and
cheering me up, giving me a push when I need it, encouraging me... a
girl couldn't ask for a better side-kick.
Katrina, I don't know what I would do without you. Your feedback is
invaluable and I appreciate every correction, and suggestion. Thank
you so much for going above and beyond in everything you do!

ABOUT THE AUTHOR

R Sullins is #1 Bestselling author of paranormal and contemporary romance as well as a voracious reader. When she's not writing you can easily find her with a book in her hands.
She grew up in California but ended up living all around the United States once marrying her high school sweetheart, who just happened to be a soldier in the USArmy. Nothing is more important to her than her family.
She is a lover of fairies, tattoos, and coffee cups, has a vast collection of them all, and receives a glare from her teenager every time she brings home a new cup to squeeze into the cabinet.
WWW.RSULLINS.COM

ALSO BY
R SULLINS

Someone from Crispin's human life reemerges

leaving us both reeling in shock.

If that wasn't enough-

My mate was *dying*,

and I was hiding a secret that would change our lives forever.

Suddenly,

the threat of someone dethroning all the leaders became very real.

We were in for the fight of our lives to save all vampirekind.

LINK: Hunter's Forever

Jared

Book 2.5 of The Hunter Series

The reluctant vampire...

This wasn't supposed to be my life

I never asked to become a *vampire*

Falling into this world of monsters turned out to be the best thing to happen to me.

The transition from human soldier to vampire sentinel was one of the easiest things I had ever done.

Now I was in for the fight of my life, convincing my *mate* to take a chance on me.

The mate in danger...

I couldn't return home no matter how much I missed it.

My mother forced me to leave for a reason.

There was an evil man after me, willing to kill anyone who got in his way.

Then a man walked through the door and set my soul on fire.

He said I was his *mate*.

I wanted to say yes.

But, how, when I had to save my mom from a killer?

The fight for their future...

I swore I would defeat all of her demons.

I wasn't going to let her go...ever.

I wanted to keep my mate safe, but what if I was the monster she needed saving from?

<u>**Contemporary Romance**</u>

Cry For Me

Paige

Loner

Outcast

Charity case

Orphan

I was all those things.

Years after my parents died, I was still being bullied, and it was all led by my cousins.

They hated me for years as children, and moving into their house didn't make

them change their minds about me.

I was counting down the days until I could finally get away from every single person in this town.

Until there was one person I wasn't so sure I wanted to leave.

Reid

My life since age 7 revolved around football and what it would take for me to get into the NFL.

I didn't have time for girls or parties.

I had never been tempted by anything that could take my mind away from the sport.

Until I walked into my new school on my first day of senior year. One look was enough to change every plan I'd made for my future.

It wasn't long before we both realized that someone didn't like that we had found each other.

LINK: Cry For Me

For more books by R Sullins visit Amazon